PRAISE FOR
GHOSTS OF MATEGUAS

"Ghosts of Mateguas joins others in the Mateguas Island saga in providing the third novel in a series that excels in blending supernatural forces with a family's relationships and the lure of an island which has changed all their lives ... Ghosts of Mateguas offers a compelling saga of grief, guilt, and perseverance that deftly combines suspense with supernatural intrigue. Prior fans of the series, especially, will find the further interactions between the characters to be engrossing and satisfying, staying true to prior events while adding deeper insights and tension and intrigue to the mix and adding a dose of revelations and truths that draw together prior events in a satisfying new story just as well-crafted as its predecessors."

~ Diane Donovan, Senior Reviewer, *MIDWEST BOOK REVIEW*

"...a vivid and poetic read that beautifully channels modern supernatural melodrama ... Watkins plays to some deeply apparent strengths in this series, and Ghosts of Mateguas is another home-run of a title. Anyone looking for something different along the lines of Shirley Jackson or Stephen King, your prayers have been answered. Ghosts of Mateguas stands as a spellbinding exemplar of modern Gothic Americana."

~ *SELF-PUBLISHING REVIEW*

"The story is fast paced; the suspense is so skillfully built into the story to have the reader turning the pages, and the characters are solid enough that any reader will care about what happens to them ... Beautifully written by a writer of a rare caliber."

~ Romuald Dzemo for *READERS FAVORITE*

"Linda Watkins' supernatural suspense novel, Ghosts of Mateguas: A Mateguas Island Novel, is dark, fast-paced and intense ... There's a marvelous Native American influence at work throughout the story, as well as appearances by a local healer and midwife. I had a grand time reading Ghosts of Mateguas and hope the author decides to write a fourth book in this terrifying and suspenseful series. It's most highly recommended."

~ Jack Magnus for *READERS FAVORITE*

'I would love to see more by Linda Watkins. Her books are fantastic. The writing is tight and engrossing. Her plots are innovative and fascinating."

~ AMAZON CUSTOMER 5-STAR REVIEW

"I found Ghosts of Mateguas to be a quick-paced psychological thriller/horror story. The various stories that made up the tapestry of the whole were equally engaging, and kept me turning the pages. If you enjoy books similar to Stephen King and Dean Koontz, be sure to check out the Mateguas Island books!"

~ J. Aislynn d'Merricksson for *READERS FAVORITE*

"I didn't see the ending coming - something that always makes me love a story. A 4th book would be very welcomed by this reader. Especially continuing the story after that ending."

~AMAZON CUSTOMER 5-STAR REVIEW

Ghosts of Mateguas

A Mateguas Island Novel

LINDA WATKINS

Published in the United States of America by Argon Press
Library of Congress Control Number 2016932222
ISBN 978-1-944815-00-4 (PB)
ISBN 978-1-944815-01-1 (EB)

www.ArgonPress.com

*"Now I know what a ghost is.
Unfinished business, that's what."*

Salman Rushdie,
The Satanic Verses

PROLOGUE
THE COASTAL ROUTE
JUNE 2005

THE FOG EMBRACED THE COAST like a desperate lover, clinging, refusing to let go. This part of the highway was precarious even in good conditions, but now, in the predawn stillness, it was almost impossible.

"This fog is as thick as pea soup," he muttered, chuckling at the image the adage conjured up. He leaned forward, gripping the steering wheel in an attempt to see what lay ahead as he tried to navigate the tortuous coastal route. He glanced toward the horizon, praying that once the sun began to rise it would burn off the fog, making the rest of his journey less harrowing. He estimated he still had another hour or so to go before he reached his destination.

As he inched his way along the highway, his mind wandered back to the phone call that had motivated him to attempt this drive in the first place. *Urgent, they said it was urgent. No details left on voicemail - just that I had to come in person.* Knowing they wouldn't have asked him to make this unscheduled visit unless the situation were grave, he'd left early, hoping to arrive just before they opened. But now the damned fog was turning the two-hour drive into four.

A series of sharp switchbacks loomed ahead, and he forced his concentration back on the road. As he approached the first, he was startled when two bright lights bore down on him from out of nowhere, blinding him. Without thinking, he swerved the car to the right onto the narrow gravel shoulder, barely missing the ditch beyond. The semi driving in his lane blared its horn at him as it hurried past.

Taking a deep breath, he brought the car to a halt and leaned back, trying to control the rapid beating of his heart. *That was a close one*, he thought.

After a few moments, feeling steady again, he put the car back in gear and, with a prayer no one was coming up behind him, steered back onto the highway.

This is crazy, he thought. *I'm going to kill myself and what good will that do anyone? Better stop for coffee. Maybe the fog will begin to dissipate.*

As if hearing his thoughts, a green sign appeared on the side of the road. The next exit was one mile ahead and there were services there - fast food and access to the beach. Nodding, he eased the car onto the ramp and, with a sigh of relief, drove to the nearest restaurant.

The lights of the golden arches cast an eerie glow in the dense mist, taking on a surreal quality. He paid for his coffee, parked his car, and followed the signs leading down to the shore.

Gazing out toward the sea, he could see the faint shimmer of the sun on the water as it began to peek over the horizon. He could hear the waves beating against the rocky shoreline and smell the salt air, but the fog still held everything else tightly in its grip.

He waited, sipping the hot coffee, letting the phone conversation that had brought him out here play repeatedly in his head.

Urgent, they said it was urgent.

Feeling the gravity of the situation, he emptied rest of his drink into the sand and returned to the parking lot, crushing the cup and throwing it into a waste receptacle as he hurried back to his car. He pulled onto the highway noting the fog ahead of him was finally beginning to lift and, smiling grimly, increased his speed.

He checked his watch; one more hour to go. He would make it.

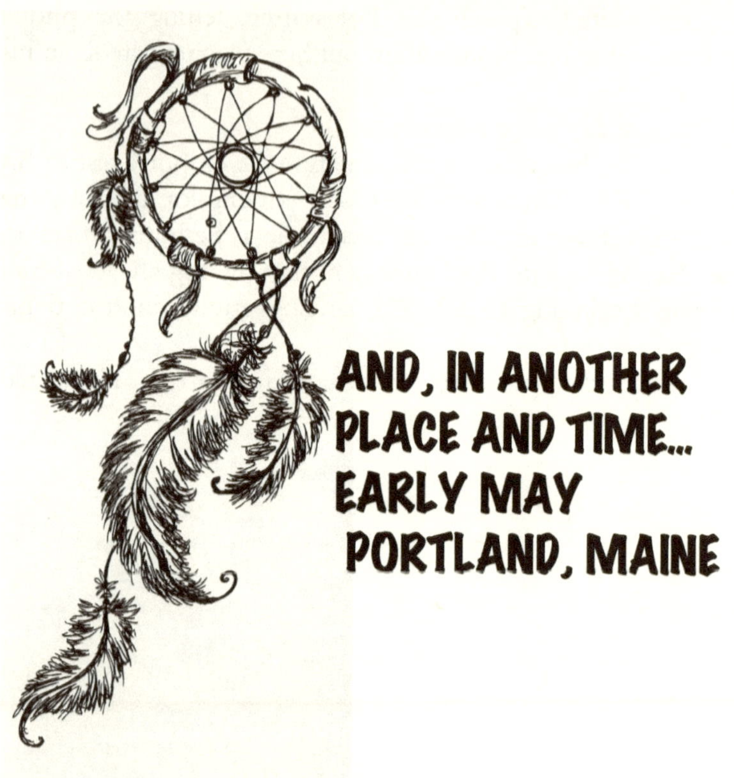

SUSAN LEVEQUE LOOKED OUT the window at the street below. A heavy mist had settled over the port city, and she shook her head in dismay.

Just my luck, she thought. *I'll have to wear a raincoat.*

She walked to the closet, stopping briefly to assess her appearance in the full-length mirror. She was wearing a red cocktail dress with stiletto heels to match. The dress, a Donna Karan knock-off, was sexy, sophisticated, and adorned with understated, but elegant, paste jewelry. Her long brown hair, usually pulled back into a scrunchie or clipped haphazardly on top of her head, was carefully coifed with wispy tendrils framing her face. Smiling at her reflection, she knew she looked lovely.

She grabbed her old L.L. Bean raincoat from the closet and, with a frown, put it on, pulling the hood up carefully over her hair. With one last glance in the mirror, she smiled, slipped her car keys into her evening bag, and headed out the door.

The restaurant was only a few minutes' drive from her apartment and, if the weather had been more cooperative, she probably would have walked. But this was early spring - "mud season" to most Mainers - so the damp, dreary weather was to be expected. Familiar with the city, she found a parking space only a half-block from the restaurant and quickly made her way to the front door.

Inside, she took the elevator to the fifth floor. As she approached the entry to the restaurant, the maitre'd greeted her warmly. This came as no surprise since, as one of Portland's local investigative reporters, she was considered a celebrity of sorts.

She spoke with the man for a moment, asking if her date had arrived. The headwaiter nodded, indicating that he was waiting for her in the lounge.

Susan glanced in that direction. The lighting in the lounge was muted, but she had no problem recognizing the man sitting at the bar. He was staring at her, a slight frown on his face.

It's the Bean, she thought. *He thinks I'm some sort of second-class citizen. Well, we'll see about that.*

Turning her back to him, she allowed the maitre'd to help her with her coat, then smiled as she slowly turned around. The expression on her date's face was priceless. Grinning, he stood to greet her as she walked over to him.

"Bill," she said, offering her hand. "How nice to see you again. How was Paris?"

Bill Andersen helped her to a bar stool and signaled to the bartender. "Paris was great. Fabulous city. Have you been there?"

Susan shook her head. "When did you get back?"

"Oh, about a month ago," Bill replied as the bartender approached. "What would you like to drink?"

"How about a Manhattan, straight up?"

The bartender nodded and turned away to fill her order.

Susan smiled at Bill. "Where are you living now? Here in the city or are you in Boston?"

Bill grinned. "Actually, I'm on Mateguas. I bought that house I used to own there."

"Which house is that?" asked Susan, a puzzled look on her face.

"You know it. It's the one where all the hoopla took place two years ago. I bought it from the Maguires."

"That old house on the hill?"

Bill nodded. "I've been renovating it. You should come over and see it. The exterior has been restored and the interior modernized."

Susan smiled, the wheels in her head spinning as she remembered.

The "hoopla" he referred to had been a big news story and included attempted murder, suicide, and arson. Susan had been the reporter on the scene, and it was at that time she and Andersen had become reacquainted.

The bartender brought her drink, and she sipped it thoughtfully. "I'm surprised the Maguires sold you that property. I heard Mr. Maguire was pretty steamed up after his daughter's death and let it be known that he blamed you and your ex-wife."

Bill frowned. "Yeah. He didn't want to sell it, but the boy - Maggie's son - was pretty messed up after his mother died and the Maguires don't have much in the way of health insurance. They sold it out of economic necessity and, well, they wanted the boy to stay with them."

"He's your kid, right? Did you agree?"

Bill looked down at his hands then back up at Susan. "Yeah, I did ... I gave up my parental rights. That clinched the deal."

Susan nodded and was silent for a moment, mulling this over. "So, is he okay now?"

"The boy?"

She nodded.

"No, he's not. You know he was in the woods when Maggie ... when she killed herself. Well, he's been amnesiac ever since. Mute, too. I think his grandparents take him to see a child psychologist in town regularly."

Susan cocked her head and pursed her lips. "Sorta strange, isn't it? It's kind of like you were when they found you on Puffin ... No memory and unable to speak."

Bill nodded. "Yeah. It is strange." He downed the rest of his drink and signaled to the bartender for another round, then excused himself to go talk to the maitre'd about a table.

As he walked away, Susan studied him carefully out of the corner of her eye. His life had been a real roller coaster ride so far. Once a rising star in Silicon Valley, he'd lost his job and sunk into the depths of unemployment. With mounting debts and a crumbling marriage, he was saved by the death of his aunt and the inheritance of a house on Mateguas, an unconnected island off the coast of Maine. Once there, he'd gotten a new job and was on the rise again when someone whacked him on the head and dumped him on a small abandoned island about five miles from Mateguas. Presumed dead by his family, his wife moved away and married a man she'd met while in Maine. Miraculously, Bill survived two years on Puffin Island and then eight more in the State Hospital - amnesiac and mute just like his son was now.

A story Susan had broadcast about him found his family, who were visiting in Maine and, again, he seemed to be on the rise - new job, new girlfriend, the whole nine yards, but then it went south again. The girlfriend shot him, almost killing him, and then killed herself and set the woods on fire.

But, true to form, he rebounded and was, once again, on top of the world. Susan wondered what calamity was lurking out there now, waiting to bring him to heel yet again.

She grinned and took a sip of her drink. "The Puffin Man," as locals called him, had already been good to her. The broadcast she'd aired about him earned her an Edward R. Murrow Award and a regular spot on the evening news.

Looking at him now as he spoke to the maitre'd, she wondered what else he could do for her career. He seemed to be settled with no disasters looming on the sidelines, but, in her gut, she knew something would happen and, when it did, she would be there to use it to her full advantage.

As dinner progressed, Susan found herself pleasantly surprised by how much she was enjoying her date with "The Puffin Man." She'd gone out with him one time before, on the evening he'd left for Paris. The man she'd had dinner with then had been bitter, angry, and looking for revenge. He blamed his former wife's husband for his exile to Puffin and had tried, in every way possible, to enlist Susan's aid in bringing about the man's downfall. She had declined to help him back then, even though his accusations piqued her curiosity about Dexter Pierce, ex-Mateguan and current husband of Karen Andersen.

But the man she was with tonight was very different from that Bill Andersen. By outward appearance, he was a witty, intelligent, and sensitive dinner companion.

Have the two years abroad really changed his outlook? she asked herself. *No, I don't think so. I bet somewhere deep down he still harbors resentment toward Pierce and the pleasant demeanor he's putting on tonight is nothing but a weak facade.*

"How about an after-dinner drink?" asked Bill, breaking into her reverie.

Susan glanced at her watch ... She had to be on the air at eight a.m. the next morning. Her head told her to politely decline, but she was having fun, and there was the possibility she could parlay a friendship with this man into something that could help her career.

"Sure, that sounds nice. A little Gran Marnier with a twist for me."

Bill smiled as he beckoned to the waiter.

Susan picked up her evening bag. "I think I'll make a quick trip to the 'ladies' while we wait for our drinks."

Nodding, Bill stood and helped her with her chair, letting his hand linger on her waist for a few seconds before letting her go.

In the ladies room, Susan checked her appearance in the mirror and applied some lip gloss. She'd wanted a few minutes alone to collect her thoughts before returning to the table. Despite her refusal to help Bill dig up dirt on Pierce two years before, she had done some Internet snooping about the man. She hadn't expected to find anything - he appeared to be a pillar of the community, well liked and honest. But, to her surprise, she did uncover a couple of mentions that intrigued her. Busy on other stories, she had quickly filed the articles away and then forgot about them. However, now, with her new connection to "The Puffin Man," she thought that maybe it was time to take another look.

Deep in thought, she checked the clips holding up her hair, then stepped back and gazed at herself in the mirror. She looked damned good. She picked up her bag and moved toward the door when another thought crossed her mind. She was attracted to the man waiting for her. Outwardly, he was just a slightly above-average looking guy, but there was an aura of danger about him and Susan found that almost irresistible.

"You really have to come see the house," said Bill as he sipped his brandy. "It needs a feminine touch and I can sense that you have impeccable taste."

Susan smiled at the compliment. "I think I'd like that. I don't get out to the islands much. Unless something is going on with the lobstering business, there's really nothing newsworthy there."

"Well, how about next weekend? Take a couple days off and let your hair down."

Susan pulled out her cell and checked her calendar. "I'm on the air on Saturday, but I have Sunday-Monday off. Would that work?"

"Sounds great."

"Okay," she answered, typing the information into her phone. "What ferry should I take?"

"Oh, no ... no ferry. I'll pick you up. I have my own boat now."

"Wow, you're really getting into island life. I'm impressed!"

Bill laughed. "Yes, I guess I am. I'm even on some of the local charity boards. Actually, I'm throwing a party to benefit one of them the beginning of June. Sort of a 'start to the summer' party. Maybe you could help me with the plans. That's the kind of thing I always left to Karen. I'm a little bit out of my depth with party planning."

Susan smiled. "Well, I don't do much in that regard either. But, sure, I'll help." She glanced at her watch then out the window at the harbor below.

"I hate to say it," she sighed, "but it's getting late and I'm on the air in the morning. Looks like the rain has stopped."

Bill nodded and signaled to the waiter for the check. "I never get tired of that view," he said, looking out at the moon as its light sparkled off the sea below. "Paris was great, but I'll take this any day."

Susan cocked her head, surprised. "You are becoming a Mainer!"

The check paid, Bill helped Susan with her coat. He smiled at her appreciatively and put his arm around her waist as they made their way to the elevator.

The restaurant was deserted at this late hour and the old-fashioned lift was empty when it arrived. As soon as the door closed, Bill stepped toward Susan, slipping his hands inside her raincoat and pulling her to him. Eagerly, she moved into his embrace, tilting her head back to await the kiss she knew was coming.

Bill leaned down and pressed his lips to hers, slipping his tongue inside her partially opened mouth.

Responding, she lifted her arms and wound them around his neck as she returned his kiss.

Emboldened by her passion, Bill moved one hand from her waist, sliding it down across her buttocks. Aroused by his touch, she moaned and moved closer to him, pressing her pelvis against his.

Slowly, fingers playing across the tight fabric of her dress, he teased her with his touch. His hand slipped tentatively between her thighs and, when she made no move to stop him, he slid it up, underneath the hem of her dress.

She wore only a garter belt and matching silk thong. Giving in to sensation, she shifted her weight so her legs were slightly apart, allowing him access.

For a moment, he hesitated, surprised by the warm, bare skin of her bottom.

"Don't stop," she moaned as she pressed herself closer to him, moving her hips against his now prominent erection.

Acquiescing to her wishes, Bill trailed his fingers down the cleft between her cheeks to the juncture where her thighs met.

Time seemed to stand still as the lift slowly descended to the first floor, finally arriving in the building's lobby. A loud 'ding' as it stopped startled them both.

Susan jumped out of his embrace, straightening her dress as she pulled her coat closed around her. She stared at him, her breathing ragged and face flushed with passion.

The doors opened slowly and she breathed a sigh of relief when she saw the lobby was empty.

"Let's go back to your place," he said, taking her hand and propelling her toward the door.

Much later, Susan rolled over and glanced at the clock on the nightstand next to her bed. It was three a.m.

Groaning softly, she moved out of the embrace of the man sleeping beside her and sat on the side of the bed. She stared at him for a moment. He was lean but well-muscled, and she noted there were several scars on his chest, no doubt painfully earned during his two years on Puffin.

Not a bad-looking man, she thought. *And a good lover ... passionate and considerate. But there's an edge to him ... something just below the surface that makes him even more exciting.*

Being careful not to wake him, she slipped out of bed and pulled on her robe. She closed the door softly behind her as she made her way to the kitchen. Liberating a bottle of water from the refrigerator, she sat down at the breakfast bar, drinking deeply. Her laptop sat on the counter and she thought about logging on, but resisted the impulse. She had to be at the studio by six a.m. and that meant she had only about an hour and a half left to sleep. Sighing, she walked back to the bedroom and crept under the covers.

"What time is it?" Bill asked, rolling over to face her.

"A little after three," she whispered. "I have to be at work at six."

Bill smiled. "Then we have plenty of time."

"Time for what?"

Bill smiled again as he slipped his hand inside her robe and fondled her breast, rolling her soft nipple between his fingers. When it hardened, he leaned forward and took it in his mouth. She moaned in response, grasping the back of his head with her hands.

"I think you know what for," he whispered as he leaned away and pulled her on top of him.

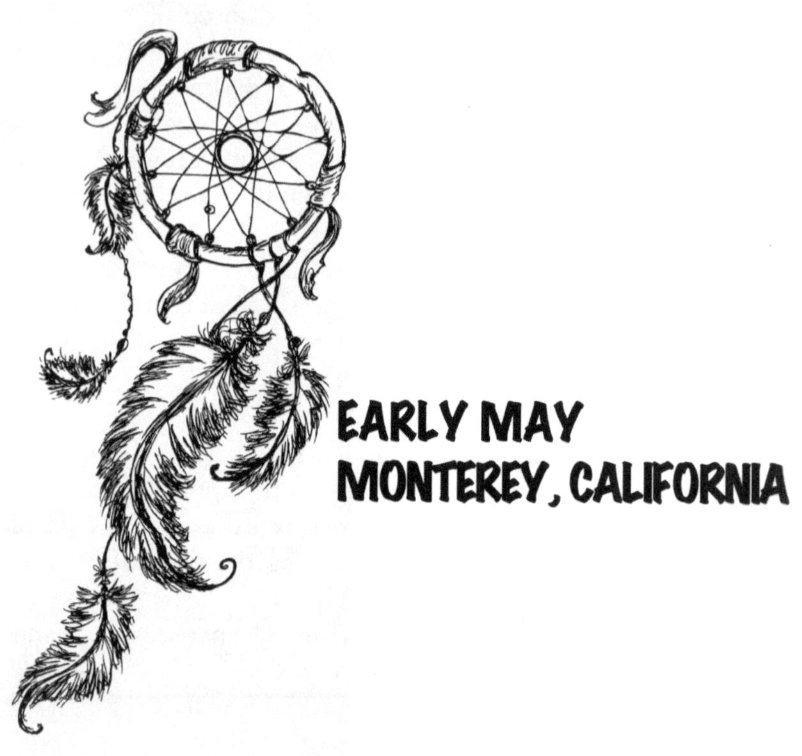

KAREN ANDERSEN PIERCE WALKED the beach alone. Her infant son, Alex, now just over a year old, was in a special preschool program for toddlers and her husband, Dex, was at work. Her other children were away at college, Terri at Scripps Institute and Sophie at Yale.

Sitting on a rock, Karen checked her watch. She still had an hour to kill before it was time to pick up Alex. Staring out at the sea, her thoughts drifted back to another shore on the other side of the country.

This time I want to go back, she thought. *I need to go back and find out the truth. Is my son special? Or is he just a normal little boy?*

She remembered the day she had given birth to him. It had been so exciting to be finally giving Dex a child of his own. But her happiness was short-lived when she saw those beautiful flecks of gold sparkling in the newborn's eyes.

Is he the child of Mateguas, Abenaki God of the Dead, a reincarnation of The Blessed Boy? Or is he the true child of my husband?

She didn't know the answers, but planned to find out. She had been struck by lightning nine months before the birth, just like the murdered acolyte of Mateguas decades before. Legend told that the lightning bolt represented Mateguas' manhood and that his acolyte, a virgin, also gave birth nine months later. But Karen had also had relations with her husband that night, so the child could, indeed, be his.

If it weren't for those damned flecks of gold in his eyes, she thought. *But I only saw them the one time. The boy's eyes are now completely normal, bright and blue, and he gives no indication of being anything other than a human child.*

Feeling restless, she stood and began walking along the shore.

Terri will be on the island this summer, too, and maybe she can hook me up with that old Indian friend of hers. Perhaps he can help me find some answers.

Thoughts of her daughter caused her to frown as she recalled their last conversation.

She just announced that she would be spending the summer on Mateguas with that boy she met there two years ago. Said she was going to be his sternman - baiting and hauling traps and other nasty stuff like that. Ugh! Said it would give her practical experience on the water. Humph! If she wanted practical experience, she could have gotten it at home. Her stepfather's a fisherman, for God's sake! Well, I'm sure she'll be getting some kind of practical experience, though I doubt it will be on a boat! At least she's smart enough to take care of herself and not get into trouble.

Karen bent down and picked up a shell that was half buried in the warm sand. She and Dex would be going back to Mateguas in early June. She wondered if her ex-husband would be there. He'd been living in Paris last she'd heard, but she knew from her daughters that he'd purchased that old house on the hill and was renovating it. He'd been bitter and resentful last time she'd seen him, but she hoped the two years abroad had mellowed him and that he no longer harbored amorous feelings for her. In addition, she prayed that he had abandoned the notion that her current husband had been the one who left him to die on that island. If he hadn't, it could make the summer on Mateguas unbearable for all of them.

Mateguas, she thought. *Once I'm back there, will all those visions start to haunt me again? The spirit of The Blessed Boy told me that that part of my journey was over. But is it?*

Thoughts of the trail behind her old house and the vicious owl that stalked her caused her to shudder with fear.

Wrapping her arms tightly around her body, she stood and stared out at the Pacific Ocean. It was so calm and peaceful, not at all like the rocky shores of Maine and Mateguas.

She checked her watch. It was time to go. With one last glance at the sea, she started back up the beach to her car. Her mind was flooded with too many questions and too few answers and she knew none of them would come clear here. She would just have to be patient and wait until they were back on the island. Once they were there, the answers would come. They had to.

SCRIPPS INSTITUTE
LA JOLLA, CALIFORNIA

THE PROFESSOR'S VOICE DRONED on and Terri Andersen found it hard to keep her attention focused on the lecture. Normally this class, *Fisheries, Ecology, and Conservation*, was one of her favorites, but today all she could think about was Mateguas and the boy who would be waiting for her there.

It had been two years since she'd been on the island and two years since she'd laid eyes on Shawn O'Dwyer. But in just three short weeks, she'd be with him again, on Mateguas, staying for the summer.

They'd kept in touch. There wasn't a day that went by when she didn't have a conversation with him either on the phone, by text, or by email. But that wasn't the same as actually being there - seeing him in person and living with him on the island for three months.

They hadn't been exclusive; both had dated others during the past two years. But for Terri, at least, none of those boys had stuck. The connection she felt to Shawn was still just as strong as it had been the night they defeated the dark magic on a deserted beach. But the thought of living in the same house with him over the summer and working with him on a daily basis was a bit frightening. She was still a virgin and wasn't sure if she was ready to take that step yet with him or anyone else. She hoped that Shawn, who was a couple years older, would understand and be able to accept that.

The student next to her gave her a nudge. Startled, she looked up and was surprised to see all the kids around her packing up their laptops and filing out of the lecture hall. A bit panicked, Terri glanced up at the board, hoping to see the next week's assignment, but it was empty.

"Don't worry, Ter," said the young woman standing next to her. "I got it all down. You can copy it back at the apartment."

Terri smiled, glad to see one of her roommates waiting for her. "Thanks, Trish. I kinda zoned out there for a while."

Trish laughed. "Probably thinking about that hunk you got waiting for you on that island up in Maine. If I had that boy on my mind, I think I'd be zoned out too!"

"Yeah, I've got him on my mind all right. We talk all the time, but I haven't seen him for two years. He may have changed. I don't know."

"Well, your dad lives on that island, too, doesn't he? If things don't work out with the eye candy, then you could always stay with him."

"Yes, I could," replied Terri, glancing at the clock on the wall. "Eye candy? I'll have to tell Shawn about that! We'd better get going, or we'll be late for Professor Stuart's class."

TO HACK OR NOT TO HACK

SUSAN BARELY HAD TIME to shower, dress, and gulp down a cup of coffee before she had to leave for the station. Grabbing her coat, she tossed her house keys at Bill, who was still lying in bed.

"Just lock up when you leave and give the keys to Jimmy, the doorman. I'll be in touch," she said as strode hastily out of the room.

"Don't forget about next weekend!" Bill yelled after her. He waited for a response, but all he got was the slamming of the front door.

Grinning, he got up and looked around the room. Susan was not what he would call a 'neat and tidy' person. Not like Karen at all. The walk-in closet had almost as many articles of clothing on the floor as were on hangers. And her shoes were strewn about haphazardly. He wondered how she ever found a matching pair.

Finding nothing of interest in the bedroom, he walked to the bathroom and took a leisurely shower. Once he was cleaned up and dressed, he explored the rest of the apartment, stopping when he found what he was looking for.

Her office was in a small alcove off the kitchen. It consisted of just a tiny desk, computer, full-spectrum lamp, and a small file cabinet. He glanced through the files, but they were ancient - paper reports from years before cloud storage facilities were the norm.

Closing the file drawer, he stared at the computer. He'd done some research on Susan LeVeque before he'd asked her out this time. Contrary to her self-assurance and swagger, she was a small-town girl, born and raised in Poland, Maine. She'd gone to state college, working her way through journalism school waiting tables at a local diner. The discovery of his abandonment on Puffin Island had been her big break. She'd been just an intern reporter back then who happened to have pulled the late-night duty call. The way she'd handled that story had catapulted her into a regular job at the TV station and, since then, she'd slowly been working her way up the ladder. And now she was close to accomplishing her dream of making it to the big time - national news - but somehow the right story kept eluding her.

Bill hoped he could help her out and, by doing so, bring about the demise of the man he saw as his enemy and rival for Karen's affections. If that could be accomplished, then he would have a chance to regain what he wanted most, his family back together again.

Sitting down at Susan's desk, he wondered if she hadn't already begun investigating Dex. He'd suggested it to her two years prior, but she had turned him down. However, he knew she was by nature curious, and he suspected that she wouldn't have been able to resist the impulse to do a little digging.

He was about to hack into her computer to see what he could find when he noticed a slight layer of dust on top of the keyboard. Staring at it, he realized she didn't use this machine much, probably preferring her laptop. He knew he could still access her files from this station, but to do that would be to disturb the dust and take the chance she might notice.

Shaking his head, he backed away. It was not worth the risk.

A bit disappointed, he moved from the office to the kitchen and put a pod in her coffee maker. Waiting for it to brew, he thought about the night before.

He'd played it just right this time. The last time he took her out, his wounds had still been too fresh. His bitterness and anger had shone through and it had scared her off. But last night, he'd kept all those feelings well hidden and she had responded to him positively.

He smiled thinking about their lovemaking. She was quite aggressive in bed, not at all like Karen. Susan knew what she wanted and made no bones about insisting that she get it. She was an exciting woman and just the thought of her lithe, firm, young body began to arouse him.

Shaking these erotic thoughts from his mind, he got up, retrieved his now full coffee cup, and walked to the window. Susan had an unparalleled view of the city from this sixth-floor apartment. There was a slight veil of fog still hovering over the wharf, but the sun was finally making an appearance, promising a nice spring day.

Downing his coffee, Bill rinsed out the cup and placed it in the dishwasher. Then he walked back to Susan's office, grabbed a post-it, and wrote a short note.

Had a great time last night. Hope you did, too. See you next Sunday. I'll be in touch to let you know when I'll pick you up.
B.

He tacked the note to refrigerator door where he was sure she would see it, then grabbed his jacket and, with her keys in hand, exited the apartment.

MONTEREY BAY, CALIFORNIA

DEX PIERCE SAT AT his desk, going over his accounts. He made his final entry, sighed, and shut down the computer. This was the part of the business he disliked. He'd much rather have been out on the water doing what he did best, fishing. But today, his new junior partner, Brad Hellmann, was on the boat and would soon be taking over the business in Monterey for the summer months while Dex and his family were on Mateguas.

Thinking about the upcoming trip to the island, Dex checked his watch. It was almost nine a.m. Pacific time, high noon on the east coast. He picked up the phone and dialed the Mateguas Boatyard, hoping the 40' Novi commercial fishing boat that he had purchased from a dealer in Fairhaven had arrived at the island safe and sound.

Ghosts of Mateguas

The call went directly to voicemail, but that didn't surprise Dex. This was a busy time of year at the boatyard with all the lobstermen getting their vessels shipshape for the upcoming season. Sighing to himself, he left a message then hung up the phone. Thinking about the new boat, he wondered if he had bitten off more than he could chew. The payments were hefty and didn't include the additional expense of gas and bait. He knew he was good at what he did, but was he that good?

The sound of a car pulling up the driveway startled him. He glanced out the window. It was Karen coming home from the daycare with their son, Alex.

Smiling, he watched as she lifted the child from his car seat.

That boy's a miracle, he thought. *It took ten years of trying, but we finally did it. At least I think we did it.*

A frown settled over his face. In the back of his mind, there was still a lingering doubt about his paternity. When the boy was conceived, they'd been on Mateguas and, after a bitter fight, had separated. They didn't stay apart long, but during their separation, she'd spent a suspicious evening alone with her ex-husband.

He'd accused her of cheating, but she'd sworn to him that nothing happened. He accepted her denial and was overjoyed when he found out she was pregnant. But still, there was always a thread of doubt nagging at his mind. He'd considered having a DNA test done but was afraid if she found out, it would be the end of their marriage and he would wind up losing both her and the child.

He watched as she hefted the toddler onto her hip and walked up the porch stairs. At forty-six, she was still a beautiful woman. He thought about the DNA testing again. He had a friend in Maine who was a doctor and, maybe, once they were on the island, he could have one done confidentially. What he would do if he found out he was not Alex's father, he didn't know. However, one way or the other, it would put his doubts to rest and he needed that for his peace of mind.

The door opened and Karen walked in carrying the chubby one-year-old.

"Here," she said, handing the boy to Dex. "You take him. He's getting heavy."

Dex smiled and took the boy from her arms, lifting him high in the air. The child squealed with delight and Dex tossed him again.

"Jesus, Dex," Karen complained. "Don't drop him. Roughhouse with him on the floor where he's not going to land on his head. I'm going to take a shower."

Leaning over to give her husband a kiss, she shrugged off her jacket and left the room.

Dex played with the child for a while, then, seeing the boy was getting fussy, put him down for a nap.

He had just settled his son in bed when Karen emerged from the bathroom, a towel wrapped around her slender body. She smiled at him as he put his arms around her, pulling her close. Her small breasts had gotten larger with childbirth and he loved how they felt pressed against his chest.

Karen leaned into his embrace, running her hands appreciatively over his body.

"Save that thought for later," she said with a smile. "I have to get dressed and you need to shower and change, too."

Dex looked puzzled. "Why? Do we have plans?"

Karen pursed her lips. "Have you forgotten? My mother and her new husband are in town and we're meeting them for dinner. The sitter will be here at five. This is the last time I'll get to see her before we leave for the summer."

Dex frowned, shrugging. "Okay, later, and I'm going to hold you to it. Guess I'd better get ready."

They returned home late and after checking on the baby, went directly to bed. Well past midnight, Karen, unable to sleep, grabbed her robe and tiptoed down the hall to the nursery. Baby Alex was asleep, his chubby fingers clutching his favorite stuffed toy, a present from his grandmother.

Karen reached out and ran her hand gently through his soft blonde hair. As soon as she touched him, the little crescent scar in the center of her palm became warm and began to slowly pulsate.

The first time this happened, she'd been frightened, not knowing whether the magic within her was reaching out to help or harm her boy. But time had eased her fears. Her magic would never harm this child; no, it meant only to protect him.

She sat in the rocking chair next to the crib gazing at him, a worried frown on her face.

Maybe bringing him to the island is wrong. Maybe we should just stay here where I know he'll be safe. Other than the flecks of gold in his eyes at birth, he's shown no signs of being anything other than a normal little boy. Will taking him to the island trigger something? Something that should stay dormant?

She thought about this for a while, trying to come up with a plausible reason for canceling their trip - something Dex would buy. But nothing came to mind.

No, Dex has too great a financial stake in this now with the new boat and all. And anyway, would staying away be the right thing to do? If Alex is The Blessed Boy, I can't deny him his heritage. And maybe in some strange way he needs the island.

Sighing, she rocked back and forth, knowing that there was no turning back now. They would go to the island and she would once again face the magic that dwelt there. All she could do was to try to protect her son using any means possible, and that she would do, even if she died trying.

JUNE - PORTLAND INTERNATIONAL JETPORT

TERRI RETRIEVED HER CARRY-ON and made her way off the plane. She was tired and, had to admit, more than a little nervous.

She'd taken the red-eye from L.A. to Detroit and then spent four hours at Metro waiting for her connection to Maine. She sent Shawn a text updating him on her arrival time but as she boarded her flight, hadn't received a reply. She prayed he'd be at the airport to meet her. The thought of him developing cold feet at this point was not an option she could entertain.

Finding her way out of the airport's restricted area, she stopped and glanced around, hoping to see a familiar face in the sea of strangers waiting to greet loved ones, but no one was there.

Well, if he doesn't show, she thought, *I'll take a cab to the ferry terminal. I can stay at Dad's. But I can't believe he'd do this to me.*

She hoisted her carry-on over her shoulder and stepped onto the escalator, heading toward Baggage Claim. She was approaching the carousel when she heard a voice calling out her name.

"Terri!"

Pivoting around, she saw Shawn striding hurriedly toward her, in his hand a rapidly wilting bouquet of wildflowers.

"Hi," she said as he approached. "I was about to give up on you."

With a grin, he grabbed her hands and swung her around. "You're not getting away from me that easily! Traffic was a bitch. There was an accident on Route 1 that backed me up for twenty minutes. I got your text. Sorry, I didn't get back to you."

He handed her the flowers.

"These are for you," he said. "They're sort of yucky now. They looked a hell of a lot better back on the island."

Terri grinned. "Thanks. It's the thought that counts."

They stared at each other for a minute.

"You look good," he finally said. "I really missed you."

Terri nodded. "I missed you, too."

Shawn reached out to take her in his arms, but the sound of the carousel starting up startled him.

He took a deep breath. "What does your bag look like?"

Soon they were on their way from the airport to the islanders' parking lot at the wharf downtown. Shawn loaded Terri's bags into his punt then helped her aboard.

It was a short trip, and before long the island's familiar shape appeared on the horizon, bringing with it memories of the last time they had been together and the magic that had threatened them.

"I can't believe I'm back here," said Terri as Shawn tied the boat to the stone pier.

"Yeah, me, too. But it's been quiet here since you left. No hocus pocus, abracadabra or anything. Just plain old boring island life. But now that you're back, who knows what will happen."

Terri laughed, glancing around the busy wharf. "I'm surprised my dad's not down here to greet us."

"Oh, he might be in Boston. He's usually there most of the week. Comes back for long weekends."

"That makes sense. You told me he's gotten involved with some of the island nonprofits. What's that all about?"

"Yeah, he works with my mom on the Hall renovation project. She loves him."

"Loves him?"

Shawn laughed. "Not that way, girl! It's just that he's been a real help to her with all the computer stuff. He's very organized."

"Yeah, that's him, for sure."

"And, he's been talking to me about boats and lobstering. Think he's going to get himself a non-commercial license."

"What's that?"

"It's an exclusive license for Maine residents. It will allow him to set a maximum of five traps. Any lobsters he catches will have to be for private consumption. He can't sell them."

"Cool. You said in your last text that he has a new girlfriend, too. Is she a local?"

Shawn grinned. "You're never going to guess who it is."

"Come on, tell me. Is it someone I know?"

"Yeah, you know her. It's that reporter who hooked you up with him at the State Hospital, Susan LeVeque."

Terri frowned. "The reporter? No way!"

Shawn laughed. "Yes, it's her. She's up here all the time."

"Isn't she a little young for him?"

"No, she's got to be thirty-five or six. Good-looking woman."

They continued chatting as they loaded Terri's gear into Shawn's truck. His house was on the far end of the island, about fifteen minutes away. Terri gazed out the window as they drove, wondering what it would be like and, more importantly, what he would expect of her once they got there.

She didn't have long to wait. Shawn pulled the truck up a winding dirt road that led to a gravel driveway. The house, a mid-sized, two-story cottage, was old and surrounded by a large new wooden deck. It wasn't on the beach but was not far from it. Lobster traps were piled high in the back, as were newly painted, shiny buoys. There were also rows of stacked wood close to the rear entrance, indicating that much of the heat came from a woodstove.

"Well, what do you think?" he asked. "I know she's old, but she's sound, and I'm fixing her up."

"I like it. It's very New England. Did you build the deck yourself?"

Shawn nodded. "Wait'll you see the inside. I gutted the kitchen this winter and remodeled the whole thing. And the upstairs ... it was three small bedrooms and a bath. I took out some walls, enlarged the bathroom, and made the rest one big room. Come on, let's go inside."

Terri smiled, the mention of the bedroom making her nervous. "Okay," she said. "Let's go inside."

SHAWN'S HOUSE

THE HOUSE WAS SMALL, but cozy. The front door opened onto the living room, which was furnished with a couch, flanked by end tables and a couple of easy chairs. In the center of the far wall sat a large fireplace that housed a woodstove insert to provide ambiance during the summer and much-needed heat during the cold winter months. The floors were wooden slats, painted a soft blue. A large circular braided rug in complementary colors adorned the center of the floor.

Beyond the living room was the kitchen. It, too, was small, and Terri noted that it would be difficult for two people to work there comfortably at the same time. But, as Shawn mentioned, it had been updated and was efficient. The appliances were Kenmore and new. The counters were Corian and gleamed in the sunlight cascading through the windows. An oak dining table sat to one side, surrounded by four chairs.

"You did this all yourself?" Terri asked. "It's nice. I like the counters."

Shawn beamed at the compliment. "Yup, with a little help from my friends. Look out here."

He gestured to the back door that led from the kitchen to the deck. Outside, sat a brand-new Weber Genesis propane grill.

"It's got a few dings on the side, but it works fine," he said. "I got a deal on it because of the dents."

Terri smiled. "Cool. Very nice."

"Okay. Let me show you the upstairs."

Terri took a deep breath. She knew this was the bedroom and just the thought of that made her anxious. "Okay," she said. "Show me."

The stairs were at the front of the house, to the left of the doorway. As they walked through the living room, Terri noted a narrow hallway just before the entry to the kitchen.

"What's down there?" she asked.

"Oh, just a half-bath and another room, but it's a mess right now."

As they climbed the stairs, Shawn kept up a running dialogue about the house and his remodeling efforts and plans. Terri remained silent, wondering what his expectations were and how she would deal with them if they were out of line.

At the top of the staircase was a small landing with doorways off to the left and right. To the left was a large bedroom, furnished with a king-size four-poster bed, nightstands, and dresser. A flat-screen TV was suspended from the wall opposite the bed. Large windows, letting in the warm summer light, surrounded the room. A small walk-in closet was situated near the far wall.

"Well, what do you think?" asked Shawn. "Think you'll be happy here?"

Terri looked at him, puzzled. "What do you mean? Isn't this your room? I think we need to talk about this, Shawn. I ... I don't think..."

Shawn smiled and shook his head. "You got it all wrong, girl. This room is YOUR room. I moved all my stuff downstairs to the spare room. That's why it's such a mess. I haven't put things away yet."

Terri breathed a sigh of relief and looked at him gratefully. "Thank you. I mean ... it's not that I don't want ... but, I...."

He reached out, taking her hands in his. "Hey, I'll be honest. There's nothing I'd like better than to share my bed with you. But, I know, it's been two years. We, and I mean 'we,' need time to get reacquainted. And when that's accomplished, if you invite me up here, well, we'll cross that bridge when we come to it."

His voice trailed off as he gazed into her eyes. Terri leaned happily toward him, resting her head on his chest as he pulled her close and buried his lips in her hair.

They stood silently in each other's arms until Terri pulled away and smiled up at him.

"I think I'm going to be happy here," she said. "It feels like home."

EARLY JUNE
BILL'S HOUSE

SUSAN POURED HERSELF A glass of wine and walked outside to the porch. Bill was standing on the front patio by the outdoor grill, unaware of her presence, preparing to broil steaks for dinner.

She stopped for a moment, studying him. She had to admit that the past few weeks had been fun. He was a good companion and lover, and she was beginning to feel comfortable in the relationship. However, she didn't completely trust him or his motivations.

He seems sincere, but I don't know. That ex-wife of his and her husband will be here soon, and we'll see how he behaves then.

She sipped her wine, thinking about Karen and Dex Pierce, going over in her mind the information she had recently found out about them.

I wonder how Bill will react if I tell him what I've uncovered.

Smiling, she stepped onto the patio. "Hey, remember back before you went to Paris when we went out to dinner?"

Bill nodded. "Yeah. It was the night I left. I had a good time. What about it?"

Susan smiled. "Well, remember what you asked me? About your ex-wife's husband?"

Bill's hand stopped mid-air as he visibly stiffened. Seconds passed as Susan watched him try to rein in his emotions.

"Yeah, I remember," he finally answered, turning his head in her direction. "You refused. What about it?"

Susan smiled, then took a sip of her wine, enjoying his discomfort. "Well, you got me curious and, without telling you, I did a little digging on my own."

"And?"

There was a hint of impatience in his tone and Susan, again, sipped her wine silently.

"I'm waiting."

Ignoring him, she sat down on one of the lounges. Finally, she looked up and met his gaze.

"I found a couple mentions. I didn't do anything with them back then, just filed 'em away. But last week, I dug a little deeper, and I think I may have stumbled onto something interesting."

Bill stared at her. She could see the excitement building in his eyes.

"Hey, don't let those steaks burn!"

Startled, he turned back toward the grill.

"Oh, Christ," he said. "I think they'll be okay ... just a little charred on the outside. Bring me a plate, will you?"

"Sure," she replied, returning to the house.

That cinches it, she thought as she pulled a plate from the cupboard. *He's still hung up on his damned ex-wife, and nothing is going to change that. Well, maybe I can still find a way to turn things to my advantage, if not romantically, then career-wise. And if what I suspect about that Pierce character pans out, it should be a real eye-opener.*

DAYBREAK

BILL POURED HIMSELF A cup of coffee and walked across the street to the beach to watch the sunrise. Susan, who had spent the weekend, had to be at the station by six-thirty and that meant motoring her over to the mainland in the predawn darkness.

Sitting on a rock, he stared at the horizon. They'd had a good time over the weekend and, for a brief moment, he'd felt happy. But, his high spirits didn't last and he was left again with an all-too-familiar feeling of emptiness in the pit of his stomach.

As he watched the first rays of the sun break over the ocean, he tried to remember the last time he'd been really happy. He knew it had been back in California before his indiscretion at that damned party caused him to lose his job. He thought about the party for a moment, picturing Julie, his boss's wife, and how close he'd come to committing an act of infidelity with her.

Frowning, he shook off those images and instead formed a different picture in his mind: Karen and the girls at the beach in Santa Cruz, building sand castles and laughing. He smiled as he visualized every detail of that day. Had it really been so long ago?

Yes, he thought, *things were good back then, but that was before keeping secrets and telling lies became a way of life for us.*

He sipped his coffee, remembering how hopeful he'd felt when they'd moved to this island. But then he'd met Maggie and gotten involved with her and, in response or retaliation, Karen formed "a friendship" with Dex.

It seemed, for a time, that their marriage was doomed, but just before the unthinkable happened, on that night of the storm, they'd made love and resolved to try to put things back together for the sake of what they once had and for their children.

He finished his coffee and stood.

Yes, he thought. *We were going to move to the mainland and make a fresh start, but someone didn't want that to happen; someone wanted me out of the way.*

His mind conjured up what he called his "list of suspects."

Suspect #1: Maggie - she was certainly capable of it. Despite her short stature, she had been in great shape and knew how to handle a boat. But she'd just found out she was pregnant and hadn't told me yet. Why would she try to kill me when, in her deluded little mind, she thought I would marry her? No, it couldn't have been her.

Suspect #2: Karen - if she had been having an affair with Dex, that would have given her a motive to get rid of me. But she knows nothing about boats and isn't strong enough to lift a body. So, if she did do it, she couldn't have done it alone. No, I can't believe she could be that callous. If she'd truly wanted me gone, she would have divorced me, not tried to kill me.

That left the only other person he knew had a motive: Dex Pierce.

It always comes back to him. He wanted my wife and did what he needed to get her. Maybe he didn't hit me over the head; the wound on my skull could have come from a falling tree branch or something. But, he took me to that goddamned island and left me there to die. But I showed him - I survived - two long, cruel years there and another eight in the hospital. And now I'm back and it's his turn to pay.

Bill took a deep breath, trying to control the anger and resentment building in his mind.

Have to keep it under control, he thought. *Can't let on how I really feel. If I do, it will only drive Karen further away. No, I have to have her on my side and, then, only then, will I get my family back.*

Feeling calmer as he again pictured what once had been his family, he watched the sun move up over the horizon, promising another beautiful day.

He smiled and turned from the sea, walking back to the house. He had work to do, and later, on the afternoon ferry, Karen would be arriving.

Just the thought of her being back on the island brought joy to his heart and he felt almost giddy with anticipation. Soon, all the players would be in place and, with Susan assuming her role, his revenge would be complete. Then he would have his family back and only when that happened would he, once again, be happy.

He grinned at this thought, then shrugged and ambled back across the street, his head full of pictures and his heart full of hope.

MID-JUNE
THE FERRY

KAREN HESITATED THEN STEPPED aboard the boat. Making her way down the center aisle into the cabin, she noted that it hadn't changed much in the past two years. However, someone had slapped a fresh coat of paint on everything and, as a result, it looked bright, shiny, and new. She shook her head, then looked back over her shoulder. Dex, carrying baby Alex, was entering the cabin after making sure their luggage was secure at the stern.

"Let's go up to the bow," he said. "It's a great day to be outside and on the water!"

Karen smiled. She usually stayed inside, but today was different. She was not dreading the island as she had in the past. No, today, she was looking forward to it - to being there with the man she loved and their little boy. And Terri would be on the island, too.

Her other daughter, Sophie, was staying in New Haven, taking classes and working at a gallery for the summer. They'd stopped to see her on their way to Maine and would probably stop again on their way back to California in September. Hopefully, she would make it up to the island for a visit sometime during the three months they would be there.

Once on the bow, Karen took a seat on a bench just outside the cabin. The wind was brisk, but not too cold, and she turned her face to the sun, relishing its warmth. Dex, with baby Alex, stood by the rail, pointing out all the sights to the excited one-year-old.

"You keep a good hold on him," scolded Karen. "Don't drop him overboard!"

Dex laughed, turning to look at her. "You worry too much. I've got him," he said, gazing down at his son, then back out to sea.

"There, Alex. Look. That's the island. That's where I was born."

The little boy stared as Mateguas came into view in the distance, its craggy shoreline glistening in the afternoon sun.

As if recognizing it, the child let out a loud squeal and began wiggling with apparent joy in his father's arms.

Dex took a step back from the rail, holding the squirming boy tightly, surprised by his animation.

"I told you so," laughed Karen.

The boy, hearing his mother's voice, turned and gazed at her, his eyes wide and sparkling, tiny flecks of gold dancing brightly in the hot sun.

Karen's mouth fell open in surprise. This was the same phenomena that had been present at his birth but had disappeared soon after. Now it was back.

It has to be the island's influence, she thought. *It's calling to him. He's excited because he's finally coming home.*

"Here, let me have him," she said, reaching out. "You enjoy the scenery."

"Okay. You ready to go back to Momma?" he asked as he handed the child to Karen.

Settling the excited little boy on her lap, she noted that the sparkles of gold had disappeared when he was looking at his father, but returned full force when his eyes met hers.

It's as if he's controlling them, she thought.

The boy finally settled down, as she cradled him close to her breast.

What lies in store for us? she asked herself, suddenly afraid. *What is this island going to do to my boy?*

She knew she needed answers and resolved to talk to Terri as soon as she could to get the name of the museum curator or, perhaps, an introduction to him. Somehow, she hoped he would be able to help her and that, together, they could find a way to keep her very special child out of harm's way.

It wasn't long before the ferry pulled into the familiar stone pier of Mateguas Island. As usual at this time of the year, the wharf was bustling. Towering piles of lobster traps sat close to its edges, waiting to be loaded aboard boats that would take them out to sea for the season.

Karen, pushing the stroller, made her way down the gangplank, onto the wharf. Dex followed with their luggage and groceries.

"You wait here with our stuff, princess. I'll get the truck. Pete said he would be sure to have it down here for us."

He kissed her lightly on the cheek, ruffled the boy's unruly hair, and strode away toward the parking lot.

Karen gazed around at the activity on the wharf. A tap on her shoulder startled her.

"Hey, Kar," said Bill as she turned her head toward him. "Didn't mean to sneak up on you."

"Bill, what a surprise."

Grinning, he leaned over and gave her a quick peck on the cheek. "Gosh, you look great! Welcome to the island! And who's this?"

As he spoke, Bill knelt down in front of the stroller, reaching out and touching the boy's soft cheek with his fingertips.

Karen laughed. "You know who that is. That's my son, Alex. Alex, this is an old friend of Mommy's. His name's Bill."

"Hey, little fella," Bill whispered as he gazed at the boy.

The child stared back with a strange intensity and Bill quickly removed his hand and stood up.

"He's a fine boy, Karen. You should be proud."

Karen reached down and ran her fingers lovingly through the boy's hair. "I am. Now, what are you doing here on the wharf? The next ferry doesn't leave for another couple of hours."

"I have my own boat now, Kar. I was just thinking of motoring over to the mainland for a bit of shopping. I'm having a big party this weekend - you, Dex, and Alex are invited, of course. It's a benefit for the Hall renovation. Helen O'Dwyer and I have been busting our butts to make this the event of the season. We're charging ten dollars a plate for adults - lobster or steak - kids eat free, of course."

Karen frowned. "O'Dwyer? Is she any relation to Terri's friend, Shawn?"

"Yeah, she's his mother."

"And, you're working with her on the Hall renovation?"

"Yes," Bill said proudly. "I'm on the Hall Committee and the Library Board as well."

Karen smiled at him indulgently. "My, my, you are becoming quite the islander. Where's the party going to be held? At your place?"

Bill nodded.

"Well, count us in."

Karen was about to say something more when she noticed the expression in Bill's eyes go cold. He was looking over her shoulder at something in the distance and she turned her head to see what had affected him so. It was Dex. He had brought the truck around and was getting out of the cab.

Karen turned back toward Bill. "Don't start anything, okay?"

Bill forced the tension from his face before responding. "Start anything? Why would I start anything? I know your situation and if you're happy, well, then I'm happy for you."

He gave her a broad smile and a wink, then brushed by her as he moved to intercept Dex, who was walking toward them.

"Dex," he said, proffering his hand. "Good to see you. Welcome back to the Island!"

Dex eyed him warily for a moment then shook his hand. "We're glad to be back. This is my *home*, you know."

Bill caught the emphasis Dex placed on the word "home" and knew the man was subtly reminding him that, try as he might, he would never really belong here. He would always be someone from "away."

Swallowing down a swift retort, Bill smiled. "Well, I've got to be getting to the mainland. See you all on the weekend if not sooner. It is a small island, you know! Nice to see you again, Kar."

With one last lingering gaze at his ex-wife, Bill turned and walked to the far side of the dock where the punts were tied up.

Karen watched for a moment as he boarded his small boat, then turned back to her husband, who was loading the truck.

"Was that really necessary?" she asked.

"What?" Dex replied, puzzled.

"You know. And I know. He's trying. Can't you give him a break? He's been through an awful lot."

Dex sighed. "Yeah, I know. But I don't like the way he looks at you. Like he'd like to gobble you right up. And what's this about next weekend?"

"He's having a party - a benefit for something to do with the Hall. You know, one of those island functions, but it's going to be at his house. A dinner, steak or lobster for ten dollars a plate. I said we'd be there. Or do you have a problem with that?"

"No, I don't have a *problem* with that. Be a good chance to say hello to everyone. I'd rather it was somewhere else, but beggars can't be choosers."

Karen shook her head slightly. "Remember how you used to get on my case about Maggie? Well, you're acting the same way about Bill. How about giving it a rest?"

"Okay," Dex said with a small laugh. "You're right. I'm acting like a spoiled princess."

Karen stared at him for a moment then grinned. "Okay, you got me there. Now, are we all loaded up and ready to go? I want to get those groceries in the fridge before they spoil."

With a smile, Dex lifted the little boy from his stroller and secured him in the car seat in the back. "Hop in, princess. Let's go home."

Bill motored slowly out to sea. Glancing over his shoulder, he frowned as he watched Dex's truck leave the wharf. When it was out of sight, he turned the punt around and proceeded back to Mateguas. He'd had no intention of going to the mainland. That was only an excuse to be on the wharf when Karen arrived.

Karen, he thought. *She's still so beautiful. God, how I wanted to take her in my arms. But that damned fisherman. What does she see in him?*

He felt a familiar surge of anger begin to build as he tied up the boat. Clenching his fists, he forced himself to take several deep breaths to keep his rage in check.

Got to keep my cool. That man's day will come, he promised himself. *Yes, soon, he'll pay.*

TERRI AND SHAWN

TERRI STRIPPED OFF HER T-shirt and shorts, leaving them in a heap on the bathroom floor and stepped into the shower. She was exhausted, every muscle in her body aching.

She stood still for a moment, letting the steaming spray relax her, then grabbed the soap and vigorously washed, wanting to remove the stench of fish and bait from her skin and hair. She'd been working on the boat with Shawn for five days and wondered if she'd actually make it through the entire summer.

Satisfied she was clean, she stepped from the shower and threw on her robe. Drying her hair, she smiled at her reflection in the mirror, knowing that despite her fatigue, she was learning a lot more about the fishing industry here with Shawn than she ever would have in the classroom. He was a good teacher, always taking time to explain everything thoroughly. And, he was patient, too - not only on the water but here at the house. She knew he wanted to make love to her, but he held back, waiting for her to signal that it was time. She thought she was almost there, but something stopped her. Fear, maybe?

Yes, she thought, *it is fear. Every time we get close, I see Mom and Dad fighting - yelling and hurting each other. It makes me feel like a little kid again, scared, huddling with my sister on the stairs. I know it's irrational; Shawn isn't Dad, and I'm for sure not Mom. But still, it's a commitment and not one to be taken lightly. Do I love him? I think I do. Being here with him feels right. It's comfortable. At times, I feel like we've been together forever; like we're the reincarnation of some past lovers from long ago.*

Shaking her head slightly, she finished her hair and walked to the windows facing seaward.

A "winter water view," she thought. *At least that's what Shawn calls it. It means that only when the trees shed their leaves, can you see the ocean clearly. Well, that's fine with me. It's only a short walk to the beach anyway.*

She turned from the window and grabbed a pair of jeans and sweater from the closet. She knew Shawn would be waiting for her downstairs. He would have bathed at the back of the house, at the outdoor shower, always careful to make sure she had her space, her privacy.

Smiling at the thought of him, she hastily finished dressing, combed her hair, and put on a dab of lip gloss.

I do love him, she thought as she ran down the stairs.

WKZTV NEWSROOM

SUSAN LEVEQUE LEANED BACK in her chair, eyes focused intently on her computer screen. The file she was staring at listed six names - all male and, with one exception, all lobstermen. Next to each name was a date and location, indicating the last time and place the man had been seen alive. All six men had disappeared without a trace and, to date, were still listed as "missing."

The oldest disappearance went back some thirty-five years; the most recent, ten. Susan scanned the dates, then pulled up a file labeled PIERCE.

When the first man disappeared, Dex Pierce was only about eleven years old. He couldn't have had anything to do with that one. But what about his father?

Susan studied her file. Dex's dad, Lonnie Pierce, born on Mateguas, had been a big wheel in the lobster business back then.

Barely making it through high school, he had turned to fishing for a living before the ink on his diploma was dry. An outspoken proponent of protecting the rights of his fellow islanders, his name often came up when violence erupted.

This did not surprise Susan. As a native Mainer, she was well aware of the "lobster wars" that periodically flared up when someone, usually from "away," encroached on what many of the proudly independent fishermen believed were their territories. To this regard, Lonnie Pierce was the rule, not the exception. These disputes would often begin with severed trap lines and shouting matches. Usually, this harassment was enough to discourage the poor outsider who would pull up whatever was left of his stringers and head to friendlier waters. However, if the intruder didn't take the hint, the dispute could escalate and turn ugly, sometimes resulting in injury or death.

Curious, Susan opened a picture of the elder Pierce and compared it to one of his son when they were about the same age.

Mmmmm, she thought. *He's got his father's rakish good looks, but there's a hint of brutality in Lonnie's face that's missing in his son's.*

She pulled up another picture, one of Lonnie and his bride, Patricia, on their wedding day. *Yeah, it's the eyes. Dex has his mother's eyes. That's the difference. There's a softness there.*

She stared for a moment at Patricia Pierce, acknowledging that the young woman was indeed a very pretty girl. She was a slender thing, with cornflower-blue eyes, and long blonde hair worn tied back in a low ponytail. Her wedding dress looked homespun, and she wore what appeared to be Birkenstock's on her feet. For a bouquet, she carried just a simple bunch of daisies.

A real child of nature, Susan thought. *A sharp contrast to the hard-drinking, tough-talking lobsterman she married. Well, they say opposites attract, and he is undoubtedly sexy in a dangerous sort of way.*

Susan scanned the wedding announcement then looked up to the header to see where it had appeared.

The Connecticut Post, she thought. *So, Patricia's family was not from Mateguas. Probably summer people.*

She quickly Googled the name of Patricia's father and was surprised at the number of responses she got. Scanning them, she nodded to herself.

Yes, her dad owned a cottage on the island. Old money. Patricia went to Wellesley. Graduated cum laude and married an uneducated, but successful, lobsterman. Interesting, I don't think her parents could have been too happy with her choice. Looks like a bad match to me.

Susan furrowed her brow, putting all the facts together in her mind. *Lonnie didn't marry a native islander. He married a summer girl, and one way above his station to boot. Mmmmm, maybe that's why Dex found himself so attracted to Bill's ex-wife. Similar looks, too, both slender, blue-eyed blondes. Like father, like son. Perhaps Dex has a mother fixation thing.*

Her curiosity about Dex's parents satisfied for the time being, she closed the file and looked back at the list of names. Only one of the men didn't make his living from the sea, Howard Nichols.

He was an environmentalist and had authored a couple of books, one on the subject of preserving island aquifers. He was also a strong believer that the waters around Casco Bay were being overfished and, as such, was an advocate for shortening the lobstering season. Naturally, this did not go over very well with men like Lonnie Pierce.

Susan Googled Nichols, looking for any articles dated in the year before he went missing. As an almost celebrity of sorts, his disappearance had gained more notoriety than those of the fishermen for whom getting lost at sea was an occupational hazard.

She clicked on one of the results and quickly scanned it. To her surprise, she discovered he, too, was a Mateguan.

No, not quite, she corrected herself. *He had a summer home there. Another summer person.*

Delving deeper, Susan tried to find out more about the man. She noted a reference to an article in the Portland Press Herald and opened another tab on her browser to pull it up. Her eyes widened when she saw the picture that accompanied the piece. Naturally, Nichols was in the photo, but it was who he was with that surprised her. He was kneeling in the grass examining some vegetation and there by his side, big as life, was Patricia Pierce, smiling broadly.

The plot thickens! I wonder what their connection was?

She bookmarked the article for later use, then went back to her file on the Pierces. Reading their obituary, she discovered Patricia was well known on the island as an herbalist and midwife.

So, her connection to Nichols, at least on the surface, would be their shared love of nature and plant life. But was there more?

Susan glanced at the clock. She was due on the set in ten minutes to tape the first segment of her new show, which would air on Sunday. Reluctantly, she shut down the computer after making a note to herself to set up a meeting with her contact at the police department the following week. She wanted to get her hands on the files pertinent to the investigations of the six missing men, most notably the one on Nichols.

She leaned back in her chair again, silently mouthing the names of the men. A theory was beginning to form in her mind and, if her hunch were right, this could be the biggest story of her career. But, to get it going, she would need Bill's help.

If only he could remember, she thought. *Well, maybe I can get him to steer that fancy shrink he sees down in Boston toward what I need. I'll talk to him this weekend. If he can give me something, anything really, that I can use to light a fire under the authorities, well, then I might be able to get something started.*

Nodding, she stood up, stretched, and turned to her assistant who was sitting at the desk behind her.

"I'm off for the taping, Arn," she said. "If anyone's looking for me, tell them I'll be back in about two to three hours. Oh, and I'll be away Friday and Saturday, too."

"Another hot date with 'The Puffin Man'?" asked her assistant, a slight smirk on his face.

"Yes, Arn, and don't knock it," Susan replied sharply. "The Puffin Man,' as you call him, has been pretty damn good to me already." As she spoke, she nodded toward the bronze

Edward R. Murrow Award for Excellence in Electronic Journalism that sat prominently on her desk.

Chastened, her assistant blushed as Susan grabbed her purse and left the room.

Outside, waiting for the elevator, she hugged herself and smiled. *Big party Saturday at Bill's. Everyone will be there, including his ex and her husband.*

Yes, the weather will be perfect and we'll all have a good time. Then comes my broadcast on Sunday. I expect that will wipe the smiles off some of their faces and, after that, I think things are going to heat up considerably on Mateguas Island.

BILL AND SUSAN

SATURDAY MORNING, BILL'S HOUSE was abuzz with activity. Helen O'Dwyer, Shawn's mother, arrived early and was busy organizing all the volunteers. Barbecues were set up in front of the house, and trucks carrying picnic tables were unloading in the back. A small tent, where tickets would be sold, was erected at the end of the driveway and another area where alcoholic beverages could be purchased was cordoned off.

Bill and Susan watched for a while from the deck, sipping their morning coffee.

"I have something to show you that I think you're going to be interested in," said Susan.

Bill smiled. "Sure. What?"

"I need the computer. Can we use one in the media room?"

Bill nodded and followed her back into the house. When he'd renovated the place, he had turned the family room into a state-of-the-art media center. The room enabled him to work from home in the consulting business he shared with his former boss, Gerry Davis.

Sitting down in front of one of the many computer screens, Susan logged into her WKZTV account, careful to shield her password from Bill. She knew that he was fully capable of hacking into it and didn't want to give him any help should he be so inclined.

"Okay," she said as she pulled up her list of six names. "All but one of these guys were lobstermen and all disappeared without a trace. The sixth guy was a writer and an environmentalist who had ties to Mateguas."

Bill studied the names for a minute. None of them were familiar. "So? What does this have to do with me?"

Susan smiled indulgently. "Just wait. Give me a minute. Okay. Now all of these fishermen set traps in the waters around here, and all five of them were not natives - three were from Canada and the other two from down south. Talking to people who knew them, I found out that each had experienced some type of harassment by local lobstermen before disappearing. Are you with me so far?"

Bill nodded.

"Okay. Now the first disappearance was thirty-five years ago and the last one, ten. No bodies were ever found, and there was never any evidence of foul play on their boats or at their homes. Authorities, therefore, assumed they were lost at sea. But I don't think they were."

Bill tilted his head, clearly puzzled. "Why? It seems logical. Except maybe for that environmentalist."

"You don't know much about 'lobster wars,' do you?"

Bill shook his head.

"It can get pretty violent. Locals are very protective of what they believe are their territorial rights. And Lonnie Pierce, Dex's father, was one of the most vocal of them. Something bad happened to those men, Bill. I found out each one of them pushed back when the harassment started, and that's something you don't do around these parts. Not if you value your life. No, they didn't simply drown."

"So, what do you think happened?"

"I think they were murdered. And, Bill, I don't believe you were the first man dumped on Puffin. It's my theory that these men were killed then dumped there, too. And I plan on proving it."

"On Puffin?" asked Bill, clearly surprised. "Jesus!"

"And there's more. As I said before, Dex's dad was very outspoken about fishing rights and he had a reputation for violence. Three of these men went missing when he was lobstering here. And, curiously, the environmentalist was a friend of his wife. Maybe more than a friend. So, have I gotten your interest?"

Bill leaned back in his chair, thinking. "Yes, you have. Good work, Susan. But how are you going to prove anything?"

Susan grinned. "That's where you come in. I need something to tell my contact at the police station so he'll take me seriously. Something that will make them go to Puffin and investigate."

"But how can I help? I still don't remember much. All that's come back is just bits and pieces."

"I know. But did you ever see any bones? Or anything that could have been the remains of a human skeleton? It doesn't have to be much. Just something."

Bill shook his head. "Sorry, nothing of that nature's come back."

"Think about it. If you said you remembered something, who could disprove it? The only one who might take issue with it would be that doctor you're seeing in Boston and wouldn't he be restricted by patient-doctor privilege anyway? If I could just tell my source that you think you remember seeing a skeleton or a pile of bones or something, then we'd be on our way."

Bill thought about her suggestion for a minute. It would be lying, but wouldn't the end justify the means?

"Okay, I'm game. Tell them I remember seeing bones that at first I thought were from a deer, but now ... now that my memory is clearer, I think they could have been human. And, don't worry about Dr. Burgess. I'll take care of him."

Susan smiled. She knew he'd take the bait.

She shut down the computer then got up and walked to the front door, locking it. She came back to the media room and pressed the button that closed all the window coverings. Smiling, she walked slowly over to where Bill was still sitting, pulling her T-shirt over her head as she moved. She dropped it on the floor, then unbuttoned her shorts and stepped out of them. Dressed now in just a lace bra and matching thong, she stood in front of him, as his eyes roamed her body.

Grinning, he reached out and put his hands on her waist, slowly moving them upward until they rested just below her bra. With one hand, she reached around and undid the flimsy garment, tossing it aside.

Bill pulled her closer as she sunk down onto his lap, wrapping her long legs around him. He moved his thumbs up to her nipples and began to slowly massage them, watching as they hardened in arousal.

Susan moaned as he moved one hand from her breast and let it trail down her back, his fingers moving under the delicate material of her thong, sliding into the crack between her buttocks. She reached down and placed her hand on his erection, grasping it through his trousers. Then she quickly unzipped him and leaned forward, whispering in his ear.

"Hurry," she moaned. "I'm so wet, I think I might drown!"

THE PARTY

THE FESTIVITIES BEGAN IN earnest around two o'clock in the afternoon. The driveway was soon full, and cars lined the road in front of the house. Karen and her family arrived fashionably late, closer to three. Dex dropped Karen and the baby off at the driveway then drove down the road until he could find an open space to park the truck.

Bill was tending to one of the barbecues when he saw her coming up the drive, pushing the baby in his stroller. Handing over his potholder and fork to one of the other volunteers, he hurried down the hill to greet her.

"Kar, you made it," he said. "I was beginning to think you all weren't coming."

Karen smiled, accepting his hug and a light kiss on the cheek. "Sorry if we're late. We got off to a slow start this morning. I hope there's still some food left. I could eat a horse."

Bill laughed, linking his arm in hers as they walked toward the back of the house. "Don't you worry about that, there's plenty. Where's Dex?"

"Oh, he's parking the car. Can we find a place in the shade to spread our blanket? I don't want Alex to get too much sun."

"Sure, how about over by that tree?"

He walked with her to the far side of the lawn, away from the picnic tables. Karen smiled when she spied the old raised beds that she had tended so diligently many years before. They were now overgrown and beginning to fall apart from disuse. Then she turned her attention to the woods beyond.

She stood silently, remembering for a minute. "It's all coming back, isn't it? The foliage, I mean. If it weren't for those charred trees, you wouldn't even know that the fire happened."

Bill nodded solemnly. "Yeah. I go back in there occasionally. The trail is overgrown now, but you can still find it. Sometimes I think I can almost see her ... Maggie. Such a waste."

His eyes had taken on an otherworldly look, distant and endlessly sad. Karen reached out and put her hand on his arm.

"Remember the good times you had with her, Bill. Don't dwell on her death or what she did to you. Just always keep the good in your heart. She did love you, you know, even at the end."

Bill smiled, then glanced down at Karen's hand resting lightly on his arm. Just the slightest touch of her soft flesh on his sent shivers down his spine and it took every ounce of restraint that he had to keep from taking her in his arms and holding her close. Tentatively, he placed his hand over hers, giving it a light squeeze.

Karen was about to say something, but was interrupted by Dex, who was striding across the lawn toward where they sat.

"Hey, Karen! What are you doing way over here? Thought you'd be at one of the tables."

Karen quickly untangled her hand from Bill's and turned toward him.

"I wanted a place in the shade, hon," she replied. "I think Alex got too much sun yesterday."

Recognizing Bill, Dex nodded in greeting, a slight look of distaste on his face. Bill caught the look and smiled.

"Good to see you again, too, Dex,"

Dex forced a smile, then leaned down and lifted his son from the stroller, hoisting the boy high in the air.

"I'll go over and see if I can put our order in," said Dex, ignoring Bill. "You still going for steak?"

"Yes," Karen laughed. "Medium rare, please. We'll probably be having lobster on Tuesday when we go to Terri and Shawn's. Where are they anyway? They're here, aren't they?"

"They're over by the lobster pit," Dex replied. "I'll send them by. But right now, I gotta show my boy off to all my old friends!"

Dex stooped down and gave her a loud smacking kiss, turned, and with one last look at Bill, headed over to the ticket booth.

"The proud papa," murmured Bill sarcastically.

Catching his tone, Karen frowned. She was about to admonish him when she noticed a young woman approaching. The woman looked slightly familiar, but Karen couldn't immediately place her.

She was slender, about thirty-five, with shoulder-length, dark-brown hair. Dressed in khaki shorts and a tight T-shirt, Karen noted she had curves in all the right places.

"Hey, Bill," the girl said as she snaked her arm around his waist. "Going to introduce me?"

Bill laughed, putting his arm around her and giving her a kiss on the cheek. "Sure. Susan LeVeque, this is my ex, Karen. Karen Andersen Pierce, this is Susan LeVeque, world-famous girl reporter."

Karen smiled as she shook the younger woman's hand, exchanging pleasantries.

"You're the reporter who interviewed Bill at the hospital, aren't you?" asked Karen.

Susan nodded. "My big story. Got a Murrow Award for that one. Bill's been my lucky rabbit's foot ever since."

"Well, I'm glad you and he have gotten together. He looks happy and, after what he's been through, he deserves it."

"Hey, quit talking about me like I'm not here," admonished Bill, laughing. "Listen, I'll catch up with you later, Kar. I think I may be needed at the fire pit. Come on, Susan. Let's go do some cooking."

He put his arm casually around the reporter's shoulders and steered her away.

Karen watched them go, a frown on her face.

Susan LeVeque, she thought. *Mmmm, she seems nice enough on the surface, but there's something about her smile that's false. Yes, it's as if she has a secret she's unwilling to share.*

As they disappeared into the crowd, Karen wondered why she felt such an instant animosity toward the girl.

It can't be jealousy, can it? I want Bill to find someone who can make his life whole again. No, it's something else ... something...

Her thoughts were broken by Dex's voice.

"Our food's just about ready," he said as he handed Alex to Karen. "I'll get it. Terri and Shawn are going to join us in a minute or two. You want a beer or lemonade?"

"Lemonade, please. And get a bottle of water, too. I forgot to put some in the diaper bag."

"Your wish is my command, princess," he laughed.

Karen smiled, thoughts of Susan LeVeque vanished from her mind. "My knight in shining armor. You're always there for me."

It was going on six when Karen and her family finished eating. Terri and Shawn gathered their paper plates and plastic utensils and went off in search of a trashcan, while Dex took a few minutes to visit with old friends at one of the nearby picnic tables. Alone with Alex on the blanket, Karen was surprised when Bill reappeared.

"Mind if I sit for a minute?" he asked.

"No, make yourself comfortable. We're just cleaning up. Nice party."

Alex, who had been looking for insects in the grass next to the blanket, turned his head toward Bill.

"Hey, little guy," Bill said, reaching out his hand to the boy.

Alex gurgled something unintelligible and crawled across the blanket, grabbing Bill's thumb tightly in his tiny hand.

Karen smiled and was about to speak when the world suddenly began to spin around her. Overcome by dizziness, she stared at her child, whose eyes were now flashing brightly, flecks of gold sparkling in the late afternoon sun. Bill seemed frozen in place, his mouth half open, eyes blank and unseeing.

A wave of nausea washed over her as everything around them disappeared, leaving just her boy and Bill, sitting on the blanket surrounded by a piercing white light.

She tried to cry out, to scream, but was unable to utter a sound as the light intensified.

Then, as swiftly as it had begun, the illusion disappeared. Her boy dropped Bill's thumb and crawled back to her, resting his head in her lap, his eyes now completely normal.

Bill shook his head as if coming out of a trance, a look of confusion on his face.

"Well, I just wanted to say how good it was to see you again, Karen," he said softly. "I hope you won't be a stranger this summer."

Karen took a deep breath and forced a smile. "Don't worry. You'll see enough of me. And thanks again for today. This was really great of you to donate your property for the event."

Bill grinned, then leaned over and again kissed her on the cheek. "Hope to see you soon."

As he walked away, Karen stared at his retreating figure, then looked down at her son, wondering what had occurred between the two of them.

As that thought crossed her mind, she felt a sharp, stabbing pain at her left temple. It was brief but intense, and tears welled in her eyes.

A childlike voice resonated across her consciousness.

"He has a shadow around his heart. I fear for his soul."

Karen's eyes widened. "Was that you?" she whispered to her son, who looked as if he were sleeping.

The child opened his eyes for a moment and nodded slightly, then closed them again.

Karen cradled him tightly to her breast, her mind swirling with disbelief. *I'll have to talk to Terri soon and find out the name of that Indian at the museum. I can't put it off any longer. I have to get some guidance about all this.*

She sat staring at her sleeping boy, her mind a jumble of confused thoughts.

"Hey, princess," said Dex returning to the blanket. "You want to move over to the fire pit and get a good seat? The band's going to start playing soon."

Karen frowned. "I think I can skip that. I'm ready to call it a day. Can you get us packed up? I'm going to use the bathroom in the house. I think he needs changing."

Dex frowned. "So soon? There's going to be dancing later."

Karen shook her head. "I feel a headache coming on. I just want to lie down for a while. You can take us home and come back later if you want. I won't mind."

"No, no. If you want to go, we'll go. They'll be plenty of other parties, and we've got the whole summer."

"Okay. I'll meet you at the end of the drive."

Karen kissed him lightly then, with Alex on one hip, walked across the lawn to the house.

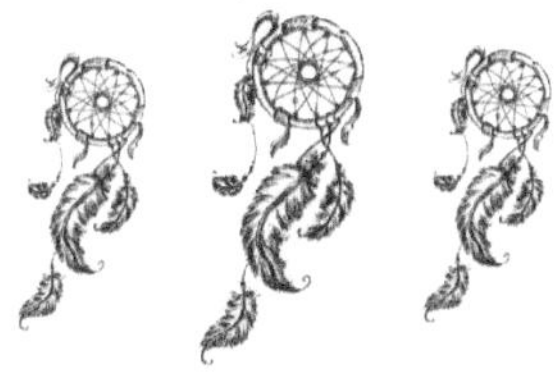

Dex watched her go, then leaned over to shake out the blanket. He was folding it when he felt a tap on his shoulder.

"Hi," said the attractive brunette standing close behind him. "Thought I'd come over and introduce myself. I'm Susan LeVeque."

It took a moment for the name to register with Dex, but then he remembered. She was the TV reporter who was keeping company with Bill - the one who had been instrumental in reuniting him with his daughters.

"Ms. LeVeque. Pleased to meet you. I'm-"

"I know who you are. Dex Pierce, best fisherman in Southern Maine. I've heard the stories."

Dex laughed. "Well, don't put too much stock in all you hear. I'm really no better than any of the other guys on this island."

"Don't be so modest. Say, I bet you'd be interested in the new show I'm anchoring. It's debuting tomorrow at five p.m. Called *Cold Cases of Southern Maine* and I think the story we're examining just might have some interest for you."

Dex frowned, puzzled. "Why? What's it about?"

Susan reached into the pocket of her shorts. "Take my card. Watch the show. You might want to talk to me afterward."

Confused, Dex gazed down at the business card she'd placed in his hand. "Now why would I...."

He stopped mid-sentence and looked up. She was gone. Glancing around, he saw her melt into the crowd over by the lobster pit. He looked down at her card again, then pocketed it and, shaking his head in bewilderment, finished packing, and headed for the truck.

At the house, Karen quickly changed the baby, then began to walk around the first floor. She'd heard that Bill had done some renovations, but wasn't prepared for what she saw. The place was beautiful. Everything had been upgraded and restored. The kitchen housed every modern convenience, yet the feel of the home was in harmony with the period in which it had been built. She was wondering if she dared peek upstairs when the door opened and Bill walked in.

"Kar, I thought you'd left. What are you doing here?"

Karen blushed. "Oh, I wanted to use the bathroom. You know me ... I'm not a port-a-potty girl. And I was just admiring what you've done with the place. It's beautiful."

Bill beamed at the compliment. "Thanks. I'd show you the rest, but the upstairs is a bit of a mess right now. Maybe you can come by some other time when things are quiet and I can give you a proper tour."

"I think I'd like that. Well, I'd better get going. Dex is probably waiting for me. Thanks, again."

She turned to leave, but Bill put his hand on her shoulder, stopping her.

"Just one more thing. Susan's got this new show starting tomorrow at five. I was wondering if you'd watch and let us know what you think. You know how much I value your opinion."

"Well, news magazines aren't really my thing, Bill."

"It's just a half-hour show. Please say you'll watch."

Surprised by his almost pleading tone, Karen smiled and nodded. "Okay, we'll watch, but I'm sure it will be great. I sense she knows what she's doing."

"Wonderful! And don't forget about that tour. Just call

me. I go to Boston usually on Tuesdays and stay till Thursday, but, other than that, I'm here."

He leaned down and, again, gave her a soft kiss on the cheek. She accepted it, smiled, and took her leave of him again promising to watch Susan's show.

By the time she got to the end of the driveway, Dex was waiting for her.

When they arrived back at the cottage, Karen excused herself and went to lie down in the bedroom. She did have a headache but, more importantly, she wanted time to think about what had happened between Alex and Bill that afternoon.

He said something about a shadow around Bill's heart. I wonder what that meant? Am I to take it literally - like Bill has heart disease or cancer? Or, did he mean a disease of the spirit? That I could certainly understand, after what he had to endure on Puffin. But he's doing the right thing and seeing a psychiatrist; at least that's what Terri tells me. Hopefully, that will help.

Unable to come to any definite conclusion, she let her mind drift away to more pleasant things. Her marriage with Dex had never been better and it looked like Bill was finally getting his life together, too. Sophie was thriving at Yale and Terri seemed content and in her element on Mateguas with Shawn. And then there was Alex, her beautiful little boy.

Karen hugged her pillow. She knew she was truly blessed but, try as she might, nagging doubts and fears threatened to undermine her joy. Closing her eyes, she finally drifted off to an unsettled sleep.

She awakened later in the evening when she felt Dex slide under the covers.

"What time is it?" she asked.

"Bedtime, babe. Around ten," he answered, pulling her to him.

She relaxed into his embrace. "I forgot to ask you," she whispered. "Did you meet that new girlfriend of Bill's at the party?"

"Yeah, Susan something. Nice-looking woman."

"Yes, she's attractive, but there's something about her I didn't like. I can't put my finger on it ... but for some reason, she put me off. She's got a show premiering on Sunday that Bill wants me to watch."

"Yeah, I know. She told me I should watch it, too. Wouldn't say why. Said I might want to talk to her after I saw it. She gave me her card."

Karen shifted her body around to face him. "That's strange. The show is about old unsolved crimes, I think. Maybe she's going to report on Bill and Puffin Island."

"Maybe. But what would that have to do with me? No, I think it's something else. Probably something to do with fishing or lobstering."

Karen sighed. "Well, I guess we'll have to wait until Sunday and watch the damn thing to find out what all the mystery is about."

TERRI AND SHAWN

TERRI AND SHAWN ARRIVED home late, having stayed at the party for music and dancing.

"That was fun tonight," Shawn said as they walked in the door. "You're a good dancer."

Terri smiled. "Listen. I'm still wound up from the party. Why don't you come upstairs with me and we can watch a movie or something?"

"Or something?"

Terri blushed, unable to meet his gaze. "Why don't you make some popcorn?" she replied, trying to ignore the innuendo. "Maybe we can find a good old movie - something from back in the days when they only came in black and white."

"Okay, sounds like a plan. Want anything to drink?"

"How about some wine?"

Shawn looked surprised. Terri was not a big drinker - a couple of beers were usually her limit.

"Sure," he replied a little hesitantly. "I've got a nice bottle of red I was saving for a special occasion, but I think popcorn and an old movie with my best girl qualifies. I'll be up in a minute."

In her bedroom, Terri turned on the television, then stripped off her clothing and slipped into her sleep shirt and robe. Combing her hair, she checked her appearance in the mirror.

I should be wearing a see-through negligee, she thought. *Instead, I'm dressed in my old Scooby-Doo shirt.*

She had decided earlier in the day that tonight would be the night. She knew she loved Shawn and wanted to spend the rest of her life with him. But, still, that didn't take away the jittery feeling that was building in the pit of her stomach.

Slipping under the quilt on the bed, she busied herself searching the listings for a movie.

"Hey, girl," said Shawn as he entered the room, popcorn in one hand and a bottle of wine in the other. "Did you find anything worth watching?"

"Yeah. It's an oldie, but a goodie. *Casablanca* with Humphrey Bogart and Ingrid Bergman. It's one of Mom's favorites."

Shawn smiled as he sat down on the bed and took off his shoes. "Sounds good."

Propping himself up on one of the pillows, he lay down next to her setting the bowl of popcorn between them.

"Here's looking at you, kid," he said in his best Humphrey Bogart imitation, handing her a glass of wine.

Terri giggled, then took a sip. Shawn slipped his arm around her as they settled in to watch the film.

By the time Humphrey Bogart and Claude Rains were strolling away into the fog, Terri was asleep, her head resting on Shawn's chest. Shawn turned off the TV and quietly moved her aside so he could get up and go downstairs to bed.

"Where are you going?" she asked, opening her eyes.

Surprised, Shawn sat back down on the bed. "Thought you were asleep. I tried not to wake you."

"I guess I missed a good chunk of that movie. Did it have a happy ending?"

"I think that depends on what you mean by 'happy.' The resistance won in the end. As for the love story, it was sacrificed in the name of France."

He leaned over and kissed her softly. "Well, good night. We're painting buoys in the morning."

Terri reached out and grabbed his hand, stopping him. "Don't go. Stay ... stay here with me tonight."

Shawn was silent for a moment, looking deeply into her eyes. "Are you sure?"

"I love you, Shawn O'Dwyer. I know it sounds corny, but I feel like you're my destiny ... that we, you and I, are meant to be together."

She gazed up into his eyes, praying silently that she hadn't said too much ... hadn't overstepped and scared him away.

"I love you, too, Terri. You've had me wrapped around your little finger since the first time I laid eyes on you at that dance. And, those two years apart ... well, they were sheer hell for me. I don't know how many times I almost jumped on a plane to come see you. But I was afraid maybe you didn't feel the same way. But, then, when you said you'd come this summer, well, I hoped ... oh, God, how I hoped."

Terri reached up and pulled him down to her. "Enough talking," she said.

Shawn hesitated. "You're sure? I don't want you to do anything you might regret."

"I'm sure. Now are you going to kiss me?"

Later, as they lay curled in each other's arms, Shawn whispered in her ear. "Was that okay for you?"

Terry rolled over facing him. "That was more than just okay. It was perfect. I hope I was..."

Shawn leaned down and kissed her softly. "You are a dream come true. And, yes, you were perfect, too."

EVIE

KAREN CAME STRIDING IN the door, baby Alex on one hip, a cooler bag over her shoulder. It was Sunday afternoon and she'd been at the beach hunting for sea glass and lost track of the time.

"Am I too late for Bill's girlfriend's show?" she asked as she walked into the living room.

Dex, who was sitting in front of the television, did not look up or respond. Karen put the baby in his playpen and took the cooler to the kitchen.

"On the way home I stopped at the store and bought a pound of scallops that they say came from the waters around here last January. They're frozen, but they keep well. I thought we'd try them for dinner later this week. I hear Casco Bay scallops are delicious. What do you think?"

Dex remained silent.

Frowning, Karen joined him in the living room, noting with displeasure a glass of either bourbon or whiskey on the table next to him.

"Dex? I asked you a question. Scallops?"

"Shhhh," he replied, taking a sip of his drink. "I'm trying to watch this."

Karen sat down beside him, irritation at his response apparent on her face. "Well, what is it? What's so God-awful important on the TV that you can't answer a simple question?"

When he didn't reply, she turned her attention to the screen. "So, what is it? Is this that new show Bill's girlfriend is anchoring or what?"

"I said I'm trying to watch this," he replied. "Can't we talk afterward?"

Karen bit her bottom lip, annoyed. "Okay, but just answer me yes or no. Is this that show?"

Dex sighed. "Yes, it's a news magazine, 'Southern Maine Cold Cases' or something like that. Now please, can I just watch it?"

Karen swallowed an angry retort, leaned back in her chair, and kicked off her shoes, waiting to see what had gotten him so riled up.

Susan LeVeque suddenly appeared on the screen. Her hair was up and she was wearing a tailored suit.

"Our first case is an old one. It's the case of a teenage girl, Evelyn LaPlante, who went missing one cold January night thirty years ago, only to wash up eight days later in Scarborough Marsh, dead, apparently strangled."

An image of a young girl flashed on the screen. Even with the outdated hairdo and makeup, she was breathtaking.

"Evie," Dex muttered, lifting his glass to his lips. "She hated being called Evelyn."

Karen stared at him. "You knew her?"

"Shush. Later, we'll talk."

Biting her lip again, Karen turned back to the television. Susan was on the screen, pictures of the young girl displayed behind her.

"An autopsy revealed that sixteen-year-old Evie, as her friends called her, was eight weeks pregnant at the time she was killed. There was no water found in her lungs, so the medical examiner determined she was dead before she was dumped in the marsh. To this day, her death remains a mystery. Who took the life of this vibrant young girl? We'll attempt to find out when we come back."

The show went to a commercial break and, once again, Karen turned to her husband.

"Okay, tell me. You knew her?"

Dex downed the rest of his drink and stood up, clearly intending to get himself a refill. "Yeah, I knew her," he answered as he walked to the bar. "I was a year ahead of her in school. She lived on the mainland. She was a good kid."

With a fresh drink, he sat down again.

Karen noted that he was avoiding eye contact with her, but she was not to be deterred.

"Okay. So, why are you so upset? This happened a long time ago. Was she a good friend? A girlfriend? What?"

Dex took a deep breath. He was about to say something when Susan's serious face appeared again on the screen.

"Tonight we're taking a fresh look at the unsolved death of Evie LaPlante, sixteen-year-old junior from St. Regis High School in South Portland."

The screen now flashed to an older man sitting behind a desk.

"Detective David Miller, then Sergeant Miller, worked the case. Detective Miller, what can you tell our audience?"

The detective glanced down at a file on his desk then back to the camera. His expression was all business. "Yes, I was assigned this case. A tragedy. Young girl killed like that."

"Can you describe the events leading up to her disappearance?"

"Yes. Evie was last seen at her place of employment, a convenience store on Route 1, not far from her home in South Portland. It was a Thursday night, cold, but clear. The proprietor, Henry Owens, told us that around seven p.m., a dark-colored truck pulled into the parking lot. The driver didn't get out of the vehicle and the proprietor didn't get the license number - there was no reason to. This same truck came by to get her every Thursday. Other days she worked, she walked home unless the weather was bad. In those circumstances, either Mr. Owens drove her home or her father picked her up."

"And the storeowner never saw the driver of the truck?"

"No. He or she always stayed in the vehicle. But Mr. Owens said he thought it was a boyfriend. He told us Evie always seemed excited on Thursdays and took special pains with her appearance. You know, put on a little more makeup. Her family was not well-to-do, but on Thursdays she dressed up, like she was going on a date."

Susan nodded. "Did Evie's parents know about this alleged boyfriend?"

"No. According to her mother, she wasn't dating anyone. Her father was strict with her and wouldn't let her go out with a boy alone until she was seventeen."

"The storeowner, Mr. Owens, was a friend of Evie's father, wasn't he?"

"Yes. The families were friends. That's the only reason Evie's father let her have the job. He knew Owens would look out for her."

"Well, then why didn't Owens tell Mr. LaPlante about this alleged boyfriend?"

"We asked him about that. He said he felt sorry for the girl. All the other kids were dating, having fun. He thought she deserved more and should be enjoying her high school years just like the others."

"Okay. So, to sum up: she wasn't allowed to date, but at the time of her death was pregnant. And, someone, possibly a secret lover, picked her up at her place of employment every Thursday night - someone her parents knew nothing about. Is that correct?

"Yeah. That's what we surmised. We spoke with her friends and classmates. No one could say for sure if she were seeing anyone. But there were rumors."

Susan smiled and turned to face the camera. "Rumors of a secret lover. We'll see if we can find out if there's any truth to that when we come back."

Dex reached up and ran his hand through his hair, a frown on his face.

"Honey, what is it?" asked Karen. "You're clearly upset. Did you know the guy she was dating? Was it someone from the Island? Talk to me, please."

Dex sipped his drink, avoiding her gaze. "No, I don't know who she was seeing."

They sat quietly for a few minutes, waiting through the commercials, then Susan LeVeque returned to the screen.

"We're examining the case of sixteen-year-old Evelyn LaPlante, who was eight weeks pregnant at the time someone brutally strangled her, then tossed her body into Scarborough Marsh. Who was the father of her child?"

The screen shifted to a man around Dex's age, standing on a dock. Karen frowned. The man looked familiar.

"I'm speaking with Andy Deegan, a lobsterman from Mateguas Island, who went to school with Evelyn LaPlante. Andy, what can you tell us about this young girl?"

The fisherman smiled. "She was a year and a half behind me in high school and she was a looker for sure. Had those big blue eyes. Half the guys in school would've given their eyeteeth to have a chance with her. But her folks were strict. She was a Frenchie - very Catholic. Think her aunt was a nun. No dating till she was seventeen."

"But there were rumors of a boyfriend, right?"

Deegan looked down at his feet, obviously uncomfortable with the question.

"Mr. Deegan, we have your signed statement right here. I can read it for you, if you want."

The fisherman took a deep breath, then looked up into the camera. "Some folks said she was seeing Dex Pierce on the sly. But I don't put any stock in that. Dex was going steady with Cindy Sue Miller, the head cheerleader. He was just friends with Evelyn."

The screen now showed what was clearly a picture of Dex from his high school yearbook. He was wearing a football uniform and had his arm around a pretty, blonde cheerleader.

"Dexter Alexander Pierce," said Susan, "Captain of the St. Regis High School football team, was indeed 'going steady' with Cindy Sue Miller, but was he also spending Thursday evenings with Evelyn LaPlante?"

Pete McKinney's weathered face now appeared on the screen, standing on the lawn behind Bill's house. Susan took a moment introducing him then launched into her interview.

"Mr. McKinney, you've lived on Mateguas all your life, haven't you?

"Ayup. Born and raised here."

"So, you would be well acquainted with Dexter Pierce, wouldn't you?"

Pete, who looked very ill at ease, nodded. "Yes, Dex is a good friend and a fine man."

"Do you recall the murder of Evelyn LaPlante thirty years ago?"

Pete shifted his weight from one foot to another, staring down at the grass, then finally raised his head and looked directly into the camera.

"Yes, I remember. It was a big story. Young girl, murdered and pregnant. Tragedy."

"Do you remember any rumors about Dex Pierce and Evie?"

Pete scratched the side of his mouth, thinking. "Yes, there was some gossip about the two of them. But that's all it was ... idle gossip. Dex was here on the island the night the girl disappeared. There were thirty people or more who could testify to that. Some sort of big party down on the beach."

"In January?"

Pete laughed. "Nothing stops a Mateguan kid from partying. They had a bonfire to keep warm and probably plenty of beer, too."

Susan was about to ask another question, but Pete interrupted her.

"And Dex, well, he's just not the sort of guy would get a girl pregnant and not man up about it. He's a straight shooter and bringing all this up again ... pointing a finger at him ... it just ain't right. Whoever killed that poor girl is long gone by now, not someone from the island."

The scene now shifted to a middle-aged woman sitting on a leather couch. There were remnants of a once pretty, young girl in her face, but time had taken its toll.

Susan again appeared for the interview. "I'm sitting here now with Cindy Sue Howard, nee Miller, cheerleader at St. Regis, and one-time girlfriend of Dexter Pierce.

"Cindy Sue, what can you tell us about Dex?"

Obviously pleased to be the center of attention, Cindy Sue flipped her dyed-blonde hair and smiled at the camera. "He was a stud. Captain of the football team, straight-A student - headed for college after graduation. He planned to be a doctor. All the girls wanted to date him."

"But he was your steady, right?"

Cindy Sue frowned, then smiled brightly at the camera. "Yeah, I thought so. I had his class ring. But, you know, he was always friendly with that LaPlante girl. When I asked him about it, he said he was just helping her with her homework and stuff like that. But now I'm not so sure."

"Did you know her well?"

"No, she wasn't in our class and, if you want my opinion, she was just some little slut."

Susan frowned. "That's pretty harsh. If Dex was stepping out on you with her, do you think they were sleeping together?"

Cindy smirked. "She was pregnant, wasn't she? And he was one hot ticket, I can tell you. Funny, if I remember right, he was always busy on Thursday's, too. Said he was working with his dad. But, now I wonder."

Susan paused, letting Cindy's words hang in the air.

"The party on Mateguas the night Evie got into that truck - were you there?"

Cindy poked out her bottom lip in a pout. "No. I lived on the mainland. Dex only invited me out to the island in the summer and on weekends. No, I can't vouch that he was on the island that night. But those island people always take care of their own. Whether he was there or not, it wouldn't matter to them."

The camera focused back on Susan, who again recapped the story, getting ready to sign off for the evening.

"So, Mainers, the case of Evelyn LaPlante still remains open with many questions unanswered. Who was the owner of the dark-colored truck that picked her up every Thursday evening? Who was the father of her unborn child? And, most important, who callously took the life of this vibrant and beautiful, young girl? If you have any information that might bear on this case, please call our hotline, listed on the bottom of your screen.

"Thank you for watching. We'll be back next week with more on the murder of Evelyn LaPlante. This is Susan LeVeque signing off."

Karen glanced over at Dex. He had gulped down the rest of his drink and looked like he was about to get another.

"Do you really want to do that?" she asked softly, inclining her head toward his empty glass. "Why don't I make us some tea and then we can talk about this rationally."

Dex looked down at his drink then up at her.

"Sure," he said. "You're right. Now's not the time to tie one on. Tea sounds good."

Karen patted his arm, then got up and left the room.

Later, they sat quietly on the deck sipping their tea. Neither had said anything much since the end of the broadcast.

Finally, Karen broke the silence. "Dex, why do you think this has come up now? You know, the timing of it all. Seems strange that she would broadcast this now, right when we've come back to the island. It seems too pat to be a coincidence."

Dex laughed harshly, then turned toward her. "Don't you get it? It's not her. It's him."

"Him?"

"Bill, for Christ's sake. It's Bill. He's put that woman up to this. Dredging up all this shit from the past. Trying to tarnish my reputation in your eyes. He still wants you, you know. And he's not going to stop trying to get you back even if it means destroying me in the process."

Karen leaned over, placing her hand on top of his. "Well, I won't let him. I'll talk to him. Tell him to stop. And I won't take no for an answer."

Dex smiled wryly and shook his head. "Nothing will stop that man. He hates me and thinks you still love him. He wants to turn back the clock. God, I wish he'd never come back from Puffin!"

"You don't mean that, do you? I know he's bitter and resentful. I had hoped his relationship with that woman would help, but, perhaps, I was wrong."

Dex shook his head. "He's using her to get at me. And, I'm afraid it's working."

Karen squeezed his hand. "Maybe you should let her interview you. Show her you have nothing to hide."

"Yeah, and then let Bill help her edit the interview, so I look even worse. No, thank you!"

Karen was quiet for a moment, thinking. "We could talk to a lawyer. Make sure the interview isn't biased. And, maybe we could get the right to approve it before it went on the air. Isn't that guy who owns the big white house down by Eagle Point an attorney? He's here for the summer, isn't he?"

Dex turned to her. "Yeah, Matt Diamond is a hot-shot lawyer down in New York. And, he likes to go fishing. Maybe I could call him and take him out on the boat, talk to him about this."

"Sounds like a plan," replied Karen. "But I'm still going to try to talk some sense into Bill. If he is behind this whole thing, maybe he can get her to drop it."

Dex sighed. "I wouldn't count on it. He's got a hard-on for me and I don't think anything anybody says is going to change that. Just wish he hadn't settled himself in here on the island."

Karen smiled. "Don't worry. You wait. This will all blow over in a day or two. After all, you had nothing to do with that girl's disappearance or murder. It's all just innuendo and rumor, isn't it?"

Dex nodded and smiled.

"Okay, now that that's settled, I'm going to start dinner. I'll bet you're starved."

She got up, kissed him lightly on the cheek, and went back into the house.

As the door shut behind her, Dex's smile faded. He glanced down at his teacup, wishing that it held something stronger, then turned his gaze seaward.

Ghosts of Mateguas

The moon was rising in the evening sky surrounded by thousands of sparkling stars. It was a beautiful sight, but he didn't see any of its splendor.

All he could see were the eyes of a young girl floating in the murky, cold waters of Scarborough Marsh, a long plaid, wool scarf wound tightly around her neck.

A WALK IN THE WOODS

THE NEXT MORNING, DEX contacted his attorney friend and made a date to go fishing around noon. After he left the house, Karen, at loose ends, decided to take Alex and do a little island exploring.

She drove aimlessly for a while until she came to an intersection. A sign, pointing to the left, said "East End Trail - 1/4 Mile." Curious, she turned down the gravel road, eventually coming to a small parking lot.

She sat in the car for a moment gazing around, the thought of being in the woods on Mateguas alone causing her some distinct apprehension.

There was a bulletin board standing at what she surmised was the trailhead and, taking a deep breath, left the car to check it out. A map was tacked on it showing a well-defined trail, suitable for a stroller, leading to the shore. The trail was only about a mile long and looked like it was well used.

Pausing for a moment, she decided it was time to put her fears aside. She returned to her car, unpacked the stroller, and loaded Alex into it.

"We're going on an adventure, sweetie," she said to the little boy as she handed him a bottle of juice and secured his diaper bag to the back of the stroller. She strapped on her *Mei Tai* baby sling, purchased in San Francisco, just in case the footpath got too rough for the stroller's wheels and, sure she had everything she might need, locked the car and started down the trail.

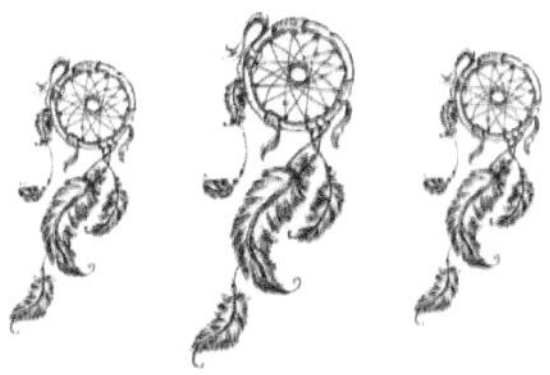

It was a lovely afternoon, sunny and bright. Alex gurgled happily as they strolled down the winding trail. At one point, as they rounded a bend, they startled a small red fox foraging for something in the middle of the path. The boy screamed in delight when he saw the animal and Karen laughed as the fox, clearly frightened by the small child, scurried away, deep into the woods.

Looking at the path ahead of her, she checked her watch.

We should be nearing the shore soon, she thought.

Alex was resting comfortably now in the stroller, eyes closed, taking a nap. Worried he might be getting too much sun, Karen pulled a hat from the diaper bag and placed it on his heavy head.

The trail now began to descend toward the beach. Moving slowly, Karen spied a narrow pathway veering off to her left. Curious, she peered down it, wondering where it led.

Mmmmmm, I probably shouldn't, but maybe just for a little bit. See if it leads to anything interesting.

The trail did not look wide enough to accommodate the stroller, so she hoisted the sleeping child into the *Mei Tai*, strapping him in securely, close to her breast. She left the stroller on the side of the main trail and stepped onto the path.

The trail was short and ended abruptly at a small clearing. In the middle sat a pond, formed by black, craggy rocks, similar to those that lined the shores of Mateguas. The water looked fresh and cold, glistening in the hot sun, and Karen stood quietly for a moment, enjoying its natural beauty. Seeing nothing else of interest in this place, she was about to return to the main trail, when something moved, startling her. She glanced around the clearing until she caught sight of a large frog sitting on a rock not far from where she stood.

It sat lazily, eyes closed as if sleeping. But every few seconds, without warning, its tongue would dart out, traveling an impossibly long distance to snag one of the greenhead flies that buzzed over the water. Then, with its prey secured, it would retract its tongue and close its eyes again, silently devouring the tiny insect.

Good for you, thought Karen. *I hope you rid the island all those nasty, biting flies.*

Grinning, she studied the creature, noting it wasn't what she would call a pretty frog. Actually, she thought it looked more toadlike, its skin brownish-green, covered with nasty-looking wart-like bumps. But its most impressive feature was its size - it was unusually large. She guessed it had to weigh at least ten pounds, probably more.

A frog on steroids, she thought, chuckling to herself.

She was about to wake baby Alex and point out the frog to him when the creature suddenly became aware it was being observed and turned its head toward her. Eyes, bulbous and red, gazed at her with ferocious intensity. Though slightly repelled by the hideous appearance of the creature, Karen felt strangely drawn to it and was unable to tear her eyes away.

As if sensing her fascination, the frog moved its obese body around until it was facing her. Its lips, bloated and dripping with spittle, moved ever so slightly, opening and closing, as it glared at her. Instinctively, Karen pulled the flap of her baby sling down to cover her child, protecting him, as a shiver of fear ran down her spine.

Not wanting to provoke the hideous creature further, she moved one foot backward intending to pivot and jog back to the main trail. But as she began to turn, the frog's blood-red eyes, glowing like hot coals, began to bulge and, without preamble...

ZAP!

A strangled cry of fear erupted from Karen's throat when she saw the slimy pink projectile moving with unbelievable speed toward her. Tearing her eyes from the creature, she started to run.

But she was too late.

The tongue lashed out and wrapped itself around her ankle, causing her to trip and fall heavily to her knees on the forest floor. Panicking, she kicked out violently to escape its grasp, but her struggles only resulted in it tightening painfully around her leg.

The creature's bulging eyes began to glow again as, along the tongue's surface, dozens of tiny barbs elongated, tearing and piercing the skin around her ankle. As they penetrated her flesh, the tongue began to pulsate, moving the spiny needle-like barbs in and out.

Karen screamed in anguish and frustration as she tried to free herself from the frog's hideous embrace. She reached back, grabbing at the tongue in an attempt to pull it off, but the barbs sunk in even deeper and a hot flame of pain shot up her leg, paralyzing her.

Breathing raggedly, she steeled herself and again tried to grasp the pulsing pink tongue. But now, to her astonishment, her arm and hand did not willingly obey her mind's command. A strange feeling of lassitude crept over her as the numbness in her limbs spread throughout her body.

The frog, observing her in this helpless state, jumped to the shore and began hopping around giddily, as if pleased with itself.

Karen again attempted to move, but, try as she might, her arms and legs refused to obey. On the edge of panic, she assessed her condition: she was breathing and could move her eyes, but that was all.

The toad watched her struggle and, apparently convinced she could cause it no harm, released its hold on her ankle. The barbs, dripping with blood, returned into their sheaths inside the tongue as the toad slowly rolled it back into its mouth. It gazed at her for a moment, then hopped out of sight.

Karen waited, praying that the creature had accomplished its purpose and had gone back to whatever hell it had come from. Minutes passed, and she was beginning to think her prayers had been answered, when something landed on her back, causing her to topple over onto her side.

The frog sat on top of her for a moment then jumped again, landing in the dirt about three feet away. It shifted its body around to face her, then waddled closer to where she lay.

Gazing hungrily at the fear in her eyes, it opened its mouth as the tongue, slowly uncurling, reached out for her. Karen tried desperately to move away, but her body remained leaden and dead.

The frog waddled even closer. Tentatively, the slimy tongue touched her face, sliding down her cheek toward her mouth. When it found her lips, the muscles hidden within it flexed and the tip began to poke and probe at her as if trying to force a way inside.

The stench of the frog's breath was horrible and Karen wanted to scream but was suddenly thankful that she couldn't. Screaming would open her mouth, giving access to the foul thing.

The frog, looking frustrated, started hopping up and down. Angry, it slapped at her mouth with the tongue, releasing one of the barbs, which pierced the tender flesh of her lip. Blood oozed from the wound, dripping down her chin.

The frog stared at it for a moment, then, closing its eyes, began lapping and sucking at her torn flesh.

Karen's stomach rebelled and she fought desperately to control her nausea knowing that in her paralyzed state, any vomit could choke and kill her. The frog continued lapping at the wound and just when she thought she could stand it no longer, stopped and hopped backward.

The creature stared at her, then turned and leapt onto her thigh and began kneading her flesh with its feet. As it moved, a sticky, whitish substance oozed out from between its toes onto her bare skin. This noxious goop burned and smelled like a combination of stale urine and feces and, again, she had to fight off the nausea that threatened to claim her.

The frog stopped and gazed at her again, its pink tongue snapping in and out, then returned its attention to the substance excreted onto her leg. With great care, it lapped at it, spreading it over and around her calves and thighs. She watched in horror as the tongue slithered this way and that, barbs pinching and tearing her tender flesh as it accomplished its mission.

The nasty creature worked on her legs for what seemed an eternity and she struggled to understand its purpose.

Then it dawned on her. *Oh, my God,* she thought. *It's like a spider. It's encasing me. Keeping me alive, but immobile. Saving me for later!*

Again, she tried to move, but her body remained limp and lifeless. Feeling she was doomed, her only thought now was of her baby and how to get him to safety. He'd been strangely quiet while all this had been going on and she feared he was injured or in shock. Not knowing what else to do, she screamed out to him with her mind.

WAKE UP, ALEX, AND RUN. GET AWAY FROM HERE! GO NOW AND FIND HELP.

To her astonishment, the child responded and began to struggle to free himself from the baby sling, his pudgy little hands deftly unbuckling it. Soon, he crawled out and stood next to her.

Again, she cried out to him with her mind.

RUN NOW, ALEX. HURRY. GO FIND DADDY. GET HELP.

The child looked down at her and smiled, his eyes golden and shining.

A lone tear slid down her cheek as she gazed at him. *Why doesn't he run*, she asked as despair threatened to consume her.

Suddenly, the frog's movement on her legs ceased, and Karen's eyes darted quickly toward it. The creature was sitting very still, eyes glowing like hot coals, staring hungrily at her child.

A new wave of fear ran down her spine as she turned her gaze back to her boy. The child's eyes, growing brighter and brighter as each second passed, were now locked with those of the creature.

Karen held her breath.

A blinding white light, so fierce she was forced to look away, began to surround her boy.

Fearfully, she looked back at the frog. It, too, had been startled by the light and she could see it struggle to regain its predatory stance.

She moved her eyes back to Alex. She could no longer see him, just the light and, again, she was forced to look away.

When she shifted her eyes back, both the light and her boy were gone - vanished. In their place sat a large golden eagle.

Karen's mind reeled.

Oh, my god! He shifted just like the spirit of The Blessed Boy!

The eagle, as if hearing her thoughts, bowed its head to her, flecks of gold dancing in its eyes, and leapt into the air, soaring high to the sky above. A feeling of relief flowed through Karen's mind. Her boy would live. She glanced back over toward the frog.

Its face was turned skyward, watching the eagle fly away. It remained motionless for a moment, then turned and stared at her, eyes again glowing hotly.

Swiftly, it became all business. Hopping this way and that, it completed the wrapping of her legs then jumped onto her torso. Again, she struggled to resist, but her body continued to ignore her mind's commands.

The frog was kneading her chest now, wrapping her arms tightly to her sides with the vile liquid it exuded from its toes. Unable to stand the horror any longer, Karen looked away and stared into the dirt, hoping consciousness would vacate her mind so whatever was to happen next would remain unknown.

Suddenly, the air around her began to move and she heard a loud shriek coming from above. In an instant, the weight of the frog's obese body was gone.

She darted her eyes this way and that, searching for the creature. Seeing nothing, she shifted her gaze toward the sky. The eagle, her son, was circling high above, the predator frog held firmly in its talons.

The boy-eagle nodded once toward her, then off it flew, over the pond, toward the forest where, finally, it flung the struggling frog deep into the woods.

Circling back to where she lay, the boy-eagle landed in front of her, eyes shining brightly. Once again a piercing white light, signaling the beginning of its bizarre transformation, surrounded it. Moments later, the eagle was gone and her little boy stood smiling before her.

Karen again tried to use her mind to warn him. *Go now and get help. Go, before that damned thing comes back. Don't worry about me. Go back down the trail to the road. Someone will come by and help.*

The boy shook his head. Without warning, Karen felt a stabbing pain in her left temple followed immediately by the high-pitched voice of her child, echoing throughout her consciousness.

"No, Mother. Open your heart and I will give you my essence, which will neutralize the poison of the Aglebemu. Then you will have your body back and we can leave together."

Not knowing what else to do and fearing the swift return of the frog, Karen stared at her son, acceptance in her eyes. A faint bluish light began to radiate from him as he reached out and pressed his hands to her heart. Warmth from his palms traveled throughout her body and, as the healing heat coursed through her, she began to move.

She struggled at first, ripping and tearing at the web the creature had used to mummify her. Finally free, she forced herself to her knees, turned and wretched into the grass at the side of the path.

Again, she felt a sharp pain in her temple and turned toward her son.

"Mother, we must hurry. I feel the Aglebemu is near and my powers are nearly replete."

Karen nodded and struggled to her feet. Her ankle was red and swollen and her legs were covered with dots of dried blood. She gritted her teeth and forced herself erect, picking up her boy and securing him again in the sling. He smiled at her, then rested his head against her chest, closed his eyes, and was almost instantaneously asleep.

She leaned over and kissed his forehead, then limped as fast as she could to the main trail. Finally, when she was back at the parking lot, she secured her sleeping son in the car seat, then hurried to the driver's side, slid in, and locked the doors. As she heard the locks catch, she let out a sigh of relief.

She rested against the seat for a moment, trying to absorb the reality of what had just happened. Then, taking a deep breath, she put the car in gear.

Ah-gluh-beh-moo, she thought as she backed out of the parking lot. *That's what he called that thing. What the fuck's an Aglebemu? I'll look it up when we get home. Or maybe this is another question for Terri's museum guy.*

As she drove the short distance to her cottage, she glanced down at her legs, still covered with the sticky substance that the frog had used to encase her.

A shower, she thought as she pulled into the driveway. *A hot shower and a drink. Yes, a good stiff drink and maybe not just one.*

Ghosts of Mateguas

At home, Karen took the sleeping boy to the bedroom and placed him gently in his crib. Gazing at him with love, she ran her fingers softly through his curly blonde hair, then covered him with a light blanket. She checked to make sure the baby monitor was turned on and, with one last glance at her child, left the room. It was time for that drink.

She pulled a half-full bottle of Jack Daniels from the kitchen cupboard, poured two fingers, and, without hesitation, tossed it back. Relishing the taste of the warm liquid as it slid down her throat, she poured another, but this time added ice and a splash of water.

Time to get clean, she thought, sipping the drink as she walked to the bathroom. Turning on the hot water as she entered the room, she was surprised when she saw her reflection in the mirror. The woman staring back at her was almost unrecognizable. Her hair was matted in places and sticking out strangely in others. Gobs of the substance the frog had exuded were woven throughout her locks, giving her a Medusa-like appearance.

Her legs were similarly covered with patches of the nasty goop and were dotted with dried blood. Her T-shirt, once white, was now a mélange of blood and dirt and her khaki shorts were wrinkled and sticky, with broad smears of red.

She leaned closer, peering at herself. Her complexion was pasty white, with no hint of tan or color. Large dark circles surrounded her eyes, which were bloodshot and rheumy-looking.

It's from that poison, she thought. *It's robbed me of my health. I had a good tan this morning. Now I look like I've spent my life living under a rock!* She sighed. *Well, maybe washing it off will help.*

The steam from the shower was beginning to fog up the mirror. Without further ado, she stripped off her soiled clothing, leaving it in a heap on the floor. Then she stepped into the hot spray.

It felt wonderful.

Picking up a washcloth, she vigorously scrubbed every inch of her body, eager to assure that no trace of the frog's venom remained anywhere. When she was satisfied she was clean, she closed her eyes and let the hot water beat the tension and fear from her soul. Once she felt in control again, all panic gone, she wrapped her hair in a towel, put on her terrycloth robe, and took her drink out to the deck.

The cottage was located on the west side of the island, and the afternoon sun streaming through the trees felt delicious. She checked the baby monitor and assured that all was well, leaned back into one of the Adirondack chairs and closed her eyes.

She sensed it even before she woke up - the presence of evil was everywhere. Slowly, with trepidation, she opened her eyes.

It was sitting before her on the rail in the late afternoon sun. Eyes closed, it looked asleep but Karen knew it was not. She tensed, ready to spring out of the chair, hoping to get back to the safety of the house.

The frog, somehow intuiting her planned escape, lazily turned its head and stared at her. A wave of terror coursed through her when she saw its eyes, glowing like hot coals. Without thinking, she opened her mouth to scream.

ZAP!

In that instant, the frog's bloated lips parted and its cruel tongue shot out.

Karen gagged as the slimy pink appendage entered her mouth and slid down her throat. Gasping, she coughed violently, trying to eject the tongue before it could do damage, but her efforts were fruitless.

The spiny barbs elongated, piercing the tender flesh of her esophagus, digging in deeply. She grasped at the tongue with her hands, trying to pull it out, but the spikes had taken root and her mouth filled with blood.

As she struggled, the familiar pulsing began and, with it, came intense pain as the paralyzing poison was injected into her bloodstream.

Eyes wide, she watched helplessly as the frog leapt from the rail onto her chest. It sat still for a moment, then waddled closer and closer to her face until its bloated and diseased lips were but inches from hers. Smiling obscenely at her, it opened and closed its mouth, making a disgusting smacking sound. Then it leaned forward...

BOSTON

DR. LIONEL BURGESS PULLED open the drapes revealing the Boston skyline. It was late and the sun was beginning sink toward the horizon, giving the city an eerie glow.

His last patient of the day sat up on the leather sofa, stretching.

"Well, doc, did we make any progress?"

Dr. Burgess smiled as he sat behind his desk. "We're chipping away at it. You know, I told you when we started this four months ago, it would be a long process."

"Yes, I know. And I think I've been patient. But I still don't remember much. Just fuzzy pictures of what looks like me digging clams or searching the seaweed for mussels or something. Innocuous stuff like that. Shouldn't more be coming back by now? I need to know how I got there and how I survived."

Ghosts of Mateguas

The doctor shrugged. "There's no set timetable for something like this. You have deeply suppressed all the events leading up to your abandonment and the two years following. As I've told you before, your mind has done this to protect you. If we open everything up all at once ... well, let's just say that your mind would not like that. No, we have to take baby steps."

His patient sighed. "Okay, you're the expert. But it's frustrating. I have nightmares, you know, bad ones. I wake up screaming sometimes, but I never know why."

The doctor smiled. "Be patient. Are you taking your anti-anxiety medication? That should help with the dreams."

"Sometimes. But when I have company, it makes me too groggy."

"Try half a dose. See if that helps."

"Okay, I'll do that. And, thanks. I'll try to be a more *patient* patient."

Dr. Burgess stood, smiling, and escorted Bill to the door. "That's the spirit. And write down anything you remember, no matter how trivial - especially after one of those bad dreams. I'll see you next week."

"I'll do that," Bill replied as he shook the doctor's hand and walked out the door.

Much later, Lionel Burgess stood at the window gazing at the city lights. He'd just finished dictating the last of his patients' notes and it was time to leave for the day. But he was troubled.

I need to speak with Malcolm, he thought.

Dr. Malcolm Machalek, Professor Emeritus at Harvard Medical School, had been the doctor's advisor, mentor, and friend during his residency and fellowship. A world-renown retrograde amnesia expert, Dr. Machalek now resided and practiced in Geneva when he wasn't on the lecture circuit.

Dr. Burgess walked to his desk and checked his calendar. Malcolm was at a symposium in Leningrad this week. After that, he and his wife were taking a cruise. They wouldn't be home until much later in the month.

I'm in too deep on this one, Dr. Burgess told himself. *I need some advice and I don't know if I can wait that long.*

He sat back down at his computer and typed in a name:

BILL ANDERSEN

The patient's chart appeared on the screen and Dr. Burgess spent some time reviewing his notes. He'd been seeing Andersen for almost four months now, using hypnotic therapy to probe the recesses of the man's mind and memory. And, contrary to what he'd told Andersen, he'd uncovered a good deal about what happened on Puffin Island. But some of it was so horrific - so traumatic - that he hadn't allowed Andersen access to those memories, at least not yet.

Maybe I should just let loose the floodgates, he thought. *Let the chips fall where they may. Maybe the man can handle it.*

But he knew he wouldn't do that. Andersen was, in his opinion, already borderline psychotic and allowing him to have access to memories of this nature would surely tip him over the precipice, sending him into total madness.

No, Dr. Burgess would keep his counsel for the time being. He would wait until his friend and mentor was home. Then, he would do whatever Machalek advised.

KAREN

KAREN FELT SOMETHING ON her shoulder.

"NO, PLEASE, NO!" she screamed as she pulled away, pushing herself back as far as she could into the corner of the chair.

"Princess, wake up! You're having a nightmare! It's me, Dex. Wake up!"

Slowly her eyes focused. He was standing over her with one hand on her shoulder, his face full of concern. It took a moment for her to realize who he was.

"Oh, Dex," she cried. "It was horrible!"

"It's okay. I've got you now," he said, wrapping his arms around her.

She leaned gratefully into his embrace as he lifted her from the chair and carried her into the house. Sitting down on the sofa, he cradled her in his lap.

"Now, what was so horrible? What was that dream about?"

Loathe to tell him the truth about the frog, Karen quickly equivocated. "I don't remember. It's gone. All I know is it was terrible."

Dex chuckled. "Well, you're safe now. I'm here. But what happened to your clothes? I found them in a heap on the bathroom floor. They were a mess. What the hell did you get into?"

Karen's mind raced. She couldn't tell him the truth; he wouldn't believe her. And anyway, all her wounds were now almost completely healed; just like those she used to inflict upon herself each month in sacrifice to Mateguas.

"Oh, that. Alex and I went exploring in the woods down the road a bit. I tripped and fell. I don't know what I landed in, but it was nasty. So, that was the end of our explorations. We came home and I showered. The shorts and shirt are ruined, but I fell asleep before I could put them in the trash."

"But what about the blood? They're covered in blood. You don't look hurt."

A look of alarm passed over his face and Karen knew instinctively what he was thinking.

"Don't worry. Alex is fine. The blood's mine. I scratched myself on some berry bushes. Karen, the klutz, strikes again! And, you know how rapidly I heal."

Dex laughed. "Well, as long as you're both okay. Where is Alex?"

"Oh, he was sleepy, so I put him to bed. Probably be waking up by now. Why don't you check on him?"

As if on cue, a loud wail erupted from the baby monitor.

"Guess you're right. I'll get him."

Karen smiled and watched as he hurried to the bedroom. Alone, she pulled her robe tightly closed, her mind reliving the dream and the horror of the frog's attack.

Pull yourself together, girl, she thought. *It was only a dream. It won't happen again.*

Later that evening, Dex was watching the evening news when Karen approached, laying her hand on his arm.

"Mute that for a minute, will you?" she asked. "We need to talk."

"Sure, princess. How about some wine?"

"No, thanks," she replied. "I've been waiting all evening for you to tell me what happened with the lawyer today. I think you're stalling."

Dex smiled sheepishly. "You're right, I have been. Let me get a glass of wine and I'll tell you all about it, okay? Sure you don't want one?"

"Okay, one glass."

He left the room for a moment and came back holding a bottle and two glasses. He poured the wine, then sat down beside her.

"I'm afraid it's not great news and that's why I was avoiding the subject."

He sipped his wine, then took a deep breath. "Matt said there isn't much we can do. Said we'd be messing around with first amendment rights and that could get sticky. His advice was just to ignore it. Told me I shouldn't respond or offer any information. He said we should just get on with our lives and that, as you said, in a couple days it will be yesterday's news."

Karen took a sip of her wine. "Well, that's not very helpful, but I suppose he's right."

"Yeah. So, that's what I'm going to do - just ignore it."

Karen nodded. "Maybe we should plan on doing something off-island on Sunday. Something that will keep us away from any televisions. Go to a movie or a play."

Dex hesitated. "Sure, let's think about it."

"And, I'm still going to talk to Bill. If he's behind this, I need to let him know what I think about it."

Dex leaned over and kissed her on the cheek. "Okay, but it won't do any good. Now, let's change the subject. We still on for dinner with Terri and Shawn tomorrow?"

"Yes, we are. We're bringing a salad. We're expected there at six. Will you be in from fishing by then?"

"Don't worry. I'll be home in plenty of time."

He lifted his wine glass, draining it. "I'm bushed. I think I'll call it a day. You coming?"

"You go on," she responded. "I just need to clean up a bit, then I'll join you."

He leaned over and kissed her softly. "Don't be too long."

"I won't."

He handed her his glass and turned to leave. Karen studied him as he walked away, a frown on her face.

Something's not right, she thought. *The way he acted when I suggested we go to a movie next Sunday. I understand he's worried about what that LeVeque woman will come up with next, but if the LaPlante girl was a friend like he says, anything Susan uncovers will be just idle gossip.*

She picked up the empty wine glasses and took them to the kitchen.

But what if Susan's right and there was something more going on between the two of them? And if that's the case, why lie about it if he had nothing to do with her death? No, I can't believe that. There has to be something else bothering him.

Sighing to herself, she turned off the lights and, trying to put her doubts and fears aside, joined her husband in bed.

LUNCH WITH DETECTIVE WALLACE

SUSAN LEVEQUE SAT IN her car in the restaurant's parking lot reviewing her notes on the six missing men one last time. She was having lunch with her contact from the city's Detective Bureau and wanted to be sure she had a convincing case put together. She knew this was her only chance to get an investigation going and if she couldn't persuade the man...

She looked at her reflection in the rearview mirror.

Snap out of it, Susan, she admonished. *Think positively. You won't fail. You've got a hunch on this and your hunches are always right!*

Smiling, she leaned over and turned off her laptop. She checked her appearance in the mirror again, applying some fresh lipstick, then, confident she had enough ammunition to make her case, grabbed her briefcase, locked the car, and headed to the restaurant.

Detective Pete Wallace was sitting at the bar when she arrived. In his forties, Pete was a seasoned officer. He'd joined the Portland Police after graduating the Academy twenty-two years earlier and his rise up the ranks had been a steady one. While not considered the most intuitive or charismatic officer on the detective squad, he was, at the very least, reliable.

Susan had become acquainted with him in her early days at the station and they had dated briefly. When the relationship failed to progress, they parted amicably and had remained good friends. She was hoping to cash in on that friendship now.

"Hi, Pete," she said, slipping onto the barstool next to him.

The detective leaned over and gave her a quick peck on the cheek. "Chivas on the rocks, Susan?"

"You know me too well."

Pete laughed and waved to the bartender, ordering a drink for Susan and a refill for himself. Then he swiveled around on his barstool to face her.

"Now, to what do I owe the privilege of your presence this afternoon? You were very mysterious on the phone."

Susan laughed. "I think I'm on to something, Pete, and, if I'm right, it could be a big break for me."

The bartender brought their drinks and they each took a sip.

"Mmmm. A break for you? And what would be in it for me?"

"It would be a real feather in your cap, too," she replied, smiling. "Might even mean a promotion."

"I like the sound of that. So, what have you got? Have you found some terrorist sect hiding out in the ladies' room of Alioto's Restaurant?"

Susan smiled and shook her head. "No, it's nothing like that. But how would you like to clear up a half-dozen cold cases - all in one fell swoop?"

Wallace was quiet for a moment, thinking. "Depends on the cases. If you're talking *penny ante* theft or stolen vehicles, forget it. Not interested."

Susan patted his hand. "What if it were murder? Would that get your heart started?"

Pete frowned. "Murder? We don't have that many that I know about. This is a quiet town."

"The cases I'm talking about may not be classified as homicides right now, but I think we can prove they are."

She pulled a printout containing her list of six names from her briefcase and handed it to him. "All these men are identified as 'missing,' but I believe they were killed. And, killed by the same man or group of men."

Pete studied the list. "Only name I remember is that of the nature lover, Nichols. The others - I've never heard of."

Susan nodded, sipping her drink. "That makes sense. The others are, or were, lobstermen who disappeared without a trace. Oldest case dates back thirty-five years; most recent one, ten. They've probably been closed by now with the assumption that the men were lost at sea."

"Well, what makes you think any different? After all, it is an occupational hazard. Who would want to kill these men anyway? I take it they weren't rich or famous."

"No, they were just regular hardworking fishermen. I'm assuming that the five were all victims of 'lobster wars.' Nichols is different. I think his death or disappearance was personal, not economic."

Pete studied the list and was about to comment further when the waitress came by to tell them their table was ready.

Getting up, Pete handed the papers back to Susan. "I gotta tell you, I can't see the Chief taking much interest in some old missing persons' files. Nichols, yeah, but the others, no. Not unless you've got something that ties them all together."

The waitress escorted them to their table and handed them lunch menus. They took a few minutes, then ordered their meals and another drink.

After she left to place their order, Pete leaned forward toward Susan. "You do have something," he said with a grin. "I can see it in your eyes."

Susan laughed.

"Come on, spill. What's going on in that devious little mind of yours?"

"You're right. I do think I'm on to something. Remember that guy who I interviewed a couple of years ago - the one they found on Puffin Island?"

"Yeah. You found his family, too, didn't you? The guy was in the nuthouse for a while, right?"

"Yes, that's him, Bill Andersen. He was amnesiac and mute. That's why he was a patient at the State Hospital. Not because he was off his rocker."

"So, what about him? What does he have to do with these missing men?"

"Patience, Pete. I'll get to it."

The waitress brought their lunches. Once she was gone, Susan resumed her explanation.

"Bill lives on Mateguas now and he has regained the memory of everything leading up to the night he disappeared. What he doesn't remember is how he got to Puffin and what actually happened to him there."

"Those are two pretty significant gaps, Susan. What are you getting at?"

"Again, patience. Pete. Over the past six months, Bill and I have become friends and I know he's seeing an amnesia expert in Boston to try to get the rest of his memory back. As a result of those sessions, things are beginning to emerge about his time on Puffin."

"So what? How does that relate to these old cases?"

Susan smiled, taking a bite of her sandwich as Pete drummed the table with his fingertips, impatiently.

"Okay," she finally said. "Entertain this supposition. What if Bill Andersen wasn't the only person left to die on Puffin? What if the skeletons of those missing men could be found there?"

Pete stared at her, surprised. "Are you saying that someone has been using that island as a dumping ground? Are we talking serial killer here?"

"No, I don't think serial killer. The crimes are spaced too far apart for it to be one man. But it could have been a group of men."

"Come on, wait a minute. A group of men? Wouldn't they be getting a little long in the tooth by now?"

Susan laughed. "Maybe one or two of them would. But, suppose they weren't all the same age. Think for a minute. One could be a boat captain and the others, hands or sternmen; younger guys who learned a way of life from their mentor. Or, perhaps, it could be a father and son team. Either way, they could span the thirty-five years and all six disappearances."

Pete took a bite of his steak and chewed for a moment, thinking.

"Okay, say you're right. A group of men have been busy eliminating their competition - permanently. What makes you think someone dumped them on Puffin? Your boyfriend getting abandoned there doesn't exactly make it a crime wave."

"I know. I know. And his memory is still a little patchy. But he told me recently that he believes he saw bones on Puffin. Bones that he now admits could have been human."

"Bones? Hmm, that's interesting."

Pete leaned back in his chair, eyes closed, deep in thought.

"You mentioned something about 'lobster wars.' Explain how bones on Puffin fit in with that?"

Susan pushed her plate aside and reached into her briefcase, taking out some photos.

"That's Lonnie Pierce," she said, handing him one of the pictures. "He was a big proponent of fishermen's rights thirty years ago - very vocal and very tough. He died in an auto accident a while back, but he was alive when the first of these men went missing and Nichols was a friend of his wife's from way back."

Pete studied the photo for a moment, then Susan handed him another.

"These two guys are Rusty Maguire and Jack O'Dwyer. They're both still alive and, though they were younger, they were tight with Pierce. Maguire still fishes off Mateguas. It was his daughter that shot Andersen two years ago and then killed herself. You remember the case, don't you? She was the same woman who found out she was pregnant with Andersen's child just before he went missing. Could be Maguire knew about the pregnancy and decided to get rid of the guy who knocked his daughter up."

"Mmmmm. That sounds like a stretch. What about O'Dwyer? That name sounds familiar."

"He's inside. Convicted of pushing drugs to kids. Got ten years to life. But before that, he was a sycophant of Pierce's. Practically worshiped the guy."

She handed him another picture.

"Who's this? Looks something like the first guy, Pierce, but not the same."

Susan nodded. "That's his son, Dex. He married Andersen's wife after Bill was presumed dead. They moved off Mateguas twelve years ago, but they're back now."

Pete laughed. "God, that little island is quite a Peyton Place, isn't it? Andersen seems to have his finger in every pie, so to speak. So, are you saying Pierce, the younger, had a motive, too? To get Andersen's wife?"

Susan nodded. "Yes. Only one man has disappeared since Dex Pierce left the island, but Rusty Maguire was there at that time. What if we have a conspiracy made up of Lonnie Pierce, his son, Maguire, and O'Dwyer who made it their mission to rid the seas around Mateguas of any outsiders who poached their territory?"

"A conspiracy?"

"Yes, what I'm really getting at is the establishment of a culture of violence, handed down from generation to generation. Starting with Lonnie Pierce protecting his territories and ending with someone, maybe his son or Maguire, carrying on the tradition by dumping Andersen on Puffin."

"Okay, but what about the nature lover, Nichols? How does he fit in?"

"Nichols had a summer home on Mateguas and he was tight with Lonnie Pierce's wife. They'd been friends since childhood. Both were summer people from Connecticut."

"Yeah, so what about it?"

"Well, what if there was more to their relationship than just friendship? For argument's sake, let's say they were having a little fling."

"Okay. And?"

"Add that together with a man like Pierce who was very protective and possessive of what he considered his property and I think you may have a pretty strong recipe for murder or, at the least, manslaughter."

Pete stared at the pictures for a moment then handed them back to Susan. "Okay, if you're right, it makes sense. But that's a pretty big 'if.' Got any other evidence?"

"Not right now, but I'm still digging. So, have I gotten your interest or not?"

Pete smiled. "Yeah. You've got me wondering. So, I suppose you want me to go out to Puffin and look for bones?"

"Yes, and if I'm right and we find some, we'll need DNA testing. On the off chance that you'll agree to take this on, I've spoken with a professor I know up at State. He will 'loan' us some of his anthropology students to help search. They've all been on digs before and know what they're doing. Said he'd give them extra credit or something for helping out, free of charge. So, all I need is your official blessing and presence on Puffin when we go."

"That's an awfully big presumption, Susan. Got any of this written down so I have something tangible to take to the

Chief? And, an affidavit from Andersen attesting to the fact that he saw human remains?"

Susan smiled and reached again into her briefcase. "It's all here," she said handing him a notebook.

Pete leafed through the pages, briefly. "Very thorough, Susan. Why am I not surprised! Okay, I'll study this tonight and, when I'm done, if I think it will hold water, I'll take it to the Chief. But don't get your hopes up. This is all pretty far-fetched, if you ask me."

"Read the material and, if you still think so when you're done, so be it. But I know I'm right about this. Puffin Island has been used as a dumping ground for bodies for more than three decades, attesting to a culture of violence that persists to this day. And, think, if I'm right, you could be the one to nip it in the bud!"

Pete smiled. "It'd be a big story for you, Susan. Could go national. Might mean a commendation for me, too. So, don't you worry. I'll read it all tonight. And, like I said, if it holds water, I'll take it to the Chief tomorrow."

Nodding to her, he tucked the notebook into his briefcase, then waved to the waitress for the check.

Susan, feeling satisfied that she'd done her best, smiled. "Call me after you talk to the Chief, okay?"

"No problem, Susan. No problem at all."

DINNER AT
TERRI AND SHAWN'S

THE NEXT EVENING AT Shawn's house, Terri and Karen worked in the kitchen while the men tended the grill outside.

"We watched that show Dad's girlfriend hosted on Sunday," said Terri. "Did you see it?"

Karen sighed. "Yes, we did, and Dex was very upset. He knew that girl, was friends with her. Their relationship was nothing like the way Susan portrayed it."

"I figured as much. Was he sort of like a big brother to her? You know, like he was with Maggie?"

Karen nodded. "Yes, I suppose. In any case, there was nothing romantic between them. But he did like the girl and being reminded of her death upset him."

Terri frowned. "Oh, come on. I bet it was more than that. Susan didn't come right out and say it, but she practically accused him of being the father of that girl's baby and possibly being involved in her death. If that happened to me, I think I'd be a little bit more than just upset. I'd be freaking out."

Karen hesitated for a moment. "Yes, you're right. He was more than just a little upset. He was angry, too. We've talked to a lawyer, but apparently, there's not much we can do to stop her without opening up another whole can of worms. And, to make matters worse, Dex believes your father is responsible for everything."

"Seriously? Why would Dad do that? I know he's not crazy about Dex and, in a sense, you can't blame him. But responsible for Susan's attack? I don't think so."

"Well, be that as it may, Dex is convinced that Bill's out to get him. I'm going to speak to your father and try to clear things up. It may be that Susan's targeting Dex out of some misguided sense of loyalty and Bill can get her to stop. But, if, as Dex believes, Bill's pushed her to do it, I'm going to let him know how I feel."

"Oh, Mom. Why can't you and Dad just get along? Other divorced people do. You always seem to be at each other's throats about something."

"This isn't my doing, Terri," Karen responded forcefully. "If your father has anything to do with trying to ruin Dex, he's got to know that we won't take it lying down. We'll fight him."

"Okay. Enough said. You're going to do what you're going to do. Let's talk about something else."

They were both silent for a moment. Finally, Karen looked up at her daughter.

"Are you still in touch with that museum curator in town?"

Terri stared at her, clearly surprised by the question. "You mean, Charlie?"

"If that's his name, then yes."

"Yeah, we try to grab lunch once a week and I usually see him on Sundays. I'm taking instruction with a friend of his, Harry Three-Feathers. Why?"

"Instruction? What kind?"

Terri hesitated. "Shamanism. Harry is his tribe's medicine man and he's teaching me. It's all about connecting the mind, body, and spirit."

Karen raised her eyebrows. "You're kidding. You're telling me you're going to be a medicine woman?"

"Sure, why not? Lots of people on the islands out here are very into holistic health. In fact, Shawn's mother is a healer and a midwife. Knowledge of the natural world can come in handy when you live in a remote place like this, you know."

Karen frowned. "Has it gotten that far already?"

"Has what gotten that far?"

"Your relationship with Shawn and this island. Are you thinking of living here forever? What about school?"

"Don't freak out, Mom. I'll finish school. Shawn wouldn't let me quit even if I wanted to. But I do intend on coming back here. For me, this is home now."

Karen absorbed her daughter's declaration in silence. Finally, she sighed. "Well, you're an adult now. I guess you need to make your own decisions and your own mistakes. So, back to your friend, Charlie. I'd like to meet with him, if that's all right with you."

Terri looked at her, puzzled. "Sure, I can set it up, but why?"

"I just want to talk to him about some of the legends. You know - things to do with that box and the objects it contains. Private things."

"Private things? Geesh, I thought we'd gotten beyond that. Don't you realize this stuff affects everyone? And have you ever talked to Dex about what really went on the night Maggie died? Or is that still one of your little secrets?"

Karen scowled. "You watch your mouth, young lady. I'm still your mother. And, no, I haven't told him and I don't intend to. Some things, well, are just better off left alone."

"Mom, don't you get it? If you and Dad had been straight with each other, who knows, you might have stayed together. And now you're doing the same thing with Dex. Aren't you short-changing him? Don't you trust him enough to tell him the truth?"

Karen stared down at her hands, unable to meet her daughter's piercing gaze. Finally, she looked up. "Listen, honey," she said softly. "There are things you don't know. I love Dex, but I don't think he would be able to accept the reality of what happened. And he's my husband and it's my call. What you tell or don't tell Shawn is your call. That's your decision and I won't interfere. All I'm asking is that you respect my decision."

Terri sighed. "Okay, I'll drop it. But I still think you're wrong. Now about Charlie, I guess, if he's willing, you can talk *privately* with him. I'll text him tonight."

"Thanks, honey. Now don't you think we'd better check on the boys? My stomach is beginning to growl."

Later that evening, after Karen and Dex had gone home, Terri received a text back from Charlie.

"I would be most happy to meet with your mother. Can you come to the museum on Thursday? My time is yours between one and four."

CHARLIE AND KAREN

"MAY I OFFER YOU a cup of coffee, Mrs. Pierce?"

Karen smiled at the older man. "That would be lovely. Thank you."

She and Charlie were alone in his office. Terri had introduced them, then excused herself saying she had errands to run in town and would be back later.

"Cream or sugar?" he asked.

"No, black will be fine."

He handed her the cup, poured one for himself, and sat down at his desk. He took a sip, then looked up. "Now what is it I can help you with?"

Karen hesitated, not sure how to begin. She had rehearsed what she planned to say hundreds of times, but now seated in this ordinary office sharing a cup of coffee with the man, it all seemed preposterous and insane. He would think she was crazy.

Charlie waited patiently, his eyes searching hers.

Finally, Karen spoke. "What's an *ah-gluh-beh-moo*?"

Charlie's eyes widened in surprise and shock. He leaned forward in his chair. "Where did you hear of this ... the *Aglebemu*?"

Karen stared down at her coffee cup for a moment. Finally, she looked up and met his gaze.

"I think I saw one the other day," she said in a voice barely above a whisper. "What is it?"

The old man sighed and leaned back in his chair, thinking as he sipped his coffee.

"In Native American folklore the *Aglebemu* is a harbinger of foul times," he replied. "In some texts, it is called a *mitche-hant*, which translates as 'evil creature.' The *Aglebemu* appears as a toad, or giant frog, and lives deep in the forest, in dark places where 'the people' do not dwell. It eschews the sunlight and exists on the flesh of other darkness dwellers – things so unclean that they are unmentionable."

Karen leaned forward in her chair, a look of puzzlement on her face.

"But the creature I saw wasn't hidden. It was sitting on a rock in the sun."

The old Indian took a deep breath and put down his coffee cup. "The toad only ventures into daylight when there is great evil about. This evil entices him, gives him the courage to leave his lair. But why do you think the creature you saw was the *Aglebemu* and not some simple frog? And where did you see it?"

Karen hesitated again, not sure how much of her encounter with the toad she wanted to reveal. "The frog I saw was unusually large, and there was something abnormal about its eyes. I searched online when I got home and found reference to this creature, the *Aglebemu*. And I saw it on Mateguas. I was taking a walk through the woods to the beach. I turned down a path that veered from the main trail. It led to a small pond where, as I said, this toad was sitting in the sun."

She stopped as an image of the frog's foul tongue lashing out at her flashed before her eyes. She shivered violently for a second, then with some effort, pulled herself together.

Recognizing her momentary distress, the old Indian took a sip of his coffee. "And you're telling me you simply saw this creature then turned and left?"

Karen said nothing, afraid to elaborate further.

"Mrs. Pierce, I fear you are not telling me the whole truth. But I will tell you what I know of this creature anyway. For from knowledge comes wisdom, and from wisdom, comes understanding and peace.

"The *Aglebemu* is a malevolent spirit who hungers for human flesh. It ensnares its victims with its loathsome tongue, which is lined with tiny spikes or needles that emit a vicious poison directly into its victim's bloodstream. This poison puts the poor unfortunate soul into a state of catatonia, unable to move, yet still fully conscious. Then, when its prey is helpless, the toad wraps it in a substance, not unlike a spider's web … a sticky filament, delicate-looking, yet strong and binding. When this is done, it drags the poor soul back to its lair - a dark, damp place deep in the forest where, in time, it will tear and devour the living flesh."

Karen shuttered as she realized how narrow her escape had been from the horrific fate he was describing.

Charlie, noticing her discomfort, leaned forward in his chair. "Are you all right, Mrs. Pierce?"

Karen took a deep breath. "Yes, I'm fine. Please go on."

"I have described the *Aglebemu* tearing and devouring the victim's flesh, but the creature does not only feed on the skin and bones of its captive. No, what it desires above all else is its victim's fear. For, while the toad is ripping and consuming the flesh, the unfortunate soul is still fully awake and aware of everything. This, obviously, engenders great terror, and it is that terror that fuels the toad's evil nature.

"Yes, the *Aglebemu* is a loathsome creature and, if it has found the courage to come into the light, then I'm afraid there is something terribly wrong on Mateguas."

Charlie spoke calmly, in a professorial tone – detached and lecturing. But, never once did his eyes leave Karen. He set his coffee cup down, leaning back in his chair.

"Are you ready to tell me the truth, Mrs. Pierce? Or do you want some other unsuspecting soul to fall prey to this evil creature?"

Karen closed her eyes for a moment, then took a deep breath. "Okay, but you'll think I'm insane."

Charlie smiled benignly. "It is not my place to judge, only to listen."

Karen nodded. "Okay. You're dead right about what it does. The tongue, the crap it wraps you in. And it was me the creature caught. Just like you said. I was watching it and then, out of nowhere, its tongue got me around the ankle … the barbs pierced me."

She hesitated for a moment, reliving the horrific experience.

"Can I get you anything, Mrs. Pierce? Water?"

"No, I'm fine, thank you. It's just … remembering it and all. I've tried to put it out of my mind."

Charlie nodded. "Yes, I can understand why. Now please go on when you're ready. Take your time. There is no need to rush."

Karen smiled, grateful for the calm acceptance she recognized in his voice. "Okay, when I was helpless, the toad let go of my leg, then wrapped me in that spider web stuff that comes from its toes. I could see and I could feel, and I was aware of what was going on, but I couldn't do anything about it. It was the most frightening thing that's ever happened to me."

"But you are here now. You were not consumed. So tell me, how did you escape?"

Again, Karen took a deep breath. "It was my son, Alex. Oh, God, now you're really going to think I'm bonkers. He saved me."

"Your son was with you? How old is the boy?"

"He's a little over a year. I had him in a sling on my chest."

Charlie raised his eyebrows. "Just a babe. And how did an infant save you?"

"This is what I really came to talk to you about. My son ... he's something special. Tell me what you know about the legend of The Blessed Boy."

"The Blessed Boy?"

"Yes, the son of Mateguas, God of the Dead."

Charlie sat quietly for a moment, digesting this turn of events.

"All right. But first, I must advise you the legend of The Blessed Boy is not part of my tribe's core mythology. This tale originates with the people who once inhabited the island of Mateguas but were forced to flee by the white man many generations ago. Only their descendants know the full tale. But I know something of it and will tell you all I know.

"It was told that Mateguas, God of the Dead, hurled down a lightning bolt, striking his virgin acolyte in her womanhood, impregnating her. Nine months later, she gave birth to a son. The child was blessed and, like your Christian deity, Jesus, had the power to heal. It was also said that he could look into a man's soul and divine the good or evil within. And, amazingly, he had the power to take on the appearance of another being, usually an animal or bird. Unfortunately, a white man, intent on stealing the sacred land, murdered both the boy and his mother. Some believe the boy's spirit still haunts the woods and shores of Mateguas and it is said he will return in human form someday, but when that day will come is unknown."

Karen nodded. "Two years ago, I was struck by lightning when I was here on Mateguas. Nine months later, I gave birth."

Charlie raised his eyebrows again. "And you believe your son is The Boy Reborn?"

"Yes, I do. When Alex was born, he had strange flecks of gold in his eyes, identical to those I saw in the spirit of The Blessed Boy when we first came to Mateguas twelve years ago. Alex's disappeared shortly after his birth but returned when we arrived here this year for the summer. And, he speaks to me with his mind and I can speak to him telepathically, too. And, oh, you're not going to believe this, but he can shift."

"Shift?"

"Change, morph. Like you said, into a bird or something else. That's how I got away. Alex shifted into the form of an eagle and picked up that creepy frog in his talons. He flew away, toward the woods, and hurled it into the trees. Then he came back to me and changed into my little boy again."

Karen slumped down in her chair, the effort of telling the truth exhausting her, then she looked up at the old man. "Okay, now I've said it. Are you going to call the men in white coats for me?"

Charlie couldn't help but chuckle. "No, I won't be calling the authorities to take you away. But what you say is hard to believe. Had he manifested any other unusual behavior before this incident?"

"No, not other than the lights in his eyes and his ability to talk to me with his mind. And when he does this, he talks like an adult, too, not like a little boy."

Charlie nodded and closed his eyes, thinking.

"If what you say is true, then I fear there is great danger for you, your son, and possibly the rest of your family on Mateguas. I think that it would be wise if you met with a friend of mine, Harry Three-Feathers. He is much more learned on these matters that I am. He meets with your daughter on Sundays at the nursing home where he lives. Would you be able to join us this week? I fear that this is a meeting that cannot be put off too far into the future."

Karen pulled out her cell to check her calendar and nodded. "Yes, I think I can do that. But, does Terri have to know? I don't want her in any danger."

"Yes, I believe you should take her into your confidence. She is wise beyond her tender years. But you need not fear for her. Harry reveres her and will not let anything or anyone harm her. He will protect her with his life if need be."

Karen looked at him, surprised, and then nodded reluctantly. "Okay. I'll talk to her. And, thank you for being willing to help us. When I made the decision to come back to Mateguas this time, I thought all of this mumbo-jumbo was over. But now, I wonder if I haven't made a terrible mistake."

"If, indeed, your son is The Boy Reborn, then you would have done him a great disservice by keeping him from the isle of his ancestors. It is his sacred home and only there will he ever be able to fulfill his potential. I fear that if he were kept someplace else, eventually, his soul would wither and die. No, you have done the right thing to bring him to the sacred land of his forefathers."

"I hope you're right."

They sat quietly for a few minutes, sipping their coffee, which now had gone cold.

Taking a deep breath, Karen stood and handed him her cup. "Would you be so kind as to show me around your museum before I leave?"

Charlie smiled. "I would be delighted."

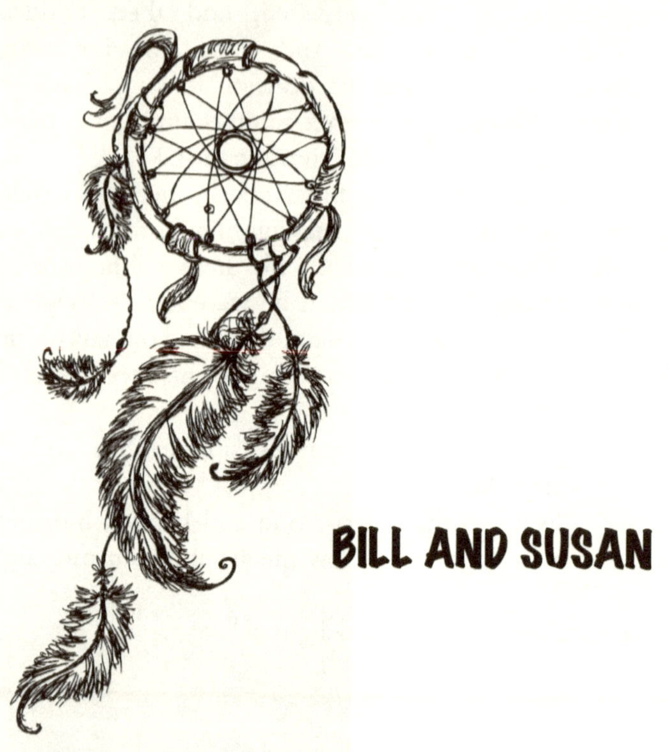

BILL AND SUSAN

THE AMTRAK DOWNEASTER PULLED noisily into the Portland terminal. Bill grabbed his overnighter and briefcase and followed the stream of passengers hurriedly exiting the train. The sun was bright and he had to squint due to its reflection off his glasses. He had a bitch of a headache.

Grimacing, he walked rapidly toward the parking lot.

"BILL! OVER HERE!"

He stopped and turned, surprised to hear someone calling his name.

Susan stood in front of the entrance to the train terminal, waving as she yelled to him.

"What are you doing here?" he asked as he approached her. "You know I have my car. I don't need a ride."

Susan frowned. "Nice greeting. I think you can do better than that, can't you?"

Despite his headache, Bill managed a laugh. "Okay," he said, wrapping his arm around her waist and giving her a lingering kiss. "That better?"

"Yes, it is," she laughed. "Much. Now let's get a cup of coffee. I don't have a lot of time and I want to let you know what's been happening."

Reluctantly, Bill followed her into the terminal. He didn't want to be with her now. All he wanted was to get home, take a pill, and lie down. But Susan was a force and he knew it would be better to accede to her demands than to fight.

Once inside, he purchased coffee from one of the many vending machines that lined the back wall. The place was now almost deserted and they sat down on one of the benches to talk.

"They bit!" she exclaimed. "They're going to look for the bodies on Puffin. And, I've enlisted the support of the Anthro Department at State for grad students to help."

"You mean the police will be going to Puffin? That's good news, I guess. Why the students, though?"

"Yes, the police and forensics. And, the kids from State - they've been on archeological digs and know how to sift through debris and dirt for artifacts. A rep from the Coroner's Office will be coming along, too."

Bill sipped his coffee, thinking. "Do you really expect they're going to find anything? I mean, it's a long shot."

Susan smiled. "I've got a hunch on this one and my hunches are usually right. Yes, I think they're going to find one, if not all, of the six missing men." She glanced down at her watch. "I've got to get going. I'm on the air in an hour, but I just had to tell you the good news."

She reached over and squeezed his hand, then stood and started for the door. Halfway across the room, she stopped and looked back over her shoulder. "Oh, Christ, I almost forgot. Saturday. Keep Saturday clear."

"Why?"

Susan grinned. "That's when it's happening. That's when we're going to Puffin Island!"

She blew him a kiss, turned, and hurried out the door to the parking lot.

Bill sat immobile for a moment staring after her as three words screamed across his consciousness, "Saturday ... Puffin Island."

Without warning, black shadows crept into the corners of his vision and the quiet terminal was abruptly filled with the vicious sound of the winter wind raging relentlessly across the ocean.

The words "Puffin Island" echoed repeatedly, bouncing off the walls and slamming into his mind over and over again. But nothing could blot out the never-ending, icy howling of the wind that threatened swallow his soul alive.

His hands began shaking violently with imagined cold, causing the hot coffee to spill over the front of his pants. The steaming liquid burned, but he was not aware of it. The shadows clouding his vision were growing larger and he feared they would soon erase all that he was or once had been, leaving his mind and his soul lifeless, devoid of all humanity.

And only one word triumphed over the roar of the bitter and relentless wind: *survive*.

Then as swiftly as the shadows and wind had appeared, they were gone. The empty terminal was back and he gazed down in shock to see his once crisp khakis soaked with cold vending machine coffee. His hands still shook and it took him several minutes to remember who and where he was.

Slowly, he stood up, trying to steady himself. As he moved, he realized there was more than cold coffee staining his pants. A look of disgust passed over his face. Swiftly, he grabbed his overnighter and briefcase and headed toward the men's room.

Once inside, he removed his soiled pants and briefs and cleaned himself as best he could. He threw the ruined trousers into the trashcan and dressed in clean ones from his suitcase. Gazing in the mirror, he noted how pale and gaunt he looked - not at all like the man who, earlier in the day, had boarded the train in Boston. His head was once again throbbing painfully and he longed for one of those magic little pills the shrink had prescribed that could make the whole world disappear.

Or Karen.

Karen could make the pain go away. He dredged up a memory from a time long ago when they lived in California. He'd had a hard day at work and was lying on the couch, his head in her lap, and she was gently and soothingly massaging his temples. They'd been so happy.

How did he lose all that? And could he ever get it back again?

As he walked out of the terminal toward his car, his thoughts turned to Susan. There were times, he had to admit, when he could almost see a life with her. She was attractive, intelligent with a good sense of humor, and, in a lot of ways, they complemented one other. But she was driven, ambitious. No, she would not be content to stand by his side and share his limelight. She wanted it all and heaven help the person or persons who stood in her way.

He thought about her planned excursion to Puffin and wondered if all her hoopla about dead bodies was just some sort of stunt she'd cooked up to draw the attention of the national media. Did she honestly care about getting justice for him? Or was he only a pawn in her greater game plan?

Shaking his head, he got into the car and, for a moment, leaned forward, resting his forehead on the steering wheel. The pain throbbing in his skull was relentless. It was always like this when he got back from Boston after a session with the doctor. If only he could remember. Maybe then the headaches and nightmares would stop. Maybe then, he could be free.

Sitting up straight, he started the car, but, before backing up, pulled out his cell to check for messages. Only one caught his eye.

Karen called! She wants to see me!

Hastily, he hit redial, but the call went immediately to voicemail. He left a message saying he was on his way home and that she could come over anytime.

Finally, he was beginning to feel better. The headache was fading and all thoughts of Puffin Island and the fear he had experienced in the terminal were wiped from his mind. All he could think about now was Karen.

He backed the car out of the stall and headed toward the ferry terminal. He would still be able to make the four p.m. boat and, maybe, just maybe, he would see her that evening.

THE FERRY

BILL REACHED THE FERRY terminal just in time. He stowed his overnighter in the stern, then entered the main cabin. He was about to take a seat when he recognized his daughter and Karen sitting on one of the front benches. Smiling at his good fortune, he made his way over to them and sat down next to Terri.

"Hi," he said. "Mind if I sit with you all?"

"Hi, Dad," Terri replied, giving him a kiss on the cheek. "You just get back from Boston?"

Karen turned in her seat and smiled at him.

"Hi, Karen," he said. "Yes, I just got in. Glad to be coming home."

"Yeah," replied Terri. "You don't really get to spend much time here, do you? What with work and that doctor and all."

"You're right about that, but I think that's going to change soon."

"What do you mean?"

"I'll tell you about it later."

He leaned over to get Karen's attention. "You called me? Something you wanted to talk about? Is it about Sophie? I hope nothing's happened."

Karen shook her head. "No, it's not about Sophie. She's fine. Can I stop by on my way home? It's not something I want to discuss here."

"Sure, like I told you before, you're always welcome at my house."

Karen nodded. "Great. Thanks."

Bill was about to say more, but she looked away and pulled a paperback from her purse.

Feeling dismissed, he turned back to Terri.

"So, what were you and your mom up to today? Shopping?"

"No, we went to see Charlie at the museum. Mom wanted to meet him."

Bill raised his eyebrows. "Is your mother getting into the whole Native American voodoo thing, too? That would be something I'd like to see."

Karen, who was listening to their conversation with one ear, looked up, laughing. "No, I'm not. One medicine woman in the family is quite enough. I just wanted to meet the guy, and, I have to admit, I found him very interesting."

"Mmmm, looks like the whole family's going native except me. Maybe I should meet these guys, too. A little mysticism might be just what the doctor ordered."

Karen smiled before turning her attention back to her book. Bill gazed at her for a moment, then looked back at his daughter.

"How's the lobstering going?" he asked.

"Oh, let me tell you what happened..."

As Terri described her week, Bill only half-listened as a feeling he thought he'd never recapture began to bubble up inside of him.

He was happy.

He was with his family again and, if he really tried, he could blot out the past twelve years and pretend that he and Karen were together and had never been apart. But deep down he knew this was just a fool's fantasy that would soon come crashing down around him.

He smiled at his daughter then turned his gaze toward Karen, who was still reading.

If only there were some Native American god willing to grant wishes, he thought. *I would give anything, all my possessions, even my soul, to stay right here and make this boat ride last forever.*

A half-hour later, Karen pulled her car into the driveway at Bill's house. He'd arrived just before she did and rushed to open the door for her.

"Still the gentleman," she said, acknowledging his gesture.

"I am my mother's son," he replied as he escorted her up the steps into the house. "Can I get you a drink? Wine or a cocktail?"

Karen hesitated, about to refuse, but seeing the eagerness in his eyes, changed her mind. "It's been a long day. How about a little Jack Daniels on the rocks?"

"You got it! Make yourself comfortable."

While he busied himself at the bar, Karen took a seat on the sofa, watching him as he prattled on about his work.

He had lost weight and there were deep, dark circles ringing his eyes.

He turned and smiled at her. "I'm probably boring you to tears with all this talk about my job. Tell me about Sophie. What have you heard from her lately?"

He handed her the drink and sat on the couch beside her.

"Thanks," she said, taking a sip. "I talked to her last night. She says she's enjoying her work at the gallery. Other than that, she didn't tell me much. I suspect she talks to Terri mostly. I hope she can get away and visit sometime this summer. Maybe you can convince her."

"I'll bet she has a young man in New Haven, Kar. I don't think work alone would keep her there. She's never been the ambitious twin. You know that."

Karen sighed. "Yes, you're right about that."

She sipped her drink, noting Bill had almost finished his and was getting up to refill his glass.

"On the boat, you mentioned to Terri that you might not be going to Boston so frequently. What's that about? Don't you see a doctor down there?"

Bill sat back down. "Yeah, I do. Dr. Lionel Burgess. Supposed to be the best retrograde amnesia specialist in New England."

"That sounds promising."

"You'd think so, but I've been seeing the great man for four months, and I still don't remember anything."

"But don't these things take time?"

"Yeah, that's what the doctor says, but I've been exploring alternative therapies and think I might have stumbled on something that might help."

"What?"

"It's called mindful meditation and articles I've read say it's been successful in restoring repressed memories."

"Are you going to be doing this on your own? Or with the doctor?"

"On my own. Can I refresh your drink?"

Karen glanced down at her glass. "No, I think I'm okay. But is that wise? I mean, what if you remember something you can't handle?"

Bill didn't answer immediately but instead stared at his glass.

"Bill?"

"Sorry. Just thinking. I haven't told anyone, but I have these nightmares. They're bad, Kar. I wake up screaming. And headaches. I don't know how much longer I can stand them. I have to do something."

Karen reached out and took his hand. "I'm sorry. I didn't know. I thought you looked tired. But don't you think it would be safer to try this meditation under a doctor's supervision? Or, if not a doctor, then someone who specializes in it?"

"That's a good idea. I'll look into that. Maybe there's someone in town. Thanks, Kar."

They sat quietly for a moment, then Bill stood and walked to the picture window. "You wanted to talk to me about something, right?" he asked as he gazed out at the sea below.

Karen turned toward him. "Yes, it's about that new TV show your girlfriend hosts on Sunday night."

"Oh, the cold case show," he replied, still looking out the window. "She's very proud of it."

"Have you watched it?"

"Yes, I have. Quite the little skeleton she found in Dex's closet, don't you think? He ever tell you about his affair with that little girl?"

Surprised, Karen slammed her glass down on the table and got to her feet. "That 'little girl' was a friend of his and any 'affair' between the two of them is a figment of your girlfriend's imagination. He was a kid and having a friend murdered affected him. And now, with your reporter friend dredging it all up again, he's understandably upset."

"Gee, I'm sorry about that. But if he's innocent, he has nothing to worry about. Just gossip."

Karen took a deep breath, trying to control her temper. "He thinks that you're behind it ... that you put her up to this slander. I told him he was wrong, but now I'm not so sure."

"Hey, I had nothing to do with it. Susan's her own woman and that show's her baby. I was as surprised as you when I saw what it was about."

Karen stared at him for a minute, wondering whether he was telling her the truth.

Bill smiled apologetically. "Listen, tell Dex I'm sorry, but I can't do anything to stop her. When she thinks she's got a story, she runs with it. In fact, she's got another little idea in that fertile brain of hers and this one involves me."

"You? What do you mean?"

"She thinks I'm not the first person to have been left to die on Puffin. She's come up with a list of men who have disappeared over the years and she's convinced the authorities that Puffin may be the place to look for them. She's dragging me out there on Saturday with a whole slew of folks to follow up on it."

Karen was silent for a moment. He had neatly sidetracked her from Dex's problem.

"I'm sorry that she's gotten you involved in that. But to get back to my husband, does she plan to go after him again this Sunday?"

Bill sighed. "Kar, I don't know. Like I said, her work is her work. I don't interfere and, if I tried, she'd be out of here. She's an independent and stubborn woman."

"Well, you can let her know that we've consulted an attorney and if she crosses the line, we'll seek legal remedy."

"I'll tell her, but I don't think it will do much good. She's ambitious and this is great TV. And, anyway, I wouldn't be surprised if she hasn't run her script by the station's attorneys. She's too smart to get caught slandering anyone."

Karen nodded. "Okay. But if you had anything to do with this..."

"I didn't. It's all Susan."

Karen glanced at her watch. "I've got to be going. I expect Dex is home by now. Thanks for the drink."

"Sure, as I said before, anytime."

He walked her to the door, then leaned over to give her a kiss on the cheek, but she turned away from him and hurried down the porch steps.

He stood quietly watching her go, wondering, once again, how he had let it all slip away.

DEX AND KAREN

DEX CHECKED HIS CELL. It was getting late and there was still no word from Karen. He'd tried calling, but her phone went immediately to voicemail.

She's turned it off, he thought. *Why?*

Concerned, he dialed Terri's number.

"Hi," she answered.

"Hey, Terri, it's me, Dex. Where the hell are you two? I thought you guys would be back long before now."

Terri hesitated for a moment. "Well, I'm at home. Mom must still be at Dad's. We bumped into him on the boat. Mom said she wanted to talk to him about something."

"And how long ago was that?"

Again, Terri hesitated. "Uh, about an hour, I guess. She should be home any time now."

Dex took a deep breath, trying to control his rising anger. "Okay, thanks. It's just that I was getting worried."

"Everything's okay. Mom will be home soon. I'm sure of it."

"Okay, thanks, sugar. You have a nice evening."

He hung up before she had a chance to respond. He knew Karen planned to confront her ex-husband about the LeVeque show and assumed that was why she was there, but in his mind, that shouldn't have taken more than a few minutes.

He leaned on the deck railing, thinking about Bill and Karen and the steps he had recently taken to try to find out the truth about their relationship.

He'd tried to dismiss his worries that he wasn't the boy's father but, after arrival on the island, his doubts had intensified. Wanting to lay them to rest, he'd contacted an old friend, Josh Rosen, who was now Chief of Neurology at the teaching hospital on the mainland. After a long conversation, Josh sent him a DNA paternity testing kit. Taking advantage of Karen's trip to town with Terri, he'd obtained the needed samples and mailed the kit back for laboratory analysis. The results would be available forty-eight hours after receipt.

Thinking about it now, he wondered why he'd done it.

What difference would it make? Even if Bill were Alex's biological father, would I stop loving him?

He knew the answer to that question was an emphatic "no." He would love that boy no matter what any DNA test said. But, Karen - could he go on loving her? That was the question torturing his mind.

Sighing, he walked back inside. His son was seated on the floor playing with his Legos, gurgling happily.

Dex smiled, watching him.

He started to kneel down beside the boy when the room was suddenly illuminated by headlights shining through the front window.

Karen was home.

She parked her car next to the cottage, turned off the engine, and sat for a moment, mentally constructing the conversation she would have with Dex when she entered the house.

There was no way she could tell him what she suspected - that Bill was behind Susan LeVeque's smear campaign. No, she would tell him that she'd confronted her ex-husband and that he had denied all culpability. And that would be the end of that.

Another lie ... another secret, she thought. *Will the need for deceit ever end? And what would Terri think?*

She laughed. *You know damned well what she'd think. She's chided you more than once for not coming clean with Dex long ago. And she's right. I should have. But how do I do that now, after so much time has passed?*

She pictured in her mind the scenario.

Yeah, I'll just march in there and tell him that the kid he thinks is his is actually the child of some Native American spirit and that, gee, he's got Christ-like powers. And how will my rational husband respond to that? Oh, he'll pat me kindly on the head then get on his cell and call the men in white coats to come get me. Off to the loony bin. Oh, then, before they cart me away, I'll tell him to talk to Terri. Tell him she'll back me up. And what will his response be? He'll just laugh and assume that insanity runs in the family. She'll be suspect, too. Nope, I can't do it. So, I'll lie again.

She bit her bottom lip, forced a smile, and opened the front door. Dex was seated on the floor, playing with Alex.

"Hi," she said.

"Where've you been? I got home about an hour ago and sent the babysitter home. I called Terri. She said you guys were on the four and that she thought you stopped off at Bill's. Is that where you were?"

She saw his eyes narrow when he mentioned Bill and knew what he was thinking.

"Yes, that's right. And you know why. I told you I was going to confront him and I did."

Dex nodded. "Yes, I know. But I guess I hoped you'd change your mind. Well, what did he have to say?"

Hearing a hint of anger in his tone, Karen tossed her purse and jacket on the table, then turned to face him. "Bill denied everything. Said this is just some stunt Susan cooked up to try to improve ratings. He said he has no control over what she does."

Dex laughed unpleasantly. "And you believed him?"

Karen leaned over and picked up her son who was now reaching for her. "Yes, I did."

"And did you discuss all this over cocktails?"

Karen held her breath for a moment, staring at him.

"Just what are you implying?" she replied. "Yes, I did have a drink with him. He looks terrible. He's lost weight and isn't sleeping well. Says he has nightmares. I don't think that doctor in Boston is doing him much good. So, yes, I stayed for a drink. I felt sorry for him. After all, he's the father of my girls. Do you have a problem with that?"

Dex was about to respond but apparently thought better of it. Taking a deep breath, he walked over to where she was now sitting with Alex on her lap. He leaned down and kissed her.

"Sorry. I was just worried when you weren't home. And Bill, well, you know how I feel about him."

Karen looked up, her expression softening. "I know. I should have called you. I didn't think I'd be there so long, but he just looked so forlorn."

Dex frowned again but didn't say anything.

Karen stood, putting the boy back down on the carpet with his toys. "Did you take anything out for supper?" she asked, changing the subject. "I totally forgot this morning."

"Yeah, I got some tuna steaks marinating for the grill. And I made a salad."

Karen smiled. "Oh, that sounds lovely. Give me a minute to slip into something more comfortable and then I'll be out to help you put it all together."

After Karen returned, they chatted idly for a while, then Dex went outside to start the charcoal.

Karen watched him as he disappeared through the doorway, knowing their discussion of her relationship with Bill had only been tabled for the time being.

Sighing, she picked up her child and put him in his playpen then grabbed a bottle of wine and two glasses and joined Dex on the deck.

"Want some wine?" she asked.

"Thanks," he said, taking a glass from her as he stirred the coals.

Karen leaned on the deck rail, her back to him. The moon peeked out from behind a cloud, shining brightly on the water below as a soft breeze blew her hair about her head.

Dex turned and stared at her for a moment, then put his arms around her waist, kissing her on the back of her neck.

"Mmmm, that feels good," she whispered, leaning into his embrace.

They stood listening as the waves caressed the shoreline below, then he turned her in his arms.

"I'm sorry for the way I behaved, princess," he murmured. "I guess I'm just a jealous guy and the thought of you and Bill together eats at me."

She reached up and laid her palm on his cheek.

"You have no reason to be jealous. I love you and only you. But you have to accept that Bill's always going to be a part of my life. We have a shared history and children together and that's not going to change."

"I know. And I'm trying."

She smiled then reached up and pulled him down to meet her lips. As they kissed, he slipped his hands around her, holding her close.

"Do we have time before dinner?" she asked.

Wordlessly, he lifted her in his arms and carried her to their bedroom. Laying her down gently, he slowly unbuttoned her blouse, opening it to expose her warm flesh. Kissing her softly, he buried his lips in her hair, murmuring her name. Moaning with pleasure, she moved her hands to the front of his jeans.

"I want you now," she whispered.

Later, Dex pulled away from her, smiling. "This never gets old, does it? Maybe we should think about giving Alex a little brother or sister. What do you think?"

Karen propped herself up on her elbow, staring at him in surprise. "What? Are you nuts? Another baby? I'll be on a walker and you'll be in a wheelchair at his or her high school graduation! No, I think you're going to have to be satisfied with the one. And, the girls - they're yours, too, you know. You raised them."

Dex nodded a bit glumly. "I suppose you're right, but I wish it had happened for us sooner. I always wanted a big family. Being an only child can be pretty lonely at times."

Karen reached out and ran her fingers through his hair. "Like I said, you have the girls, too. Especially Sophie. She adores you. And Terri loves you, too. She's just a little wrapped up with her dad right now."

"Yeah, Bill leaves his mark wherever he goes, doesn't he? God, I'm sick of that man."

As Dex spoke, she could feel the tension in his body return. Swiftly, he let her go and stood, pulling on his jeans.

"Now, I don't know about you, but I'm feeling pretty damned hungry. How about I finish fixing dinner?"

Karen forced a smile. "Do you think we still have any coals left? They're probably burned to ash by now."

"We can always broil," he muttered as he left the room.

Karen watched him as he walked down the hall, toward the deck. Sighing, she grabbed her robe from the closet and wrapped it tightly around her. In the living room, she retrieved Alex from his playpen and cradled him in her arms.

"Well, little guy," she whispered. "I don't think your father is ever going to believe me about Bill."

The child smiled and stared at her, flecks of gold dancing merrily in his eyes.

Karen laughed. "Yes, he may still harbor the thought that Bill might be your biological father, but he's dead wrong. Bill's not your father, but then neither is he. Your father is something quite different and I hope the day will never come when I have to explain that one!"

BILL

LONG AFTER KAREN LEFT the house, Bill sat alone on the porch steps. A drink in hand, he silently cursed himself knowing that somehow he'd exposed his involvement in Susan's schemes to her.

Maybe it was an edge of sarcasm in my tone of voice or a slight sneer that danced across my face. But whatever it was, the damage is done. And to make matters worse, we'd been getting along so well, almost like old times.

He took a sip of his drink then looked down at the amber liquid swirling around in the glass. He was drinking too much again and knew he ought to cut back. He thought about pouring the liquor into the shrubs and getting a glass of water but took another sip instead. The alcohol helped to keep the dark dreams at bay, and that was worth whatever brain and liver damage he might be incurring.

He turned his gaze toward the night sky. As if summoned, the crescent moon slipped from behind a cloud, silently admonishing him for his foolishness. Sighing with resignation, he let his mind wander.

Karen.

They had met at a party at San Jose State. He remembered how she looked when he'd caught sight of her across the room.

Tall, slender, wearing faded jeans and a Stanford sweatshirt.

Her long blonde hair had been pulled back loosely into a ponytail, wispy tendrils escaping and curling around her face. She was the most beautiful thing he'd ever seen.

He remembered approaching her and all the silly small talk they'd made, "what's your major?", "where are you from?", yadda, yadda, yadda. Then the music had started and he'd asked her to dance.

They'd danced to several fast numbers first, delighting in how well they moved together. Then a slow number played.

What was it?

Frowning, he searched his memories for the song. Then he smiled.

An oldie but a goodie. "Only You" by the Platters.

He closed his eyes, humming the melody, silently mouthing the words and picturing their dance in his mind.

It wasn't really dancing. More like swaying to the music.

He remembered how he'd put his arms around her waist as she draped hers across his shoulders, their bodies pressed tightly together, her head resting against his chest.

He smiled as he let that dance linger in his mind, knowing he would give anything to go back in time and hold her like that again.

Only you, Karen, only you.

DINNER WITH THE O'DWYER'S

TERRI DRESSED CAREFULLY. IT was Friday night and Shawn's mother had invited them to dinner. While she'd met Helen O'Dwyer once before, that meeting had been brief, and they'd had little chance to get acquainted. Tonight would be different and Terri wanted to make a good impression.

She was wearing a neatly pressed pair of white linen shorts and a silk peasant blouse. To complete her look, she wore large, gold hoop earrings and a pair of flip-flops from L.L. Bean, embroidered with lobsters.

She was appraising her appearance in the mirror when Shawn came up behind her, putting his arms around her waist.

"You look beautiful," he said.

She turned her head to look at him. "Don't I wish. But, seriously, do I look okay?"

"You have totally captured and tamed 'island chic,' my dear. My mom will love you." He glanced at his watch. "That is, she'll love you if we get there on time. Mom is a stickler for promptness. You ready?"

"Just let me put on some gloss and grab my purse. I'll meet you at the truck."

Fifteen minutes later, they were pulling into the O'Dwyer driveway. The house, like many island homes, was old but well-tended. A large vegetable and herb garden sat on the side along with several rows of blueberry bushes. A fine netting had been erected over the berries to keep birds and other predators from decimating the summer's crop.

As they entered the house, they could hear music coming from the backyard.

"I'll bet everyone's out on the patio," said Shawn. "Come on. I want you to meet my brother, Jason, and his wife."

Shawn grabbed Terri's hand and quickly led her through the house. As they moved from room to room, Terri smiled, noting the place was tastefully decorated, Maine cottage style. The floors were painted a pale green and were adorned with braided rugs woven in complimentary colors. A door at the back of the kitchen was propped open and they were about to step through to the yard when Shawn stopped abruptly.

A middle-aged man with black hair, peppered with gray, stood on the patio in front of the doorway. He wore tight faded jeans, ripped at the knees, and a cut-off T-shirt. His arms and neck were muscular and covered with tattoos.

"Well, if it ain't my youngest," he said with a grin. "Get over here and give your old man a hug."

Shawn ignored the comment, turning toward his mother, who was standing by the barbecue, a worried expression on her face.

"What the fuck's he doing here, Ma?"

"Your father got out today, Shawn. Good behavior, he says, though I doubt it. Surprised us all. Said he wanted to see you boys so I invited him to dinner."

Terri peered around Shawn to get a better look at the man.

Jackson Thomas O'Dwyer, known to his friends as Black Jack, stood about ten feet away, hands on his hips, a sly smile on his face. Seeing Terri, he stepped forward, closer to where they stood.

"And who's this lovely lassie, Shawn?"

Shawn didn't move, still shielding Terri with his body. "She's my girlfriend, Jack."

The elder O'Dwyer raised his eyebrows and smiled. "Well, good for you, boy. So, how about that hug?"

He took another step toward Shawn and held his arms out.

Shawn didn't move.

Jack O'Dwyer laughed. "Okay, I guess you think you're too old to hug your old man. How about a handshake then?"

He waited for a moment, offering his hand, but when Shawn didn't take it, stepped closer.

"Listen, boy," he said, anger apparent in his voice. "I've served my time and from here on out, I'll be walking the straight and narrow; an honest man. And I'm your father. You need to show some respect."

Shawn stared at the man, still not moving.

"Shake it, Shawn," pleaded Helen. "For Christ's sake. Just get it over with."

Shawn turned toward his mother and, after a minute, nodded. Reluctantly, he reached for Jack's hand, but, as soon as they touched, Jack stepped forward and pulled him into a fierce bear hug, lifting him off the ground.

Angry, Shawn pulled away, a look of disgust on his face.

"Now that wasn't so bad, was it, son?" said Jack, grinning as he took a couple of steps back, giving Shawn the once-over. "You sure got the O'Dwyer look about you. Not like that other one, the firstborn. He looks more like his mother."

Shawn was about to respond when Jack sidestepped around him and approached the doorway where Terri stood alone.

"And what's your name, little girl?" he asked.

Terri's eyes darted back and forth from Shawn to his father.

"Terri Andersen," she said. "Pleased to meet you."

Jack looked back over his shoulder at his son. "She's a polite one, I'll give you that. And pretty too."

He smiled then looked back at Terri, who was about to step out of the doorway to join Shawn. Without warning, Jack intercepted her, grabbing her and lifting her off her feet. He twirled her around once then set her back down on the ground in front of his son, keeping one arm wound around her waist.

Shawn, his face flushed with anger, stepped in front of her.

"Shawn, don't," cried Helen, reaching out and grabbing her son by the arm.

Shawn glared at his father and was about to shake off his mother's restraining hand, when he was startled by a voice coming from the patio doorway.

"I think you should unhand the young lady, Jack. NOW."

Terri turned toward the speaker. He was a burly-looking young man, tall and fair-haired. His belly protruded a bit over his pants, but Terri could tell from the way he held himself that the rest of him was all muscle.

Recognizing his eldest son, Jack quickly released Terri and stepped back.

"Well, if it isn't my firstborn. Good to see you, lad. Is that your wife behind you? Amanda, isn't it? And do I see a bit of a bump on her? A grandchild?"

Ignoring his father, Jason O'Dwyer took Terri gently by the hand.

"You must be Terri," he said. "You're as beautiful as my brother said you were. I'm Jason and this is my wife, Amanda."

As he spoke, he deftly maneuvered Terri back into the house behind him.

Staring at his son, Jack laughed.

"Okay, okay," he said, grinning. "I see I've been put in my proper place. No harm, no foul. Helen, me love, how about another beer? And when's that food going to be on the table? I'm about dying for a home-cooked meal after all that prison chow."

Without waiting for an answer, he reached into a cooler and grabbed a bottle of Coors, then, ignoring his children, stretched out on one of the lounge chairs.

Helen stared angrily at him then walked firmly to where Terri and Amanda waited in the doorway.

"You girls come with me. The sooner we eat, the sooner he'll be gone. Jason, I want you to make sure he's on the last boat. The smell of him is already polluting this island."

Jason nodded, then ambled out onto the patio and sat down next to his father.

"Why is he even here, Ma?" asked Shawn. "Why'd you let him stay for dinner?"

Helen sighed. "Thought you boys should have a chance to see him, that's why. He is your father. I hoped he'd changed ... that maybe prison had done him some good. But that was just wishful thinking. Now you go out there with Jason and try to make nice. The girls and I will take care of dinner."

Later, when they were home and in bed, Terri turned to Shawn.

"You're upset," she said. "Don't try to hide it. It must have been difficult seeing him after all these years. Do you want to talk about it?"

Shawn rolled over, facing her. He was silent for a moment, then let out a deep breath.

"Yeah, you're right. It was. You know, he wasn't always like that. When we were little, he was good ... always playing with us, horsing around. He was sort of like a big kid himself. There was a lot of laughter in our house then."

"What happened? When did it change?"

"I think it was when I was around eleven or twelve. Jack was never the greatest at lobstering, you know; just did enough to make ends meet and when the prices were high, that was okay. But then the cost of gas went up at the same time the price for lobster went down and, well, Jack, he just couldn't keep up. Mom had to get a job, so we didn't lose the house, and things between them went sour. He'd stay out to all hours with his new 'friends,' drinking and doing drugs. And there were other women, too."

"Who do you mean by new 'friends'? People from the mainland?"

"Some of them were, but some were islanders and they were a rough crowd. Dex's dad was one of them. He was successful as a lobsterman, but he was a tough guy. And he liked to have a group of younger men around him, looking up to him, making him feel like a big man. My dad was one of those guys."

"Was Dex's dad into drugs, too? Dealing?"

"No, I don't think so. He did okay fishing. But there were rumors of other stuff not quite so legal. Hey, don't say anything about this to Dex. It's just island gossip."

Terri leaned over and kissed him. "I won't say anything. Don't worry. But how did Jack wind up in jail?"

"Oh, that was when I was fifteen. Right around the time we found your dad on Puffin. Mom and Jack had a big blow-up and she kicked him out. Seems he'd gotten some mainland girl pregnant. Well, once he was out of the house, he had no means of support. Mom was paying all the bills. So, he started dealing and made the mistake of pushing to kids at the school."

Shawn laughed bitterly. "He was never the sharpest knife in the drawer if you get my meaning. I thank God I have his looks and not his intellect. Well, to make a long story short, he got caught. He had no money for a lawyer, so he pled guilty and the judge threw the book at him, ten to life.

"And that's about it. He's out now, but Jason will make sure he doesn't come sniffing around here again, you can bet on that!"

Shawn reached for Terri and pulled her close. "Thanks for making me talk about it. I needed to get it out. When he grabbed you, I thought I would go berserk! Good thing Mom stopped me or I'd probably be the second O'Dwyer in the slam."

Terri smiled as she snuggled in his arms. "I wouldn't have liked that at all!"

He held her closer, kissing her neck. "I love you, you know. I'll never let anything bad happen to you."

"I love you, too, Shawn O'Dwyer, and it'll take more than a man like Jack to scare me away."

VOYAGE TO PUFFIN ISLAND

BILL ROLLED OVER IN bed, the sound of the phone jarring him awake.

"Hello?"

"Hey, sleepyhead! It's me. We're on our way over to pick you up."

It took Bill a minute to realize who was calling. It was Susan and today was Puffin Island day. Inwardly, he groaned as he sat up running his free hand through his hair.

"Yeah, I remember. Sorry, I took a pill last night and it makes me groggy in the morning. Can you give me an hour? I need a shower and some coffee."

Susan was silent for a moment. "Bill, I've got the police and forensics here and we can't waste their valuable time. Can't you hurry? I can stall them for a few minutes, but that's all. Remember, I'm doing this for you."

Bill had a hard time suppressing a laugh. Susan never did anything that wasn't ultimately for Susan. "Okay, okay. Give me a half-hour and I'll meet you at the wharf."

"That's better. See you soon."

She hung up abruptly, obviously irritated.

Fuck her, he thought as he made his way to the bathroom.

He took his time and kept them cooling their heels on the wharf, waiting. When he finally arrived, he smiled broadly, shaking hands and making small talk. Susan tolerated his brief kiss on the cheek, her eyes icy and unyielding.

Later, he stood at the bow of the Coast Guard cutter as it approached Puffin Island. The sun was shining, but, despite its warmth, he hugged himself trying to ward off an imaginary chill.

Susan, busy getting her crew and equipment ready, did not notice his apparent unease. Periodically, he glanced over at her, his mind questioning the soundness of his decision to go along on this wild goose chase.

Is this all really necessary? he wondered. *Isn't the Evelyn LaPlante thing enough?*

He felt the boat begin to slow as they maneuvered to anchor off what once had been the island's dock. Suddenly repelled by the sight of his former prison, he turned away from the bow and entered the empty cabin. Taking a seat on one of the bunks, he stared out the doorway. Everyone else was on deck, preparing their equipment. He frowned as he watched them - they all looked so eager and enthusiastic.

But how can I fake this when I don't remember anything? And I don't even know if I can set foot on that place. Just thinking about it gives me the creeps.

His thoughts were interrupted when Susan came down the steps, displeasure apparent on her face.

"You're not getting cold feet, are you?" she asked. "We've talked about this. I know you can do it. You're stronger now."

Bill stared down at his hands, unable to meet her unflinching gaze. "I know. I'll do it. I just didn't realize it would be so difficult. I mean, I know no one's going to leave me here, but still, I have to admit, it scares me."

Susan tried unsuccessfully to hide her impatience. She took a deep breath.

"I'll be there beside you all the time. If it comes to a point where you can't stand it any longer, you just say so and you can come back and wait on the beach. Okay? I mean we've gotten them here and that's what's important anyway."

Bill nodded and forced a smile.

"That's more like it," she said, grinning. "The launch will be leaving in a few minutes. Meet you on deck."

Bill nodded then watched her turn and leave the cabin. He gazed out the window, seaward, hoping the open ocean would erase the image of Puffin Island from his mind. Then, he, too, walked out on deck.

Once ashore, Susan was all business. Barking orders at her camera crew, Bill wasn't surprised that she had all but forgotten her promise to stay by his side. He watched her for a moment, then turned. The police department representatives and anthropology students stood dutifully behind him.

"Well, Mr. Andersen, I guess we're all waiting on you," said Det. Wallace. "Can you tell us approximately where you remember seeing a skeleton or bones while you were here?"

Bill stood motionless, trying to get his bearings. Flashes of darkness clouded his vision as an unbidden memory began to surface:

Shivering in the dark, cold, damp cellar, trying desperately to get a fire started.

"Bill," said Susan, sharply. "The detective asked you a question. Are you all right?"

The anger in her tone brought Bill rapidly back to the present. "I'm sorry," he replied, turning toward the police officer. "What did you ask?"

"Just wondering where you might have seen bones. We need a place to start."

Bill glanced around. Everyone was staring at him, waiting

Again, dark shapes crept into the corners of his eyes, blotting out the glow of the sun. The winter wind was howling in his ears, its ferocity accentuated by the booming of thundersnow.

A surge of bile rose up in his throat and he turned from the crowd of anxious faces, fell to his knees, and retched violently into the sand.

"Oh, for Christ's sake," murmured Det. Wallace as he turned toward Susan. "Can you do something? I mean, look at the man."

Susan took a deep breath. "Just be patient. I'll handle this."

She walked over to Bill, who was crouched in the sand, dry heaves racking his body. A look of distaste passed over her face as she reached out and placed her hand on his shoulder.

"You okay?" she asked. "All you need to do is give us some direction. You don't have to go with us. Just give us some idea of where to start."

Bill wiped his mouth with the back of his hand as he turned to look up at her. "The ridge. Try over by that ridge."

As he spoke, a fresh bout of nausea overcame him and he turned away from her.

Susan frowned. "Okay, thanks. If you need to, stay here. Get some water from the cooler and clean yourself up."

Bill nodded, not looking at her. She stood watching him for a moment, apparently waiting to see if he could pull himself together. When he didn't move, she patted him again on the shoulder and walked away.

"He says to start up by that ridge," she yelled, indicating the steep outcropping of rock that Bill had pointed to.

The detective and his forensics man nodded and, with the students, started climbing. Susan followed with her camera crew, leaving Bill alone on the beach.

He sat in the sand for a few minutes, catching his breath. He gazed down at the remnants of his breakfast, now mixed with bile, sinking into the wet sand.

What made me think I could do this, he thought as he turned to look at Susan's retreating figure. *And what's up with her? Christ, doesn't she have any compassion whatsoever? Karen would never behave like that. Karen wouldn't have let me suffer like this.*

Thoughts of his ex-wife calmed Bill's feverish mind and, picturing her, the dark shadows quickly disappeared.

If I keep focused on her, maybe I can do this. Yes, I'll go along with this masquerade and, when it's over, perhaps everything will work out.

He took a deep breath and got to his feet, careful to keep a picture of Karen in his mind's eye. Taking a step, he weaved unsteadily and barely managed to stagger over to the cooler left on the beach. Grabbing a bottle of water, he rinsed out his mouth, spit into the sand, then downed several cool swallows. When he felt in control again, he gazed around. He was alone. A wave of fear passed over him. He didn't want to be alone anywhere on this island and, with no other alternative available, knew he would have to rejoin the search party. Accepting this, he finished the bottle of water, then jogged over to where Susan stood with the news crew.

Surprised to see him, she smiled. "I knew you could do it," she said reaching down and squeezing his hand.

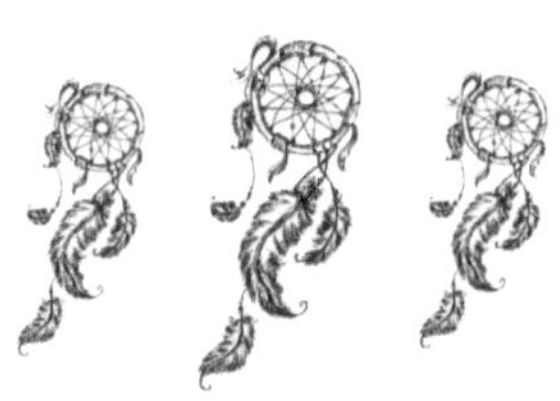

They spent the greater part of the morning scouring the terrain around the ridge, finding nothing but the carcasses of a few deceased seagulls.

Again, everyone turned to Bill for guidance. Feeling more comfortable now and strangely in his element, he led them over to the east end of the island. As they traversed the rocky landscape, he began an amiable conversation with one of the students, an attractive young woman. Susan followed behind, watching him as he laughed and joked with the girl.

For another hour or so, they sifted through dirt and sand at the new site, again finding nothing. Det. Wallace was having a hard time hiding his increasing impatience and agitation, constantly looking at his watch.

"I've about had it," he finally said to Susan. "I don't think Andersen has any idea about any bodies other than his own. This has just been a wild goose chase."

Susan looked at him sympathetically. "I know it's frustrating, but I'm sure I'm right. Let me talk to him again."

Wallace grimaced. "Okay. One more time, but if he doesn't come up with the goods, we're out of here."

Susan nodded and walked over to Bill and the student.

"Bill, can I talk to you for a moment?"

"Sure," he replied.

She took him by the arm and led him out of earshot of the students and police. "Listen, we have to come up with something. Wallace has just about had it. Can't you remember anything that might help?"

Bill stared off toward the horizon. "You know, I think I was right the first time. If there's anything here, it's over by that ridge."

"But we scoured that area and found nothing."

Bill was silent for a moment, staring at the rocks, the sound of the waves beating against the shore reverberating in his ears.

Suddenly he laughed. "Damn it! Why didn't I think of that?"

"What?"

He put his arm around her shoulder, turning her toward the ridge. "Don't you get it? It's the tide. We looked too close to shore. When the tide's in, it covers that whole area. It's out now so we were searching in the wrong place. That ridge is the best spot for a boat to come in here unseen and, if it were high tide, they could come right up to those rocks, dump a body, and be gone in no time."

"You could be right," Susan exclaimed. "Round up the students. Let me handle Wallace."

She leaned forward on her tiptoes and gave him a quick kiss, a bright smile on her face, then hurried away to placate the detective.

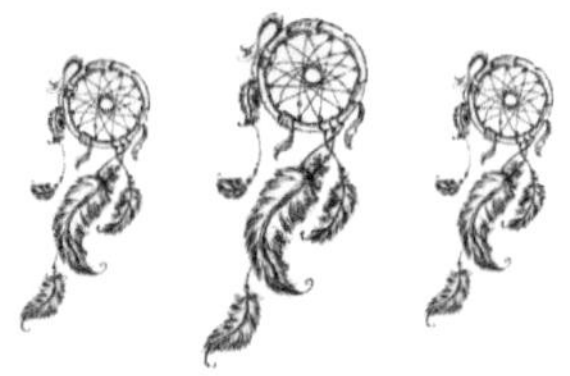

It happened several hours later when everyone was tired and hungry. Bill, beginning to feel nervous and edgy again, volunteered to go down to the beach to retrieve snacks and water for the hard-working students and police. As he was loading the contents of the cooler into his backpack, he heard someone yelling.

Swinging the backpack over his shoulder, he jogged up the hill to the site where the students were digging. One of them, the young girl he had been talking with earlier, held in her hand what looked like a femur bone.

"And there's more," she was saying. "I think possibly a whole skeleton."

The other students crowded around to get a better look as Susan tried to create an opening for her cameraman. Everyone was laughing and smiling now, but that mood would soon change.

"Okay, everyone, out of the way," barked Det. Wallace. "This is now officially a crime scene. Sergeant Miller, you secure the area. I want this whole ridge cordoned off with tape."

Quickly, the forensics experts took over, shooing away the weary students and forcing Susan and her cameraman back behind the crime scene barriers that were rapidly being erected. Wallace stood apart, on his cell to the mainland, requesting a full crew to excavate the area.

Bill stood well away from the group, watching the activity. The sight of the human remains brought on a fresh bout of nausea and he struggled to keep from succumbing to it. To steady himself, he once again mentally conjured up a picture of Karen, focusing on her smile. After a few minutes, he felt in control again and glanced around, trying to locate Susan.

She was standing with Wallace, just outside the now roped off "crime scene." Her face was flushed and anger was apparent in her stance and gestures. Watching her, Bill surmised that the detective was restricting her access, something he knew she would not take lightly.

"Are you okay, Mr. Andersen?" asked one of the students.

Bill smiled at her. "Yeah, I'm good. You want a water or an apple or something?"

The young woman nodded. "Yeah, that'd be cool."

Bill dutifully opened the backpack and handed the girl a bottle of water and a piece of fruit. "How much longer do you think we're going to be stuck here?" he asked.

"Oh, the cop radioed for more help. They don't want us touching anything anymore. Think once the cops are on their way, they'll take us back to the mainland. Your reporter friend is pretty pissed."

"Oh, why?"

"Cops won't let her film anymore."

Bill laughed knowingly. "You're right - that would piss her off."

The girl sat down next to him, taking a bite of her apple. "What was it like? You know, being here all that time?"

Bill took a deep breath. He thought about lying, but the girl's face was so open and innocent.

"I really don't know," he answered. "I actually don't remember anything. Finding those bones, well, that was just dumb luck."

The girl's mouth fell open in amazement. "You mean you didn't have any idea where they were ... or even if there were any?"

Bill laughed. "That's right. Just dumb luck."

Soon the other students, police, and TV crewmen were instructed to return to the beach. Bill passed out water and snacks as they waited for the outcome of the ongoing verbal sparring match between Susan and Det. Wallace. Finally, they saw Susan nod, turn, and walk over to where they were sitting.

"Everything okay?" Bill asked as she approached.

"What a fuck-up!" she exclaimed. "That bastard has the nerve to restrict my access to the crime scene that I led him to. Well, I'm not going to let that happen."

"What can you do?" Bill asked. "It's his show now."

"You just wait and see."

She pulled out her cell and walked several feet away from the crowd, looking for some privacy. After several minutes, she came back, a self-satisfied smile on her face.

"My boss is going to call his boss. I'll be back out here tomorrow with a full crew!"

"So is this it then? You won't be needing me anymore?"

There was a sense of finality in his tone and Susan stared at him, surprised.

"You don't have to come with us tomorrow, if that's what you mean. But, I do need you. You are important to me, Bill. I know this was hard today and I'm sorry if I wasn't more understanding."

Bill smiled, stood, and put his arm around her waist. "I'm glad. Let's get out of here. I'm just about sick to death of this island."

Later that evening, Bill sat on his porch sipping a glass of wine while he listened to the soothing sound of the waves pounding the shore.

How'd I know where to look for those bones, he asked himself. *I still don't remember much. But I was spot on when I said they were up on that ridge.*

He thought about this for a bit, then put it aside, deciding it would be best to wait and discuss it with the doctor that coming week. He stared at the sea, remembering how close he'd come to losing all control on Puffin.

Karen ... only her image kept me from going round the bend. I need her. Hopefully, Susan can dig up more dirt on Dex and his family. Something that will open Karen's eyes so she can recognize what a bastard he really is.

He grimaced as he conjured up an image of Karen's husband, mentally picturing the man being arrested and hauled off to prison.

Somehow, it has to work out. And, once he's gone, I'll get my family back and it will be as if the past twelve years never happened. Karen and I will be together just like before. We'll remarry; take all the same vows over again.

Yes, I just have to be patient. It will be Karen and me, here on Mateguas, till death us do part.

HARRY
THREE-FEATHERS

ON SUNDAY, AS PLANNED, Terri and Karen took the morning ferry to the mainland. The drive to the nursing home where Harry Three-Feathers lived was one that Karen remembered well. Harry was in the same hospital that old Madge Parker had been a resident of so many years before. As they drove, Karen reminisced about the woman.

"You would have liked her," she said. "She was an honest, plain-speaking woman who was extremely knowledgeable about Mateguas and its folklore. Without her, I don't think we would have survived back then."

"I wish I had had the chance to know her, Mom."

Upon arrival, a nurse escorted them to the back of the building where a large teepee was erected.

"Harry likes it out here," the nurse explained. "We can't allow all that smoke and incense inside, but we know it has

157

important religious significance for him. So, to accommodate his beliefs, our director let his family put up this wigwam. Occasionally, we do bend the rules a bit. No one's hurt."

"What do the other patients say about it?" asked Karen, noting a wisp of smoke coming from the top of the tent. "Don't they complain?"

The nurse chuckled. "No, it's really a curiosity. On Friday's, Harry's family and members of his tribe usually come to visit. Some of them dress in tribal costumes and put on quite a show. Since they started doing this, the other patients actually have had more visitors. It's really quite entertaining and educational. So, it's been a good thing for everyone."

"This place is very cool, Mom," said Terri, indicating the teepee. "And it's real spiritual. You'll see once we're inside."

Karen raised her eyebrows, giving her daughter a skeptical look, then turned and thanked the nurse.

"Come on, Mom," said Terri. "Time to go."

Karen rolled her eyes. "Okay, let the fun and games begin."

Shaking her head at her mother's sarcasm, Terri leaned over and opened the teepee's flap, allowing Karen to stoop and enter. Charlie, sitting near the entrance, stood and greeted them both.

"Welcome, Terri and Karen," he said, hugging Terri warmly. "Karen, let me introduce you to my friend, Harry Three-Feathers."

He led her over to a wizened old Indian, sitting cross-legged next to an earthenware pot from which smoke was rising. The old man was slowly tearing up some leaves or herbs and placing them haphazardly into the pot. When Karen and Charlie approached, he looked up.

The color of his eyes was concealed by milky white clouds and Karen realized he was blind. She was about to speak, to let him know where she was, when he turned his face to her, his unseeing gaze penetrating.

"Mrs. Pierce, my friend Mekwi Mikoa, who you know as Charlie, tells me you have seen the *Aglebemu* and that the toad has marked you as his own. Is this correct?"

Karen started, surprised by his statement. "Well, I don't know about the bastard marking me, but, yes, I have seen the toad."

Terri sat down beside Charlie on the opposite side of the teepee. "What's all this about a toad, Mom?" she asked, obviously puzzled.

"Hush, child," replied Charlie. "All will be revealed in its own time."

Harry Three-Feathers nodded then gestured for Karen to take a seat on the ground beside him.

Once she was comfortable, he picked up a feather and waved it briefly over her head before turning his attention back to the pot in front of him. Slowly, he moved the feather through the plumes of smoke, and began to chant:

Nana nay yahya,
Nana nay yahya,
Na yay toki nana yahya,
Nana nay, nana nay

As he intoned the words, the old shaman tossed more herbs into the pot and soon the aromatic smoke began to fill the tent. Karen was surprised she could still breathe as the smoke surrounded her, making it difficult to see anything clearly.

The chanting became louder and seemed to no longer be coming from just the old man beside her, but from the walls of the teepee itself.

The smoke continued to thicken and Karen felt the onset of claustrophobia build in her chest. Involuntarily, she took a deep breath, and, when she did, the sweet smoke slipped down her throat and entered her lungs.

Almost immediately, the sense of panic dissipated and a strange feeling of calm washed over her. Now, relaxed and accepting, she glanced over to her right to where the old man sat, but he had disappeared - vanished in a cloud of the soft, sensuous smoke.

The chanting droned on, but now it was coming not from without, but from within. It was as if the mantra had become a part of her and she found her lips moving as she whispered the strange and powerful words.

The smoke continued to billow around her, becoming almost a solid wall. She reached out to touch it, surprised to find that it was soft and silky like the skin of a newborn infant. This made her think of her son, and a smile broke out on her face.

The sound of the chant was now joined by the steady beat of a drum and with each repetition, became louder and louder. The smoke around Karen began to swirl and the peacefulness she had felt suddenly vanished. Her hands gripped her knees as wispy plumes of smoke moved with purpose, as if painting a picture before her eyes.

At first, there was just a vague outline, then the drawing gained dimension and color. Fear coursed through her body as she recognized what the smoke was revealing. It was an image of the *Aglebemu*, vast and horrific, sitting on a rock, its red eyes staring at her with ferocious intensity.

She tried to get up but was unable to move. The toad in her vision blinked its eyes once, then began to slap its feet in time to the cadence of the drum, one after another, on the wet river rock.

Terrified, Karen shrank back. The toad, as if sensing her fear, smiled, then opened its mouth, flicking its tongue in and out in time to the drumbeat.

Again, she tried to get up but it was as if she were glued to the floor of the tent. The sound of the drum quickened and the tongue, moving with it, inched closer and closer to her face.

The chanting reached a deafening pitch, drowning out everything else, and Karen could feel it pounding painfully in her head. She pressed her palms to her ears, trying to blot out the sound, but it only got louder and she feared that if it didn't stop soon, she would go insane.

As if reading her mind, the chanting and drumbeat abruptly ceased.

In the eerie stillness that followed, all Karen could hear was the sound of her ragged breathing and the pounding of her heart.

The smoky toad sat motionless, staring at her, its red eyes bulging out of their sockets. It smacked its swollen lips once in anticipation and then, without warning, leaped into the air.

Karen gasped as the creature hurtled through the smoke toward her, its tongue darting out with ferocious speed and determination.

Unable to move and expecting the loathsome creature to land on her at any moment, she did the only thing she could. She screamed.

Abruptly, the thick smoke dissipated to a wispy thread and the vision of the toad dissolved, fading quickly away.

Surprised, Karen gazed around. Harry Three-Feathers was back sitting beside her and, across from her, sat her daughter and Charlie Red Squirrel. Everyone was looking at her.

"I...I saw..." she stammered.

"Hush," commanded the old blind shaman. "All in good time."

He gave her a hard stare with his sightless eyes then turned toward her daughter. "Tell me, young one, what did the Great Spirit show you in the smoke dream?"

Terri glanced quickly at her mother, then back at Harry.

"It was strange. I saw two little girls at the beach. They were about two or three years old, with blond curls. And I think they were twins! At first, I thought it was a memory, you know, of Sophie and me at the beach in California. But it was the wrong beach. The beach in my vision was the one across from Dad's house on Mateguas. So, it couldn't have been us. We were much older when we were there. And that's it. That's what I saw."

The old Indian nodded his head solemnly. "It may be a vision of the future or of the past. Or it may be nothing at all. Only time will tell."

He turned his head toward Karen. "Now, tell us what the smoke gods brought you."

"I think you already know," she answered testily. "It was that nasty frog. What was in that freaking smoke anyway? Some sort of hallucinogen? What I saw was very scary and I'm not at all happy about it."

A look of concern passed over Charlie's face and he reached out his hand to her. "Please, Mrs. Pierce, try to keep an open mind. These things happen for a reason and the images that appear in the smoke are sent there to help you on your journey, not to hinder you."

"Well, if you don't mind, I think I'll sit this particular journey out. I've had enough of that toad to last a lifetime."

"Will someone please tell me what this is all about?" asked Terri. "I mean, what is this toad? Everyone seems to know what's going on but me."

Harry smiled. "Patience young one. It will all come clear."

He turned his head back toward Karen.

"Now, Mrs. Pierce, could you recount for me your experience with the *Aglebemu*? Not the smoke dream, but your encounter on Mateguas. And, please, don't leave anything out. Not the slightest detail. For if you do, I will be unable to help you."

Karen, still visibly irritated, sighed. "Do you think I could get something to drink?"

Charlie smiled and reached over to a cooler that sat near the entrance to the teepee. "We've got Coke or bottled water. Which would you prefer?"

"Just water, thank you."

Charlie handed her a cold bottle of spring water and watched as she drank deeply. Then she ran her fingers through her hair, sat up straight, and locked eyes with Harry. "Okay, I'll tell you. And, I'll tell you everything."

The old Indian nodded as Karen closed her eyes for a moment and took a deep breath.

"All right. It started when I decided to take Alex, that's my son, with me on a walk..."

Ghosts of Mateguas

It took some time and gentle prodding, but Karen finally related the whole unbelievable story of her encounter with the strange frog.

When she finished, Terri looked at her incredulously. "I can't believe you didn't tell me about this, Mom. Maybe I could have helped."

Karen smiled. "You weren't there, honey. How could you have helped? In any case, it's over now. No harm, no foul."

"Do not be so quick to dismiss this creature, Mrs. Pierce," said Harry Three-Feathers. "As my friend Mekwi Mikoa has undoubtedly told you, the toad is a harbinger of evil times."

"But why on Mateguas?" interrupted Karen. "There's plenty of evil in the world. And I'm sure there are far more tasty pickings here on the mainland than there are on that small island."

"You may be right about that, but you forget the special nature of Mateguas."

"Special nature? What do you mean?" asked Karen.

"Since ancient times, Mateguas has been steeped in dark magic. 'The People' recognized this when they settled there. Haven't you felt it?"

Karen sat quietly for a moment, thinking. "Well, yes, I suppose I have. There seems to be an undercurrent of energy there and, in some places - like at our old house - it's stronger."

"Yes, energy," replied Harry, nodding. "There are many energy centers, or swirling currents of subtle power, located on and around Mateguas. The property you speak of - is it the one that 'The People' once held sacred?"

Karen nodded. "Yes, it is."

The old Indian smiled. "That land may contain the strongest of all the vortexes on Mateguas and it is no surprise that you and your daughter once lived there.

"The spiritual power that emanates from this place and other centers in and around the island is great and can serve to uplift and inspire the soul of a person whose heart remains open and pure. Haven't you noticed how some Mateguans live longer and healthier lives than their counterparts on the mainland? How they seem to prosper no matter what happens in the outside world?"

Karen nodded. "Yeah. A lot of the women are in their eighties or nineties. And there are a couple of residents who are over one hundred and are still pretty active. But if that's the case and all this energy is positive, then why do so many bad things happen there?"

Harry Three-Feathers nodded solemnly. "There are always two sides to every coin, Mrs. Pierce. The same healing energy, when disturbed by outside influences, can create vortexes that have the opposite effect."

Karen sighed. "Outside influences? All right, here it comes. It's all my fault, right?"

Harry laughed. "No, Mrs. Pierce, it's not ALL your fault, but your presence on the island does mix things up a bit."

"But what about Terri? She's got some of this power or magic or whatever it is, too. Doesn't her being there also stir things up?"

Harry smiled and nodded toward Terri. "Your daughter is in tune with the spiritual power that comes from the Mother. She is in harmony with the earth."

Terri smiled shyly at him, blushing at the compliment.

The old Indian nodded to her, then turned his attention back to Karen.

"You, however, fight against it. This creates negative energy that swirls in and out of the vortexes, creating disharmony and a fertile ground for evil."

"Then it is my fault?"

"No. You can no more help being as you are than the moon can cease to rise each night in the sky. You are the acolyte of Mateguas; his chosen one; the one he has entrusted with the care of his son. It is not you, Mrs. Pierce. It is the energy of the God of the Dead that resides within you that has altered the environment around Mateguas. And The Boy himself - can you imagine what courses through him?"

"Then maybe it would be best if we left. Dex wouldn't like it, but I can think of something. I'll take him back to California."

"And watch him wither and die? No, The Boy is part of Mateguas and Mateguas is part of him. It is right that you brought him here. How it will end, only the gods know. But right now we must deal with the threat of the *Aglebemu* for, to be sure, that toad hungers for your flesh and will not stop until he has it."

Karen shuddered at the thought of the toad and how she almost became his victim. "You're not suggesting that I have to kill that thing, are you?"

Harry chuckled. "Not kill. No, even you with your power could not kill that ancient creature. But wound him - yes, you can do that."

"I'll help you, Mom," cried Terri. "And Shawn will, too. We won't make you face it alone."

Harry shook his head at Terri. "Have you not listened, young one? It is your mother who has been marked by the toad. It is she it hungers for. Thus, it is she who must strike fear in its heart. Not you, not your mate. This is something that only she can do. Otherwise, all may be lost."

Karen bit her bottom lip, then took a deep breath. "Okay. I'm game. Tell me what I have to do."

MEMORIES

DEX CARRIED HIS SLEEPY son to the bedroom and laid him down in his crib. The toddler was exhausted after spending the day on the boat with his father. Once the boy was settled, Dex helped himself to a beer from the fridge.

What the hell is keeping Karen? he wondered, glancing at the clock. *She went with Terri to see those two old Indians. I hope she's not getting mixed up in all that mumbo jumbo again.*

He walked out to the deck and sat down. It was twenty to five - almost time for Susan LeVeque's show and, although Karen asked him not to watch it, he knew he wouldn't heed her advice.

He leaned back in the Adirondack chair and took a pull on his beer. Quietly gazing at the summer sky, he thought about the broadcast.

Evie.

He closed his eyes, picturing her. They had become friends when she'd transferred to his school in the tenth grade. She was beautiful, but also intelligent with a quick sense of humor and he'd enjoyed talking with her. They didn't date - she wasn't allowed to - and, anyway, he was going steady with Cindy Sue at the time.

Then came the day when everything changed.

It happened in the library, sometime just after her sixteenth birthday. He'd been joking with her saying if she didn't watch out, she'd end up being sweet sixteen and never been kissed. He remembered how she'd laughed, her beautiful face lighting up as if just being with him was the best present in the world. Then she'd motioned him to come with her to the back of the library, into the stacks.

When they were well away from prying eyes, she'd leaned back against the shelves, smiling at him. Unable to help himself, he'd reached out and touched her face, running his thumb slowly down her cheek, over her jaw line, coming to rest on her full lips. She'd stared deep into his eyes for a moment, then opened her mouth and slowly, teasingly, drew him in.

The memory was so vivid, he could almost feel the warm wetness of her cheeks and tongue as she moved his thumb in and out, occasionally brushing it against her soft, swollen lips. It was the most erotic thing that had ever happened to him. Up to that point in his romantic career, all he'd accomplished was five to ten minutes of vigorous petting and dry humping, followed by inserting his dick into a barely moving Cindy Sue and ejaculating.

But this, with Evie, was something quite different.

Eyes still closed, Dex reached down and pressed his hand against his crotch.

Just like when I was a kid, he thought *Just thinking about her can give me the hard-on of all hard-ons.*

He remembered how she'd moved one of her hands to the front of his jeans, pressing it against his obvious and painful erection. She'd smiled at him once, then unzipped his fly and slipped her small hand inside, encircling his engorged penis with her fingers. Squeezing him gently through the thin fabric of his boxers, she'd moved her hand slowly up and down.

The feeling was exquisite and more sensuous than anything he'd ever felt with Cindy Sue. In no time, he found himself gasping for breath as his excitement peaked. Unable to stand it any longer, he'd pulled Evie to him, crushing his lips to hers as he ejaculated into her palm.

Afterward, she'd unwrapped her hand from his limp member and moved her wet fingers up to her lips. She'd hesitated only for a moment, never breaking eye contact with him, then, slowly, licked his warm sperm from her fingertips. When she was finished, she'd taken his hand and pressed it between her legs.

Her skirt was short and it was easy for him to slide his fingers up her warm thigh and under the soft cotton leg of her panties. He'd hesitated for a moment there, knowing instinctively that if he continued there would be no turning back. But the temptation was too great and he moved his finger between her folds, slipping it cautiously inside her. Her warm wetness astounded him and, feeling more turned on than he'd ever been in his young life, he moved his hand rhythmically, wanting desperately to give her as much pleasure as she'd given him.

The ecstasy of this crude finger-fucking seemed to last forever, but, in actuality, it was only moments before he felt the pulsing of her orgasm. As she reached her crescendo, she moaned and, again, he pulled her close, covering her mouth with his.

When it was over, she'd reached her arms up around his neck and whispered in his ear.

"I tasted you; now it's time for you to taste me."

He grinned now as he remembered how shocked he had been and how he had pulled away from her in surprise. But there was a hint of a challenge in her bright, blue eyes, and he'd finally smiled and slowly removed his hand from her and brought his wet fingers to his lips.

Evie.

How sweet she'd tasted. Never before and never since had he tasted anything quite as wonderful as her. His erection had returned and he reached for her again, but she'd pulled away, her eyes darting to the clock on the wall.

"I have class," she'd said.

Seeing the look of disappointment on his face, she'd reached out and touched him, feeling his renewed hardness. Then she retrieved her purse from the floor, pulled out a pen, and, taking his hand, wrote something quickly on his palm.

"Pick me up after work," she said, kissing him lightly on the cheek. He stared down at the address scribbled hastily on his hand, then back to her and nodded. She gave him one more sweet smile, then turned and quickly walked away.

Later that evening when they were parked at a deserted beach, he remembered how scared and confused he'd felt. The experience in the library had, for him, taken on a surrealistic quality, almost as if it had been a dream. He was sure she didn't date and that she was innocent. Yet, how did she know so much? Tentatively, he'd asked, almost afraid to hear her answer. He remembered now how she'd blushed and smiled.

"I read," she'd said softly.

He'd looked at her puzzled and, in response, she reached into her backpack and pulled out a book. *The Story of O* by Pauline Réage. She opened it at random and in a quiet voice began to read.

He didn't touch her that night. But, somehow, just sitting with her, just listening to her, was almost as exciting as what they'd done in the library earlier that day. He'd hoped it would last forever.

But it didn't.

Six months later, she was dead.

Feeling regret, Dex sat quietly thinking of her and, at the same time, longing for Karen. His erection was now fading and he stood and walked to the kitchen for another beer, only stopping briefly in the living room to turn on the TV.

When he came back, Evie's image, taken from her high school yearbook, was on the screen. Gazing at her with undisguised longing, he took a pull on his beer and sat down. Susan LeVeque's "Cold Cases of Southern Maine" had begun.

KAREN AND TERRI
DEX AND KAREN

THEY LEFT THE NURSING home around four o'clock and drove quietly for a time. Finally, Terri broke the silence.

"I don't care what Harry says. You don't have to do this alone. Shawn and I can help."

Karen grimaced. "Why do I feel like the heroine in some bloody adventure comic? You know, going off to slay the evil toad creature. Christ, I thought all this was over when Maggie torched herself. But why should today be different than any other day? As usual, I'm wrong."

Terri reached over and patted her mom's knee. "I said we'd help. I can come over tomorrow and show you how to throw a knife. Shawn's been teaching me and I'm getting pretty good at it."

"Oh, great. Is he going to teach you how to use a gun next? Soon, you'll be a regular Annie Oakley."

"Mom! Understand, he has skills and I have skills. We share things. Isn't that the way it's supposed to be?"

Karen sighed. "I guess you're right. But as for this toad thing, Harry was pretty adamant. I'm the only one who can put the fear of God into it. I can't kill it - it's too old and steeped in ancient wisdom and all that crap. But I can scare the shit out of it and that's what I intend to do. But why do I have to use a knife? Why can't I just throw a rock or, better yet, get a gun and blast away?"

"You know what Harry said. A rock won't inflict enough damage and the *Aglebemu* will sense a gun - smell it - and disappear before you get a shot off. No, it has to be a knife."

"Okay, okay. A knife it is. And, I'll take you up on those lessons. The worst harm I've ever inflicted with a knife was on a turkey and I think you know how that turned out!"

They arrived at the ferry terminal in time to catch the five-thirty commuter boat and had an uneventful ride back to the island.

At the cottage, Karen found her husband slumped in front of the TV, asleep. There was a beer bottle on the arm of the chair and another empty one on the floor.

He watched that damn show, she thought, shaking her head.

Frowning, she picked up the bottles and took them to the kitchen, then went to the bedroom to check on their son. He was still asleep but was showing signs that he would soon wake up. Comforted that at least Alex was okay, she walked back to the living room where Dex, too, was beginning to stir.

"Hey," he said groggily. "You're finally home. I was beginning to get worried. How are all the old Indians doing?"

Karen laughed. "They're okay and, I have to admit, it was kind of interesting. They actually erected a teepee in the hospital's backyard. I'll tell you all about it later. So, what's up with you? I take it you ignored my advice and watched that show anyway."

Dex looked at her contritely. "Yes, I did. I know you said not to, but I couldn't help it."

"Well, what's done is done. Did Bill's girlfriend dredge up anything new?"

"Not much. She interviewed a couple of my classmates who were at the party the night Evie disappeared. Ones who swore back then that I was there all night. Now they say they can't remember for sure when I arrived. Said I might have come later. Also, she interviewed Evie's dad. That's about it. And, you were right when you said this would be over soon. Next week Susan's moving on to something new. Evie's case has been shelved again."

"Thank God for that," replied Karen, leaning down and kissing him lightly on the cheek.

In response, he reached up and pulled her into his lap, wrapping his arms around her. Holding on to her tightly, he closed his eyes as he moved his hand to her face and gently ran his thumb along the side of her cheek, over her jaw line to her mouth.

Surprised by the sensuousness of his gesture, Karen closed her eyes and rested in his arms as he moved his thumb in a soft, circular motion over her lips.

She could feel his breath quicken as he caressed her and she opened her eyes and looked up at him.

He was staring off into space, a strange faraway look on his face. It was as if he were no longer there with her, but somewhere else, in some distant place and time.

Confused, she put her hand on his, pulling it away from her face.

"Dex? Are you all right?"

For a brief moment, a look of unbearable sadness appeared in his eyes, but quickly it was gone.

"Yeah, I'm fine now," he said, smiling at her.

They gazed at each other for a moment as he tightened his arms around her.

"If you ever leave me, I don't think I could go on," he whispered.

Karen pulled slightly away from him, reached up, and took his face in her hands.

"I'll never leave you. I love you. So, for better or worse, I guess you're stuck with me."

He grinned at her in response. "I have no problem with that."

He embraced her again, kissing her deeply.

She could feel his hunger and wanted nothing more than to strip off all her clothing and lie with him right there on the living room floor. But she had a fussy one-year-old in the next room. Romance would have to wait.

She sat up, nodding toward the bedroom where her son slept. "I think someone else is awake, too. Maybe we can table this until later tonight."

Dex laughed. "No problemo, princess. It's a date."

Smiling at him, she stood. "Now, I know you've been with him all day and may need a break, but I also know you're probably hungry. I know I am. Could you please check on him while I get some steaks ready for the grill and make a salad?"

Dex performed a mock bow. "Your wish is my command," he replied.

He started to walk toward the bedroom, but stopped and turned back toward her.

"Hey, I need to ask you something. When we were out today, we bumped into Ruth Slocomb and her grandkids. One of them is about Alex's age."

"So, what of it?"

"That kid was jabbering away ... you know, 'ma-ma, da-da, doggie' - baby talk like that."

"And?"

"Well, Alex ... he doesn't do that. Ruth remarked on how quiet he was. Is that normal?"

Karen's mind raced. She knew Alex was fully capable of speaking telepathically in complete sentences, but verbally, Dex was right, he was quiet. Whether that was by choice or not, she didn't know.

"Was Ruth's grandchild a boy or a girl?"

"A little girl, I think."

Karen sighed. "Haven't you been reading your parenting magazines? Alex is a boy. Boys develop their verbal skills later than girls. He'll catch up in time, you'll see."

Dex nodded. "Makes sense, but Ruth also said something about how he plays. You know, he doesn't scream and run around like other little kids."

"And you're complaining about that? Listen, again, he's a boy and he's smart. He's ahead of other kids in manual dexterity and spatial skills. He's a problem solver. His favorite toys are those he can build with."

"Yeah, I know, and sometimes I think he's more like a little old man than a fourteen-month-old child. Do you think we should have him tested?"

"Tested?"

"You know, IQ?"

"No, definitely not. All those tests are too subjective. The examiner can skew the results. What would you do if he proved deficient in some area? Or, at a genius level in another? No, I don't want him labeled in any way. He's developing just fine. And don't be surprised if one day he just starts speaking in full sentences. He may actually skip the 'ma-ma, da-da' phase entirely."

Dex grinned. "You're probably right, princess. He's happy and healthy and that's what's important."

A wail coming from the bedroom startled them both.

"I guess he's vocalizing now!" laughed Dex. "I'll go check on him."

Karen watched him as he turned and walked away, glad that she had been able to satisfy his curiosity about Alex's development.

Walking to the kitchen, she noted the TV was still on, the volume muted. Remembering Dex's strange, melancholy mood when she'd arrived home, she picked up the clicker and checked their DVR recordings. Susan's show was listed.

He recorded it! Why? Why would he want to watch it again?

Puzzled, she turned the TV off.

As she prepared a salad, she thought about the look of sadness or regret she had glimpsed in his eyes.

Maybe, there was something more to his relationship with that girl, she thought. *Maybe it's not the show he wants to see again, but the girl.*

KAREN

THE NEXT MORNING, DEX was off early fishing and Karen settled young Alex on the floor in the living room with his toys. When he was well occupied, she sat down in front of the television and searched for the tape of Susan LeVeque's Sunday show. Finding it easily, she punched the 'play' button.

After the introduction, a picture of young Evie LaPlante appeared. Karen paused the broadcast, studying it.

The sixteen-year-old was smiling. She had big blue eyes, a long slender face, full, pouty lips, and abundant blonde curls that cascaded down over her shoulders.

I always wanted hair like that, Karen thought. *Mine was straight as a stick.*

She pressed the play button again. Susan LeVeque appeared on the screen, talking about the murder, as other pictures of the young girl flashed behind her. Karen only half-listened, focusing her attention on the photos.

The program went to a commercial break and Karen hit the rewind button until the first high school yearbook picture of Evie LaPlante again appeared. She paused the tape and sat back quietly staring at the photo. After a few minutes, she got up and walked to the bathroom.

Standing before the mirror, she searched her face.

Yes, she thought. *She looks like me, or like I used to when I was her age. Same shape face, eyes, and lips. Just the hair's different.*

Puzzled, she returned to the living room and looked at the TV screen. The girl's picture was staring at her as if trying to tell her something.

Is that why he was attracted to me? Because I reminded him of her?

She recalled the first time she'd seen him - it was on the wharf the day she and Bill arrived on Mateguas twelve years before. She remembered how intently he had stared at her.

Is that why he pursued me? Loved me? Am I just a surrogate for a girl he lost long ago?

She looked back up at the TV. Not wanting to see any more of Evie LaPlante, she abruptly turned it off and joined her son who was playing on the floor. Sitting down beside him, she idly picked up one of the Legos and rolled it over in the palm of her hand.

I need to know more about that girl and the night she disappeared. But how? I could ask him, but if he's lied about it for thirty years, what would make him tell the truth now?

She thought for a moment, then smiled. *I'll talk to Louise McKinney. She knows everything. Maybe she can shed some light on Dex's relationship with that girl.*

Again, the image of Evie LaPlante danced before her eyes.

Evie, she thought. *What did you do to my husband?*

BECOMING ANNIE OAKLEY

LATER THAT DAY, KAREN stood at the window, watching as Shawn's truck pulled up the drive. Turning around, she surveyed her house. The day was half gone and she'd accomplished nothing. Legos were scattered everywhere and a pile of dirty clothes stood in the hallway outside the laundry room. The breakfast dishes were still sitting in the sink, unwashed.

All she'd been able to think about the whole morning was that damned girl and Dex. She'd searched through unopened boxes of belongings that they'd sent from California, hoping to locate his high school yearbooks, but found nothing.

Either he threw them out or they're back at the house in Monterey, she decided. *But maybe I can find copies at the library here.*

Nodding to herself, she put her thoughts about the girl and her untimely death aside. Shawn and Terri were here and she had to focus on something entirely different.

Taking a deep breath, she walked over to the door to welcome them.

"Busy morning, Mom?" Terri asked, nodding toward the pile of laundry in the hallway.

"What I did this morning is none of your business, young lady. I'll get to the chores before your stepfather gets home. Now would anyone like some lemonade? I made it fresh and I believe knife throwing could be thirsty work."

Terri laughed and nodded. "Sounds good."

Karen grabbed a pitcher from the refrigerator, put it on a tray with three glasses, and handed it to Terri. "Let's go outside, around back where no one will see me make a fool out of myself."

Again, Terri laughed. "Mom, you're going to do fine. Quit worrying."

Karen frowned, turning to Shawn. "Right. And I suppose my daughter's told you everything, Shawn. All about the nasty toad, the vortexes, and how my polluted energy is to blame for all the world's troubles?"

"Yeah, that's pretty much it," replied Shawn with a grin. "Except for the part about your polluted energy. I think you might be exaggerating a bit there. Come on, knife tossing's easy. Let's give it a whirl."

Outside, behind the garage, Terri placed the tray on a tree stump while Karen spread a blanket on the grass and settled Alex on it with some action figures.

"You sit and play with him, honey," she instructed Terri. Then she turned to Shawn, who had pulled three knives from his backpack and placed them on the fence rail.

"Okay," he said. "Lesson one: what kind of knife are you going to throw? See these three?"

Karen nodded.

"Pick each up and tell me what you feel."

Karen gingerly took hold of the first knife. "What am I supposed to be feeling for?"

"Check the balance. Where is the most weight?"

Karen rolled the knife over in her hand. "I think the blade. Yeah, the weight is in the blade. Is that right?"

"Yes, that's right. Now try the second."

She put the first knife down and picked up the second one. After a few seconds, she smiled. "This one has more weight in the handle. The blade is lighter."

"Good. Now the third."

Karen picked up the last knife and spent some time handling it. "I don't feel any difference. Is that right?"

"Yes, that knife is what they call 'balanced.' It has an equal distribution of weight. Now, why do you suppose it's important to know where the weight is?"

Karen bit her bottom lip, thinking. "It must have to do with how you throw them. Does the heavy end go first?"

Shawn smiled. "I knew you were going to be a natural at this. Yes, if you're tossing a blade-heavy knife like the first one, you want the blade to be thrown first so you hold it by the handle to toss it. Similarly, if it were a handle-heavy knife, you would hold it by the blade to throw it. The balanced knife you can toss either way; whichever is more comfortable for you."

"Okay. But which knife should I use?"

"We're going to try all three and see what's most comfortable for you. Now, let's talk about the grip."

Shawn lectured for a while about the hammer and pinch grips, then he picked up each knife and demonstrated.

"Okay, now you try and let me know which grip and which knife feels the most natural."

Karen took her time getting acquainted with each knife. "I thought at first I'd like the balanced knife, but I think I actually like the handle-heavy knife best. Is that okay?"

Shawn grinned. "That's my choice, too. Okay, now let's see you throw."

For the next hour or so, they tossed the knives, until Karen was consistently hitting her mark. Then they took a break, sitting in the soft grass, each sipping a tall, fresh glass of lemonade.

"So, when's this going to go down, Karen?" asked Shawn.

Karen studied the young man who she could see was completely enamored with her daughter.

"Well, according to Harry Three-Feathers, the *Aglebemu* is a late sleeper and doesn't get up for his morning coffee till close to noon. So, I'm assuming around one or two o'clock might be the best time."

Shawn pulled out his cell and checked his tide table. "How about Tuesday? Terri and I can get our hauling done early and meet you here at say one-thirty?"

Karen smiled. "You two don't have to come with me. I'm a big girl. I think I can handle this by myself."

Shawn frowned, his face now all business. "No, you're not doing this alone. I, we, understand that it's you that has to do it, but you might need back up and we're going to be there to protect you. Right, Terri?"

"Shawn's right, Mom. You're not going after this thing alone."

Karen stood and poured more lemonade for each of them. "You really believe all this crap, don't you, Shawn. You know, evil toads, swirling vortexes, ancient curses."

Shawn looked at her, his face serious. "Your daughter doesn't lie. If she says something's true, then it is. I've learned not to question her judgment. So, your answer's yes, I do believe it all."

Karen patted him lightly on the shoulder, looking over at Terri. "I think you might be right, honey, this one could be a keeper."

Terri blushed. "Mom!"

"Okay. I've said enough," said Karen, smiling. "And, I think I've had enough practice for today."

She picked up the handle-heavy knife in her hand, again mimicking her throwing motion. "You know, honey, it's probably a good thing I didn't know how easy this was when I was married to your father. There were times when I would have been tempted..."

Terri's mouth fell open in shock. "Mom! You wouldn't have!"

Karen walked over and ruffled her daughter's hair. "I'm just joshing with you. No, I wouldn't have. At least I don't think I would have. Now, give me your brother. I think it's time he got in out of this hot sun. Can I make you guys something to eat?"

"I think we're good, Mom. Shawn has to go to the mainland and I have chores to do at home. So, we'll meet up with you on Tuesday, okay? Any change in plans and you call me."

"Yes, honey. I won't go without you. And, Shawn, thank you so much for helping me. I really appreciate it."

"No problem, Karen. Glad I could be of service. Come on, Terri, let's get a move on."

Karen hefted her son up into her arms and walked with them to their truck. She kissed Terri lightly on the cheek and, on impulse, did the same with Shawn. He blushed but looked pleased by the gesture.

When their truck disappeared around the bend, Karen took her child back into the house and put him down for a nap. Then, with a rueful sigh, grabbed the pile of dirty clothes took them to the laundry room.

AN UNWELCOME GUEST

SHAWN DROPPED TERRI AT the front of the house and headed for the wharf. After waving goodbye, Terri skipped up the steps and reached under the flowerpot for her house key. Although Shawn didn't think it was necessary to lock the doors on the island, for Terri, old habits died hard, and hiding the key under the pot was her way of compromise.

Surprised to find it missing, she wondered if Shawn had taken it with him. A bit puzzled, she tried the door. It was open.

She hesitated for a moment, then stepped over the threshold. The aroma of stale tobacco greeted her and since neither she nor Shawn smoked, she knew someone was either in the house now or had been there recently.

"Who's there?" she called as she walked cautiously into the living room.

No one answered.

On the coffee table were a half-lit cigar and an empty beer bottle.

Wrinkling her nose in disgust, she bent down to clean up the mess.

"Holy crap," she whispered.

Hidden by the bottle, on her hand-held mirror, was a razor blade next to a pile of white powder, some of which had been carefully molded into lines.

Alarmed, she reached into her pocket for her cell phone when the sound of a toilet flushing caught her by surprise.

She whirled around.

Jack O'Dwyer was standing in the doorway.

"Help yourself," he said, grinning. "It's wicked good blow."

"What are you doing here?" she demanded.

Jack ignored her, sauntered over to the table, and snorted a line.

"You can't do that in here," said Terri. "We don't do drugs. Take your stuff and leave. If you go now, I won't say anything to Shawn."

"Now, you don't really want me to leave, do you?" he asked, taking a step toward her.

Terri backed away as he approached.

"Yes, I do," she said firmly. "Take your drugs and get out. Shawn will be back any minute."

Jack laughed. "Naw, I don't think he'll be returning soon. I heard Jason say he was meeting his brother on the mainland at the marine store this afternoon. I think they'll be gone for quite a while."

He paused for a moment, then took another step toward her.

Terri's eyes darted toward the front door, which she had left ajar.

Catching her gaze, Jack swiftly moved into the entryway, casually kicking the door shut with his foot.

"Not thinking of leaving, were you?" he taunted. "No, I think not. You and me, we need to get better acquainted. You know, seeing you and my boy are keeping such close company and all."

As he spoke, he moved nearer.

Terri stepped away again but found she was out of space, her back against the living room wall.

She glanced down at her cell, which was still in her hand.

"I'm calling him right now," she said. "Just get out."

Catlike, Jack closed the distance between them and grabbed her by the wrist, causing the phone to fall to the floor. He leaned his body toward hers, placing his palms against the wall on either side of her head.

"Please leave," she begged. "I don't want any trouble with you."

Jack laughed and slapped her across the face with the flat of his hand.

"No, honey," he whispered. "You and me are going to have us a party this afternoon. After all, it's my duty as Shawn's father to see that you're properly broken in. And it will serve the boy right for refusing to shake my hand, don't ya think?"

Terri inched herself along the wall, moving toward the doorway to the kitchen.

"Please," she said. "Don't do this."

Jack moved his body even closer, then slapped her again, but this time with more force. Tears welled in her eyes.

"Now, you're going to cooperate, aren't you, honey?" he sneered. "Although it might be more fun if you didn't."

He reached up and cupped her chin with one hand, squeezing painfully and forcing her to look at him.

His face was now only inches from hers. He stared at her for a moment then leaned forward and ran his tongue along her cheek.

His breath smelled of stale tobacco and alcohol and a wave of disgust and anger shot through her. Violently, she twisted out of his grasp and pushed him with all her might.

"NO!" she cried.

Startled by the ferocity of her response, Jack lost his balance and had to back up a step, releasing her. Seeing the opportunity to escape, Terri sprinted away from the wall, toward the kitchen.

Jack quickly recovered and followed.

Frantic, she opened the cutlery drawer, looking for something to use as a weapon, but she wasn't fast enough. Jack was right behind her and grabbed her around the waist, lifting her off the ground. She screamed as he swung her around and slammed her head into the wall.

Tears of pain and rage ran down her cheeks as he pressed his body tightly against hers and grabbed her face, pinching her cheeks forcefully together.

"Now, you'd better start behaving, missy," he snarled, grinding his pelvis against hers.

Desperately, she struggled to free herself but her efforts only seemed to arouse him further.

"Ahh, yes," he moaned. "I bet you're a tight one. My Johnson's going fill you up, that's for sure."

"Please," she cried. "Don't do this."

Jack laughed unpleasantly. "Maybe I'll put a little of that coke on Mr. Big here and let you lick it off. Think you'd like that?"

She tried to knee him, but he anticipated her intent and deflected her blow.

"None of that now!" he yelled, slapping her again, this time using the back of his hand. "Time for you and me to get a little more comfortable."

He laughed again, then grabbed her around the waist and lifted her into the air, carrying her struggling body up the stairs to the bedroom. Once there, he tossed her on the bed and slammed the door shut.

He stared at her for a moment, smiling, then reached into his pocket and pulled out a folded white paper she assumed held more drugs. He placed it carefully on the nightstand and opened it. Grinning at her, he dipped his finger into the white powder, then leaned over and forced it into her mouth.

"Maybe this will loosen you up a bit," he said as he wiped the potent drug across her gums.

She tried to bite him, but he quickly pulled his hand back and grabbed her by the hair.

"None of that biting shit. Try that again and you'll regret it."

He pushed her back down on the bed and, laughing, moved his hand to his crotch and began to stroke himself.

Terri's eyes darted around the room. She could try for one of the windows, but the fall might kill her. Frantic, she knew she was stuck - there was no way out. Fighting him would only end with her being injured or worse - he was just too strong.

Realizing she was close to panic, she forced herself to take a deep breath. She knew she needed to get back in control or all would be lost. Remembering the lessons learned from Harry Three-Feathers, she closed her eyes and focused on her breathing.

Jack, momentarily diverted by the drugs, turned his back to her, preparing more of the white powder.

Quietly, she sat up on the bed, crossing her legs in front of her and placing her hands, palm up, on her knees. Taking another deep breath, she closed her eyes and began to move her lips in a silent chant.

Jack, oblivious, leaned over the nightstand and snorted a couple more lines then swiveled around to face her, a leering grin on his face.

But that grin was short-lived.

"What the f-," he exclaimed.

The room, once brightly lit by the sun, was now full of shadows and fog and he could barely see the bed in front of him. Confused, he moved closer, reaching for Terri, but she was no longer there.

He whipped his head back and forth, searching for her, but could see nothing but the heavy mist, which was growing denser by the minute.

"Where'd you go, girl?" he cried taking a step forward, moving into the middle of the room.

Suddenly, the fog around him parted.

She was sitting cross-legged, floating five or six feet off the floor as if suspended on a cloud, a strange white light surrounding her.

He stared at her in wonder and growing fear. The room was deathly quiet except for the sound of his ragged breathing and, suddenly feeling nervous, he took a step toward where he thought the bedroom door was.

But it was gone.

A strangled cry issued from his throat as he realized that the once spacious room was changing - slowly shrinking, its walls closing in on him.

He edged himself again toward what he thought might be the doorway, looking for an escape from the young woman who, surrounded by that eerie light, was floating effortlessly in front of him.

Then, it began.

SHAWN

JASON AND SHAWN WERE standing at the counter at Northeast Marine Supply inspecting chart plotters.

"I sure would love to have one of those," said Jason wistfully.

"Yeah, me, too, but they sure are pricey."

"Yeah, Amanda'd have my hide if I put that on credit. Everything extra's being set aside for the little guy when he comes."

Shawn smiled at his brother's reference to his wife's impending birth.

"How's she doing?" he asked. "It must be soon."

"Yeah. We met with the midwife yesterday. She says we got about another week to ten days and I can tell you that didn't sit too well with Mandy. She can't wait to get rid of that load she's carrying!"

Shawn laughed and patted his brother on the back. "I'm with her on that. I, for one, can't wait to be an uncle..."

He was about to say more when a strange tingling sensation ran down his spine. Then, without warning, his mind was blasted by a vision of cold, blue fire.

"Shawn? What's with you? You look like you've seen a ghost."

Shawn shook his head violently. "I've got to get home. Something's wrong."

Jason stared at him, puzzled. "Huh? How do you know?"

"I just do. Listen, you pay for the line and stuff and I'll settle with you later. I gotta go."

Without waiting for a reply, Shawn turned and hurried out the door.

Jason walked to the store window and watched as his brother jogged across the parking lot to his truck then took off, burning rubber as he tore out of the lot.

TERRI

"*TANKASHILA, MYA, KYA,*
Tankashila, mya kya,
Che wo kielo,
Wakan chelo heyo,
Ah hey wa hey cheyo,
Wachio hey hey."

The chant was so soft at first that Jack was unaware of it, but, soon, the ancient song began to swell.

"It must be bad drugs," he mumbled to himself. "What the fuck did they cut this stuff with?"

Rubbing his eyes in disbelief and shaking his head, he took a step toward Terri. Her face was slack as if she were in some sort of trance, but her lips were moving, intoning the mantra that now seemed to be coming from all around him.

"What do you think you're doing, girly?" he snarled, an edge of fear creeping into his voice.

His words hung in the air as the song abruptly ended.

In the stillness, Terri's eyes became alive and filled with a painful white light that pierced him with deadly intent.

"You had better leave now," she whispered. "I don't want to hurt you and I don't know how much longer I can control them."

As she spoke, she glanced down at her hands and involuntarily his eyes followed.

Dancing between her fingertips were tiny balls of cold blue fire and he watched, transfixed, as they jumped and played from one finger to another, swelling and shrinking at will.

"Stop that!" he yelled, pointing at her hands as he took another step toward her, his mouth curled in a vicious snarl.

As if sensing imminent danger, the fiery orbs leaped from her fingers and danced in front of her, hovering menacingly before his eyes.

Jack stopped mid-step. The white light emanating from her had now turned icy blue to match the strange flames that, somehow, she had created and, he knew, she controlled.

She stared at him silently for a moment, her eyes now icy and cold.

"Please don't," he begged, backing away from her.

But it was too late.

With a slight nod of her head, one of the fierce, hot flames launched itself at him, streaking effortlessly across the room.

He stared at it, mesmerized, as it slowly flickered in front of his eyes, then swiftly transformed itself, taking on the elegant shape of a woman's long, thin finger.

Entranced by the delicate beauty of the flame, Jack stood frozen as it reached out and caressed his cheek.

At first, he felt nothing but cool fire, then the smell of burning flesh stained the air around him and an intense pain pierced his consciousness.

Screaming in agony, he reached up to try to put out the flame ... to stop the burning.

"Don't touch it!" she cried. "You'll make it worse. That flame is a part of you now. You'll never be free from it. Leave before any more of them come for you."

He stared down at her hands. There were dozens of the balls of blue fire there now and they looked, to him, extremely agitated and angry.

Watching them, he knew he had only seconds before they, too, would come for him.

He turned to run, as the strange song began to resonate again, filling the room.

"Tankashila, mya kya,
Tankashila, mya kya,
Che wo kielo..."

Knowing this was his only opportunity, he sprinted toward the door, which was now clearly outlined by a glowing white light. Throwing it open, he hastily disappeared down the stairs.

As soon as he was no longer in the room, the song ended.

Terri listened carefully, waiting for the sound of the front door opening. When she finally heard it open and slam shut, she breathed a sigh of relief and slowly returned her body to the bed. The blue flames dancing between her fingers were beginning to flicker and die, and she felt a profound weariness take their place.

Exhausted, she stretched out her legs and gazed around the room. The walls were now where they should be and the sun was streaming through the windows, bringing with it much-needed warmth.

She hugged herself and said a silent prayer of thanks to Harry Three-Feathers, for she knew it was he who sent her the smoke dream that, in turn, had ignited the cold fire that burned within her.

She grabbed a pillow and curled her body around it. Glancing at the clock, she smiled. Shawn would be home soon.

TERRI AND SHAWN

SHAWN MOORED HIS PUNT and raced to his truck. The feeling of impending disaster was still with him as he backed swiftly out of the parking lot and drove down the winding road to his house. He tried again to reach Terri on her cell, but there was still no answer.

He was almost home when he rounded a sharp bend. Directly in front of him, a man was jogging in the middle of the road, weaving from side to side.

Shawn slammed on the brakes, swerving the vehicle onto the shoulder. Heart pounding, he looked out the window at the man who was approaching the truck. He recognized him immediately.

It was his father.

Jack stopped next to the cab and stood still for a moment, surprised to see his son's face staring down at him.

Shawn idled the truck. "What are you doing here?" he asked.

Jack moved his hand spasmodically to the bright, red scar Terri had left on his cheek, as if trying to remove something painful and foul. Then, without a word, turned and took off running toward the woods on the side of the road.

What the fuck's he doing? Shawn thought. *And what was that on his face?*

Shawn watched until Jack disappeared into the trees then put the truck back into gear.

Oh, Christ. Our home is right around the corner. Was that bastard coming from there? Oh God, what's he done?

Fueled by adrenalin, Shawn pulled the truck back onto the road and stomped on the accelerator, covering the short distance to his house in minutes. Leaping from the cab, he ran up the steps.

"Terri, Terri!" he called.

No one answered.

He glanced around the living room, noting the cigar stub and ash sitting on a plate on the coffee table.

Fearing the worst, he sprinted up the stairs.

Terri was lying on the bed, her eyes closed, hugging a pillow to her breast. A fresh blue bruise adorned her cheek and dark circles shadowed her eyes.

"Oh, baby," Shawn crooned, kneeling next to her. "Did he hurt you? Are you okay?"

Recognizing his voice, Terri opened her eyes. Tears welled up and spilled over onto her cheeks. "Oh, Shawn," she cried. "Hold me, please, hold me."

Shawn sat on the bed and pulled her into his arms as she sobbed, clinging to him.

After a few minutes, he pulled away, looking deeply into her eyes.

"Did Jack do this?" he asked, brushing the skin next to the bruise very lightly with his fingertips.

Terri nodded.

Shawn took a deep breath. "Did he do anything else?"

Terri stared at him, comprehending what he was asking, and shook her head. "No, he didn't. He wanted to. Was going to ... but ... but, I stopped him."

Slowly, in a voice barely above a whisper, she recounted what happened; how she had, through meditation, sent a message to Harry Three-Feathers and how the old Indian sent her the strength to prevail.

"But how did you know it was Jack that was here?" she asked when she'd finished her story.

"At the marine store, I got this feeling. You know, like a premonition. It was strong, babe, and I just hightailed it outta there. I didn't know what it was, but I knew something bad was happening. On the way here, I saw Jack on the road. He was running like a madman. I almost hit him. Wish I had now. But he saw me and took off through the woods. Ran like he had the fear of God in him."

Terri smiled. "He does. I left him with a little going away present."

"Huh? What do you mean?"

"When I was in the smoke dream Harry sent, the cold fire that burns within me reached out to Jack and, now, that fire is a part of him. He'll never be free of it nor will he be free of the pain it can inflict. Trust me, he won't be back. And he won't be hurting any other girls either."

Shawn stood and walked to the window, fists clenched by his sides. "If I ever see him again ... if I get my hands on him, he won't be doing much of anything to anyone!"

Terri joined him, putting her arms around his waist. "Don't talk like that. It scares me. I don't want you to do anything that could get you in trouble, you hear? It's over and, believe me, he won't be back."

Shawn looked down at her and nodded. "I know you think that, but let me make sure. I'm going to call Jason if that's okay with you."

Terri nodded. "Sure, it's fine."

Shawn pulled out his cell and walked to the opposite end of the room. Terri could only hear fragments of the conversation; something about getting the boys together to make sure no one harbored Jack on the island and calling his probation officer.

When the call was over, Shawn came back. "If it's okay with you, I'm going to call my mom. She needs to know about this. Also, she can bring something that will help ease the pain of that bruise. Do I have your permission to call her?"

Again, Terri nodded. "But this time, let me in on the conversation, please."

Shawn smiled. "Sorry, about that. But that was man talk with Jason. He's going to make sure no one on this island takes Jack in and is going to call his probation officer and let him know the man's using drugs again. That okay with you?"

Terri smiled. "Yeah, that's okay. Now let's call your mom."

Twenty minutes later, Terri and Shawn watched as a beat-up blue Subaru pulled into the driveway.

Slamming on the brakes, Helen O'Dwyer didn't even wait for the car to come to a full stop before she threw open the door and jumped out.

"Shawn, you get over here," she yelled as she unlatched the hatchback.

Shawn ran to help his mother who was lifting a heavy cast-iron casserole from the rear of the car.

"Take this inside," she said, handing him the pot. "It's the last of the venison stew I put up last winter. You and Jason sure better plan on getting me another doe or two come hunting season, you hear!"

"Yes, Ma," Shawn replied taking the heavy casserole from her hands.

"Put it in the oven on 350. And, give me a few minutes out here. I want to talk with Terri, alone!"

"Yes, Ma," he intoned again.

"Wait a minute. Is she okay?"

Shawn glanced over his shoulder at Terri, then back to his mother. "She's good. Shaken up, but good. I'll give you some time."

Helen nodded and walked with him to the deck where Terri sat waiting.

"Mom's brought us some stew. I'm going to put it in the oven," said Shawn, kissing her lightly on the top of her head. Then he went inside.

Helen sat in the seat next to Terri. She was silent for a moment then turned to face the girl. "Look at me. Let me see what that sorry son of a bitch did to you."

The bruise on Terri's cheek was now dark purple and the surrounding tissues were swollen. Her eye on that side of her face was half shut.

"Sweet Jesus!" exclaimed Helen as she tenderly touched Terri's cheek with her fingertips. "Don't worry, I've got something in the car that will take down that swelling and help you heal."

She got up and returned to her car, quickly coming back with what looked like an old toolbox. Opening the lid, Terri was surprised to see it filled with numerous bottles, vials, and Ziploc bags full of various dried herbs.

Helen rummaged through the bottles, finally finding what she was looking for.

"I'm going to put this on your cheek," she said as she dipped her fingers into a jar of ointment. "It will feel warm, then cool. It's a little greasy, but it will reduce the swelling and numb the pain. It will also help the blood vessels heal faster so the bruising will fade quickly. Okay?"

Terri nodded and bit her bottom lip as Helen applied the ointment.

"There, how does that feel?"

"Nice. Just like you said, warm then cool. Thank you."

"Good. Now, honey, after I spoke with Shawn, I talked to Jason and he told me what Jack tried to do to you."

Terri's back stiffened. "I ... Nothing really happened ... I'm sorry..."

"Shush, now. Let me do the talking," replied the older woman. "And you have nothing to be sorry about. I'm the one should be apologizing to you. If I suspected that bastard would try something like that, well, I can tell you he would have had a date with the business end of my twelve-gauge!

"I want you to know that we've reported it to the police along with the fact that he's drinking and using again. Jason told me they went to pick him up at the boarding house where he was staying but, apparently, he's hightailed it outta there. They've got an APB out on him, but I suspect he's gone deep into the backwoods up north or down into New Hampshire. However, if he hasn't, Jason has put the word out on Mateguas that Jack O'Dwyer is *persona non-grata* here and that anyone who helps or harbors him will have to answer to us. I know that doesn't make up for what he did or what he tried to do, but you won't have to worry about him in the future. Quick thinking of yours, tossing that boiling water on him."

Terri averted her gaze, trying to hide her surprise. The boiling water must have been a story Shawn made up to explain the burns on Jack's face.

"The police are probably going to want to interview you," said Helen. "I asked Jason to tell them to hold off a couple of days so you could get your bearings, but they'll be calling."

Terri smiled. "Thank you. Really, nothing much happened. He tried, but I let him know that I wasn't having any of it."

"Good for you!" said Helen, smiling. Then she became serious again. "He wasn't always like that, you know. He was a good man once. I married him when I was just out of high school. He was older than me and my family wasn't happy about it, but Jason was already on the way, so we got hitched. I thought I loved him and that he loved me."

She glanced down at herself. She was wearing a bulky sweatshirt and blue jeans, tucked into heavy work boots. Her steel-gray hair was short, cut in a no-nonsense style. Her face was deeply lined, but she wore no makeup to try to camouflage her age.

"I didn't always look like this, you know. I was a pretty thing back in those days."

Terri was about to say something but Helen, again, cut her off. "I know what I look like and I'm at ease with my appearance, so don't feel you need to say anything to make me feel better. Okay?"

Terri grinned, recognizing the intelligence and kindness in the older woman's eyes. "I think you're beautiful."

Helen blushed and patted the young girl's hand. "You're a good kid."

Their conversation was interrupted by the sound of the front door. Both women turned as Shawn came striding toward them, holding a pitcher of lemonade and three glasses.

"Thought you all might like something to drink," he said.

Both women smiled and thanked him as he pulled up a chair and sat down.

"Your mom was telling me about Jack back when they first got married."

Helen laughed. "Yeah, as I was saying, back then, Jack was a lobsterman but he wasn't too good at it. Just didn't have the patience. He always wanted things fast and wasn't willing to put in the hard yards. We had some good years when the boys were young, but when the economy went sour, he started in with the drugs and alcohol. At first, he just used, and we went further and further into debt. That's when he started dealing. Once that happened, he rarely spent time with us. He was always in some bar on the mainland, hanging out with guys like Lonnie Pierce and Rusty Maguire. He was selling hard stuff ... heroin and cocaine ... to kids and that's what got him busted. For the boys and me, it was a blessing. I divorced him while he was away. His showing up here last week was a total surprise."

Terry nodded. "Tell me about Lonnie. He was Dex's dad, right?"

"Yup, that's him."

"Dex never talks much about his family. I know his parents died in a car wreck back when he was in college. But he never speaks about it, at least he hasn't to Sophie or me."

Helen sighed. "Lonnie was a hard case. A good-looking man, but there was a mean streak in him. I don't think he did drugs - oh, maybe a little weed here and there, but then who doesn't. No, if he had a substance issue it was alcohol. He was known to tie one on and that's when he got mean. Then and if someone crossed him on the water. God help the man that set a stringer in his territory."

Helen paused and took a sip of her lemonade. "Does Dex ever talk about his mom?"

Terri shook her head.

"Well, let me tell you, she was a wonderful person. A saint, really. Patricia was a summer girl, came to the island with her family. Met Lonnie at one of the dances. Think, for her, it was love at first sight. They married right after she graduated college - Barnard, Bennington or some fancy place like that. She was a smart cookie. Her parents weren't very happy about her marrying an islander. They disowned her, you know.

"In any case, she settled in here on the island, like she was a native. She'd been a botany major in school and knew just about all there was to know about plants and herbs. In no time, she was helping when folks got sick and couldn't make it to town. Took classes in midwifery, too, and, I can't tell you the number of babies she helped come into the world on this rock."

"Yours, too?"

"Ayup. I went into labor with Jason during a bad nor'easter. Patricia delivered my boy, easy peasy! She stayed with me after for a while and we talked. When I was back on my feet, she took me on as an apprentice, teaching me all about plant life and natural remedies."

"She sounds great. I wish I could have met her. I wonder why Dex never talks about her."

Helen sighed. "He was her only child and oh, how she loved him; doted on him really. And he loved her, too. Used to call her his 'princess.'"

Terri frowned. "Princess? That's what he calls my mom."

Helen bit her bottom lip, thinking. "Well, mayhap your mom reminds him of her in some way. Patricia was blonde, too, and tall like your mother. She was a very attractive woman, but her real beauty came from inside ... from her soul. Anyway, as I was saying, she and Dex had a close relationship and I think there were times when Lonnie resented it."

"What do you mean?"

"It's not something I can put my finger on and point to, but sometimes I'd catch him looking at the two of them and it wasn't fondly. No, I think he was jealous of his own son and that colored the way he treated him."

"Are you saying he was abusive to Dex?"

Helen hesitated for a moment. "No, not physically, but mentally, maybe. He worked Dex hard, too. Sometimes too hard, in my opinion. Anyway, all in all, they lived a pretty good life here until about two months before the car accident that killed them."

"What happened then?"

"I can't say for sure, but it was something dark. Patricia changed. She wasn't the same afterward."

"Something dark? What do you mean?"

"Don't know any specifics. But I'm sure it was something between her and Lonnie - something bad. Things changed after that. She called me in and told me there was no more that she could teach me. Told me I was ready and that she was retiring. Gave me this box full of dried herbs and potions along with all of her notebooks that detailed her recipes for remedies. She said I was on my own and that she had confidence in me."

"Didn't you ask her why she was retiring?"

"No, I didn't. If you had seen her face, you would understand. She was like a broken woman. No, something dark happened in that house and I believe it eventually led to her death."

"What do you mean? I thought they died in an accident."

"Yes, that's the official version. Lonnie and Patricia were driving up north to see Dex at college. Police said something ... an animal, maybe a deer or moose ... must have caused the car to swerve into oncoming traffic. Both Patricia and Lonnie were killed instantly. But some of the facts just don't add up."

Terri leaned forward, intent on the woman's story. "Tell me."

"Okay. First off, witnesses say they stopped at a tavern on the way for lunch. Lonnie, not surprisingly, had several drinks while Patricia just sat in one of the booths, watching and barely touching her food. According to some of the other patrons, Lonnie was partying hard, flirting with the waitresses and all. By the time he and Patricia left, the bartender said Lonnie could barely walk and had to be helped to their car. The barkeep also said he admonished Patricia not to let her husband drive and she assured him that she wouldn't. The man said he watched them drive away, Patricia at the wheel. Said he couldn't put his finger on it, but that there was something very sad about her."

"Okay, but what's suspicious about that?"

"Well, I knew Patricia and let me tell you, she would've NEVER let Lonnie get shit-faced when he was on the way to see his son. No way! And, because of the nature of the accident, they did tests on the bodies. Lonnie's blood, as expected, was way over the legal limit but, interestingly, they also found barbiturates in his system. Patricia's blood was completely clean."

"Sleeping pills? Why would he take sleeping pills if he was going to be driving?"

"I know - it makes no sense. And, that's what makes me wonder."

"Wonder, what?"

"I think Patricia had a plan when she suggested they take that drive. I think it was her idea to stop at that tavern and while he was busy with the waitress, I think she slipped him a Mickey."

"A Mickey? What's that?"

Helen laughed. "I guess that expression is before your time. A *Mickey Finn* is slang from my day for a drink laced with a drug. Don't know where it came from."

"So, you're saying you think she drugged him? Why?"

"I think she wanted him passed out so they'd be no way he could drive. She wanted to be behind the wheel. And I don't think there was any moose or deer on that road. No, I think she swerved the car intentionally."

"Suicide?"

"Yes, and I think she planned to take Lonnie with her. Something happened that she couldn't live with anymore ... something to do with Lonnie. I think she believed that by dying, somehow, she was protecting her son."

Terri leaned back, clearly shocked. "That takes us back to the child abuse angle, doesn't it?"

"Honey, I don't know. I never saw any signs of that. There were no bruises or broken bones that I can remember. But Lonnie could be a hard one so, I guess, anything's possible. And, like I said, he made Dex work. He was always dragging the poor kid out on the boat to haul and set traps, even when he had schoolwork that needed to be done. But don't you go spouting off on this to your stepdad, you hear? Whatever happened, he's put it in his past and become a good man and made a good life for himself."

Terri nodded. "Don't worry, I won't. He was a great dad to Sophie and me and my mother loves him very much. And now they have Alex."

Helen smiled and took a sip of her lemonade, then turned to her son. "You've got yourself a fine young woman here, Shawn. Don't do anything to screw it up!"

Shawn laughed, putting his arm around Terri. "I won't. She won't let me."

"Well, she's family now."

Terri gazed into the kind eyes of the older woman, leaned over, and hugged her. "Thank you, Helen," she whispered.

Helen gave her a squeeze, then, wiping her eyes quickly with the back of her hand, turned to her son again.

"How about a bowl of that stew? I didn't bring it over here just to let it dry out in your oven."

"Sounds good," replied Shawn. "Come on, let's go inside. I think I can handle setting the table."

SUSAN LEVEQUE

SUSAN SAT AT HER desk, finishing up for the day. She was pleased her broadcast had gone well and was excited about the one she would be preparing for the following week.

Yes, she thought. *It's time to put Evie LaPlante to bed. I've done as much damage as I can to Mr. Dexter Pierce and fulfilled my promise to Bill. Now it's time to see where the missing men can take me.*

She leaned back in her chair, going over her notes. To date, the bones unearthed on the island had been determined to come from five different men. Samples had been sent out for DNA analysis, but that could take a week or two. No other clues to the identities had been found except for one signet ring that the police were following up on.

Susan thought about the six men on her list. They were the focus of her next show, in which she planned to reveal her theory about Puffin Island and 'lobster wars.' She hoped that when the identities of the remains were revealed and if it proved she was right, that the story would be picked up by the national media, catapulting her into the limelight.

But if she were wrong?

She didn't even want to think about that. She would be an embarrassment to the station and would be lucky if she could get a job reporting on lobster eating contests. Picturing that in her mind, she cringed in horror.

But that won't happen, she thought. *I know I'm right.*

Nodding, she put her fears aside and focused back on the bones found on Puffin.

Five skeletons and six missing men. Which one haven't we found? Maybe it's the guy who's been gone the longest. Perhaps they just haven't dug deep enough or the body could have washed out to sea. Or it could be the environmentalist, Nichols. He's the only one that doesn't fit the pattern.

With no answer forthcoming, she decided to switch gears and retrieved her file on Lonnie and Patricia Pierce. Quickly scanning the contents, she stopped when she got to the police report of the accident that killed them both.

Something doesn't ring true here, she thought as she carefully read the report. *It's too pat; too perfect. Why would Lonnie Pierce get drunk on the way to see his son? And, why were barbiturates found in his blood work? He was the one driving when they left Mateguas. Was he trying to get them killed?*

She made some notes in the file margins and set a reminder to contact the witnesses at the tavern the Pierces had stopped at for lunch.

She glanced at the time on her computer. It was going on eight p.m. and she felt she needed a break.

If I hurry, I could catch the last ferry to Mateguas. Bill's forgoing his trip to Boston this week and a couple of days on the island might be just what I need to revitalize myself. And he's a good sounding board, too.

Smiling, she shut down the computer and grabbed her coat. On the way out the door, she pulled out her cell and speed-dialed Bill. He answered on the second ring.

"Hey, feel like some company tonight," she crooned. "I can just make the last boat."

She could almost see him smiling on the other end of the line.

"Sure, that'd be great," he replied. "Nice broadcast on Sunday. I'll bet Dex enjoyed it. Have you eaten yet?"

"No, hope you've got some leftovers."

Bill laughed. "I was just going to nuke a hot dog, but in honor of your visit, I'll run down to the Shack and pick up burgers and fries."

"Sounds good. Get me a cheese and bacon burger. See you soon."

Hanging up the phone, she rushed out of the building to her car. As she drove to the ferry terminal, she wondered how much longer this relationship would last.

It's going to end for you and him, you know, and probably sooner rather than later. He's never going to give up on his ex-wife and you know that. In any case, you wouldn't really want him if he did, would you?

She sighed as she pulled up to the terminal parking lot. Swiftly, hopping from the car, she jogged to the wharf just in time to catch the last boat.

Burgers, fries, and hot sex, she mused to herself. *Nothing too shabby in that! If it's going to end eventually, I might as well enjoy it while I can!*

BILL

BILL CALLED THE ISLAND Burger Shack and placed their order. Glancing at the clock, he had just enough time for a quick wash before picking up the meal and meeting Susan at the evening boat.

As he showered, he thought about Susan, wondering how long it would be before they went their separate ways. In his mind, she'd already served her purpose and he didn't know what, if anything, more she could do to further incriminate Pierce. Unfortunately, despite all she'd uncovered about the LaPlante girl, the police had taken no interest, leaving it all to rapidly fading rumors and innuendo.

I have to refocus on regaining my memory, he thought as he toweled off.

He'd canceled the last couple of sessions with the doctor in Boston, discouraged by his lack of progress. He spent his time, instead, researching lost memory on the web, focusing on various meditation techniques that were reported to help with amnesia. Delving into the efficacy of each method, he'd finally narrowed it down to one or two that he planned to experiment with later in the week. At the same time, his nightmares had gotten worse, causing him to wake up almost nightly, shivering and in a cold sweat.

I just have to tough it out, he thought. *Take those damned pills if I need to. And, when my memory returns, if I find out it was Dex who dumped me there, I'll see he goes to jail where he belongs.*

Nodding to himself, he jogged out to his car. The Burger Shack was at the opposite end of the island and he drove quickly, picked up his order, and arrived at the wharf just as the ferry was pulling in.

He sat idly eating a French fry as it docked, waiting.

One of the last passengers, Susan stepped off the boat, an overnight case in her hand. She was wearing a tight black pencil skirt and a flimsy silk blouse. On her feet were bright-red stiletto heels. Bill smiled. She looked very sexy.

He watched as she slowly made her way up the steep gangplank, trying to keep her balance.

Chuckling at her apparent discomfort, he hopped from the truck and jogged to the wharf, arriving just in time to help her up the remaining steps.

"As much as I like them, I don't think those shoes are island-tested," he said, taking her hand.

Susan laughed. "Don't worry. I have my flip-flops in my bag. Now let's get going. I'm starved and I don't mean just for burgers!"

KAREN AND DEX

LATER THAT EVENING, KAREN lay in bed hugging a pillow to her chest. Dex slept on the opposite side, snoring slightly.

What happened to all that passion he displayed earlier? she thought, gazing over her shoulder at him.

She closed her eyes, reliving in her mind how sensuously he had caressed her that afternoon after she'd come home and, more importantly, after he'd watched Susan LeVeque's show. He'd been amorous then, but when they'd gone to bed and she'd reached for him, he'd rolled away, murmuring something about being too tired and asking for a rain check.

She buried her face in the pillow, willing sleep to come, but her mind was clouded by a mass of long blonde curls framing a face so like her own.

Evie. What's the real story behind your murder? And what, if anything, did Dex have to do with it? He's hiding something. I'm sure of that. But what will I do if I find out he was involved? Do I really want to go there? What will finding out about it do to my life and my marriage?

Sighing to herself, she relinquished the pillow, rolled over, and wrapped her arms around the man she loved, knowing it might be better to just forget everything and let that young girl from his past rest in peace.

But as these thoughts ran through her mind, she knew she wouldn't heed them. No, the answers, as horrible as they might be, were out there somewhere, and it was up to her to find them and face them, regardless of what consequences they might bring.

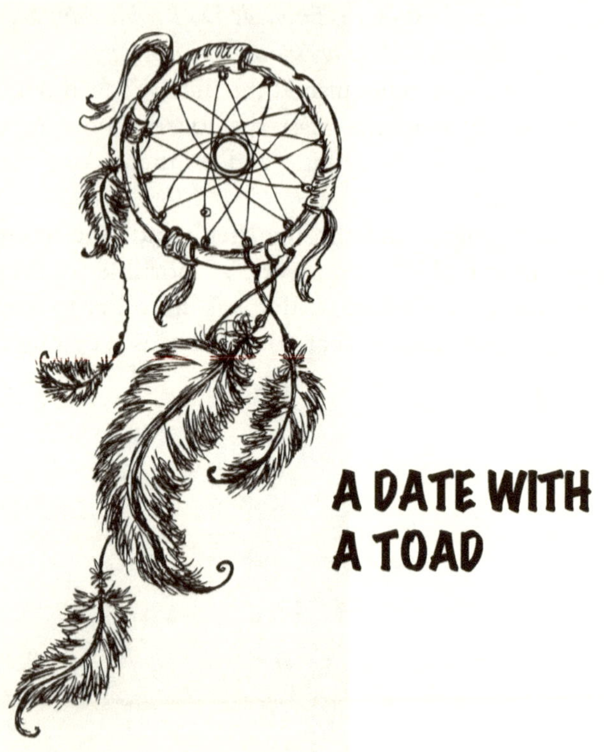

A DATE WITH A TOAD

TUESDAY MORNING, AFTER DEX left for the boatyard, Karen took Alex out back. As the boy busied himself chasing butterflies and birds, she practiced her knife throwing. Convinced she was as good as she ever was going to be, she finally put the blade away and fixed lunch.

At one o'clock, she heard Shawn's truck pull up the driveway. Peering out the window, she couldn't help but laugh when she saw the look of grim determination on her daughter's face.

Sweet Jesus, she thought. *Am I really going to do battle with an evil toad? Or is this all part of that malignant tumor that's been hiding somewhere in my brain for the last twelve years? I just can't believe that those two kids can take this hallucination so seriously. If I don't believe me, how can they?*

Chuckling nervously, she walked to the door and took a deep breath.

Better put on my game face. They might be offended if they see me laughing.

Pulling herself together, she opened the door. "Hi, guys," she said with a smile. "Come on in."

Terri gave her mother a hug.

Karen hugged her in return then stepped back and stared at her. "What's that on your cheek?" she asked, reaching up and laying her finger on the bruise still visible on Terri's face.

When her daughter didn't answer immediately, Karen shot a hard look at Shawn.

"Mom, it's nothing," said Terri, catching her mother's gaze. "I had an accident on the boat. I tripped and fell."

Karen didn't blink. "Is that right, Shawn?"

"Yes, ma'am," he replied firmly. "I stupidly left some line loose on the deck. Terri tripped and fell into one of the stanchions. We came right home and I had my mom take a look at her to make sure we didn't need to go to the ER. It won't happen again."

"Is that correct, Terri?"

"Yes, Mother," she replied, taking Shawn's hand in hers. "I was just clumsy."

Karen breathed a sigh of relief. "Okay, but be more careful in the future. I don't want to hear you've gone overboard or something."

Terri laughed. "I won't. Now, where's Alex?"

"Oh, I put him down for a nap about an hour ago," Karen replied. "He should wake up soon. I want you to stay here with him."

"No, Mom!" Terri exclaimed. "I'm going with you!"

"Now, honey, be reasonable. I'm not putting Alex in jeopardy by bringing him along and someone has to stay with him. It can't be me and, if I have a say in who's going to be my back-up, then I pick Shawn. He has to be better in the weapons department than you. And, anyway, I'd rather put him in harm's way. No offense, Shawn."

The young man smiled. "None taken, Karen. And, I agree with you. I'd rather have Terri here, safe, than out in the woods where anything can happen."

Terri pushed her bottom lip out in a pout. "Well, looks like I'm outnumbered. Okay, I'll stay. But you call me, Shawn, as soon as it's over."

"Will do. Now are you ready to go, Karen?"

"Just let me check on the baby for a minute."

She came back five minutes later holding the tired toddler. "Here, you stay with your sister," she said, handing the boy to Terri.

"Okay, I guess it's toad time. Let's go."

Shawn followed Karen's directions to the trailhead and parked his truck. Helping her out, he scanned the area, a puzzled look on his face.

"You know, I've lived on this island my whole life," he said, shaking his head. "And I think I know it pretty damned well. But I've never seen this trail before. Doesn't make sense."

Karen grinned. "Welcome to my world, Shawn. Strange paths no one else can find, evil spirits ... It's a wonder we're not all in the loony bin."

Shawn shook his head again. "Okay, guess I'm about to head down the yellow brick road and since you know this road so well, I'll let you take the lead."

Karen laughed wryly. Then, with Shawn right behind her, began walking down the trail. It wasn't long before they reached the juncture where it forked.

"This is it," said Karen. "This is where I veered off the main trail and found the pond. It's not far. I think you should probably wait here. If Harry's right and that creature sees or senses you, then all this will have been for naught."

Shawn nodded. "Okay. But if you need me, yell."

"Don't worry. If I need you, I'll scream my bloody head off."

She smiled, then impulsively put her arms around him and gave him a fierce hug.

"I'm counting on you," she said.

"I know and don't worry," he replied. "I'll be here for you. You just stay steady. You can do this. Pretend you're in your backyard."

Karen nodded and reached out and squeezed his hand. "Remember, if you hear screaming, you come pronto, okay?"

"I've got your back, Karen. Don't worry."

Nodding, she turned around. Hesitating for a moment, she took a deep breath, then walked down the trail and out into the clearing.

TERRI AND ALEX

TERRI STARED OUT THE window watching Shawn's truck back down the drive. When they were out of sight, she turned and walked back to the living room where she'd left the baby happily playing with some toys.

"Okay, let's see what mischief we can get into, little brother," she said, glancing around the room.

His toys were scattered about on the floor, but Alex was no longer sitting on the carpet playing with them.

Holy shit, I only left him for a minute, she thought. *Where'd he go?*

"Alex!" she cried, looking behind the sofa. "Where are you? Are we playing hide and seek?"

She searched the room and, finding it empty, was about to check the kitchen when a loud, sharp BANG came from the bedroom.

What the hell was that, she thought.

Bracing herself, she opened the bedroom door.

"Sweet Mary, Mother of God, how the fuck?"

Standing by the window was a miniature unicorn, shaking its head and stomping its hooves happily on the painted wooden floor.

With some trepidation, Terri approached the creature. "Alex, is that you?"

The unicorn gazed at her, grinning, flecks of bright, shiny gold dancing in its eyes, and nodded.

Astounded, Terri sat down on the bed remembering what her mother had said about how she had seen him change into an eagle.

The unicorn-boy stomped his hoofs again, sending yellow flecks of paint flying.

"Uh-oh, your mother's not going to like that," scolded Terri looking at the damage he was inflicting on the once beautifully painted floor. "Can you change back? And, why a unicorn?"

The unicorn-boy pranced over to the far side of the bed and began nodding his head up and down. Sitting on the pillow was a stuffed animal. The boy had copied it exactly, right down to its long eyelashes and sprinkles of glitter on its nose.

"Okay," laughed Terri. "You decided you wanted to be your bedtime buddy. I get it. But now it's time to change back. Right?"

The unicorn-boy stuck out his lower lip in a very comical pout but nodded again. The gold in his eyes grew brighter as a shimmering white light surrounded him. As it increased in intensity, Terri watched in wonder.

Christ, she thought, smiling. *It's almost too beautiful to believe.*

Then in an instant, it was gone. On the floor sat Alex, flecks of yellow paint on his baby sneakers, a happy smile on his face.

Hugging the stuffed unicorn to her breast, Terri slipped down on the floor beside him.

"How'd you do that?" she asked. "I mean, doesn't it hurt to change like that?"

The boy grinned at her.

She was about to say more when a sharp, stabbing pain hit her in her left temple.

"Yikes!" she cried, her hands going to her head as a child-like voice began to echo through her mind.

"No, sweet sister, it does not hurt. It is a gift from my father. But using it does tire me. I think I would like to sleep now."

The little boy held out his arms, waiting to be picked up.

It took Terri a minute to comprehend that he had just spoken to her telepathically. She stared at him blankly, then grinned, marveling at the strange child who was her brother.

"Okay," she said, picking him up and carrying him to his bed. "You nap now. And no more shenanigans. I've had enough already for one day."

The child smiled at her, then closed his eyes.

Terri leaned down and kissed him on the cheek, noting that he had already fallen asleep. Reluctant to leave him alone, she pulled the rocking chair close to the crib and sat down beside him to wait for Shawn's call.

A TOAD'S KISS

THE POND WAS AS she remembered it, water glistening in the bright sunlight, colorful dragonflies dancing above its surface. And, sitting on the same rock, was the toad, eyes closed as if sleeping in the warmth of the sun.

ZAP!

Its loathsome tongue darted out from between swollen lips to snag a blue bottlefly that made the mistake of hovering too close. The sight of that pink appendage made Karen shudder as she stood near the pond's edge.

The toad lazily opened one eye, as if sensing the presence of an intruder. Slowly, it scanned the area around the pond. When it caught sight of Karen, it stopped.

She stared at the creature, which had now opened both eyes and was glaring at her with menace.

Smacking its lips together in apparent delight, the toad shifted its ponderous, bloated body around to face her.

Karen gripped the knife carefully by the blade, holding it out of sight behind her back. Her heart was pounding and, as she watched the toad, she feared she might faint. Every instinct told her to flee, to run back to the safety of the car and let Shawn take care of this evil creature.

But she pushed those thoughts aside.

The old Indian had said that this was her responsibility. Somehow, she had awakened this creature from its dark slumber and only she could wound it so severely as to send it back. She knew it was she who had done the damage and it was up to her to fix it, not Shawn. And, if she didn't follow through, any harm this creature inflicted on the innocent would be on her head.

She steeled herself, remembering the instructions Harry Three-Feathers had given her.

"You must be strong. Do not move too soon. For the toad is ancient and with such revered age, comes wisdom. If you rush, it will know and anticipate your intent. No, you must act as if you have fallen under its influence ... as if you are ready to succumb to its will."

She stood still, watching, as the toad began to move, shifting its impressive weight from one foot to another. It looked, to Karen, almost as if it were dancing, celebrating some mad rite of spring. But she knew that was not its intent. It wasn't dancing. It was anticipating the wondrous feast it would have later ... her fear and her flesh devoured slowly and painfully.

The creature's eyes began to glow as they bulged from their sockets. The tongue now moved in and out so fast that all Karen could see was a blur.

She ached to throw the knife and run, but knew it was not yet time.

I'll count to ten, she thought. *Then I'll do it.*

Tensing her muscles and gripping the knife tightly, she began to count.

One, two, three...

The tongue lashed out, moving in her direction with electrifying speed. She gasped in surprise and brought her hand from behind her back and, as Shawn had taught her, hurled the knife.

End over end, the blade sailed through the air toward the creature.

The toad involuntarily turned its gaze to the knife, which glistened in the afternoon sun.

In a flash, the tongue, guided by instinct, darted swiftly away from Karen toward the brightly shining object, snatching it from the air and wrapping tightly around it. The blade, honed to acute sharpness, sliced neatly through the foul appendage, severing it in two places. Then, dripping with the toad's black blood, the knife then fell harmlessly into the pond.

The toad began to hop about, guttural gurgling noises emanating from its throat. The segment of tongue that had been sliced off catapulted from the beast, landing in the dirt near the edge of the pond not far from where Karen stood.

"Take that, you fucking bastard," Karen whispered.

Hearing her taunt, the creature turned its face to her one last time, staring with malignant intensity, then hopped from its rock into the water and disappeared beneath the surface.

Karen watched the toad leave, then turned her attention to the piece of severed tongue lying in the dirt several feet away. With a smile of grim satisfaction, she walked purposely toward it.

The piece of bright, pink tongue lay in the sunshine and was beginning to shrivel like a slice of bacon sizzling in a hot fry pan. Smiling, Karen raised her foot to stomp on the vile thing, wanting to grind it to dust.

ZAP!

Without warning, the severed tongue launched itself into the air.

Karen's mouth fell open in surprise as it hurtled toward her. It landed on her shoulder and, before she could react, the tiny barbs elongated, tearing her blouse and piercing her flesh.

Like an inchworm, the severed tongue moved down her arm, not stopping until it wrapped itself tightly around her wrist. Once secure, the tongue's barbs dug in. As they penetrated, one of them punctured her ulnar artery, causing a hot spray of blood to erupt, spattering her face and blouse.

Karen screamed as the needle-like spikes began their pulsing. Tearing at the tongue with her other hand, she cried out in fear and frustration, knowing the paralyzing poison was entering her bloodstream.

Her vision blurred, causing her to stagger as numbness spread to her arms and legs. Finally, losing consciousness, she fell to the forest floor.

BILL

HE LAY NAKED ON wrinkled, sweat-soaked sheets. It had been another difficult night, the nightmares intensifying. When he'd awakened for the second time, screaming, Susan had insisted he take one of his anti-anxiety pills. Once it took effect, he slept and did not wake again until mid-afternoon.

Rolling over to check the clock, he groaned when he saw how late it was. He sat up and rubbed his eyes, still groggy from lack of sleep and the effects of the drug. As his vision cleared, he surveyed the room around him. Susan was nowhere to be seen. He took a deep breath and called out her name, but the house was quiet except for the sound of brightly chirping birds outside the bedroom window.

Getting unsteadily to his feet, he grabbed his robe and made his way to the bathroom. He urinated noisily then downed three aspirin with a glass of water, hoping to dull the incipient hangover from the sedative he had taken.

Coffee, he thought. *And lots of it.*

In the kitchen, he noticed a new note pinned to the refrigerator door.

Sorry, you were sleeping so soundly, I didn't want to wake you and I had to leave. Hope you are okay this morning. Talk to you later. S.

He put a pod in the coffee maker, then took the note, crumpled it in his hand, and tossed it in the wastebasket. When the coffee was brewed, he grabbed his cup and went outside to the front porch. Sitting on the steps, he sipped, thinking about the night before and the dark terrors that continued to lay claim to his soul as soon as he closed his eyes.

There's something, a memory, he thought. *It's right there - right on the edge of my consciousness. I can almost touch it. If I can just remember whatever it is, maybe the night terrors will stop.*

Putting his coffee cup aside, he leaned back on his elbows and turned his face to the sun, his headache soothed by its warmth.

Again, he glanced at his watch. It was time.

His investigations into mediation techniques had finally borne fruit and he'd settled on one method in particular that had documented evidence of the ability to jumpstart repressed memories.

Excited by what he'd found in the literature, he'd begun experimenting with the technique, called "mindful meditation," the week before.

This method of meditation was best performed in a quiet space and he'd chosen the spare bedroom as the best place to practice. No one ever stayed in that room and it was pleasant with plenty of light from the windows at the back of the house.

A methodical man by nature, Bill felt it was important to keep his meditation practice to a regular schedule and, despite his headache and fatigue, was determined not to vary from it.

Tossing the rest of his coffee in the bushes, he re-entered the house and, after rinsing out his cup in the sink, returned to the second floor.

He'd taken some care to adapt the room into a space conducive to meditation. He'd moved the furniture to open up an area facing the corner where the walls met. There, he placed a low table, kitty-corner, to serve as a focal point or altar. On the table, he positioned photos from a time when he'd been happy. There was a picture of Karen on their wedding day, another of her at the beach, one of the two of them holding their newborn daughters, and one with their girls taken at Christmas. Next to these, he'd placed his wedding band and other small mementos of his life with her. The table was crowded, but it gave him a sense of peace - as if she were there with him, helping him, encouraging him on his journey.

On either side of the photos, he placed incense burners and two white candles - white selected for what he felt was the purity of his love for her.

Fearing that this display might seem strange to anyone other than himself, he'd installed a deadbolt on the door to the room and now kept it locked all the time. Susan, naturally inquisitive, had remarked on it shortly after he'd installed it.

"What's that for?" she'd asked. "You hiding someone or something in there?"

Bill remembered laughing uneasily. "This isn't Manderley, Susan. I don't have a mad woman stashed away in the spare bedroom if that's what you're getting at. I had an infestation in that room and it had to be fumigated. Smells disgusting and I don't want anyone breathing the stuff. So, I added a lock as a precaution. Islanders can be awfully nosy, you know."

He knew this explanation was flimsy, but, surprisingly, Susan seemed to accept it without question.

Now, ready to begin his meditation, he inserted the key and opened the door. The room was stuffy, so he turned on the ceiling fan and opened the windows to let in the salty sea breeze.

On the floor in front of his altar sat a densely packed, rectangular cushion called a *gomden*. All other furnishings that had once decorated this corner of the room had been removed. The result was austere, but peaceful. Sitting down on the cushion, Bill was encouraged by the sense of calm he felt.

This was a change from his first couple of meditation sessions. Tense with anticipation, he'd found the *gomden* and meditative pose uncomfortable. His leg and back muscles cramped after only a few minutes and his mind had longed for a reprieve. But determined, he'd stuck with it, and by practicing every day, the discomfort lessened, replaced by a wondrous feeling of serenity.

He took a deep breath, then leaned over, placed a couple of joss sticks in the burners, and lit them along with the candles. Then he straightened his back and sat cross-legged, hands on knees, and took a deep breath, turning his gaze to the blank wall in front of him. Focusing his mind inward on his breath, he started the process he hoped would transport him to a state of pure thought.

As usual, at first, it was difficult to rid his mind of the events of the day and he struggled to settle in. His body resisted his rigid posture, but he persevered and soon could feel his mind relaxing.

He sat still for a time, breathing in and out, allowing a jumble of unconnected memories to rise up in his mind - Karen at the beach, laughing; Susan the night they first made love; his daughters, as children and as adults. These were pleasant memories and he was loath to leave them. But, as his mind longed to concentrate on his past life, he knew he had to bring it back to the present, so he returned his thought processes once again to his breath, focusing on inhaling and exhaling the fresh, salty air.

Soon, images once again began to crowd his mind, but these were not so amiable - Dex with his arms around Karen, kissing her deeply; himself, lying in a hospital bed, barely alive, his body emaciated from the effects of his abandonment on Puffin.

As these memories danced across his consciousness, he felt his anger begin to rise and, once again, forced himself to come back to his breath, eliminating the bad karma the images brought with them. Soon, he felt himself relax, and again random thoughts began to waft across his mind. After a while, he became so caught up in these images, he forgot he was sitting on the floor of his spare bedroom, but instead felt he was floating on some sort of strange, astral plane.

A beautiful memory of Karen nursing their girls drifted before his eyes and he smiled as he gazed at it lovingly with his mind's eye. But it was soon replaced by another more frightening picture of a scarecrow of a man, sharpening a shard of rock into some semblance of a crude knife.

He felt his body tense as the remote memory began to flee, but, unwilling to let it go, forced his mind to hold on to it fiercely.

I made a knife! he thought.

As he grasped this recollection, more pictures of himself using the knife flooded his consciousness. He was prying open clams and cutting brush. He saw himself adapting the blade so that, tied to a stick, it became a sort of spear, and with it in hand, he waded waist-deep into the ocean, eventually returning to shore holding a wiggling, silver, fish.

He smiled at what he saw as his prowess, but his pride in his ingenuity was short-lived as another memory surfaced that caused him to grip his knees tightly in shock.

He was standing on the beach, holding a fat, squirming vole by the tail as he put it, still alive, in his mouth.

As soon as this image flooded his mind, an acidic stream of bile erupted from his stomach, breaking his concentration.

Jesus Christ, he thought, *I ate those nasty rodents. And I ate them alive!*

Knowing his trance was irreparably broken, he got to his feet, ignoring the pain caused by his cramped muscles, and hurriedly left the room. Running to the bathroom, he knelt over the toilet, his body racked by dry heaves.

When he'd purged himself of what little food he had ingested over the last twenty-four hours, he stood up, rinsed out his mouth, and brushed his teeth.

Finally, feeling back in control, he tried to recapture all the images of his imprisonment that the deep meditative state had revealed. Slowly, they flashed before his mind, one by one.

This meditation works, he thought, smiling. *It's hard, but it's a hell of a lot cheaper than that charlatan who calls himself a doctor in Boston. Every day I'll sit there until it all comes back. Then I'll know for certain who did this to me, and if it was that damned fisherman, I'll stuff a fucking vole down his throat and see how he likes it.*

Nodding, he returned to the spare bedroom, snuffed out the candles, and locked the door securely. Feeling a profound weariness, he decided it was time for something to eat. Walking down the staircase, he pictured again the knife he'd made on Puffin.

It's the first clear memory I've had.

Suddenly, another image appeared before his eyes, causing him to grip the stair rail to keep from falling.

A man, huddled on a dirt floor, roasting something over a small fire.

He studied the memory for a moment, shaking his head in wonder, as he made his way to the kitchen. There was leftover pizza in the refrigerator and, suddenly famished, he reached for the plate.

As he took it from the shelf, the image again rose up in his mind, but this time in more detail. Shocked by what he saw, the plate slipped from his hand and shattered when it hit the floor. But he was too intent on the memory to notice or care.

What the fuck? he thought. *I'm wearing a sailor's pea coat. Where the hell did that come from?*

He stood for a moment, concentrating on the picture of himself by the fire, then, shaking his head, glanced at the broken plate and pizza that now decorated the kitchen floor.

Leaning over, he began to slowly pick up the pieces of stoneware, his mind still bewildered by what he had remembered.

I need to talk to someone about this, he thought as he put the broken dish and spoiled food in the wastebasket. *But who? Susan's working and Lord knows she doesn't like to be disturbed at the studio. Terri? No, I don't think she can give me the insight I need.*

He got out the vacuum and began to go over the floor, hoping to pick up any errant shards of crockery that might still remain. When he finished and was satisfied the floor was again spotless, he grabbed his windbreaker and car keys and headed out the door.

He knew who he needed to talk to. He always knew.

# KAREN

SHE FELT A SHARP pain. Startled, Karen opened her eyes. She was lying in the soft grass on the side of the trail with Shawn bending over her, his hand poised to slap her again on the cheek.

"Finally," he said when he saw she had regained consciousness. "Can you sit up?"

Karen nodded as Shawn helped her to a seated position.

Slowly, she gazed around at the pond and the forest beyond. The memory of the attack by the severed tongue flashed across her mind and she shrunk back, leaning into Shawn's arms.

"You're safe now," he said, trying to quell the panic he could see building in her eyes. "It's okay. It's gone. Look."

He lifted her hand in front of her face. Her wrist was now wrapped in a white handkerchief that was dotted with blood.

"It's gone? Really gone?" she asked. "How?"

Shawn smiled. "That was one hell of a scream you put out. When I heard it, I came running. When I got here, you were yelling and pulling on that thing attached your wrist. Blood was spraying everywhere, but before I could help you, you passed out."

"But how did you get it off me? It was dug in with those barbs."

"I cut it with my pocketknife. Those needle-like things had pierced your skin and I had to pull some of them out with tweezers. Sorry if it hurt, but you were bleeding like a stuck pig. I thought I'd have to call 911, but as soon as that thing was off you and the needles out, the bleeding stopped. Wouldn't be surprised if you're not completely healed by now."

Karen unwrapped the bandage and examined her wrist. It did look normal except for some bruising. "Where ... What did you do with it?"

"You mean that thing?"

Karen nodded.

"I burned it. See over there."

He gestured to a pile of ashes about a foot away.

"Burned it, why?"

"Burning is an act of purification. At least that's what my mom says. So, I lit that bastard on fire. You should have seen it. Flame shot up about six feet in the air. Stunk like hell, too. But it was gone in a flash. You don't have to be afraid anymore. What was that thing anyway?"

Karen shuddered at the thought of it. "It was a piece of the frog's tongue. I threw the knife, just like you taught me. The frog's instinct took over and it went for it. The blade sliced its tongue in two and a piece of hit landed over there. I thought it was harmless and was going to stomp it. I guess I was wrong. Can you help me up?"

Shawn took her arm and helped her to her feet.

"You okay? You're not going to faint again, are you?" he asked.

Karen shook her head. "No. I think I can walk now. Let's get the hell out of here."

Shawn smiled and, giving her his arm for support, led her back to the main trail.

On the drive to return to the cottage, Shawn called Terri on his cell.

"Hey, girl, it's all over. We're on our way home."

"Is everything okay?"

"Yeah. Everything's fine, but I don't want you to be alarmed when you see your mother. She's okay. We should be there in ten."

He hung up, not waiting for Terri's response.

Karen watched him, smiling.

"You didn't give her a chance to question you, did you?"

Shawn grinned sheepishly. "No. How was I going to explain about that tongue thing and all the blood? You look a mess, you know. Blood on you shirt, in your hair, on your face."

Karen reached up and ran her fingers through her hair. It did feel sticky. She pulled down the visor to look in the mirror.

"Jesus H. Christ!" she muttered. "I look like something out of the *Texas Chainsaw Massacre*!"

She checked her watch. "Shawn, can you speed it up? I've got to get cleaned up before Dex comes home."

"Sure," he replied, laughing as he pushed the pedal to the floor. "Now we'll be home in seven!"

Terri was waiting for them on the porch when they arrived. Her shock at seeing her mother's condition was immediately apparent despite Shawn's warning and Karen spent a few minutes convincing her daughter she was okay.

Once inside the house, Karen poured herself two fingers of Jack Daniels and tossed it back.

"That's better," she said. "Okay, honey, now I'll tell you what happened."

Sitting on the couch, she related to Terri in detail what had occurred in the woods.

"It was just like that old Indian said it would be," she concluded, referring to Harry Three-Feathers. "The toad's instinct took over when it saw that shiny knife sailing through the air. The tongue forgot all about me and went after it."

"But you were lucky, weren't you? That piece of it almost got you."

Karen sighed. "Yes, once again I was foolish and thought for a moment I was invincible. But Shawn was there and I'm thankful for that."

"Let me see your wrist again," demanded Terri, still fearful that her mother's injuries might return.

Karen held out her hand. The bruises were beginning to fade.

Terri shook her head in amazement.

"Now, I'm going to have to excuse myself and send you all on home," said Karen, gazing down at her bloodstained clothing. "I need to take a shower and get cleaned up before Dex gets here. Otherwise, I'm going to have to come up with some sort of excuse for my appearance."

Terri gave her mother a reproachful look and was about to speak, but Karen cut her off.

"I know. You think I should just blurt out the truth. Tell him everything. Right?"

Terri nodded.

Karen raised her eyebrows. "Sure, and he'll say 'Let me see your hand, princess, you know I went to medical school and all.'"

Terri laughed; her mother's impersonation of her stepfather was spot on.

"And then I show him this hand and wrist."

Again, she held up her arm. The bruises were gone and the skin looked pink and healthy. There were no remaining signs of the tongue's vicious attack.

"And what do you think he'll do when he sees this? He'll pat me on the head and excuse himself to go call the men in white coats to haul me off to the same loony bin your father was at for so many years. He'll visit me on weekends to wipe the drool off my chin and try to comb my matted hair."

"Okay, okay," conceded Terri with a laugh. "You get cleaned up so you don't have to lie to him. But someday, you're going to have to tell him everything. It's not right keeping him in the dark like this."

Karen stood. "You tend to your business and I'll tend to mine. Now, again, Shawn, thank you for saving me. I'm in your debt. And, honey, thanks for taking care of Alex. You must have worn him out but good; he's sleeping so soundly."

Terri opened her mouth to say something but thought better of it.

Karen walked them to the door gave them each a hug, then watched until their truck disappeared down the drive. Closing the door, she checked one more time on her baby then headed to the bathroom for a hot shower.

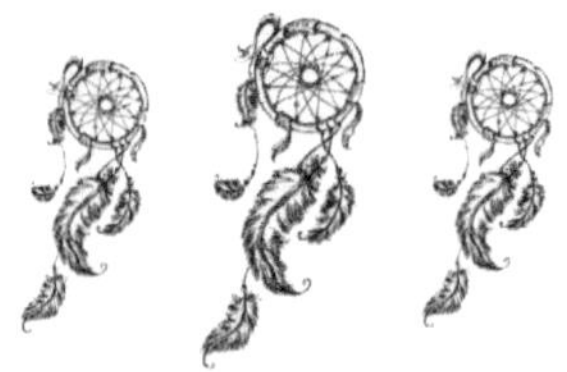

On the way home, Shawn again recounted the events that took place in the woods, providing more detail.

"Seriously, when I heard your mom scream, I took off. When I got to the clearing, it looked like the end of one of those slasher movies, blood everywhere. Really gross. And that piece of tongue or whatever it was - that was totally obscene. I had to cut it off her with my knife, then pull out the spikes it left behind in your mom's skin. I almost lost my lunch. They were totally nasty."

Terri laughed. "I'm glad you were there for her. It might have turned out really bad if you hadn't been."

Shawn nodded. "And that's about it."

"Okay," said Terri, a grin on her face. "Now it's my turn. Wait till I tell you what happened at the cottage while you guys were gone..."

BILL AND KAREN

TWENTY MINUTES AFTER SHAWN and Terri drove off, Bill pulled up the driveway. As he parked, he noted that Dex's truck was nowhere to be seen, but that Karen's car was in the garage. Sure she was home, he bounded up the steps and knocked lightly on the door. He waited for a minute, but there was no answer. He knocked again.

She's home. I know it, he thought. *Maybe she's out on the deck and can't hear me.*

Hesitantly, he tried the doorknob. It was unlocked. Convincing himself he was doing nothing wrong, he entered the house, shutting the door noisily behind him. He stood for a moment gazing around the empty foyer looking for Karen. A voice from the back of the house startled him.

"I'm in the bathroom, Dex!" she yelled. "I just finished showering."

Confused for a moment and feeling a strong sense of *déjà vu*, Bill took a step toward the voice.

The bathroom door was ajar and, peering inside, he could see Karen standing in front of the mirror. She was bent over drying her hair, her face obscured by the towel. She was wearing a white terrycloth robe, which hung loosely around her slender body, and, as she moved, he could see flashes of her bare skin beneath.

Feeling as if he were in a dream, he crept into the room, silently coming up behind her. Without hesitation, he wound his arms around her waist, pulling her to him as he slipped his hands under her robe.

"My, my, but you're the frisky one today," she said dropping the towel and leaning back into his embrace. Her eyes were closed and she gave the impression of enjoying the sensation of his hands on her naked body.

Encouraged, he moved one hand to her belly and gently stroked her while his other hand journeyed lower. Finding her mound, he spread his fingers, entwining them in her damp, silky hair.

She moaned as he ventured further, searching out the cleft he had once known so well. His rested his thumb on what he used to call her "sweet spot" and, when she gasped in response, began to gently caress her.

Her hips were now moving sensuously against his and he leaned over and bit her lightly on the neck as he continued to move his thumb rhythmically.

Moaning with passion, she turned in his arms facing him, her eyes opening.

"What the f-!" she cried. "How dare you!"

With anger etched across her face, she shoved him violently with the flat of her hands, pushing him away from her as she pulled her robe tight, knotting the sash.

Surprised by her response, Bill tripped and fell backward, landing on the wet tile floor. He stared at her blankly as the reality of what he had just done washed over him. He was about to say something, to apologize, but she silenced him with a wave of her hand.

"Have you lost your mind? Coming in here. Violating me that way. You're damned lucky Dex didn't come home to see that."

Bill pulled himself to his feet. "Kar, I didn't mean ... I just came over to talk to you, but you looked so..."

"Shut up. Now I'm giving you thirty seconds to get the hell out of here before I call Dex or the police."

She picked up her cell phone, which had been lying on the counter next to the sink.

"Time starts right now."

Seeing the determination in her expression, he muttered a quick apology and hastily ran to the front door.

He jogged down the steps and leapt into his car, backing quickly down the drive.

Once he was clear of the house, he slowed and pulled the car onto a road marked "Right Of Way to the Shore." The winding dirt lane was deserted and he parked at its end.

Taking a deep breath, he leaned back in his seat, silently listening to the sound of the waves as they pounded against the rocks.

Slowly, he lifted his hand to his face. He could still smell her. He moved his fingers to his nose and breathed deeply, his mind reliving the feel of her warm, damp skin as he'd caressed her.

He moved his other hand to his crotch.

Just the smell of her got him hard.

He unzipped his fly and, releasing himself, began to move his hand up and down his turgid shaft, feeling transported to a height of ecstasy he'd never known existed. Again, he breathed deeply, delighting in her pungent aroma.

When he felt he could stand it no longer, he slipped his fingers into his mouth, sucking greedily on the last remnants of her sweet juices as he bucked his hips forward and ejaculated into his hand.

He leaned back in his seat, his wilted member lying limply in his palm, beads of spent sperm dripping down his fingers.

She's mine, he thought. *All mine.*

At the cottage, Karen stared out the window as Bill's car rapidly disappeared from sight.

Sweet Jesus, she thought. *Has he lost his mind?*

She pulled her robe closed, hugging her body, as she remembered how he'd touched her so intimately. *Should I shower again? I feel dirty now.*

She started to walk back to the bathroom, but turned and stared at the front door. Decisively, she clicked the deadbolt into place.

To hell with that "we're on the island, we don't need to lock the door" crap. I don't care what Dex says, that door is staying locked from now on.

Nodding, she started back to the shower but was stopped by the sound of her child crying.

Oh shit, she sighed. *Guess I'll just have to live with the grease from his fingers on me. It's not like they haven't been there before. Thank God, he stopped when I recognized him and didn't try to go any further.*

She turned toward the bedroom and her child but stopped when she heard the sound of a car pulling up the drive. Warily, she peered out the window. Dex was home.

Breathing a sigh of relief, she gazed at the locked door and, biting her bottom lip, pulled back the deadbolt. She couldn't tell him what happened and she didn't have the energy to get into an argument with him about home security. That would have to wait for another day.

Feeling suddenly very weary, she took a deep breath and turned to answer the cries of her now very distressed child.

BILL

IT WAS BEGINNING TO get dark when Bill arrived back at his house. Tired and hungry, he poured himself a drink then went to the kitchen to prepare something to eat. He took a frozen meal from the refrigerator, put it in the microwave, then sat down at the kitchen table and pulled out his cell phone. Turning it on, he noted he had two messages.

One was a text from Susan. She was meeting with the detective who had accompanied them to Puffin to go over preliminary DNA results. She asked did he want to meet her for dinner the next evening to review the findings. He texted her back that he would meet her at The Harbormaster's Restaurant at eight p.m.

The thought of the remains found on Puffin ruined his appetite and he got up and poured himself another drink.

The second message was a voicemail and he recognized the area code as Boston. It was from his psychiatrist. There was concern and almost a hint of panic in the man's voice as he questioned Bill about the advisability of canceling his appointments. The doctor pointed out again that restoring memory was a long process and one not to be taken lightly. He urged Bill to call him back or, at the least, to make another appointment.

Bill smiled as he deleted the message.

Wouldn't the good doctor be surprised to find that I can reclaim my memory on my own? And why is he so concerned anyway? Probably afraid of missing a payment on his yacht or something.

The microwave signaled his meal was ready and Bill found his appetite restored by deleting the message from the doctor. Spooning the casserole onto a plate, he sat down to eat. As he chewed his food, his thoughts returned to his encounter with Karen.

You shouldn't have wasted your time with all that foreplay, he chided himself. *She was ready and willing. She could have been yours.*

He chuckled softly, imagining sneaking up behind her, lifting her robe, and entering her roughly. He held on to that image for a moment, savoring it, when a voice from somewhere in the back of his mind began screaming at him.

"This is not you! You love her. You can't violate her!"

As this voice echoed across his consciousness, Karen's image began to blur and fade. He tried desperately to recapture it, but it was gone.

"NO!" he screamed as he pushed the voice away, burying it until it was only a muted buzzing, like an annoying mosquito on a hot summer's night.

Again, he pictured himself taking her by force, but this time the image held no pleasure. This time he recognized it for what it was ... rape.

Disgusted with himself, he threw the rest of his meal into the garbage disposal, leaving the plate in the sink. He poured himself another drink and walked outside to the porch.

Sitting on the steps, he wondered what was happening to him.

I've never done anything like that ... never even entertained the thought of abusing someone that way. What's wrong with me? Maybe I've made a mistake canceling Dr. Burgess. But how could I tell him about these thoughts? They're too obscene.

He sat quietly for a while, thinking about what he'd almost done to Karen. Finally, he stood and walked back into the house.

It was an aberration brought on by the situation. I'd never do it again, would I? No, it was just a lapse in judgment. It doesn't mean anything's wrong with me. I don't need to see that shrink. I'm doing just fine on my own.

KAREN

THE NEXT MORNING, KAREN took Alex out back and settled him on a blanket playing with his toys. It was a pleasant day and she planned to work on some new jewelry designs.

After studying the colorful shards of glass that she'd recently found on the beach, she quickly set to work sketching out her ideas. Alex was content playing on the blanket and, every so often, Karen would put her work aside and join him for a few minutes.

They passed the morning this way. Happy with what she'd accomplished, she decided to call it quits and go back to the cottage for lunch. She was packing her sketchpad and bag of glass into her carryall when a scream of delight from Alex caught her attention.

"What's up, sweetie?" she asked, turning her head toward the boy.

He was bouncing up and down on the blanket, his chubby arms raised in the air, fingers pointing at something in the woods beyond.

"What is it?" she asked. "What do you see?"

Eyes following her boy's fingertips, she gasped when she saw what he was pointing at. A large owl was perched on a branch in one of the trees closest to them, a small creature clasped in its talons.

Alarmed, Karen dropped her bag, letting pieces of sea glass tumble out.

"Stay still, Alex," she whispered. "Don't move."

With care not to disturb the raptor, she cautiously crossed the distance from her chair to the blanket. But, as she reached out toward her child, the owl spread its wings and swooped down off the branch, landing between her and the boy.

Panicking, she tried to move around the creature and get to her child, intending to shield him and, if possible, pick him up and run to safety. But as she neared him, he turned and stared at her with eyes no longer those of an excited one-year-old.

"Alex, what...?"

A blinding pain assaulted her left temple, causing her to fall to her knees in the grass, as a small childlike voice penetrated her consciousness.

"Fear not, sweet mother. This creature is my kinsman and bears me no harm."

As he spoke, brilliant streams of golden light began to glow around his small body and Karen watched in wonder as the owl bowed its head to him as if in homage. In response, Alex nodded slightly and reached out his palm. Seeming to understand the gesture, the raptor unclenched its talons, releasing the small rodent it had apparently brought as tribute.

The tiny creature froze for a second, lifted its head and sniffed the air, then turned and darted toward Alex, settling itself gratefully in his palm. Alex stroked its tiny head with his finger then leaned over and whispered something softly in its ear. The creature looked at him once more, nodded, then scurried rapidly away toward the house, apparently unharmed.

Alex smiled benignly as he watched it go.

The owl observed all this, then turned its gaze to Karen.

A wave of fear pierced her heart as the creature locked its eyes with hers. She sat frozen, her mind in turmoil, wondering what was going to happen next. Seconds passed as they stared at each other, then to her surprise, the raptor blinked once and lowered its head in a gesture of submission.

Astounded, Karen held her breath as another stab of pain pierced her temple and her child's voice again echoed in her mind.

"Do not worry, sweet mother. My kinsman only wishes to pay homage to you and, since he is a noble creature and blessed by my father, it is only right that you acknowledge his fealty."

Nodding, Karen let out her breath as she tried to comprehend what her boy was telling her. The owl meant her no harm.

Biting her bottom lip, she turned her eyes back toward the raptor. She stared at it for several seconds, then, conceding to her son's wishes, nodded slightly.

The raptor gave her a soft hoot in response, turned its gaze back to Alex, then launched itself into the air. As it ascended to the sky above, the boy lifted his eyes to it, sending out streams of golden light to surround and shadow it in its flight.

When it was out of sight, the light disappeared and the boy turned his head back to his mother, eyes once again normal. Smiling, he reached out for her.

Karen lifted him in her arms, relieved that he was her little boy again.

Shaking her head, she leaned down and tried to collect the pieces of sea glass that were now hidden in the grass. When she had all she could find, she grabbed her carryall and, with her child on hip, walked hurriedly back to the house.

BILL AND SUSAN

BILL ARRIVED AT THE Harbormaster's Restaurant early and, after checking on his reservation, went into the bar to wait for Susan.

As he sipped his cocktail, he thought about the evening ahead and Susan's dogged insistence that her investigation of the missing men would ultimately benefit him.

None of those men were fishing at the same time as Dex. He was just a kid then. So, what difference does it make if they were killed and their bodies dumped on Puffin? I'm only interested in who took me there, not in some ancient history. But Susan will expect me to be all excited about it and, I guess, I'd better not disappoint.

He checked his watch. She would be arriving any minute. Mentally, he conjured up a picture of her, comparing her to Karen. He was lost in thought when he felt a tap on his shoulder.

"Hey, you," Susan exclaimed. "Are you off on another planet or something? I've been standing here for a couple of minutes already."

Startled, Bill quickly recovered, turned, and smiled at her. "Just thinking. Sorry. Have a seat. Our table should be ready in a few minutes. What do you want to drink?"

Susan slipped onto the barstool next to him as he placed her order. They chatted briefly about mundane matters until the hostess came over and informed them their table was ready. After placing their dinner order, Susan turned the conversation to her meeting with Detective Wallace.

"Okay, here's the gist of it. We think that the skeletons found on Puffin came from at least five different people, right?"

"Yeah, that's your supposition and the police sent samples out for DNA analysis to confirm it. You already told me all that."

Susan bit her bottom lip, a slight scowl on her face. "Yes, I know. I'm just summarizing. You have a problem with that?"

Bill smiled contritely. "Sorry. Go on."

Susan took a deep breath, apparently a bit miffed by his attitude. "Okay. So, yesterday, I met with Wallace and the results are back. They confirm the five body hypothesis."

"So? Now we know for sure five different people died on Puffin. How does that tie in with your theory? I'd be surprised if there were ever any need for DNA testing on any of these guys when they were alive and I doubt that their wives kept strands of hair or wads of dried spit on hand waiting for someone to come along and find a bunch of bones."

Susan frowned again, aware of the veiled sarcasm in his tone. "Just wait," she responded. "Let me finish. Be a little patient, okay?"

Bill took a sip of his drink. "Sure. Sorry. Go on."

"You asked how we checked the DNA on these deceased men since there are probably no viable hair, skin or other samples to compare to, right?"

Bill nodded.

"DNA runs in families, Bill. It's likely that we can get a match if the sample from the bones is compared to that of a close relation, say, a son or a daughter. And, that's what we're doing. Five of the six men were married and had children. Wallace has talked to these offspring and has obtained permission to run analyses on them. When we get those results back, we'll know."

"But you said only five of the six men had children. What about the sixth? And which one was he anyway?"

"The environmentalist - the outlier of the group. However, he is survived by a sister and she's also agreed to be tested."

"And how long will all this take?"

"It's being expedited. We should have our answers in a few days."

The waitress returned, bringing their entrees, and they sat quietly eating, the tension between them almost palpable.

"So, what's your problem, anyway?" asked Susan, slapping her fork down on the table. "I'm doing all this for you."

Bill laughed. "For me? Explain it to me. How does any of this benefit me?"

Susan held her breath, trying to rein in her temper. "Pay attention. If these bones are identified as belonging to any of the six men, then we have evidence that Puffin was used as a dumping ground. Assume that happens, okay? Then the question becomes 'who did the dumping?' Right?"

Bill nodded. "But, how..."

"Don't interrupt. I'm not through. With the exception of Howard Nichols, the nature guy, all of these men had ties to the lobster industry and all of them had documented run-ins with local fisherman. If it can be proven that those locals were from Mateguas, then we will have established a culture of violence that spans decades. And, if we can prove one of those fishermen was Lonnie Pierce, then we have a direct link from this culture to your ex-wife's husband. In other words, if Lonnie dumped one or more of these men on Puffin, it stems to reason that Dex knew about it or, at the least, suspected it. Ergo, when he needed to get rid of someone - namely you - he knew just where to do it. Do you understand now how this affects you? Is there anything I haven't made clear?"

Bill lifted a forkful of food to his mouth, taking his time before responding. He could see she was angry and, perversely, wanted to stoke the fire a little bit more before acknowledging the logic in her explanation.

Susan drummed her fork on the table waiting.

"Okay, I get it now," he said, reaching out and taking her hand. "Sorry, I was so obtuse. It's been a rough week and I'm tired and a little testy."

Susan pursed her lips, nodding.

"Okay, I forgive you. But I'm not finished. What I didn't mention is about the environmentalist. He has direct ties to the Pierce family. He was friends with Dex's mother from way back when they were children. If it can be proven that his bones were found on Puffin, that's even more concrete evidence that Lonnie Pierce may have been involved."

Bill nodded. "I get it now. Good work, Susan. If it all plays out, it should be quite a feather in your cap down at the station."

As he spoke, he raised his drink glass in a mock salute, a sarcastic smile on his face.

Susan angrily pushed back her chair and stood. "I don't know what your problem is, but I'm not going to sit here and be the butt of your jokes. I've worked my tail off to help you and, yes, it IS going to benefit me, too. But what's wrong with that? We both end up winners, but you're too self-absorbed to see that."

Without waiting for his response, she threw her napkin down on the table, grabbed her purse, and started to walk toward the restaurant's entrance.

Realizing that he had gone too far mocking her, Bill jumped up and followed, grabbing her by the elbow.

When she felt his hand, she whirled around, her face a mask of hurt and anger.

"I'm sorry, babe," he said softly. "I really am. My behavior was out of line. You're right, I should be grateful, and I am. It's just that ... no, no excuses. Please forgive me."

Susan's face softened. "Okay. But don't start again. I really want this to work out for both of us. All right?"

Bill nodded. "Now let's go back to the table and I'll order a bottle of bubbly. Would you like that?"

"Sure."

He put his arm around her shoulders and steered her back to the dining room. As he pulled out her chair, he motioned to the waitress.

"A bottle of your best champagne, please. We're celebrating."

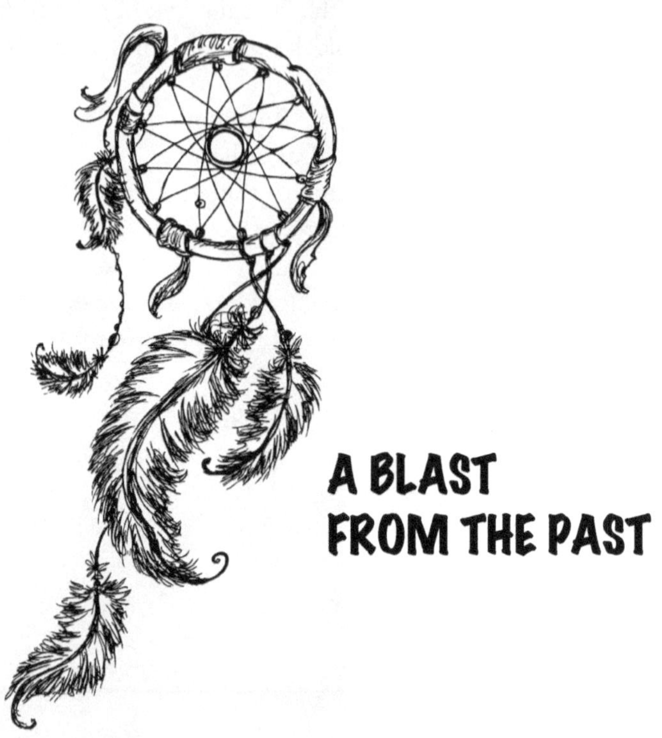

A BLAST FROM THE PAST

THE NEXT MORNING, KAREN swiftly cleaned up the breakfast dishes and loaded Alex into his car seat. She had spoken with Louise McKinney the night before, asking if she could come by for a visit, and Louise had happily agreed.

Driving the short distance to the older woman's house, Karen considered how to approach her about the subject of Dex and the LaPlante girl,

I can't just blurt out my suspicions, she thought. *Louise is a nice woman, but she is a bit of a busybody and, if I let on that I'm concerned, it will be all over the island in no time. I'll have to come at it sideways, somehow. Let her think it was her idea to bring it up.*

Pulling into the drive, she was pleased to see Louise waiting on the porch. The woman was now well into her sixties but still looked the same as she had twelve years before when Karen first met her on the ferryboat.

254

"Karen!" exclaimed Louise. "How nice to see you again."

Karen hopped from the car and gave the older woman a hug. "Good to see you too, Louise. You look great."

"And is that the little one? Here, hand him to me."

Karen smiled and took Alex from his car seat, placing him in Louise's waiting arms.

"My goodness, he's a big boy," she declared, settling him on her hip. "My grandbabies won't be here until later this summer and they're all grown beyond this stage now. Sure is nice to be holding a toddler again."

"Well, if he gets too heavy for you, let me know."

"Don't you worry about that. Pete says I'm strong as an ox. Now, why don't we go around back to the garden? I've got a pitcher of iced tea cooling in the fridge and some freshly baked cookies to go with. Your boy can play while we catch up."

Karen nodded and followed her around the house to the patio. While Karen settled Alex on a blanket, Louise went inside and came back a few minutes later with a tray laden with iced tea and cookies.

After pouring the tea, Louise sat down, chatting amiably about her children.

"And where are your boys?" asked Karen.

"Brian's in California and Pete Junior is in Alaska. He works the pipeline. Both are way too far away for my liking. But kids have to do their own thing, as they say. I'm just glad they still see fit to visit every summer. And this winter, Pete and I might just take a trip out west."

"That sounds good."

Louise smiled and took a bite of her cookie. "Now, you said you wanted to talk to me about something. Seemed serious."

Karen nodded. "Yes, but it's not really a big deal. You've known Dex for a long time, right?"

"Yes, his whole life, actually. Pete and I were friends with his parents."

"Exactly. I don't know if you're aware of it, but he doesn't talk about them much, probably because of the way they died. So,

I don't know much about them and was wondering if you could fill me in a bit. Now that we have a child of our own, I like to know a little more about his background."

Louise frowned and took a sip of her drink. "Sure, let me tell you about his mother. Her name was Patricia and she was a good woman. Smart, but a bit on the shy side. You look like her, you know."

Karen couldn't hide her surprise. "I do? How so?"

"She was blonde like you; wore her hair long and, most of the time, tied it back in a ponytail or braid. She had big blue eyes and a beautiful smile. She was a summer girl; her family lived in Connecticut. She met Lonnie, that's Dex's dad, at a dance."

"What was he like?"

"Good-looking man. Dex has his coloring and features. Hard worker, too. But he could cross a line now and then."

"What do you mean by that?"

Louise sighed. "He could get a little rough. A barroom brawl wasn't out of character with him, if you know what I mean."

"Tell me more."

Louise prattled on for a while about Dex's father and lobstering, but Karen only half-listened. She wanted to steer the conversation around to the LaPlante girl but was at a loss as to how to go about it. Finally, she decided to just blurt it out.

"Have you been watching that new TV program the LeVeque woman hosts on Sunday nights? The one about cold cases?"

Louise hesitated for a moment. "Ayup, guess the whole island's been watching that and wondering what that fool woman will come up with next. I'll wager Dex has been glued to the screen."

"Yes, I'm afraid he has. It's been unpleasant for him, to say the least."

Louise chuckled. "I'll bet. All that stuff about that poor girl. And that reporter trying to insinuate that Dex had something to do with her murder. I'll bet that riled him up some."

"Yes, you're right about that. He was upset. Did you know her? The LaPlante girl?"

Louise shook her head. "She wasn't an islander and I don't believe she ever came over here to visit. Still, her death was a shock back then. We don't have many murders in this part of the country and a young girl, pregnant and strangled, well, it got everyone's attention, for sure."

Karen leaned back in her chair, trying to look casual. "She was a very attractive young girl."

"Ayup, she was," replied Louise, cocking her head to the side and frowning. "You know, she kind of looks like you, too. All three of you, blue-eyed blondes. Interesting."

The two women were silent for a moment, then Louise stood. "You want to see some pictures?"

"Pictures?"

"You know, of Patricia and Lonnie, and some of Dex from back then."

"I'd love to," Karen replied.

"I'll be right back."

Karen watched as Louise went inside the house.

That cinches it, she thought. *Louise sees the resemblance, too. But it's not just Evie and me. It all starts with his mother. Does he have some sort of Freudian fixation?*

Her thoughts were interrupted when Louise returned, carrying a large photo album.

"This is from the time before all that digital stuff," she said placing the album in Karen's lap. "Real Kodak photos. Take a look."

Karen opened the scrapbook at random. There were numerous photos of Louise, Pete, their children, and other unidentified family members.

Louise reached over and flipped the pages until she came to a picture of a young woman holding an infant. The photo was faded, but Karen could see the woman was blonde and had features much like her own.

"Is that Dex and his mother?" she asked.

"Yes. That was taken after his christening. And, here," she said as she again flipped the pages. "That's Lonnie, the proud papa."

Louise pointed out more photos, spanning the years between Dex's birth and his parents' death.

"And that's about it," she said, closing the album. "It was a sad day when they died. Senseless."

Karen nodded. "Yes, but don't you think, in the more recent pictures you just showed me, his mother looks sad. I mean, her smile in those last shots, it seems forced."

Louise frowned. "You know, you're right. In those last months before they died, she retreated into herself. She'd always been very active in local events, but that last winter, she was hardly seen. Some thought maybe she had a sickness."

"And Lonnie, did he retreat, too?"

Louise laughed as she reached for the pitcher. "No way. He was always larger than life. Nothing kept him down. More tea?"

"Oh, no, I'm fine," replied Karen. "And thank you for sharing those pictures. It looks like Dex had a good family. It's too bad that LeVeque woman is trying to stir things up. It brings back all kinds of bad memories for him. Say, were you and Pete at that beach party the night that girl disappeared?"

Louise's eyes narrowed as she thought for a minute.

"No, we weren't. That was a kid's party. Pete and I were grown-ups. We weren't invited!"

"Seems strange to me; a beach party in January?"

"Not strange here, honey. Mateguan kids will party whenever they have a mind to. No, I can't shed any light on what went on at that shindig. Why, do you think Dex is lying when he says he was there?"

Louise's question caught Karen off-guard and she stiffened visibly. "Oh, no," she stammered. "Nothing like that. I just thought it was strange, that's all."

As she spoke, she glanced at her watch. "Oh, my, it's getting late. I've taken up enough of your time. Thanks so much for having me."

She quickly gathered up her boy and walked with Louise back to her car.

"You and Pete will have to come over for dinner some night soon. I know Dex would like that."

"Sounds good," Louise replied, giving Karen a hug. "Just let me know when."

A while later, sitting on the deck at the cottage, Karen thought about the pictures Louise had shared with her.

They looked like a real family on the surface, but what if they weren't? From what Louise said, his father was a badass, but his mother was educated and shy. Oil and water - it doesn't mix and could have been a recipe for disaster.

She closed her eyes, picturing Dex's mother and then Evelyn LaPlante.

We all look the same. I wonder if he even realizes it.

She sighed and stared out at the sea.

We used to always take time on Sundays for ourselves, go to the movies, dinner, or just exploring. But now, all he wants to do is stay home and watch that damned show.

She thought about Susan's last broadcast. As predicted, the LaPlante case had been dropped in favor of reopening an investigation into six disappearances spanning thirty-five years. Karen had found the cases slightly boring, but Dex had been glued to the screen, especially when Susan spoke about the last man, Howard Nichols.

He was a summer person, too, Karen thought. *But, when I asked Dex if he knew him, he equivocated and said he'd heard of him, but that was all. Then Susan posted that picture of Nichols with Dex's mother. Boy, did his face turn red. He had to backpedal and say maybe the guy had been out to the house once or twice. But why would he lie in the first place? What difference does it make whether he knew the man or not? Unless, he knows something about his disappearance that he's not telling.*

Karen thought for a moment about Patricia Pierce, mentally comparing Susan's photo with the ones Louise had shown her earlier.

Susan's photo didn't do the woman justice. I think it must have been from an old newspaper print, grainy and in black and white. That's why I didn't see the resemblance. The pictures Louise has are much better quality.

Feeling troubled, she leaned back in her chair and closed her eyes.

Dex has been out of sorts ever since that show premiered and it's affecting our lives in so many ways. We used to laugh all the time, but now he's moody and sullen. It's affecting our sex life, too. Things were very intense between us after the first LaPlante broadcast, but since then he's always too tired. We had a very healthy relationship before we came here, but now he laughs and says he's getting old. For Christ's sake, he's only forty-eight!

Yes, everything dates from that Evelyn LaPlante show and yet he still says she was only a friend. Well, I'm beginning to think that he's not telling me the whole truth.

She sat up and leaned forward, looking over the rail at the sea below.

Things here should be good for us for a change. There've been no murderous owls, deadly trails into the woods, or swamp hag waiting to pounce on us. Oh, there was that stupid toad, but I haven't seen hide or hair of him since the knife throwing. And Alex is acting normal again, too, just like any regular little boy. Even the girls seem to be doing okay ... Terri here, with Shawn, and Sophie in New Haven, working and going to summer school. Yeah, everything's good, except for Dex. And what I'm going to do about it, I don't know, but something has to be done and soon.

SUSAN

SUSAN'S PRODUCTION ASSISTANT ANSWERED the phone, spoke for a minute, then handed the receiver to her.

"I think you're going to want to take this one," he said.

Susan scowled at him as she grabbed the phone from his hand.

"This is Susan."

"Hi, glad you're in. It's Pete, Pete Wallace."

"Hi, Pete. What you got for me?"

The detective laughed. "You always get right to the point, don't you? I called to let you know I forwarded you an email. Did you get it?"

Susan's heart began to race. This could be it.

"Just a minute," she said as she opened her mail folder.

She groaned inwardly when she saw her mailbox was full. There had to be over fifty new messages.

"You said you forwarded it. Who did it come from originally?"

"Maine State Police Crime Lab in Augusta. It's addressed to the Chief with a carbon to me."

Susan nodded and did a quick search of her messages. Finding the one she wanted, she leaned forward, scanning its contents.

"Find it?"

"Hallelujah!" she exclaimed. "I was right!"

"Yes, you were," laughed Pete. "Hit the nail right on the head. Even the writer matches and that's the one I had pegged for missing."

Susan read the email again, focusing on the details.

"Funny thing, though," she said. "It's the man who disappeared most recently that's missing. I thought for sure his bones would be there."

"Probably drowned at sea, Susan. But five out of six isn't bad."

"Do I have the okay to put this on the air?"

"Yeah. Chief has already spoken with all the families. Files on the five are being reopened, too. Chief is especially anxious to put to rest the Nichols' case. The family is influential and is applying pressure. If you can dig up anything about him that might help, it will be appreciated and remembered."

Susan grinned. "I'll work on it. And, thanks, Pete. This wouldn't have happened without your help. Now, I've got to get cracking. I have a lot of revisions to make to my script for the broadcast on Sunday. Thanks again."

"Thank you, Susan. Let's get together for a drink real soon."

"Sure. Just let me know when and where."

After hanging up, Susan re-read the email again. She leaned back in her chair, mentally congratulating herself, then pulled up her script for Sunday's show and began hastily making revisions. When she was satisfied, she searched her files for headshots of the men whose bones had been identified. When she got to Nichols, she also pulled up the picture she had of him with Patricia Pierce. She studied it for a moment, then shook her head and closed the file. She'd used that picture in her last broadcast. For this one, she'd need something different.

Searching online, she finally found one of Nichols speaking at a State House hearing related to his proposal to limit the length of the lobstering season. It was a good photo and she quickly copied it to her file, but it wasn't exactly what she needed. Determined, she sifted through the rest of the pictures taken during at same hearing. Most of them were boring and she leafed through them rapidly until one photo caught her eye.

Holy crap, she thought. *This is too good to be true.*

She leaned forward staring at a picture of Nichols being confronted by a very angry-looking Lonnie Pierce. Pierce appeared to be yelling at the writer and was poking a finger into his chest. People in the background looked alarmed.

Smiling, Susan copied the picture then went back to her file and pulled up the photo of Nichols and Patricia. Placing the two side by side on the computer screen, she grinned. These pictures would be the cornerstone of her Sunday piece, "Lobster Wars: The Bones of Puffin Island."

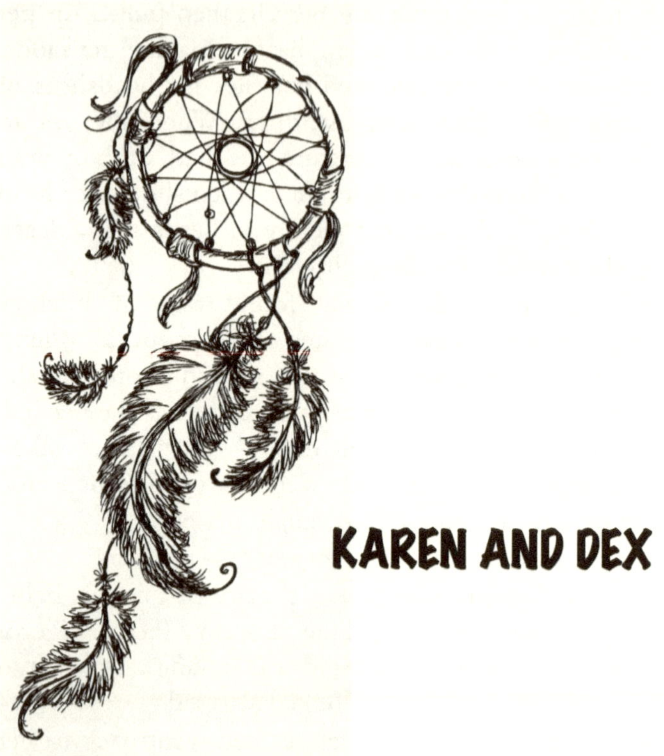

KAREN AND DEX

ON SUNDAY, KAREN SUGGESTED they go to the mainland for a movie and dinner, but Dex declined again, saying he had maintenance work to do at the boatyard. Not surprised by his refusal, Karen bit back a bitter retort and contented herself with working in the shed behind the house. The previous owner had used that structure for his gardening tools, but Karen hoped to turn it into an artist's studio.

The hours passed swiftly and it was late afternoon when she heard Dex's truck pull back into the driveway. She hastily gathered up her baby and walked back to the cottage wanting to be there to greet him.

I don't know why I'm hurrying, she thought. *I know exactly what he's going to do. First, he'll shower and shave, then he'll help himself to a beer, and sit down in front of the TV. And guess what he'll want to watch? Why, Susan's crime show, of course.*

Hoping she was wrong, she walked into the house.

"Dex? Is that you?"

There was no answer, but she heard the sound of the shower and smiled. She settled the boy in his playpen then went to the bedroom to change. When she returned, Dex was seated in his easy chair, beer in hand, in front of the television.

"Hi," she said. "Have a good day?"

He muttered something unintelligible, not looking at her.

Karen held her breath, trying to keep her anger under control, then poured a glass of wine and joined him in front of the television.

An ad for toothpaste was playing.

"I think I made some headway in the shed today," she said. "Got most of it cleaned out. Alex was trying to be my 'helper.' You should have seen him. I think I would have gotten a lot more done if I hadn't had a 'helper,' but it was more fun with him there."

"That's good," Dex replied, then turned up the volume on the television.

Karen bit her lip in frustration.

The commercial ended and was replaced by a shot of the rocky Maine coastline.

"And now, WKZTV is proud to present *COLD CASES OF SOUTHERN MAINE* with Susan LeVeque."

Dex put down his beer and leaned forward.

"Good evening, Mainers," said Susan. "I'm Susan LeVeque and welcome to *COLD CASES OF SOUTHERN MAINE.* Tonight we're going to examine several different cases that span some thirty-five years. Six men, five of them lobstermen, all who disappeared without a trace. Were they simply lost at sea? Or did something more sinister happen to them?

"We'll answer those questions and more when we come back and take a look at: 'Lobster Wars: The Bones of Puffin Island.'"

"Oh, Christ," moaned Karen. "Those missing men again. I'd hoped she'd come up with something better this week."

Dex frowned angrily. "If you don't mind, I happen to be interested in those men and what happened to them. I fish these waters, you know. What happened to them affects us all."

Karen stared at him surprised by his tone. "What the hell is your problem? I'm on your side, you know. Why are you treating me like I'm the enemy?"

Dex took a deep breath. "I'm sorry," he said. "I guess I've been behaving like a jerk. All this old stuff being rehashed ... first Evie and now this. I guess it's upset me more than I thought."

Karen leaned over and took his hand. "It's okay. Just remember I love you. And what's past is past. You can't change it now no matter how much you might want to. And remember, I'm a good listener if you want to talk about any of this."

Dex smiled. "I know. I love you, too."

He was about to say more, but Susan was back on the screen.

"Today," she said solemnly, "I received word that the five bodies found on Puffin Island earlier this month have been positively identified through DNA analysis."

Headshots of four of the men flashed on the screen as Susan read off their names and the dates of their disappearances. She then switched to taped interviews with surviving family members who all attested to problems with local lobstermen prior to their loved ones going missing.

Susan then displayed a graph that illustrated how the disappearances of these men coincided with some of the more ugly periods in Maine's "lobster wars."

They went again to a commercial break and Karen leaned back in her chair.

"Did you know any of these guys?" she asked.

"No," Dex replied. "I was just a kid when most of them disappeared."

"What about your dad? Did he ever say anything about them?"

Dex was silent for a moment. "No. My dad didn't talk much about the business at home. But, yeah, sometimes things got rough, especially back in my dad's day. It's different out there now."

"But I thought you sterned with him during the summer after school was out. Surely, you knew some of his cronies."

Dex didn't answer, just stared at the screen. Susan was back on camera, behind her the familiar picture of Howard Nichols and Dex's mother.

"That brings us to our fifth body and probably the most mysterious disappearance of all, Howard Nichols. Nichols, a Harvard graduate who authored several highly regarded books on the environment, lived in Connecticut but maintained a summer home right here in Maine - on Mateguas Island."

Several more pictures of Nichols flashed on the screen as Susan described his upbringing and education. Finally, the picture of him speaking at the State House appeared.

"Nichols was an outspoken proponent of lobster conversation and, to this end, advocated for a shorter season, allowing the lobsters to repopulate. He argued that a targeted lobster fishery outside the summer season could result in a higher quality product which in turn would mean higher prices."

The camera shifted to an interview with Nichols' sister, who summarized her brother's views and then stated that she believed he had, prior to his disappearance, expressed concern about comments made by some of the local lobstermen after his appearance at the State House hearing. Susan asked if he had ever mentioned any names.

The woman answered, "Yes, one. Lonnie Pierce."

At this point, the photo of Nichols and Lonnie appeared on the screen.

Karen took a deep breath. "That's your dad arguing with him, isn't it?"

Dex said nothing but stared intently at the photo.

A second later an ad for mouthwash began.

"Dex? Did you hear me? Nichols was a friend of your mom's, wasn't he? It doesn't look like he was any too friendly with your dad, though."

Reluctantly, Dex turned to face her. "Yeah, Nichols and Mom were tight. They knew each other when they were kids. Pop never really cottoned to him, though. Called him a 'summer complaint' and other things not quite so nice."

"So, they didn't like each other. You can tell that from that picture. Your dad looks ready to punch him out."

Dex didn't respond.

"You can see where Susan's going with this, can't you?" said Karen. "She's implying that your father may have taken that man to Puffin and left him to die there."

"I'm not stupid, Karen," Dex retorted angrily. "I know what she's doing and I know who put her up to it!"

Karen was about to respond, but he ignored her. He finished his beer in one gulp, slammed the bottle on the counter, and walked toward the door. "I've had just about enough of this for one night," he said. "I'm going for a walk."

Karen looked at him, speechless. He was running away from her again.

She began to get up, to tell him she'd go with him, but all she got for her trouble was the sound of the door as it closed behind him.

She stared at it for a minute, then turned back to the TV screen. The picture of Nichols and Lonnie was again displayed with Susan standing in front of it, talking.

Karen stared at the image of the father of the man she loved and wondered if he had been responsible for at least one senseless death, and, perhaps, others. And, if that were true, what, if anything, did her husband know about it?

She shook her head as a shiver ran down her spine.

Oh God, Dex, what did you do? What did you do?

SUSAN

SUSAN WAS FEELING GOOD. She was sure she'd achieved just the right balance between mystery, suspense, and outrage over the deaths of the five men investigated in her broadcast.

Checking her Twitter account, she was gratified to see the number of tweets and retweets that had registered about the show and, more importantly, the number of congratulatory communications that had come in from colleagues both locally and throughout the country. Her number of followers had also increased substantially and all this, she knew, was to her benefit.

Still fueled by an adrenaline rush from being on the air, she grabbed her coat, said goodnight to everyone, and left the station, acknowledging to herself that she was too wired to simply go home and go to bed. She thought about venturing downtown and splurging on a meal at a five-star restaurant but somehow knew that wouldn't satisfy her.

I don't want to be alone, she thought as she pulled out her cell and speed-dialed Bill.

After a brief conversation, she dashed back to her apartment, grabbed her overnighter, and got to the wharf just in time to meet his punt.

Once on the island, they enjoyed a leisurely dinner at one of the B&Bs then headed down to the Hall where a local band was playing. They danced, drank, and had a good time, Susan's ebullient mood being infectious. They stayed at the Hall until the band quit, then returned to Bill's home on the hill.

Finally, as the clock struck one a.m., they went to sleep.

"No, no, nooo..."

Susan sat up. The moon was shining through the open window, illuminating the room. Bill was huddled on the far side of the bed, curled in fetal position, crying and moaning pitifully.

Slowly, trying to shake off her fatigue, Susan slid over to where he lay and put her hand on his shoulder.

"Bill," she said gently. "Wake up. You're having another nightmare."

His skin felt clammy and cold and she could see the sheets around him were drenched in sweat. He seemed oblivious to her presence and continued to rock and moan as if he were in great pain.

She sat back on her heels watching him. He had had nightmares before, his experience on Puffin haunting him, but never like this. Usually, he would scream, then wake up and it would be all over. But this time, this dream, was different.

Maybe he's actually remembering, she thought. *I'll bet finding the bones on Puffin helped stimulate him.*

She sat still for a moment, thinking, then scooted back across the bed to the nightstand and grabbed her cell phone.

Maybe I can tease it out of him and, if I record what he says, I'll have it to play back when he wakes up. That would help him, wouldn't it?

She stared at him again, knowing she was just kidding herself. What she really hoped was that whatever he was experiencing could be of use to her and help advance her career. A twinge of guilt ran through her mind, but she pushed it aside, set the cell to record, then moved back across the bed and placed it on the pillow near his head. Taking a deep breath, she leaned close to him.

"Bill, it's okay," she whispered. "Tell me what you're seeing."

Hugging his knees even tighter, his body was suddenly racked by silent sobs.

"Hush, now. You're safe," she crooned softly. "Tell me what's happening. What do you see?"

Slowly, his sobbing subsided and he reached over and placed his hand on her arm, gripping it tightly.

"Oh, Karen," he cried.

Her first instinct was to pull away in anger, but she steeled herself. If he wanted to think she was his ex-wife, then so be it. She'd be happy to be part of his delusion.

"I'm here, Bill," she responded in a whisper. "What's happening?"

He rolled over and wrapped his arms around her waist, laying his head in her lap. "I can't. It's too ... too ... I can't."

Susan placed her hand on his head, petting him like a dog, and spoke soothingly. "You can tell me anything. It's okay."

He sighed and began to relax as she stroked his brow and whispered to him gently, encouraging him.

For a while, he seemed to have fallen back to sleep, then, without warning, his body started shivering violently.

"What do you see, Bill?" she asked.

Hesitantly, he began to speak, his voice just a whisper. Unable to make out what he was saying, she leaned over, closer to his face. His eyes were squeezed tightly shut as if trying to obliterate whatever vision he was experiencing.

"A storm," he whispered. "Oh, Kar, so cold, so much snow ... lasted days, weeks ... not sure ... wind ... too much wind ... food all gone ... hungry."

He hesitated, his hands gripping her painfully. Biting her bottom lip, she began massaging his shoulders, trying to get him to relax.

"Go on, tell me."

He was silent again for a few minutes, then he shuddered.

"I had to go ... find food ... dying ... so cold ... hold me, Kar."

Susan put her arms around him, cradling him like a child.

"I'm here. I'll keep you warm. Tell me what happened."

He again relaxed in her embrace, his shivering abating as she held him.

"The wind ... oh, God ... howling ... beach frozen ... no clams ... no crabs ... no fish ... wanted to die. Then..."

Again, he shuddered and held her closer as tears rolled down his cheeks.

"Make it go away, Karen!" he screamed. "Make it go away."

Susan rocked him gently in her lap.

"I will. Don't worry, I will. But first, you must tell me what happened, then it will all go away. I promise."

As she spoke, she could feel him relax and his grip on her lessened.

"A boat ... two men. I hid. They had a bag ... swung it off the bow."

"I don't understand. What do you mean?"

"Tossed it ... to shore."

"But why did you hide? Why didn't you call out to them?"

Violently, he shook his head. "Hurt me ... hurt me ... same boat ... same man. Hurt me ... kill me."

Susan's heart began to pound.

"The man on the boat, was it the one who took you to Puffin?"

Bill's body began to shake and his hands once again gripped her thighs.

"Yes!" he screamed. "It was him!"

Susan took a deep breath. "Who was it? Tell me."

He raised his head and opened his mouth, but no words came out. He stared blankly at her for a moment, then let go and rolled away, burying his head in a pillow.

Angry with herself, Susan realized that she had pushed too hard and, as a result, let the identity of his kidnapper slip away. But he was still in a deep dream state, and, perhaps, there was something more she could gain by continuing to probe him.

She lay down beside him, putting her arms around his waist.

"Okay, you don't have to remember. Tell me about the bag? What was in it?"

Her question appeared to upset him and he began to moan and shiver again. She gently pulled him from the pillow he was clutching, turning him to face her. Holding him close, she stroked his back, whispering gentle endearments, until she felt some of the tension leave his body.

"Not a bag," he murmured. "A man..."

It took all of Susan's strength not to jump up and scream in triumph. Instead, she forced herself to stay calm.

"Was he dead?" she asked, trying to hide her impatience.

Bill was becoming more agitated and she could feel his heart pounding as she held him.

"Don't know. Body ... warm. Alive? Say he was dead, Karen ... please, say he was dead."

His voice had taken on a pleading quality and Susan tried to soothe him.

"Yes, you're right," she whispered. "He was dead. Now tell me what happened."

"Oh, Kar ... my knife ... I..."

Susan held her breath. "What did you do with the knife, Bill?"

In response, he pulled away from her, his body rigid, hands again clutching at the pillow.

"The knife. What did you do with it?"

Moments passed, then he sat up, dropping the pillow and kneeling over it. He stared at it for a moment, then turned his head toward her.

His mouth was slack, but his eyes were intense, focused on something that only he could see.

"I knew what to do," he finally said in a voice calm and devoid of emotion. "My father taught me how to gut and dress a deer..."

Susan inhaled sharply as he stared past her with unseeing eyes. Minutes that seemed like hours slipped by until he finally sighed and lay down on the bed.

Fighting to choke back a surge of bile that rose up from her gut, Susan tried to assimilate the horror he had just revealed. She reached toward him, but pulled her hand back, overcome with a sudden aversion to touching him. She forced herself to take several deep breaths, knowing that her job here was not finished yet; there was still more information to be gleaned from this man - a man she had almost loved and who had apparently committed the most heinous of crimes.

Back in control, she reached over to him and began massaging his shoulders.

"It's okay, Bill. You did nothing wrong. Get it all out. Tell me."

Later, when she was sure she had gotten enough detail about what happened on Puffin, she let him go back to sleep. When she was sure he was out, she grabbed her phone and tiptoed into the bathroom. Closing the door, she sat down on the toilet, opened up her contacts, and dialed. The phone was answered on the fourth ring.

"Pete Wallace and this had better be good."

"Pete, it's Susan."

"Susan? Susan LeVeque? What the fuck are you calling about? Do you know what time it is?"

Susan waited for his tirade to end. "Listen, I'm sorry about the late hour, but I think, no I'm sure, I know where the sixth body is."

Det. Wallace sighed. "Susan, we've been over this. There is no sixth body. That guy must have drowned. Give it a rest, will ya?"

"No, you're wrong, Pete. Tell me, when we were at Puffin, did anyone check out the root cellar?"

"Root cellar? You mean the place where your boyfriend hung out? No, why would we?"

Susan smiled. "That's where you'll find the bones. I'll bet my career on it."

The detective was silent for a moment. "Are you saying the sixth guy died in that cellar?"

"No, that's not what I'm saying. But his bones will be there. Think. How did Bill survive that last winter? You know it was a hard one and there was no food to speak of on that island. Think about it."

Again, there was silence on the line. It lasted so long, Susan thought that maybe she'd lost the connection. Then there was a loud sigh.

"Jesus, are you saying what I think you're saying? Christ, you mean Andersen...?"

"Yes, Pete. I got it straight from the horse's mouth and it's on tape, too. We need to get back out there before he realizes what he's told me."

"I guess you're right. But it won't be a big production this time. Can you get your hands on a boat?"

"No problem. The station will foot the bill."

"Okay, you arrange it and let me know when. I think I can grab one of the forensics' guys to come along and keep everything on the up and up. Where are you now?"

"On Mateguas - at Andersen's."

"Christ, you get yourself outta there, okay? No telling what that guy might do if he realizes what he's revealed to you."

"Yeah, I know. I'll be on the first ferry. And, I'll call you when I have the boat arranged."

"Okay. You take care and thanks for calling me. Sorry I was so brusque when I answered."

Susan laughed. "Don't worry about it. Talk to you soon."

She stood, shutting down her phone, and opened the door. Everything was quiet. Slowly, she tiptoed down the hall to the master bedroom. Bill was still tangled in the bed sheets, dead to the world. She stood for a moment in the doorway staring at him, then walked to the dresser and began to toss her belongings into her overnight case. She glanced wistfully at the closet. She had clothes in there, some that she really liked, but there was no room in her bag for them.

Fuck it, she thought. *They're just fabric. They can be replaced.*

She slipped into the jeans and T-shirt she had worn the night before then gave the dresser one last look to make sure she had all her jewelry and other personal items.

As her eyes scanned the surface, they came to rest on a small bowl into which Bill routinely dumped the change from his pockets before he went to bed. Beside the pile of coins lay a key.

Susan glanced back at the bed, then at her watch. She still had time to kill before the five-thirty commuter boat and Bill wouldn't be waking up anytime soon.

She zipped up her bag, tossed it over her shoulder along with her purse, then grabbed the key and left the room. As a precaution in case she was wrong about Bill's condition, she placed the overnighter at the head of the stairs where she could grab it easily if she needed to make a quick getaway.

Satisfied, she walked back to the landing, stopping before the door to the spare bedroom.

He's hiding something in there, she thought as she slipped the key into the lock.

The click of the latch was so loud in the quiet house, she involuntarily jumped and turned around, sure she would see Bill coming to get her. But the hallway was empty. Laughing at the state of her nerves, she opened the door and entered the room.

The windows faced west and, in the predawn darkness, let in very little light. She reached for the switch on the wall just inside the doorframe that controlled the lamp over the ceiling fan and turned it on.

At first, she glanced around puzzled, wondering why he had shoved the bed, paintings, and other attractive furnishings he had so painstakingly selected against the back wall of the room. She took a step or two inside, surprised to see what looked like a small, uncomfortable cushion sitting in the empty space where the bed had been.

What the hell? she thought. *Is he doing yoga or something? If so, why hide it?*

She walked over to the *gomden* and sat down. It was facing the corner where the back and sidewall came together. In the shadows, she could see a small table positioned kitty-corner there. On the table, she could make out several picture frames flanked by two candles and incense burners.

The light was too dim for her to identify the people in the photos, so she pulled a penlight from her purse and shone it on them.

"Jesus H. Christ!" she muttered. "He's erected a fucking shrine to her."

Slowly, she leaned forward shining her light on each picture and, in every single one, she saw Karen's smiling face.

Later, outside in front of the house, she breathed a sigh of relief.

She stood quietly for a moment gazing at the sky. It was almost dawn.

She glanced at her watch. She would still make it in time for the morning commuter ferry.

She started walking down the driveway but paused for a moment, looking back over her shoulder at the house she was leaving forever. There had been times when it had felt like home and something deep inside her wished that somehow she could turn back the clock and recapture that feeling. She wondered briefly if she had made the right decision. Was her career worth the damage she was about to inflict on this man whom she had taken as her lover and grown to care for?

Smiling ruefully, she knew the answer. It was a no-brainer.

Hoisting her bag onto her shoulder, she turned away from the house. She reached into her pocket and ran her fingers idly around the small trophy she had taken from the shrine in the spare room and then, without a second thought, quickly jogged down to the road.

BILL

BY THE TIME HE woke, the sun had already climbed high in the sky and was shining brightly through the bedroom windows. Groaning, Bill glanced at the clock, then got up, put on his robe, and staggered to the bathroom.

His head was pounding and he swallowed four aspirin, hoping to dull the pain. The house was quiet and he assumed Susan had already left for the studio. There was probably a note saying so tacked to the refrigerator. He would call her later.

He stripped off his robe and stepped into the shower, letting the hot spray relax him. As he bathed, he tried to remember what had happened the night before. He was sure he'd had another nightmare. He had a vague memory that he'd thought Karen was with him, but it was wispy and he hoped he hadn't called out her name or done anything to piss Susan off.

And, as usual, the details of the dream that made it a nightmare were missing.

After drying off, he slipped his robe back on and gazed at his reflection in the mirror. The pain at his temples was easing and he was beginning to feel more alert.

Intending to get dressed and do some work in his media room, he stepped out into the hallway. The sun was streaming in the windows and in the bright morning light, he could see the door to the spare bedroom door was open, the key still in the lock.

Oh, shit, he thought as he entered the room. *Susan.*

At first glance, everything looked normal. The furniture was still against the wall and the *gomden* sat unassumingly in the empty space he had created. But that's where the normalcy ended.

He stared in disbelief at the altar.

His pictures were scattered on the floor, their glass frames smashed to bits. The photo of Karen from their wedding day had been destroyed - torn to pieces and strewn about the room. His wedding band was missing and other mementos that were fragile were now broken or torn apart.

He knelt down, gathering up the pieces of the picture, trying desperately to put them back together again. But it was hopeless.

Feeling depressed and angry, he sat down on the *gomden* and stared at the wall, his body involuntarily assuming his meditative position. Soon, random thoughts and memories began to surface. Knowing he was entering a trance-like state, he focused his mind on his breath and let the process begin.

He didn't know how long he sat there, only that it was calming to his troubled mind. Most of what passed through his consciousness was benign - memories from times long ago when he was young and carefree.

He smiled as these images floated by, wanting them to go on forever, but that was not to be.

Suddenly, an icy wind began howling in his ears and he saw himself huddled behind a rock, watching two men on a boat as they tossed what he thought was a duffle bag to the shore. He waited patiently, instinctively crouching low to avoid detection, as the men turned the boat and motored away. A shiver of fear ran down his spine as he recognized the burly, redheaded man standing in the stern and knew that that man had once wielded a shovel aimed at his head. Frightened, he waited until the boat was out of sight, then crept silently up the snow-covered rocks to where the bag lay.

He rolled it over. It was not a bag. It was a man.

Inhaling sharply, he placed his hand on the man's chest and thought he could feel the faint beating of a heart. Slowly, he examined the body. There was a large gash on the man's forehead and one of his legs was broken badly, a shard of bone jutting out just below the knee.

He stood outside of himself, watching as he sat back on his haunches, breathing heavily and wondered if, in that pivotal moment of time, he had actually been thinking. Had he been weighing the pros and cons, making a moral decision?

He didn't know. A year and a half on Puffin had seriously eroded his thought processes and, after two months of cruel, unrelenting weather, he knew his brain functioned only on the most primitive of levels. Therefore, it was no wonder what he did next.

He took his knife from the sheath he had strapped to his leg and, kneeling on the man's chest, slit his throat.

KAREN

SHE CHECKED HER WATCH. It was close to nine and she was beginning to get worried. They'd just sat down to dinner when Pete McKinney called. Apparently, a fellow islander's boat was stalled out to sea and Pete was going to his aid and asked Dex to come along. Of course, Dex said he would be glad to help. But that had been over two hours ago and there had been no word from either of them since.

Karen tried calling him, but his cell went directly to voicemail. Knowing there was little coverage where they were, she left a brief message and then called Louise.

"Hi. It's Karen. Have you heard from the boys?"

Louise laughed. "Just got off the marine radio with Pete. It took longer than they expected. Sea's getting rough out there. Looks like a storm's coming in fast. They're on their way home now. Should be back to the island in about an hour."

Karen thanked Louise and hung up. Determined to wait up for him, she brewed a cup of tea and sat down with her sketchbook.

Pencil in hand, she stared at the blank page, unable to concentrate, her mind filled with thoughts about Evelyn LaPlante and Patricia Pierce and their untimely deaths.

Thinking about these events, she had a vague sense that, somehow, they were connected, but that led to an even more disturbing thought. The common denominator in both women's lives was her husband, Dex Pierce.

BILL

AS THE CRUDE KNIFE pierced his skin, the man began to struggle, fighting for his life.

Bill held the blade firmly in place, calling on the last of his reserves, knowing it wouldn't take long until his own strength was depleted. Viciously, he sawed at the man's neck, cursing himself for not having the foresight to keep the knife sharpened and ready.

How long this went on, he couldn't say. But soon, the blade slipped through, severing the external and internal jugular veins, causing hot, black blood to spurt out, splashing onto Bill's face.

The blood was warm and, instinctively, Bill reached out with his tongue and tasted it. It was salty, and it was good.

Without hesitation, he buried his face in the man's neck, drinking deeply, savoring the taste and feel of the hot blood sliding down his throat. In no time, his stomach, empty for so long, felt full to bursting and he turned and vomited into the cold, frozen sand.

As the regurgitated blood dripped from his lips, he heard the sounds of carrion birds coming to join in the feast. Knowing that time was now of the essence, he quickly stripped the man of his clothing.

He slipped his arms into the warmth of the man's wool pea coat and pulled on his jeans over the tattered remains of the ones he had worn for so long. The boots were too big, but they were better than the cloth wrappings he now wore for shoes, so he stuffed the man's socks into the toes so that he wouldn't stumble over the jagged rocks on the way back to his shelter.

The body, now stripped down to an undershirt and boxer shorts, lay lifeless in the sand and Bill hoisted the man's legs under his armpits and began to drag him back to the root cellar he called home.

As he moved away from the shore, gulls and other predator birds landed on the ridge, furiously vying for the congealed pool of bloody vomit he had left for their enjoyment.

It took time and was tedious, but he finally got the body back to the ruins of the old manor house. There, he abandoned it briefly to retrieve from his cellar lair a faded blue tarp that had washed ashore the previous summer. He rolled the body onto it and began the arduous process of eviscerating it.

Once the entrails were removed, he wrapped them in the man's shirt and carried them to a place near the shore where he dumped them on the beach and spread them as wide as he could with a stick. Then he picked up the bloody shirt and jogged back to the body he'd left wrapped in the tarp.

He crouched down next it, catching his breath, and gazed toward the horizon. It wasn't long before the sky turned black with hungry birds, their cries echoing loudly over the howling of the wind.

Bill stared down at the tarp and the body wrapped within it, the horror of what he had done finally becoming real to him.

He leaned over, hands gripping at the covered corpse, as tears cascaded down his cheeks.

Then a faint voice pierced his consciousness. Surprised, he looked up, cocking his head to the side, listening.

"Hurry, son, that deer needs to be dressed before nightfall."

Recognizing the voice, Bill smiled and nodded, knowing what he had to do. He unfolded the tarp and stared at its contents. To his eyes, the body was no longer that of a man. No, it was a doe, taken legally during hunting season.

Wiping away his tears with the back of his hand, he took a deep breath, picked up the knife, and, obeying his father's command, went to work stripping meat from the bones and "packaging" it as best he could in dried seaweed. As he steadily skinned and cut, he could almost see his father standing behind him, encouraging him, telling him to hurry.

As he severed the last joint and packaged the final cut, he looked up. The moon had risen in the winter sky and was peeking out from behind dark clouds that promised yet another storm in the morning.

Quickly, he stored the packaged meat in an old cooler he'd found washed up on the beach. Once it was full, he wrapped the tarp around it and covered it with rocks to keep predators from raiding it. The bones, he tossed into the cellar, having some vague notion about carving or whittling them into useful tools.

Standing and surveying his work product, he felt proud, satisfied that, at least for the remaining weeks of winter, the meat would stay frozen and not spoil.

Exhausted, he now retired to his cellar to start a fire and, for the first time in a long time, eat dinner.

All these memories came rushing back as Bill sat rigid, eyes closed, on the *gomden*. When he finally looked up, he remembered everything - what had happened in the woods, how he'd gotten to Puffin, and the horrible things he had been forced to do to survive there for two years. But as he sat in the moonlight that now streamed brightly through the window, he acknowledged that none of it mattered anymore. All that mattered was that he regain his life and, to do that, he had to eliminate anyone who stood in the way of him bringing his family back together.

Nodding, he tried to stand, but his legs, cramped from sitting in one position for so long, failed him and he fell to his knees on the floor. Tears of frustration and pain streamed down his face as he massaged his calve and thigh muscles trying to get the blood flowing again.

Soon, when he was able to stand, he walked unsteadily to the bathroom to take another shower. As he vigorously scrubbed his body, washing away a multitude of sins, he knew that when he was cleansed and refreshed it would be time to begin - time to bring his family back to him.

TERRI AND SHAWN

IT WAS EARLY EVENING by the time Shawn returned home. He'd been at the boatyard all day repairing a faulty bilge pump and Terri could see he was exhausted.

"You sit," she commanded, handing him a beer. "You've had a long day. I'll put the burgers on the grill."

"Thanks, babe," he said as she grabbed a plate laden with raw meat and headed outside to the deck.

Turning on the grill, she gazed up at the sky. Thunderheads were rapidly moving in from the mainland, promising a storm later that night.

Hope our food's cooked before it gets here, she thought.

Turning back to the grill, she put the hamburgers on the rack and closed the lid. With the empty plate in one hand, she intended to return to the house, but a strange rustling sound in bushes beside the deck caught her attention. Afraid it might be a raccoon or a fox coming to steal their food, she leaned over the rail to get a better look.

A crack of thunder pierced the stillness of the night.

ZAP!

The vile, pink tongue lashed out.

Before she could react, the barbed appendage, whole again, encircled her knee, causing her to lose balance. The plate flew from her hand, shattering when it landed. In shock, she reached out to grab the railing, hoping to break her fall, but she missed. Instead, her head hit the wooden rail hard and, losing consciousness, she crumpled to the deck.

The toad hopped out of the bushes, grinning evilly as it let loose the vicious barbs that elongated and pierced her skin, sending their terrible poison into her bloodstream.

The creature, using the tremendous musculature hidden in its tongue, now proceeded to drag her lifeless body down the deck's stairs and across the yard, anxious to return to a secluded spot where it could enjoy its evening's meal uninterrupted.

KAREN AND BILL

KAREN HEARD THE CAR in the drive and leaped to her feet, relieved.

Thank God, he's finally home safe.

She quickly crossed to the door, unlocked it, and threw it open, expecting to see Dex coming up the porch stairs.

But the man standing in front of her was not her husband.

Shocked, Karen took a step back. "Bill, what are you doing here?"

A clap of thunder shook the house and the skies opened as heavy rain began to fall.

Bill stood silently in the wind and rain, a look of anguish painted across his face.

Karen hesitated, knowing she should slam the door on him, but he was the father of her children and was clearly upset about something. And he was getting soaked standing in the sudden downpour.

"You're getting all wet," she said. "If you promise to behave, you can come in. I thought you were Dex. He'll be home any minute."

She moved to the side and waved him into the house.

Bill stepped over the threshold, still silent, standing in the shadows of the doorway.

Karen watched him, puzzled. "Are you all right? Did something happen? Are you hurt? Talk to me, Bill."

He didn't respond, but slowly walked forward into the light of the living room, a strange smile on his face.

Karen gasped recognizing the madness in his eyes.

Now regretting her decision to let him in, she took a step back, searching around the room for a weapon or a way to escape.

"Bill, I-" she started, but before she could finish, he was on her.

He grabbed her around the waist and lifted her into the air, tossing her onto the couch. Momentarily stunned, she didn't see him pull a roll of duct tape from one jacket pocket and a knife from the other.

Shaking her head, she started to get up, but he pushed her down, grabbing her arms and forcing them behind her back. She kicked at him, struggling to free herself, but she was no match for the madness that now fueled and empowered him.

Swiftly, he bound her wrists with a piece of tape.

"What the fuck to you think you're doing?" she screamed in outrage.

In response, he took a piece of tape and slapped it roughly over her mouth.

She lay still for a moment, chest heaving with fear and exertion as he reached down and grabbed her ankles.

Knowing that if she let him bind her feet, she would be helpless, she kicked at him viciously, catching him on the hip with her heel.

Knocked off-balance, he staggered back a step, but recovered quickly and soon was on her again, binding her ankles together.

When he finished, he stood and, for a moment, surveyed his handiwork, then wordlessly left the room.

As she struggled to get free from the tape, Karen's eyes flashed around in panic. The house was silent except for the sound of the rain beating against the windowpanes accompanied by an occasional clap of thunder.

Seconds that seemed like hours passed until she heard footsteps coming from the hallway. Her body tensed, waiting.

Finally, he stepped in front of her, smiling.

Her eyes widened in shock. He had her baby, settled on his hip, his arm gripping the boy tightly.

Without a word, he leaned over and cut the tape around her ankles.

"Get up," he said in a voice barely above a whisper. "You're coming with me."

Vigorously, she nodded and, with difficulty, got to her feet. Her arms were still bound behind her back and Bill took hold of them and shoved her forcefully toward the front door.

The rain was coming down hard and lightning flashed across the sky as he pushed her out the door and guided her down the steps into the front seat of his car. He placed the child on her lap, securing him in place with the seatbelt.

He stared at the two of them for a moment, oblivious to the pounding rain, then turned and jogged around to the driver's side.

Behind the wheel, he leaned over and yanked the tape off her mouth. Tears welled in her eyes as the adhesive tore at her skin.

She took a deep breath, trying to calm the rapid beating of her heart. She knew her only chance was to reason with him, to bring him back from whatever dark place his mind had gone to.

"Bill," she said tentatively. "Where are you taking us?"

He turned and gazed at her. "We're going home, hon," he cooed. "Like before - just you, me, and the girls. It'll be good. You'll see."

He smiled, then turned on the ignition and backed out the driveway onto the road.

The windshield wipers slapped against the glass, pushing the rain from side to side, as Karen's mind raced, searching for a way, any way, to escape from this insanity with her son.

"You said we're going home," she said in a soft voice. "But this isn't the way to your house. Where are you taking us?"

Bill laughed. "We have one stop to make before we go home, honey."

"Where, Bill?"

He took a deep breath, nodding toward her son. "You see that little boy? He's not mine."

"What does that have to do with anything?" she asked, terror gripping at her heart.

"The only way we can be happy is if things go back to the way they were before. You understand that, don't you? It has to be you, me, and the girls."

He spoke in a calm, patient voice as if lecturing a child, but it was tinged with madness, causing Karen's fear to escalate.

"Okay," she said. "We don't need him. Let's drop him off at Terri's. Then it will be just you and me, like when we were dating. You'd like that, wouldn't you?"

He didn't seem to hear her but kept looking straight ahead.

Minutes passed until he finally slowed the car and made a quick left turn. Karen now recognized the road they were on. It led to Eagle Point with its towering rocks, jutting precariously out toward the sea beyond.

"I could have had a son," he whispered. "But you killed him, didn't you? Now it's my turn..."

The intent in his words shocked her. Desperately, she screamed out to Alex with her mind, begging him to use his powers to escape, but the child was strangely silent.

Desperate, she twisted in her seat so that her back was kitty-corner between the upholstery and the door. Like most island cars, Bill's was an older model and in the passenger armrest sat a metal ashtray that was damaged. There was a sharp edge on one side and Karen moved her bound hands across it, hoping to tear the tape.

Bill was quiet again, concentrating on the road. They were only minutes from their destination and Karen struggled frantically to free herself.

The car made an abrupt turn and she could see they were now entering the Eagle Point parking lot. Bill pulled the car to a halt and moved the gearshift into park.

At that same moment, Karen felt her hands come free. She held her breath, steeling herself, and shielding her son with one arm, lashed out at Bill with the other.

SHAWN

HEARING THUNDER, SHAWN GOT up and looked out the window. The storm was coming in fast.

"Terri!" he yelled. "What's taking you so long?"

He looked out the window again. Smoke was coming from the grill, but Terri was nowhere in sight. Puzzled, he walked outside to look for her.

The hamburger meat was sizzling furiously as black smoke billowed from the barbecue. Shawn stopped and turned down the gas, then gazed about trying to locate Terri.

Shards of the broken plate were scattered on the deck and, when he knelt down to pick them up, he saw drops of fresh blood, mingling with the rain on the deck's railing.

Frightened, he called for her again, but the only response he got was the sound of distant thunder.

Jack, he thought as he ran back to the house. *If that bastard's got her, I'm going to kill him.*

Once inside, he threw open the closet door, revealing a locked gun case. He hastily opened it, taking out his rifle. He loaded the gun, then, from a drawer below, retrieved his favorite hunting knife.

The knife, an old blade carved from bone, had been a present from his mother. She'd given it to him for his seventeenth birthday and told him the seller said the knife was Abenaki and had been used in sacred rituals. She'd gotten it at a flea market and didn't put too much stock in the vendor's stories, but thought that he might like it anyway.

For reasons he couldn't fathom, he'd used it more than any of the other, newer blades he'd acquired over the years. Now, feeling the urgency of the situation, he felt strangely drawn to it and slipped it silently into its sheath.

Another clap of thunder echoed, breaking the silence of the house. Noting that the light outside was swiftly diminishing, Shawn reached back into the drawer and grabbed a headlamp.

Then he threw on his slicker and walked out into the storm to search for the woman he loved.

DEX

HE ARRIVED HOME ABOUT twenty minutes after Bill's car backed down the drive. He was tired, wet, and wanted nothing more than a hot shower and a cup of coffee.

Bounding up the porch stairs, he was surprised to find the front door open, the entryway floor wet from the pounding rain. He hesitated a moment, then quickly walked into the house, closing the door firmly behind him.

"Karen," he called as he entered the living room.

The room was dimly lit, but he could see her half-filled cup of tea resting on the end table and her sketchbook on the floor beside it.

Thinking that perhaps she'd gone to bed and that the wind had blown the door open while she slept, he stripped off his coat and walked to the bedroom, but it was empty.

Puzzled, he looked in his son's room, but there was no one there either.

Methodically, he checked the house, finding no sign of Karen or Alex.

Maybe they went over to Pete's to wait, he thought as he pulled his cell from his pocket and quickly dialed.

Pete answered promptly.

"Hey, buddy. Sorry to bother you, but are Karen and Alex there?"

Pete was silent for a moment. "They're not at home?"

"No, the house is empty and the door was open when I got here. Thought maybe they went over to your place to pass the time till we got in."

"No, they're not here. Louise says Karen called a couple hours ago and wanted to know if she'd heard from us. You need me to come over?"

"No, I don't think so. Just can't figure out where they'd go in all this weather."

"Well, you let me know if you need to rustle up a search party. Okay?"

Dex laughed. "Will do and thanks."

Hanging up the phone, he grabbed his jacket and jogged outside to the garage. Karen's car was still there.

Now, with warning signals going off in his gut, he ran back toward the house and, hoping he could find a note somewhere, turned on all the lights. In the living room, he saw a roll of duct tape lying on the floor.

Sweet Jesus, he thought. *What happened here?*

KAREN

SHE RAKED THE SIDE of his face with her nails, drawing blood. Her back was to the door and she turned to open it and escape.

But Bill recovered too quickly. With one arm, he reached out and grabbed her by the thin cotton fabric of her T-shirt. With one swift motion, he pulled her toward him, then reversed his movement and shoved her forcefully back against the passenger side window.

Her head slammed into the glass and for a moment, black spots danced before her eyes. Instinctively, she grabbed the back of her head, which was now sticky with blood. As she struggled to maintain consciousness, she felt the weight of the child on her lap disappear and heard the car door slam.

She bent forward, holding her head between her knees, to keep from fainting. After a few seconds, she sat up. Feeling in control again, she jumped from the car.

The rain was still coming down hard, and she strained to see where Bill had gone with her son. Fearfully, she turned her gaze toward the rocky outcropping that she had climbed so many times. This had always been a place of peace and serenity for her, but now, with one cruel act, it was turning into her worst nightmare. Slowly, not knowing what else to do, she began to climb the rocks, struggling to keep her footing on the slippery seaweed and eel grass.

As she made her way up the cliff, she desperately scanned the area above, hoping to locate Bill and Alex through the driving rain. Feeling on the edge of panic, she forced herself to climb faster, unmindful of any danger to herself. Finally, for a brief moment, the rain let up and she caught sight of a figure in the distance above her. It was Bill, her child balanced precariously on one hip.

"Bill!" she cried. "Don't do this. Please, don't do this!"

He hesitated for a moment, turned, and gazed down at her, then cupped his free hand around his mouth and yelled, "I have to! Don't you see? Everything has to go back to the way it was. You'll understand when it's done. Things will be better soon."

She was about to respond, to try to reason with him, but he had already turned and was continuing his ascent up the cliff.

A renewed wave of fear washed over her and she again began to scramble up the rocks toward her child. She called to the boy with her mind, begging him to change into an eagle and fly away to safety. But he remained silent and unresponsive. Not knowing what else to do, she continued climbing, praying she would reach them in time.

She yelled again at Bill, hoping to distract him and slow him down when, suddenly, a sharp pain stabbed at her left temple. It was intense and she fell to her knees, gripping the rocks to keep from falling. As she steadied herself, the boy's voice flooded her consciousness.

Do not fear, sweet mother. All is as it should be. The evil foretold by the appearance of the Aglebemu has borne fruit and my father says the time is not right for me to walk the earth again in human form. The heart of this man, once pure and light, has turned black and only by my physical death can this evil be extinguished.

So, I go now to wait by my father's side for another day, another time, when I can once again walk in the light of the sun. But, always, dear mother, my spirit will be with you, in your heart.

"NO!" Karen screamed as she tried to plead with him, begging him to come back to her. But somehow, she knew her words would not change anything. It was over. She would lose her precious son.

Tears welled in her eyes as she sank onto the rocks in despair. The boy's voice once again echoed throughout her mind.

Sweet mother, open your heart, for my father wishes to enter and speak to you in a vision.

Karen took a deep breath, frightened by the thought of giving the God of the Dead entry to her mind and soul. But it was her child - her flesh and blood - asking, so she steeled herself, nodded, then closed her eyes and opened herself to him.

BILL

HOLDING THE BOY SECURELY, Bill finally reached the top of Eagle Point. Carefully, he edged his way out onto the rocks until he was standing on the farthest ledge, overlooking the churning sea below. He stood still for a moment. Even over the sound of the wind and rain, he could hear Karen's voice in the back of his mind, pleading with him to return the boy to her.

He listened but dismissed her cries. He had to turn back time and, to do so, the boy had to die.

Resolved, he stepped closer to the edge, watching the waves crash furiously against the rocks below.

He hesitated and raised his face to the sky, watching as storm clouds passed swiftly over the island. He cocked his head to one side, listening. Another voice was calling to him, coming from deep within the recesses of his soul. The voice was soft and only vaguely familiar at first, and he strained to hear it. As he concentrated, it became louder and clearer, resonating across his mind, until, finally, he recognized it. It was his own voice, coming from a time years before ... before Mateguas, and, most assuredly, before Puffin.

He stood listening as the voice admonished him to remember who and what he once had been. It begged him to renounce the stranger he had become and, deep down in his heart, he yearned to heed to it.

All he really wanted was to leave this place, go home, and lie down. He was tired. He knew all he had to do was return the boy to Karen, and maybe he'd be free.

But another voice, louder and more strident, overshadowed this desire. This was the voice of the person born and raised that cruel winter on Puffin, and it tore at his heart and blackened his soul.

The conflicting voices screamed at him, blotting out the sound of the rain and wind. Finally, heeding one, he stepped closer to the edge, taking the boy from his hip, raising him to his chest, and holding him tightly.

The child was strangely quiet, as if he'd already made peace with his fate and was content.

Taking a deep breath, Bill reached out and dangled the child over the angry sea below.

A bolt of lightning split the sky and, for a moment, Bill thought he could see heaven. Then a loud clap of thunder shook the earth and he knew what he had to do.

SHAWN

SHAWN QUICKLY RECONNOITERED THE yard and recognized immediately that someone or something had been dragged from the deck, across the grass. The trail led to the far edge of the property, stopping at an old shed where he kept the lawnmower and other gardening implements.

Moving swiftly and stealthily, he approached the structure. The door was slightly ajar.

Taking a deep breath, he pulled the bone knife from its sheath. He gripped it firmly by the blade and, without hesitation, pushed open the door.

DEX

HE KNELT IN FRONT of the sofa, picking up the discarded roll of duct tape. Puzzled, he stared at the couch. One of the pillows was on the floor; the others were tossed about haphazardly.

Unbidden, his mind traveled back to the incident two years before when he had come home to find a similar situation: pillows strewn about the floor, half-empty wine glasses on the table.

Bill.

Dex stood, fists clenched in anger. *Could she have finally done it? Left me to go back to her no-good ex-husband? I know I've been insensitive and distracted lately, guilty of ignoring her, but could that justify her betrayal?*

Duct tape forgotten, he walked to the bedroom, throwing open the closet door expecting to find it half-empty. But it wasn't. All her clothes were still there, hanging neatly beside his.

He reached over to the nightstand and pulled open the drawer. Her best jewelry, one-carat diamond earring studs and matching pendant, were still safely tucked away behind some lingerie.

She wouldn't leave without those, he thought.

Shaking his head in frustration, he returned to the living room and noted her cell phone sitting on the side table. He picked it up and checked for recent calls. There was nothing to or from Bill.

The last call she made was to my cell when I was out to sea with Pete.

He stared again at the sofa then down at the almost forgotten roll of duct tape he still held in his hand.

Something happened here, he thought. *Something bad. And now Karen and Alex are missing.*

Quickly, he speed-dialed Pete and described the situation to the older man, trying to keep the panic out of his voice.

"I'm calling 911," said Pete. "You sit tight. I'll be right over."

About fifteen minutes later, Pete's truck pulled up the drive, followed almost immediately by a police car, sirens blaring.

The officers questioned Dex and Pete then walked around the house and property looking for any possible clues that could lead them to Karen and the baby's whereabouts.

Impatiently, Dex waited for them to conclude their investigation.

"We should be out there looking," he said to Pete. "It's a small island. They can't have gotten far."

"If it were Andersen like you suspect," reminded Pete,

"he has his own punt now. He could have taken them to the mainland."

"Jesus, when I think of Karen and Alex in the hands of that man..."

"Take it easy, Dex. Karen's smart. If Bill's gone off his rocker, she'll figure out a way to handle him."

Dex nodded, anxiously watching the police officers who were now walking back toward them. One was busy talking on the phone.

"Just heard from dispatch," he said, tucking the cell into his pocket. "Something fishy's going on down at Eagle Point. Some kids were driving up that way to watch the storm and, when they got out of their car, they thought they heard someone screaming. It came from up on the rocks. And there's a lone car parked there. They said it looks like it might be Bill Andersen's."

Dex clenched his fists and turned abruptly, intending to jog to his truck, but one of the officers physically restrained him.

"Settle down, Dex," he said. "We don't want you going off half-cocked and getting yourself or your wife and boy injured or killed. Leave this to the professionals. I've already radioed for backup. They're on their way and will meet us in the Point's parking lot. You and Pete can ride with me, in the back. But you have to stay out of our way. Otherwise, I'll be forced to put the cuffs on you."

Dex looked about to protest, but Pete raised his hand, gesturing him to stop. "The boy's right," he said. "That temper of yours might make matters worse. Calm down and let them do their jobs."

Dex took a deep breath and slowly unclenched his fists. "Okay. I get it. But let's get going. My family is in danger."

SHAWN AND
THE KNIFE

BEFORE HE ENTERED THE shed, Shawn turned off his headlamp, not wanting to surprise or startle whoever or whatever might be hiding inside.

Slowly, he inched the door open then stepped over the threshold, waiting in the doorframe for his eyes to adjust to the lack of light. Tuning out the sounds of the storm, he listened carefully for any unusual noise or disturbance, but everything was still and quiet.

A clap of thunder echoed outside.

Suddenly, Shawn's ears perked up. There was a faint lapping or sucking sound coming from the far corner of the shed.

He took a step toward it as a flash of lightning lit up the interior of the building. For a split second, in the blinding light, he could see the outline of a body lying behind the lawnmower. But it was not alone. On top of it, on its back, sat some sort of animal.

Without hesitation, Shawn turned on the beam of his headlamp, illuminating the corner.

Terri was lying in the dirt, unconscious, an obese frog or toad covering her back. The creature, unaware of Shawn's presence, was flicking its obscene tongue in and out, lapping at the blood that was oozing from a wound on her forehead.

In an instant, Shawn acted.

The bone knife flew through the air in a blur of motion, its blade surrounded by a cold white light.

The toad, sensing the intrusion, turned its head toward Shawn, ready to attack. The loathsome tongue contracted as the beast prepared to enslave another victim.

But the creature was out of time. The bone blade, shining brightly, entered its skull, slicing through like butter to its ancient brain.

As it pierced the cerebral cortex, the toad let out a hideous, croaking cry and leaped into the air. Flashes of brightly pigmented light streaked from its wound, painting the walls of the old shed with an aurora borealis of color. The toad hovered in the air for a moment, surrounded by the light, then fell silently to the dirt floor below.

When it took its final breath, the strange, brilliant light went out and the shed was once again cloaked in darkness. Shawn trained his headlamp on the creature's carcass. The bone knife was protruding from its head, the blade now dull and ordinary-looking.

Shawn kicked the toad's remains aside and rushed to Terri. Relieved that she was still breathing, he took her in his arms and carried her back to the house. He lay her on the sofa, noting the wound on her head was still bleeding. Desperate, he grabbed his cell and called his mother.

"Mom, you have to come quick. Terri's hurt. No, no, it wasn't him. It was something worse and she needs you now! Bring all your stuff."

Ten minutes later, Helen's car squealed to a stop in the driveway.

KAREN

A STRANGE FEELING OF lightness passed over her as she felt the power of the ancient God enter her being. For a moment, it felt as if every nerve in her body were on fire as his essence traveled through her, permeating every muscle, every bone. Adrenaline surged and she felt the life within her take on a frenzied quality, but swiftly the sensation diminished as he presented her with a vision - a vision of what the future could hold.

It lasted only seconds then was gone. Abruptly, the old God left her and when the last vestige of his spirit oozed from her pores, she felt as if she were being ripped apart.

Empty and devoid of all emotion, she opened her eyes trying to remember who and where she was.

In an instant, it all came rushing back and, with trepidation, she looked to the rocks above. Bill was standing on an outcropping over the angry sea, Alex dangling helplessly from his hand.

"NO, BILL! DON'T!" she screamed, unable to reconcile herself to her child's senseless death. "Please ... he's just a baby."

Bill didn't respond. In a state of panic, she scrambled up the rocks wanting to reach him before he did something that would scar them all forever. Shoeless, she could feel the ledge tearing at her feet and toes, but she couldn't let that deter her. She felt no pain, only an urgency to reach her boy and save him.

She was close to the top and a glimmer of hope washed over her.

If he just keeps standing there for a minute or two longer, I'll reach them.

As if hearing her thoughts, Bill looked back over his shoulder. He stared at her with eyes filled with regret, then turned once again to the sea and let the boy go.

A cry of anguish erupted from her throat as she watched the child she had given birth to float for a moment on air, then hurdle down to be crushed by the rocks and sea below.

She stared at her child's executioner as he stepped away from the cliff's edge. Desiring nothing more than to inflict upon him the same punishment he had meted out to her son, she flew over the rocks, rapidly covering the distance between them. But as she neared him, Bill sat down on the ledge, shoulders slumped, knees hugged tightly to his chest.

"Bill?" she whispered as he began to rock slowly back and forth, his eyes unseeing and his face a mask of pain.

A wave of pity washed over her and she stood quietly staring at him, knowing that this was not the same man who had just taken the life of her child. That man, a stranger whose persona had been re-shaped by two years of bitter exile on Puffin Island, was gone and, in his place, sat the shell of the man she had once loved.

She moved silently toward him and hunkered down beside him. He didn't seem to recognize her but stared straight ahead, his eyes haunted by ghosts that only he could see. He was moaning, tears scarring his cheeks, as he continued rocking back and forth.

She watched him for a moment and then, as if he were the child she'd just lost, took him in her arms and held him close.

DEX

HE STARED OUT THE window of the police cruiser, wishing desperately that they could go faster. His rational mind chided him that the officer driving was just being careful and that visibility was limited due to the heavy rain. But that didn't stop him from wishing the man would forget about safety and put the pedal to the metal.

As they pulled into the parking lot at Eagle Point, Dex noted only two other vehicles were there - a Subaru Outback that he immediately identified as the type of car Bill Andersen drove and an old pickup truck.

The pickup was parked next to the trailhead leading up to the rocks and outside it, huddled together, was a group of teenagers wearing bright yellow, marine slickers. The kids were staring and pointing to the top of the tallest rock outcropping.

Dex leaped from the car before the officer brought it to a full stop and sprinted to where the group was standing.

"Did you see them?" he yelled. "A woman and a small child? Are they up there?"

One of the teenagers stepped forward. "There's a woman on the rocks," he said, hesitantly. "And a man, I think. A child..."

His voice trailed off, reluctant to relate what he thought he'd seen.

Dex stepped forward, white-hot anger apparent in his expression, and grabbed the front of the young man's slicker, pulling him roughly forward. "You tell me. Tell me what you saw! A little boy, a baby. Where is he?"

A hand reached out from behind Dex, grabbing him by the shoulder.

"Let the kid go, Dex," said Pete.

Dex whirled around, pushing his friend away. "He saw something. He knows where Alex is. I can feel it. He's going to tell me or I'll beat it out of him! You stay outta my way."

He turned, about to begin interrogating the boy again, when one of the officers approached, his hand resting lightly on the butt of his pistol.

"MR. PIERCE!" he yelled. "You stand down now or I'm going to have to arrest you!"

Dex stared at the policeman, fists clenched, jaw set. He was about to challenge the man when he saw two more officers approaching, their hands ready to draw if he gave them any reason to.

He took a deep breath, realizing he was outnumbered. He nodded helplessly at the officer, admitting defeat. Slowly, he unclenched his fists and, for a moment, it seemed as if all the air went out of him as his shoulders slumped and tears welled in his eyes,

"Please," he pleaded softly. "This kid saw something. Please, you have to find my wife and son."

Tears were now streaming down his face and the officer, recognizing the agony he was in, removed his hand from his gun and reached out, patting Dex on the shoulder.

"Don't worry, Mr. Pierce," he said calmly. "We've got everything under control."

As he spoke, an ambulance and another police van screamed into the parking lot.

The officer glanced at the vehicles as they parked, then turned back to Dex.

"See? That's the back-up I told you about. They've got a portable, battery-operated spotlight that can reach the top of those cliffs. And we're ready in case anyone's been hurt."

Dex again nodded.

"And, look behind you, out to sea."

Dex turned and gazed where the man was now pointing.

"That's a Coast Guard cutter and they've got Search and Rescue on board in case it's needed."

Dex watched the boat maneuver itself through the heavy seas toward the rocks of Eagle Point. He knew how dangerous this was and felt his heart fill with gratitude that they were there.

The officer, convinced that Dex was not a threat, waved to Pete, who was standing a few feet away.

"Now you and Mr. McKinney take yourselves over to where my cruiser's parked and wait. This is a police operation and we'll handle things."

Pete stepped forward and put his arm around Dex's shoulders.

"Come on, pard," he said. "Let's do like the man said. Leave this to the professionals."

Dex again nodded and let himself be led away by his friend. The officer then approached the group of teenagers and instructed them to get into their truck and move it to the far end of the lot. They quickly complied as the police proceeded to cordon off the area.

In no time, they moved the spotlight out of the van and set it up in the parking lot. After turning it on, it took a few moments to adjust the beam and train it on the rocks at the top of the point.

The rain was letting up and, after a brief search, Dex saw the light focus on two figures huddled together on the shiny, seaweed-covered, rocks. As the spotlight illuminated them, one of the figures turned her head and slowly stood. It was Karen.

SHAWN'S HOUSE

HELEN KNELT IN FRONT of the couch, examining Terri's head wound. The bleeding finally stopped and a large goose egg was forming at her temple.

"I don't think the damage is extensive," Helen said to her son. "But she may have a concussion. It's important that we wake her up."

She reached into her case of remedies and pulled out a small brown bottle. She shook it slightly, then poured a dollop of the oily liquid onto her fingertips. The smell was atrocious.

"This should do it," she said as she dabbed the medicine on Terri's nostrils.

The result was immediate. Terri's eyes popped opened and she began to cough.

"Where ... where am I?" she asked, trying to sit up.

Helen pushed her gently back to the pillows.

"You may have a concussion, honey," she said. "Just lie still for now. Shawn's going to make you some tea."

Shawn leaned over and kissed Terri softly.

"Welcome back, girl," he whispered. "You had me worried there for a moment."

"Make her a cup of tea," said Helen, handing him a box of loose tea leafs. "Use these."

"My knee," said Terri. "Is it all right?"

Puzzled, Helen looked down at the young woman's leg. Just below the hem of her shorts was a thin line of red dots that encircled her knee. On examination, Helen recognized that the dots were actually individual punctures that were already beginning to heal.

"My God, what got you here? Those can't be spider bites, they're too symmetrical."

Helen waited for an explanation, but Terri remained silent. Sighing, Helen turned toward her son.

"Okay, Shawn," she demanded. "Are you going to tell me what happened here?"

Shawn looked at Terri as he handed her a cup of tea.

Terri smiled and nodded slightly. "Go ahead. Tell her. She needs to know."

"Okay, Mom," said Shawn, taking a seat on the couch next to her. "But you're going to have to put all your rational beliefs aside. And, if you can promise to do that, I'll tell you what happened."

Helen looked at him skeptically for a moment.

"All right. I can do that. Tell me."

KAREN

SHE STOOD ON THE rocks, waving toward the police in the parking lot below.

"Is that you, Mrs. Pierce?" asked the officer in charge through a loudspeaker.

"Yes, it's me."

Her voice was barely audible over the wind, but the officer could catch the gist of what she was saying.

"Is that Mr. Andersen behind you?"

"Yes, it's Bill."

"Is he armed? Does he have a weapon?"

Karen shook her head. "No, he doesn't. He's sick and needs help."

The officer nodded to the EMT's standing by the ambulance, calling them over.

"Sick? Is he hurt?"

Karen again shook her head. "He's ... his mind ... he's not right in the head."

"Is he dangerous?"

"I don't think so. Not to me, at least. But to himself..."

"Can you make your way down here?"

Karen looked back over her shoulder at Bill, who was still rocking and moaning.

"No, I can't leave him."

The officer was silent for a moment, then nodded. "Okay, we'll come up. You just stay put. We'll come get you."

Karen nodded, then turned and sat back down beside Bill, putting her arms around him, as the officers began to climb the rocks.

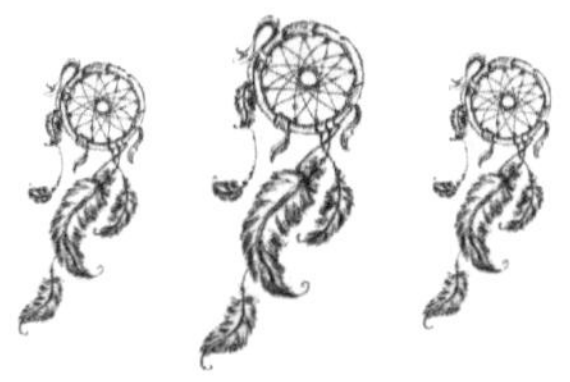

Dex watched and strained to hear the exchange going on between Karen and the police.

"What the hell is she doing, Pete?" he asked. "Why doesn't she come down? If Andersen is unarmed, why is she staying up there?"

"Now calm down, buddy," said Pete, recognizing that his friend was beginning to lose control again. "Maybe she can't. Looks like she's barefoot. Mayhap she's cut herself on the rocks or is afraid she'll fall."

Dex nodded. "Yeah, that could be it. But where's Alex? Why isn't anyone talking about him?"

Pete shook his head silently, not knowing what to say. The lack of concern for the boy's welfare had puzzled him at first, too. But now, watching the search and rescue team from the Coast Guard combing the area at the base of the cliff, he feared the worst.

"Look. They've reached the top," he said, changing the subject. "She'll be down soon."

Karen stood again as the police approached.

"Mrs. Pierce, are you all right?"

She nodded. "I've got some cuts on my feet but, otherwise, I'm okay. It's Bill - Mr. Andersen - who needs help. I was afraid to leave him, afraid of what he might do to himself."

The officers looked at Bill, who was still sitting on the rocks, oblivious to their presence.

"I have to ask, Mrs. Pierce, did he drop your son into the sea?"

Tears sprang into Karen's eyes as she choked back a sob. Unable to speak, she nodded, her body swaying slightly with emotion.

"Easy, Mrs. Pierce," said the officer, taking her by the elbow.

Karen breathed deeply. "I'm okay. But, Bill, you have to understand, he's not responsible. He's insane."

Saying those words proved to be too much and, overcome with fatigue and despair, she staggered, black dots clouding her vision. The officer stepped in and caught her before she fell to the rocks, then helped her to a seated position.

"Put your head between your knees, Mrs. Pierce. Let us know when you feel okay to start back down."

Karen did as he instructed, breathing deeply to try to calm the hysteria that threatened to consume her.

As she settled, the officer turned and spoke with the other policeman who had climbed the rocks with him.

"You place Andersen under arrest. Cuff him, but be careful. If he's loony tunes like Mrs. Pierce says, he could do anything. And he killed a kid. Don't forget that."

THE KNIFE

IN PAINSTAKING DETAIL, SHAWN related to his mother and Terri, the events that had occurred earlier that evening. When he finished, Helen looked at him, eyebrows raised in disbelief.

"A giant toad? A tongue full of poisonous barbs? Are you on drugs, son?"

Shawn laughed. "No, Ma. You know I don't do drugs. This is real. Right, Terri?"

Terri sat up, nodding. "When I went outside to put the burgers on the grill, that toad attacked me. I hit my head and must have passed out. It's the same creature that went after my mother, too. Harry Three-Feathers calls it a 'harbinger of evil.'"

Helen shook her head. "Either the both of you have gone crazy or this is just a dream and I'll soon wake up."

She looked back and forth from Terri to Shawn, waiting

for them to laugh and yell "April Fool's" or something similar, but, instead, their faces remained solemn.

"Okay," she said finally. "Show me this toad."

Shawn led them outside to the deck. The rain was letting up and they walked briskly over to the shed.

"I left that creature in here. I think it's dead," said Shawn as he approached the door. "I know I should have burned it, but I had to get Terri to safety. So, I don't know what we'll find. I harpooned it with that bone knife you gave me, Mom. But that toad is a supernatural being and I might have needed silver bullets or something to actually kill it. Both of you stay behind me."

He pushed open the door, turning on his headlamp as he stepped inside with Helen and Terri following closely.

At first glance, everything looked ordinary. Trying to remember just where the toad had landed, Shawn carefully scanned the floor with the light.

The carcass lay in the dirt by the lawnmower, the bone knife still protruding from its skull.

"Jesus H. Christ," whispered Helen. "That thing's bigger than Mabel Brewster's dog!"

Shawn leaned over and pulled the knife from the creature's head. As the blade slipped from the skull, a black noxious fluid began to seep out, staining the dirt floor.

Helen instinctively covered her nose with her hand. "That stinks to high heavens!" she exclaimed.

"I think we can safely conclude that it's dead," Shawn said. "Now, Mom, look at this."

He took the knife and pried open the toad's mouth, using the tip to spear the creature's tongue. Pulling it out, he turned it over, showing his mother the barbs hidden within.

Again, she shook her head in wonder. "I wouldn't have believed it if I hadn't seen it with my own eyes," she said. "Burn it, son. Burn it but good."

Shawn smiled as he wiped the blade on a rag that hung on a peg behind the lawnmower.

"Don't worry. I'm going to light him up. You two stand back. If he goes up anything like that tiny piece of his tongue did, we're going to have quite some fireworks."

Later, Helen reheated a lobster casserole that she'd brought with her. As they sat down to eat, Shawn remarked on how quiet his mother had been since they'd come back to the house.

"Are you okay, Mom?" he asked.

Helen stared at her plate, then took a deep breath. "I'm getting there, son. This has been an awful lot for an old woman to take in, you know. Evil frogs, smoke dreams, Abenaki curses. Not your everyday cup of tea."

Terri smiled, reached out, and grasped the older woman's hand.

"It doesn't happen every day, you know. But when it does ... watch out!"

Shawn chuckled. "What do you think Harry Three-Feathers will say when you tell him what happened?"

Terri laughed. "I'll bet you he'll say he already knew everything. He'll say it came to him in a smoke dream!"

Shawn grinned. "Yeah, but you told me he said that the toad couldn't be killed. That it was too ancient or something. If he's right about that, then how did I manage to destroy it?"

Terri leaned forward, suddenly serious. "You didn't use your regular hunting knife, did you?"

"No, I used that old bone one Mom gave me. I don't know why I grabbed it. Just seemed right, I guess."

Terri nodded. "Show it to me."

Shawn carefully pulled the knife from its sheath and placed it on the table in front of her.

Terri studied it for a moment, then reached out and touched the bone blade, running her finger lightly across it. She could feel it warm to her touch.

"Can you see it?" she asked, looking from Shawn to Helen. "Look closely and you can see the heat radiating from it."

Both Shawn and Helen leaned forward, staring at the knife.

"Holy crap!" exclaimed Helen. "I see it. Is it burning you?"

"No," said Terri with a smile. "It's a cold fire. It only burns what it needs to burn. Like the brain of that creature."

She picked the knife up and rolled it over in her hand, studying the handle. "This blade has some of the same carvings as the little bone knife that was in that old box Sophie and I found when we were kids. You know, the one that haunted me two years ago. I'll bet this one is related to it in some way."

"But I found that knife at a flea market in Augusta," said Helen. "It wasn't anything special. Just a cheap relic."

Terri handed the blade back to Shawn and smiled at Helen. "You say you found the knife, but I'll say to you that it was the other way around. This knife found you. It was looking for a way home and found it when you came into that market. And I believe it was meant to go to Shawn so that someday he could use it to protect me."

Helen frowned, clearly puzzled.

Terri reached out and took the older woman's hands in hers. "Don't you see? It's all related. That knife belongs on Mateguas. And, it was meant to protect me, to keep me safe. That's why it found its way to you and, through you, to Shawn."

"But why?"

"It saved me from the toad, for one, but my gut tells me there's something more. Something bigger. Maybe my mother or

Harry can shed light on it. In any case, we need to keep this knife safe. Right, Shawn?"

"You got it, girl," he replied. "That knife stays right here with us and, if need be, I'll use it again."

KAREN AND DEX

SLOWLY AND WITH CARE, the police escorted Karen and Bill down to the parking lot. Dex watched impatiently, every instinct telling him he should be the one with his arm around Karen, helping her make the perilous descent. But a line of cops standing just inside the crime scene tape told him that if he approached, he would be arrested. So, he stayed where he was and waited.

All eyes were on Karen, Bill, and the police, when Dex caught sight of a man running out of the water at the base of the cliff, in his arms a small bundle.

"I've got him!" the man yelled as he ran toward the ambulance. The EMTs took the bundle from him and quickly went inside their van.

Dex turned and stared. The man was wearing a Coast Guard Search and Rescue jacket.

It took Dex a moment to understand what he had just seen.

"ALEX!" he screamed and, shaking off Pete's restraining hand, ran toward the ambulance.

The sailor, wrapped in a blanket and holding a cup of coffee, cut Dex off before he could reach the van's rear door.

"Whoa, there, buddy," he said. "Identify yourself."

"Is that my son? Is he okay?"

"Settle down. First things first. What's your name?"

Dex took a deep breath. "Dex Pierce. Now, was that my son?"

The sailor, recognizing the name, looked down at his coffee. "Yeah, I think so," he said softly. "It was a little boy. But I'm afraid he's gone."

"Gone? I don't know what you mean. Let me see him."

The sailor put his hand on Dex's shoulder. "Take it easy, man. I'm sorry, but it looks like the fall killed him instantly. He's dead. I'm sorry."

Dex stood stock still as the words penetrated his consciousness. At that moment, Karen came rushing toward him.

"Dex!" she cried, throwing herself into his arms.

Later, they stood together watching as the police brought Bill to the cruiser. He was flanked by two officers, hands cuffed behind his back. His face held no expression and his movements seemed forced and unnatural. Dex took one step in his direction, fists clenched, but Karen restrained him with a hand on his arm.

"Don't," she said. "You'll only make things worse."

Dex turned toward her, his face etched with pain and anger.

"How can you be so calm about this? He killed our child!"

Karen's face contorted as if she had been struck. Tears welled in her eyes.

"How can you say that? I had to watch..."

Her voice broke and she turned away. She leaned against the side of the police van, trying to keep from collapsing onto the ground. She took several deep breaths, then reached out to Dex.

"My baby's gone. I'll never hold him again or..."

She choked back a sob, overcome with emotion. Dex ignored her, staring angrily at police cruiser as it sped away with Bill inside.

"Dex, please, I need you. Your anger won't bring him back. Honey, can't you see? Bill's sick. And, he's not going anywhere but to a hospital where he'll spend the rest of his life."

Dex turned and stared at her coldly.

"Okay, you give him your pity, but I can't. He's a murderer, plain and simple. A hospital's too good for him and I hope he fries for this."

Karen was about to say more, but their conversation was interrupted by a young woman from the paramedic team who was swiftly approaching.

"I'm sorry," she said. "But I need one of you to identify the body."

Karen nodded.

"I'll go," she said.

"No, Karen. We'll both go. He was our son."

AFTERMATH

THE PHONE RANG SHRILLY. Karen looked down at her watch. It was seven a.m.

It had been two days since the tragic events at Eagle Rock and, consumed by grief, she found it hard to leave her bed. Everywhere in the cottage were reminders of her lost child and, unable to face them, she let herself drown in the oblivion brought on by sedative-induced sleep. Dex as rarely home, handling his grief and anger by throwing himself into his work. Most of the daytime and early evening hours, he was down at the boatyard or out on the water. When he was home, he barely spoke to her, either unwilling or unable to seek comfort in her arms.

Karen tried to convince him they should go back to California to bury their boy, but Dex was adamant. His son would be buried in the island cemetery, next to his parents.

With no strength to fight him, she conceded to his wishes.

The phone rang again. Afraid it might be a reporter, she glanced at the caller ID. It was Terri.

"Hi, honey."

"How are you doing, Mom?"

Karen took a deep breath, holding back the tears that threatened to erupt again. "I'm okay."

"You don't sound like it. How's Dex?"

Karen hesitated. "He's taking it hard as you would expect. He's angry and right now that's overshadowing his grief. He'd kill your father if he could get his hands on him and I can't say that I blame him."

"Mom, you don't mean that, do you? Dad ... he's sick. He needs help."

"Yes, I know. And I agree. Actually, I'm planning on going to the mainland to see him today if they'll let me. I've hired a lawyer for him, too. Do you want to go with me?"

"Yeah, I would. I'll get Shawn to take us over. What time?"

"Around eleven? Will that work?"

"We'll make it work. Have you spoken to Sophie?"

"No, not since the day before yesterday. She called again last night and talked to Dex. I was asleep. She'll be here for the funeral."

"Good. Okay, I'll see you at eleven."

"Thanks, honey."

"Give Dex my love."

"Will do."

Karen hung up and sat down at the table. The house was so quiet without the boy. She thought again about the words he'd left her with and the feeling of joy she felt when his soul washed over hers in the final moments before he'd left the earth. And then there was the message or vision sent to her by Mateguas. She would have to deal with that, too. But not now. Now was time for grieving, both for her son and for the man she once loved.

Deep in thought, she was startled by a hand on her shoulder.

"Sorry I scared you," said Dex. "Who was that?"

"Just Terri."

"Well, Louise called on my cell. There's a bunch of folks getting together down at the church ... sort of a support group. I think we should go."

Karen shook her head. "I can't."

"Princess, it will be good for us. They're all good people. And they want to help."

"It's not that. I have to go to town."

"Town? Why?"

Karen sighed, bracing herself. "I have to meet with Bill's attorney."

"WHAT? What are you doing meeting with that bastard's lawyer? He killed our boy, Karen! Dropped him down on those rocks like he was so much garbage. His head was crushed! You saw it! And now you're going to try to help his murderer?"

Karen sat still for a moment, letting him vent his anger, then she stood and faced him.

"Yes, I am. Be reasonable. You know he's insane, don't you? You've seen all the news reports. We watched them together, for Christ's sake. You heard that bitch LeVeque revealing what he had to do to survive. A memory like that would unhinge anyone. Yes, he killed Alex, but he wasn't responsible. The person responsible is the one who left him on Puffin in the first place. And why is it so wrong that I just want to make sure he gets a fair deal? He'll be locked up for the rest of his life anyway. I think that and what he's doing to himself right now are punishment enough."

"Are you listening to yourself? I can't believe you're making excuses for him. Okay, you go - go and give comfort to the man who killed our son. But don't expect me to understand or sympathize. If I had my way, he'd be in the morgue right now, not in a cell wasting the taxpayers' dollars."

Karen reached out to put her hand on his arm, to try to reason with him, but he pulled away and walked to the hall closet, grabbing a jacket.

"Go to town. See that bastard, hold his hand. I'll be at the church."

Without giving her a chance to respond, he walked out the door, slamming it behind him.

Deflated, Karen leaned against the counter, tears streaming down her cheeks. How could she make him understand? Bill was lost and should be pitied, not vilified.

She reached for a tissue from the side table and blew her nose, then poured herself a cup of coffee. She sat down and closed her eyes, thinking about her little boy, remembering him. She stayed like that for a while, not moving. Finally, she picked up her cup to take a sip, but it had grown cold.

She poured the coffee into the sink and glanced around the room. This place held only sadness now. She thought about returning to California alone. She could do it. She had her own money and there was nothing holding her here on this island anymore. But, deep in her heart, she knew that was wrong. Those swirling vortexes or forces that lay buried beneath this island's surface weren't finished with her yet. No, there would be more grief to come, of that she was certain.

She checked her watch. It was almost ten. Shawn and Terri would be there to pick her up in an hour. Sighing, she put the cup in the sink and walked to the bathroom. She had to get ready.

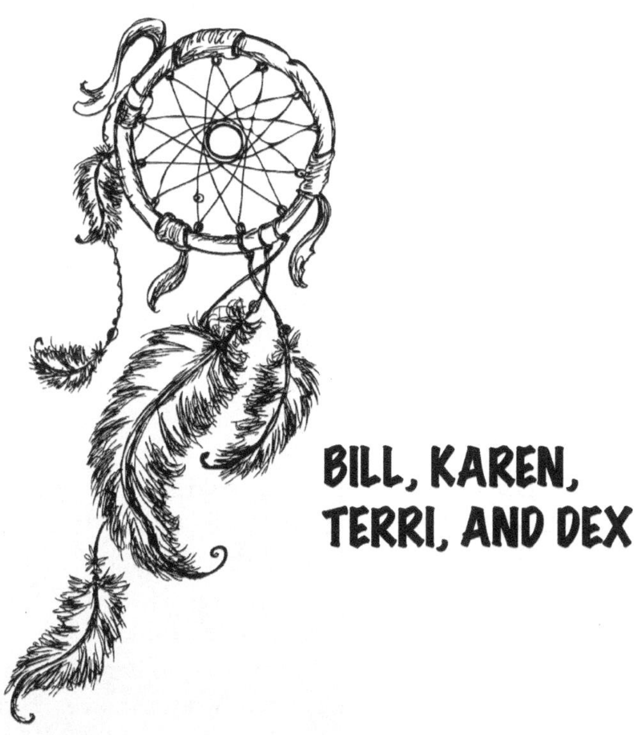

BILL, KAREN, TERRI, AND DEX

AT THE POLICE STATION, Karen conferred with the attorney she had hired for Bill.

"And you'll make sure they get him out of here as soon as possible, won't you?"

"Yes, Mrs. Pierce. I've already set up a meeting with the judge in chambers. Mr. Andersen's been examined by two psychiatrists, one representing the State. They both concur in their diagnoses. I don't think there'll be any difficulty getting him transferred immediately back to Bangor State. I've also spoken with the Chief Medical Officer there, a Dr. Todd, and, since he knows your ex-husband well, he volunteered to come down here and accompany him back to the hospital."

"That would be good. Bill always spoke highly of Dr. Todd. Thank you for all you've done. When this is over, please send your bill directly to me, not to my husband. Now, is it possible for my daughter and I to see Bill?"

The lawyer frowned. "I'm afraid our doctor says he's entered a state of catatonia and isn't communicating with anyone right now. But, if you want to sit with him, I think I can arrange it."

"Thank you."

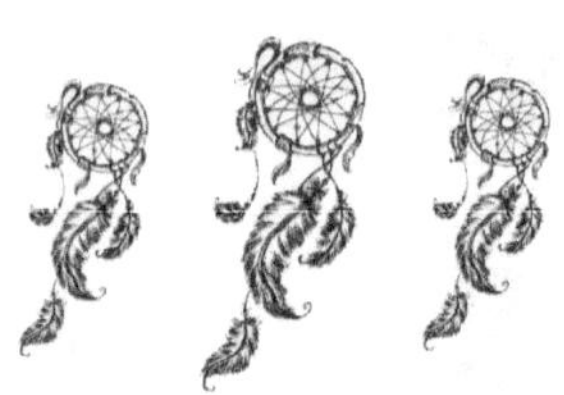

Later, Karen and Terri were led to a small, cold room inside the jail. An empty table sat in the middle, two chairs on one side, one chair on the other. Bill was already seated there, handcuffed and shackled. He didn't seem to notice their arrival. His eyes stared blankly at the wall as his body rocked from side to side.

Karen reached over and put her arm around her daughter, who was apparently shocked by her father's appearance. Terri clutched at her mother's hand, then approached the table.

"Dad?" she whispered. "It's me, Terri. And Mom. We've come to see you."

Bill gave no indication that he even knew she was in the room. He continued rocking, humming softly as he stared into space.

Karen squeezed her daughter's hand. "This is how he was after he..."

Her voice broke. Terri gazed at her mother's sad eyes. "It's okay, Mom. I want to just sit with him a while. You don't have to stay."

Karen gave her a small smile. "Yes, I do. This is not his fault. It's my fault. I didn't pay enough attention to what was going on. Maybe, I could have stopped this."

"No, don't say that. Don't torture yourself that way. Dad's fate was decided the day someone left him to die on Puffin. No one could have foretold what would happen and you did everything you could to help him."

Karen looked gratefully at her daughter. "Let's sit down."

They each took a chair opposite Bill. Terri reached out and grasped his limp hand while Karen leaned across the table, toward him, a curious look on her face.

"I know that song," she said in a voice barely above a whisper. Slowly, she began humming the plaintive tune along with Bill.

"What is it, Mom?" asked Terri.

Karen didn't answer immediately, but just kept humming, then she turned to her daughter.

"Back before you were born, your father and I went to a movie. It was a tragedy about war and separation. This tune is the love theme from that film. We made it our song that night."

"What was it about?"

"Oh, the usual, love and promise. It was about two people who were torn apart by war ... two people who vowed they would wait for each other forever. Of course, that didn't happen. Hence, the tragedy."

Terri nodded then gazed back at her father, again taking his hand.

They sat quietly until the guard came and told them they had to go. Terri embraced her unresponsive father and Karen kissed him lightly on the cheek, then they were escorted out the door to the hallway.

When they reached the entrance, Karen stopped short. Susan LeVeque, her cameraman, and sound recording crew were rapidly making their way through the security checkpoints.

Karen turned to Terri. "You stay here and, no matter what happens, don't interfere."

Terri opened her mouth to respond, but Karen was already striding in Susan's direction.

Susan was talking to the cameraman when Karen came up behind her, tapping her on the shoulder. Whirling around, Susan looked surprised to see the mother of the slain child standing in front of her.

"Mrs. Pierce, I..."

With a resounding "CRACK," the back of Karen's hand connected with Susan's face. The reporter, caught off-guard, stumbled backward and fell on her backside on the courthouse floor.

Before the cameraman could put down his gear and restrain her, Karen leaned over the reporter and spoke in a voice too soft for any live microphone to catch.

"You fucking bitch. You ever come near any member of my family again and I'll see that it's you dangling over those rocks! And if you repeat this to anyone, I'll deny it and sue your bony ass for slander. Are we on the same page?"

Without waiting for a reply, Karen stood and gave the cameraman a brilliant smile before walking back to her daughter.

"Let's get the hell out of here," she said, steering Terri toward the door.

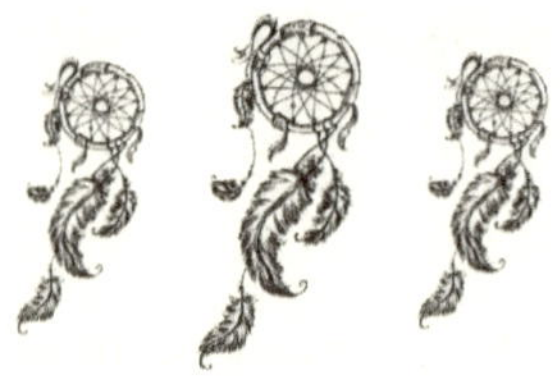

When they arrived at the cottage, the house was dark.

"Do you want us to stay with you, Mom?" asked Terri.

"No, honey. I'll be okay. I'm sure Dex will be home soon. You and Shawn run along now. I do need to talk to you both about something, but it can wait until tomorrow. I'm bushed."

She kissed her daughter and embraced Shawn. "You take good care of her, okay?"

"Not a problem. You call us anytime, day or night, if you need anything."

Karen smiled, hugged her daughter again, and went into the house.

Once inside, she tossed her bag on the couch, turned on some lights, and poured herself a drink. Sitting alone, she turned on the TV. It was a little after six. Not wanting to see the local news, she switched to CNN.

They were in a commercial break, so she leaned back, closing her eyes. When the ad ended, the anchorman's words jarred her back to reality.

"Tragedy in Maine."

She opened her eyes and leaned forward, surprised to see pictures of Bill, Dex, Alex, and herself flashing across the screen. The anchor said something about turning things over to the news reporter on the scene and the somber face of Susan LeVeque stared back at her.

"For Christ's sake!" Karen cried, leaping from her chair. "That fucking woman's profiting by all this."

She picked up the clicker and turned off the TV, restraining the urge to throw her shoe at the screen. Tears were beginning to flow again and, wishing her husband was by her side, she walked to the window and gazed out.

She stayed there for a moment, hoping to hear the sound of his truck in their drive, but all was quiet. Sighing to herself, she turned off the lights and, exhausted, decided to lie down.

She was jarred awake from a deep sleep by movement on the bed. For a brief instant, Karen was terrified. Bill's recent attack flashed across her mind as strong arms reached out for her. Her first instinct was to pull away, but, as the fog of sleep cleared, she recognized Dex's masculine scent and surrendered herself to him in relief.

He didn't say anything, just pulled her close, nuzzling her neck as he turned her in his arms so she was facing him.

She started to speak, but he silenced her by pressing his lips forcefully against hers. She could smell the liquor on his breath and, realizing that this was not a good time for conversation, opened her lips, inviting him inside.

Too tired to undress, she was still fully clothed, wearing a cotton shirt and shorts. Dex pressed his body close to hers and slid his hand down to her chest, fumbling with the tiny buttons on her blouse. She moved back slightly, intent on helping him, when, in apparent frustration, he ripped the shirt apart.

She gasped as he pushed the thin material aside and burrowed his head between her breasts. Surprised by the depth of his need, she moved her hands soothingly over his back, hoping to calm him.

In response, he pushed her away and rose up on his elbows for a moment, staring at her, his face expressionless.

"Dex, what..."

Again, he silenced her, his hands reaching for the zipper on her shorts.

"Dex, please..."

Ignoring her pleas, he unzipped her fly and in one swift motion yanked off both her shorts and panties. She tried to move away from him, but he held her down, using his knee to spread her legs.

Without saying a word, he entered her roughly. She was barely ready for him and cried out as he forced himself inside.

It didn't take long, just a few hard pushes before his body tensed and he let out a long, painful groan as he ejaculated.

His hands gripped the sheets on either side of her head and she lay frozen beneath him as he caught his breath and relaxed. Still silent, he rolled away from her, turning his back.

Karen stared at him, confused by his callous and crude behavior. She was about to say something, to ask him why, but heard his soft snore and knew he was already asleep. Shaking her head, she got up, left the bed, and walked wordlessly to the bathroom to clean herself.

When she was through, she stood in the doorway, staring at him as he slept. There had been no love in the act he had just forced her to perform, only anger. In acknowledging this, she knew they had come to a crossroads.

He was the man she'd loved and lived with for twelve years and, in all that time, he had never made her feel the way the way she felt now - soiled and badly used.

DEX

HE ROLLED OVER, EYES opening. The room was still dark. He checked his watch. It was almost five-thirty. He sat up and glanced around, at first not sure where he was, then recognition set in. He was home.

Sighing to himself, he tried to put together the pieces of what had happened the night before. He remembered spending most of the day at the church with friends whom he had known since childhood. Later, at night, there'd been a vigil down by Eagle Point and, while there had been plenty of psalm singing and prayers, there'd also been plenty of alcohol and he knew that he'd had his fair share of the hard stuff. One of the O'Dwyer boys had driven him home - not Shawn - the older one, Jason.

Dex glanced around the room. He was alone. Karen was nowhere to be seen. Again, he searched his memory of the night

340

before and was sure she had been there, in this bed, when he finally got home.

She was asleep, he thought as he remembered her laying on the bedspread, still dressed in shorts and a cotton blouse, her blonde hair spread across the pillow like a fan.

He had wanted her so badly at that moment that just touching her lit him up like a Christmas tree. But he'd also been angry and knew that somehow that anger had eclipsed his need and carried over into their lovemaking.

Slowly, he got up off the bed and pulled on his jeans, making his way to the bathroom. He relieved himself and splashed cold water on his face.

Still feeling the effects of the night before, he walked toward the kitchen to make some coffee. On his way, out of habit, he opened the spare bedroom door, meaning to check on his infant son, but stopped, remembering that this was a chore he no longer had to perform. A picture of the boy lying lifeless on the ambulance stretcher passed before his eyes, and he had to brace himself to keep from screaming.

Karen, he thought, knowing he still needed her, more than he could admit. But would she still want him after what he'd done to her the night before?

He knew he had used her - used her like some one-night-stand or whore from down on the waterfront. And he knew why.

I wanted to hurt her like she hurt me when she'd left to help her murdering ex-husband. My actions were fueled by anger and jealousy. But now, all that seems so senseless. I need her. I want to hold her in my arms and never let go.

He brewed a cup of coffee, wondering where she had gone and if she had left him for good. He glanced over to the living room, now partially lit by the sun, which was streaming through the curtains.

She was there - lying on the couch, her body covered by a lightweight afghan. He could see she still had on her blouse, open in the front where he had ripped it. And, even with her eyes closed, he could tell they were puffy and swollen from crying.

Was she crying for our lost child or because of what I did to her the last night?

He didn't know the answer and couldn't ask. All he wanted to do was go to her and hold her close, but now, he didn't know how. So, instead, he sat at the breakfast bar, watching and waiting for her to wake up.

The sound and smell of bacon sizzling in a fry-pan caused Karen to stir. Her stomach growled and she sat up, aware that she had eaten next to nothing for the past twenty-four hours. She glanced over to the kitchen and saw Dex busy at the stove. Pulling her blouse closed, she remembered how he had treated her the night before. She picked up the afghan and wrapped it around her body like a robe, not wanting him to see her nakedness.

Hearing her movements, he turned and leaned on the breakfast bar.

"Hi, sleepyhead," he said. "I hope you're hungry 'cause I've got bacon, eggs, and pancakes ready to go."

Karen bit her upper lip, then forced a smile as she got off the couch.

"Yes, I could use some eggs. And coffee. But I'm going to get washed and dressed first."

Holding the afghan tightly around her, shielding herself from his eyes, she turned and walked away.

He stood watching her go, knowing somehow, in the night, he might have lost more than he could have ever imagined.

KAREN, TERRI, AND SHAWN

SOMEHOW, KAREN AND DEX got through the morning.

Breakfast was always a happy time in their house, filled with laughter and good conversation. But today, the kitchen table was draped in silence. Karen only picked at her food and Dex was unable to find a way to bridge the gap that his behavior the night before had created. Finally, he muttered something about needing to go down to the boatyard, grabbed his coat, and, giving her a peck on the cheek, left the house.

Karen watched as he drove away, saddened by their failure to communicate.

He seemed slightly contrite, she thought as she gazed out the window. *But he didn't apologize.*

That omission on his part ate at her soul.

Trying to put her fears about her marriage aside, she

checked her phone for messages. There was only one. It was from her daughter, Sophie, saying she would come to the island for the funeral, which was scheduled for the next day at noon. She would be arriving that night on the five o'clock boat.

Karen smiled at the thought of seeing her again. She'd missed spending time with Sophie this summer and knew that her arrival would be good for Dex, too. He had a close relationship with her - closer than he had with Terri.

Her spirits lifted a bit, Karen was about to shut down the phone when it chimed.

"Hello?"

"Hi, Mom. It's me, Terri. How are you doing this morning?"

"I'm all right. I got a message from Sophie. She'll be on the five o'clock today."

"Yeah, I know. I talked to her last night. She's going to stay with us."

"Oh," said Karen, disappointment apparent in her voice. "I thought she'd stay here."

Terri hesitated. "We didn't think you'd want company. We thought that you and Dex might want to be alone. But if you want her to stay at your place..."

"No, no, that's okay," Karen interrupted. "She's only going to be here for a couple of days anyway. It will be good for you girls to catch up."

"Yeah," said Terri, laughing. "Twin stuff. Now, is there anything you need in town? Shawn's going over later today."

"Actually, I do need something, but not in town. I need to speak with you AND Shawn. Do you have time this morning?"

"Sure. But what about?"

"I'll tell you when I see you. And, I'll bring a list for Shawn, too. Can I come over in about an hour?"

"Yeah. We'll be here."

"Okay, see you then."

When Karen walked up the deck stairs, Terri was waiting to greet her.

"You look tired, Mom," she said, hugging her. "Come on in. You want some lemonade?"

Karen smiled weakly. "Sure. Is Shawn here?"

"Yeah. You said you wanted to speak with both of us. He's upstairs. He'll be down in a second."

Karen nodded. "Good."

Terri ushered her into the living room as Shawn came stomping down the stairs.

"How are you holding up?" he said, embracing Karen. "If you need anything..."

Karen returned his hug.

"I'm okay, thanks. Now sit down. I need to talk with the both of you."

Terri brought in a tray holding a pitcher of lemonade and three glasses and busied herself pouring drinks for everyone.

"Sit down, Terri," said Karen. "And don't look so worried. This isn't necessarily a bad thing."

Puzzled, Terri obediently sat on the sofa next to Shawn and waited for her mother to begin.

Karen took a sip of lemonade, then turned her gaze to Shawn.

"Do you love my daughter?" she asked.

Terri's mouth fell open, shocked by her mother's bluntness. "Whoa, Mom! I don't think..."

Shawn interrupted, taking Terri's hand in his. "It's okay, babe," he said. "I don't mind answering that question."

Nodding to Terri, he looked back to Karen. "Yes, ma'am, I do, with all my heart."

Karen smiled. "And do you intend to marry her?"

Again, Terri looked shocked. "MOM! That's none of your business!"

Karen reached out and took her daughter's hand.

"You're wrong about that, honey. It is my business. Now, Shawn, can you give me an answer?"

Shawn met her gaze for a moment, then stood and left the room. He came back a minute later.

"I planned on doing this sometime this summer," he said. "I don't know when exactly. I was waiting for the right time. But, seeing you've asked, I guess that this is the right time."

He knelt down in front of the sofa and took Terri's hand in his. "Look at me, girl," he said softly. "I want nothing more than to spend my life loving you. I know you have school to finish and I won't stand in your way. In fact, I insist that you do finish. But I want, no, need to know that you're coming back to me.

"So, Theresa Marie Andersen, will you do me the honor of becoming my bride? Will you wear this ring as a token of my love and commitment?"

As he spoke, he removed from his pocket a small velvet box. He held it out to her and opened it. Inside sat a small solitaire diamond ring.

Tears sprang into Terri's eyes as she realized what he was asking. She held out her hand to him.

"Yes. I'll marry you Shawn O'Dwyer. I love you with all my heart. And I'll be proud to wear your ring."

Smiling softly, Shawn slipped the ring on her finger, leaned forward, and kissed her, then he turned back to Karen, surprised to see tears welling up in her eyes.

"Good," Karen said, smiling at him. She took Terri's hand in hers and gazed down at the ring. "How beautiful. See, honey, I was right. He is a keeper."

Terri was about to speak when Karen, her face once again serious, held up her hand. "

"And you're going to need him standing steadfastly by your side if you choose the path I think you'll choose."

Terri stared at her. "What path? What is this all about?"

Karen leaned back in her chair, sipping her lemonade, collecting her thoughts.

"Humor me for a minute. Shawn. I take it Terri's told you everything."

Shawn looked puzzled. "Everything about what?"

"About the hocus pocus. Mateguas, the ancient box, the knife - everything, not just the toad stuff, but everything else."

Shawn nodded. "Yes, Terri's filled me in on all she knows and I'm on board with it."

"That's good. There can be no secrets between you two. I know Terri understands that, but do you? Secrets are what ruined things for her father and me. And secrets and things kept hidden are to blame for what happened the other night. My life has been full of lies, betrayal, and deceit. That can't happen to you two. Understand?"

"I understand, ma'am," replied Shawn. "And, no, we don't keep things from each other. Right, Terri?"

Terri smiled. "We're straight with each other, Mom. You know that."

Again, Karen nodded, pleased with both the young man's and her daughter's response.

"Okay. Now that that's out of the way, I need to tell you both what actually happened the other night on the rocks. Not about Bill and what he did to Alex, but what Alex shared with me before he left."

"Shared? What do you mean, Mom?"

"You know I told you he could send his thoughts to me telepathically, right?"

Both Shawn and Terri nodded.

"Okay, well just before Bill..." She hesitated, wiping away an errant tear that was sliding down her cheek. She bit her bottom lip and took a deep breath.

"Alex spoke to me before he died. He told me not to grieve, that things were as they should be. He said that the evil foretold by the *Aglebemu* had come to pass and that his father had called him home."

Terri stared at her, confused. "You mean, Dex? I don't get it."

Karen smiled and patted her daughter's hand. "It is confusing, honey, but you need to know that Dex is not his biological father. No, his father was and is Mateguas, God of the Dead. Alex was The Blessed Boy reborn, but, for many reasons, the time was not right for him to walk the earth in human form again. So, he was called home. Are you following me?"

Again, the young people nodded in unison.

"Good. Before he left, he let his soul wash over me. Oh, honey, it was beautiful. I can still feel him. He's right here in my heart."

Tears were flowing freely now although Karen seemed unaware that they were sliding down her cheeks. Terri leaned forward and embraced her. "I'm glad you have that memory, Mom."

Karen reached into her pocket for a tissue and blew her nose. "Okay, but there's more. Alex told me his father wanted to speak to me and asked if I would open my heart to let him in. Well, let me tell you that threw me for a loop. The God of the Dead wanting to talk to me. But what could I do? So, I opened myself to him."

"Oh, Mom, what did he say?"

Karen smiled. "He didn't really speak to me. It was more like he sent me a vision. And that vision is why I'm here talking to you two. Remember when Harry Three-Feathers sent each of us that smoke dream or whatever it was?"

"Yeah. You screamed."

"Well, yes. Mine wasn't very pleasant as I'm sure you remember. But what about yours?"

Terri frowned. "I saw two little girls, blondes with curls, playing at the beach. I thought it might be Sophie and me, but it was the wrong beach. Harry said it could be an image of the future or nothing at all. What has this got to do with Mateguas?"

"Patience, dear. I'll explain. You were right. It wasn't you and Sophie. The vision Mateguas sent me was of you, Shawn, and those little girls. They're going to be yours - your daughters, yours and Shawn's."

Terri and Shawn looked at each other, surprised. "We're going to have twins?" exclaimed Terri.

"Yes," said Karen, nodding. "And you'll be living at your father's house, the one on the hill where all of this started. It's still sacred land, you know. Let me describe the vision, okay?"

Terri and Shawn nodded, leaning forward, intent on her words.

"I saw you, Shawn, sitting on the porch on one of those old-fashioned glider swings. Next to you, one on each side, were the twins - little girls about two years old, with long blonde curls. You were reading to them."

"Wow," said Shawn, a broad smile on his face.

Karen smiled back then turned her attention to Terri. "You were there, too, honey. You were standing on the lawn, under the waning crescent moon. And you were pregnant."

Terri stared at her mother. "I'm going to have three children? Is that what you're telling me? What's the catch?"

Karen laughed. "Yes, the catch. There always is one, isn't there? Okay, you're right. There is a catch and this one's a dandy. The third child, if you choose to have him, will be Him."

"I don't understand, Mom. Him?"

"Oh, sweetie, he will be The Blessed Boy. He'll come back ... back this time to a house full of love and trust, not to a place full of lies and deceit. But it has to be your decision. That, you see, was part of the problem this time. I wasn't given a choice. His birth was forced on me."

"But you loved him."

"Yes, and I wouldn't trade the time I had with him for anything in the world. But for it to work, it has to be voluntary. It has to be done with love. It's a sacred responsibility ... you have to swear to protect and cherish him so, this time, he can fulfill his destiny. And that's what I came here to tell you."

Terri and Shawn were silent for a moment, then Terri got off the sofa and knelt in front of her mother.

"Oh, Mom," she said. "Of course, we'll do it. The world needs him. And we'll keep him safe, won't we, Shawn?"

Shawn nodded. "You can count on us, Karen. He'll be my son and I'll shelter and protect him just as I will my daughters and my wife."

Karen smiled and squeezed her daughter's hands. "You don't have to make this choice now. You have to finish college. After that will come marriage and the twins. You both need to keep your minds and hearts open, for, you know, life can do strange things to people. You may find that when the time comes, you're not quite as willing to sacrifice as you are now. And, if that becomes the case, then it is as it should be. No guilt. You do what's right for your family."

Karen stood, pulling Terri to her feet. "Now, I have to go. There are lots of details about the funeral tomorrow I have to take care of."

"Where's Dex?" asked Terri. "Is everything okay with you two?"

Karen hesitated before answering.

"He's down at the boatyard. We're having a bit of a rough patch. He doesn't understand why I don't hate your father. But we'll get through it. We've been through worse before. Don't you worry. And why don't you, Shawn, and Sophie come over for dinner tonight? It would be nice to have my family all together again."

"Sure, Mom. We'll pick Soph up on the five, then be over. Okay?"

"Great."

Karen gazed down at her daughter's hand, the tiny diamond solitaire sparkling in the sunlight.

"I think I like the looks of that," she said softly. "We have something to celebrate."

Smiling, Shawn and Terri walked her to her car and stood, arm in arm, as she backed down the drive.

Once away from the house, Karen turned the car around and headed to the far end of the island. Parking at a deserted beach, she got out and slowly walked the shore.

Tonight my girls will be with me again, she thought. *And that will be a cause for celebration. But tomorrow, I'll have to endure the funeral and all its religious trappings. The whole island will be there to lay my child to rest and Dex will be surrounded by all his old friends. But what about afterward? There are still so many questions that demand to be answered.*

She picked up a stone and tossed it, watching as it skipped across the water.

'*The truth will out*,' she thought, remembering a line from Shakespeare. *Yes, whatever fate has in store, it's time for the truth to bare its ugly head and finally lay all the old ghosts to rest.*

FAMILY REUNION

SOPHIE ARRIVED AS PLANNED and, after settling in at Terri's, they drove to the cottage for dinner. Karen was waiting for them at the door.

"Hi, Mom," said Sophie, embracing her. "I'm so sorry. This is all so awful."

Karen hugged her daughter, holding her close.

"Thanks, honey," she said. "It's been rough. The house is so empty without him."

Sophie hugged her again. "I can't believe that Dad could do what he did. What's wrong with him?"

Karen took her daughter's hand. "Your dad is sick, honey. They're taking him back to the hospital in Bangor tomorrow. If you want, we could go to the mainland before he leaves if you want to say goodbye."

Sophie shook her head. "No, I don't want to see him. What he did can't be forgiven. I think we'd all be better off if he'd just stayed dead."

Karen stared at her, shocked by the harshness of her declaration. "Sophie, have some compassion. He is your father."

"Not anymore, he isn't. Let's go inside. I want to see Dex."

Karen was about to say more but thought better of it. She put her arm around Sophie's waist and escorted her into the house.

Dex was standing just inside the entryway. When he saw his stepdaughter, he stepped forward and pulled her into a tight embrace.

"Missed you, honey," he whispered. "So glad you could make it."

Sophie kissed him on the cheek. "I missed you too, Dad,"

Dex pulled away from her, startled. "Dad? You've never called me that before."

"Do you mind? You know, I've always thought of you as my father and now I think it's time that I said it."

Dex hugged her again. "Do I mind? Not in the least! Come on, let's sit down. Tell me all about New Haven."

Karen listened to this exchange, surprised, but said nothing. She stood in the doorway watching the two of them laughing and talking.

Terri came to her mother's side. "I don't get it, Mom. What's up with her?"

Karen shook her head. "I don't know, but let's not discuss it here. Everyone handles grief differently. I'm sure she doesn't really mean what she said about your father. Now, come and help me in the kitchen."

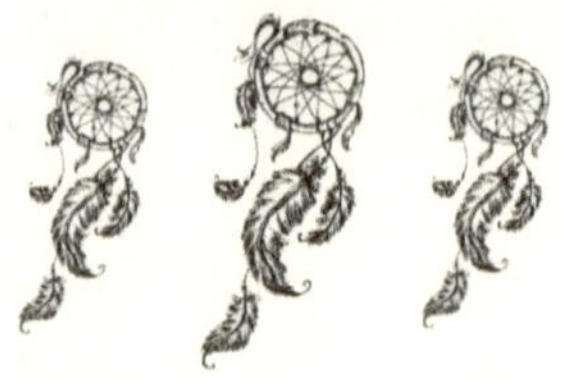

After dinner, everyone went out on the deck while Karen cleaned up. When she was finished, she joined them.

"I've convinced Sophie to stay here with us, princess," said Dex. "She can only stay for tonight. She has a test in a couple of days and a new exhibit opening at the gallery. She has to leave tomorrow after the funeral."

Karen smiled. "I wish you could stay longer, honey, but I'm glad you'll be here. I'll make up the spare room for you. Shawn, can you get Sophie's things and bring them over?"

"Sure, Karen. I'll be right back."

"I'll go with you," chimed Terri, hurrying along behind him as he left the house.

Sophie grinned at her mother. "I can't believe they're engaged. What does she see in him? I mean, he's good-looking but, overall, he's really quite ordinary. You think this engagement's going to last?"

Karen frowned at her daughter's curt dismissal of Terri's young man. "Yes, I do believe it's going to last. They love each other very much and they make a good couple. And, Shawn is not ordinary. Actually, I'd say he's quite an extraordinary young man."

Sophie looked surprised. "Boy, you've done a turnaround on him. Guess I'll have to try to get to know him better."

"That would be a good idea. Now you and Dex chat while I make up the bed."

When she finished in the bedroom, Karen stood in the doorway observing her family. Terri and Shawn had returned and were in animated conversation with Dex and Sophie.

Watching them closely, Karen wondered about Sophie's apparent total rejection of her natural father.

She and Dex have always been close and finding Bill two years ago was really Terri's idea, not Sophie's. Maybe being on her own, away from her twin, has given Soph a new sense of confidence or something.

Sighing, she turned from the doorway and sat down on the sofa, leaning back. She was tired and tomorrow would be a difficult, if not impossible, day. She closed her eyes.

Just one more day to get through, she thought. *Then Sophie will return to school and Terri and Shawn will be back on the water. That will leave me with Dex. We'll be alone for the first time, no children running around. No, it'll be just the two of us and maybe, if we try, we can sort things out and see if we can find a way to go on together.*

THE FUNERAL

THE FUNERAL WAS HELD at the island church. Most of the year-round residents turned out as well as a number of summer people who were acquainted with Karen and Dex. There was a brief sermon followed by hymns and songs selected by Karen. Following this, the pastor turned the floor over to the islanders, to share their remembrances and feelings about the young boy. Since Alex was just a baby and new to the island, there were not too many people who knew him well. But most everyone knew Dex and they spoke to and of him, offering their support and condolence for his loss.

Charlie Red Squirrel and Harry Three-Feathers came over on the morning ferry. Harry sat stoically in a wheelchair, a wool lap robe across his knees despite the heat. He looked old and frail and Karen's heart went out to him.

After the church service ended, Charlie took Karen aside.

"Harry would like a few minutes of your time, Karen, if that's all right with you."

Karen nodded. "Of course. Anything he wants. I'm in his debt."

Charlie smiled and took her arm, leading her to a place behind the church where Harry sat under an old oak tree.

"Sit, Mrs. Pierce," he said as she approached. "I have something for you."

Puzzled, Karen knelt down at the foot of his chair.

The old man leaned over, pulling a tissue-wrapped package from under his lap robe. Slowly he unfolded the paper, revealing its contents. It was a pendant, which he placed in Karen's hand.

Surprised, she studied it.

The clasp and bale were made of hammered, highly polished silver. The pendant hung from a braided rope made of some kind of fiber Karen couldn't identify. But it was the subject of the necklace that held her attention. It was an intricately carved owl made out of what she believed was mother of pearl.

"It's beautiful," she said softly. "But why are you giving this to me? It looks like an antique and is probably worth a lot of money."

Harry smiled at her. "Because it belongs to you. It is your totem."

Karen frowned. "My totem? An owl? I don't think so. Owls here have always been out to get me."

Harry reached out and took the pendant from her, holding it up in front of her face.

"Look with your heart, Mrs. Pierce, and truly see for the first time. This rope that holds the owl is made from the hairs of the sacred moose. It is strong and binding, like your love for your family. Run your fingers over it. It is centuries old yet still is as strong as the day it was woven."

Karen did as he asked and moved her fingers over the ancient braid.

"Now look at the pendant. It is made from the nacre of a giant oyster, pulled long ago from the waters around Mateguas.

The owl itself was carved using the sacred knife that you have wielded so many times. Touch it. Do you not feel its warmth?"

Tentatively, Karen ran her fingers over the carving. Like the little bone knife, the owl warmed to her touch, sending heat up her arm and into her heart.

She nodded. "I feel it, but I don't understand."

Harry smiled. "This is your totem, Mrs. Pierce, your spirit guide. Have you never wondered why the owl that harassed you could never really hurt you? Why it shadowed your every move?"

"Yes, I guess so. It wounded me once, but that was the only time. And the cut, it was superficial, not life-threatening."

The old Indian nodded. "That is because the owl was sent by Mateguas to guide and lead you on your journey. At times, it had to frighten you to move you in the right direction. At others, unseen, it watched over and protected you and your little ones."

As he said this, he nodded toward Terri, who was standing with a group of young people in front of the church.

"This pendant is yours. It is a part of you. Will you accept it and let me place it around your neck?"

Karen stared at the carving for a moment, remembering the incident with Alex and the owl in her backyard, then slowly smiled and nodded.

Harry, though blind, felt her acceptance. Smiling, he leaned over and reached out, placing the pendant over her bowed head.

Karen gasped as the mother of pearl owl touched her skin, its heat flowing through her. Relishing its warmth, she looked up at Harry and smiled.

"Thank you. Thank you for everything. But most of all, for keeping my daughter safe. Will you promise me that, whatever happens, you will continue to protect her?"

"I could not abandon her even if I tried. For she is the Bringer of Light."

Karen frowned, puzzled, and was about to ask him what he meant, but, at that moment, Dex came striding over.

"Karen, people are asking for you," he said impatiently. "I think it's only polite that you join your family."

Karen bit back an angry response and instead smiled up at him. "I'll be there in a minute. I'm just saying goodbye to Charlie and Harry. Could you ask Shawn to take them back to the ferry?"

"Sure, but I expect you to join the rest of us in the next few minutes."

"Don't worry. I'll be there."

She watched him walk away, then turned back to Harry. "I'm sorry about that. We've been having a rough time lately."

"No need to apologize," said Harry. "You go to your husband. Charlie and Shawn will help me get back."

Karen leaned over and kissed the old Indian's wrinkled cheek. "And, thank you again for your gift. I will wear it always."

She stood and walked briskly away, joining Dex on the church lawn.

The old Indian watched her go, a solemn expression on his face.

"You look troubled, old friend," said Charlie. "What is it?"

Harry continued to stare silently at Karen and Dex, then he sighed. "I fear we will never see her again, my friend. She has chosen a path and should she walk upon it, her fate will have been decided. But maybe that is as it should be for then the circle will be unbroken once again. Come now, help me down to the parking lot where the young man waits for us. It is time to go home."

Dex, Karen, and the girls waited at the graveside as the tiny coffin was interred in the island cemetery. The service was mercifully short. Afterward, the mourners proceeded to the Hall where a potluck luncheon was being served.

Karen endured all of this, staying close by her husband's side. By mid-afternoon, people were beginning to disperse and, feeling exhausted, she suggested they go home.

"You go," said Dex. "I'm going to stay a little longer. I want to make sure I've shaken everyone's hand and thanked them for their kind words."

"Okay, you stay," she said. "But I need to lay down. Can someone drive me?"

Shawn stepped forward. "We'll take you. I think Terri's ready to go, too. What about you, Sophie? Do you want to come with us or stay here with Dex?"

"I'll stay with Dex. I don't leave until seven. There'll be plenty of time to say goodbye before then."

Back at the cottage, Karen stripped off her black dress and lay down on the bed, thinking about the events of the day, mostly, remembering her lost child. Tears began to flow again and she wrapped her fingers around the small carved owl that now rested between her breasts, and was comforted by its warmth.

As tears dried on her cheeks, her thoughts turned to her husband who had been so cool to her lately.

Why isn't he here to hold me? I know he's still angry because I tried to help poor Bill, but does that justify this behavior? Or is it something else? Has Alex's death reopened some old wound that's now festering?

Wanting only to sleep, she closed her eyes, pushing aside her questions and letting her mind go blank. Finally, she drifted off, her hand still clasped tightly around the little carved owl.

DEX AND SOPHIE

DEX STAYED AT THE Hall until the last of the mourners were gone. Afterward, he spoke quietly with the minister for a few minutes, thanked the choir, and left a sizable offering for the collection plate.

Sophie was by his side throughout, holding his arm, giving him love and support. Finally, they left the church grounds.

"Are you okay?" asked Sophie as they got into his truck.

"Yeah, honey. What say we go down to the shore? I don't feel like going home just yet."

"Sure, whatever you want."

Dex drove to the west end of the island and parked near the shore. There were only a few people on the beach, none of them familiar. Taking Sophie's hand, Dex walked in silence for a time, only stopping occasionally to skip a stone across the water or examine a shard of shiny sea glass. Sophie, respecting his privacy, stayed by his side until, finally, she broke the silence.

"What's up with you and Mom, Dad?" she asked.

Dex stopped and turned away from her, facing the sea. "What do you mean, sugar?"

"You know. I thought you two would be a united front, not leaving each other's side. But you're barely speaking to one another. I've never seen you two like this before. It's like you're strangers."

Dex didn't answer immediately, just leaned over, picked up a rock and skipped it across the water. After a few minutes, he turned to face her.

"Sometimes I think we are strangers, honey. I've never been able to really figure out what makes your mom tick though God knows I've tried."

Sophie smiled. "I know. All that Indian mumbo-jumbo. I don't get it either. But you've always been able to live with it. But now ... don't you need each other now?"

"It's difficult to explain. The day after..."

Dex's voice broke and he struggled to suppress a sob as his eyes filled with tears.

Sophie put her arms around him, holding him. "It's okay to cry. There's no shame in it. I'm here."

Dex sobbed softly in her arms, releasing the emotion he had kept in check all day. After a few minutes, he pulled away, wiping his cheeks with the back of his hand.

"Thanks, Sophie," he said softly. "I guess I needed to let that out."

"It's okay. Now, what were you going to tell me about Mom?"

Again, Dex took a deep breath. "You know what she did. Our boy was barely cold and all she could think about was helping the man who murdered him. While I was at the church mourning my son, she went to town to get that bastard a lawyer! I'm sorry, honey, I know he's your father, but he killed my boy ... your brother. And she hired him a lawyer to make sure he didn't have to pay for his crime. So, now he's going to live out his life in luxury up at Bangor State instead of the State Pen where he belongs!"

Sophie reached out and placed her hand on his arm.

"Take it easy. I'm sure she only did what she felt was right. And, yes, he is my biological father, but you ... it's you I really think of as my dad. I know I was happy when we found him. No one should have had to go through what he did. But you are the one who raised me and there was always a lot of love in our house when you were there."

Dex looked at Sophie gratefully then put his arms around her and hugged her.

"Thanks, sugar," he whispered. "Hearing you say that means the world."

Sophie pulled away and smiled. "You know, you and Mom should think about getting away. Take a trip somewhere ... Europe or South America, somewhere far away."

Dex smiled at her. "You know, that's not altogether a bad idea. As much as I love this rock, it does hold some bitter memories. And maybe if we get away, we can work this all out."

"How about the Azores or maybe Majorca? There's lots of fishing and stuff going on there. Mom's done all the cities in Europe. Maybe a little foreign island adventure would be just what the doctor ordered."

Dex laughed. "You make me feel good, sugar. I'm so glad you came. Wish you could stay longer."

"I do, too, Dad, but I have a test the day after tomorrow and you know the gallery is opening a new exhibit this weekend and I have to be there. I'll visit again when you and Mom come back from your trip and you can tell me all about it."

Dex leaned over and kissed her on the forehead. "It's a date. Now, I think I have to get you home to pick up your things. It's getting close to seven."

Sophie nodded and, together, they walked arm in arm back to his truck.

Later, when the ferry was finally out of sight, Dex walked slowly back to the parking lot. It was time to go home and face his wife.

KAREN AND DEX

IT WAS DARK WHEN Karen woke up.

Oh, Christ, she thought. *What time is it? I may have missed Sophie.*

Hurriedly, she dressed, throwing on a long peasant skirt and sweater, and rushed into the living room hoping to find her daughter still there. But the room was empty. The door to the deck was open and she could see her husband, silhouetted in the moonlight by the rail.

"Dex?" she asked.

"Yeah, it's me," he replied without turning.

"Has Sophie left?"

"Yeah to that, too. You were sleeping so soundly we thought it best not to wake you."

"Well, I wish you had. I would have liked to have had a chance to chat with her."

Dex turned and leaned his back on the rail. "She was here all day. You had plenty of opportunities."

Karen frowned, wondering where this was leading. "Sorry, I meant that I wanted to have some time with her alone. I wanted to really talk to her, not just make polite conversation."

"Well, I guess that's too bad. She's gone now. You could have stayed at the Hall, but you wanted to come home."

"What's that supposed to mean? What are you inferring?"

Dex didn't respond, but turned his back on her again, leaning on the rail.

"Dex, I'm talking to you. If you've got a bug up your ass about me, let it out. I'm all ears."

Dex turned to face her, an angry scowl on his face. "I still can't understand you; why you had to go to town to help that murdering bastard. And, yes, that's the bug up my ass."

Karen took a step back and stared at him, taking a deep breath.

"Okay. You win. I'm too tired to fight. Let's just agree that I'm callous and cruel because I didn't want to let a man, who has clearly lost his sanity, get swallowed up by the judicial system. A man, who, I might add, was my husband for ten years and is the father of my two children. A man whom someone took against his will and left for dead on a God-forsaken island. Will that satisfy you? Christ, I'd thought you'd already done your best to punish me. Now can we please get over it?"

"Punish you? Are you referring to the other night?"

He waited for her to respond, but she just stared at him.

Moments passed. Neither of them blinked.

Finally, Dex stepped away from the rail, toward her.

"Okay, I'm sorry about the other night. I was drunk and insensitive. And a little angry, but don't worry, it won't happen again."

Finished, he again turned his back to her and gazed at the sea below.

Karen walked out on the deck, not willing to let this go.

"What is it with you? You treat me like a whore and then you just say 'gee, I'm sorry.' Don't you think I'm grieving, too?

We should be together in this, mourning our son. But, instead, you're pushing me away. And don't tell me it's just because of Bill. You've been pushing me away ever since..."

She hesitated for a moment, afraid of what would happen if she said what she was thinking. But it had to be said.

"...since that broadcast about your dead high school girlfriend."

Dex whirled around.

"What the fuck! What does she have to do with anything? And I told you, she wasn't my girlfriend."

"I don't believe you. Every time you look at her picture or hear her name, something comes over you ... a sadness, a look of regret or longing. She was more than a friend and you know it."

Dex, anger written across his face, opened his mouth to speak, but apparently thought better of it. Instead, he gave her a cold, hard stare, then abruptly pivoted and walked back into the house, slamming the door behind him.

Karen, her anger mounting, threw open the door and followed.

Dex spun around and took a step toward her.

The look of hatred in his eyes was alien to her and suddenly, fearing she had gone too far - that he might be on the verge of using physical violence - she stepped away from him, into the kitchen. Scanning the room, she noted the butcher block was to her right and, on it, within reach, sat a large carving knife.

Dex stopped mid-stride, seeing her eyes dart toward the knife. He stared at her for a moment, then turned and walked to the bar.

Pulling a bottle of Jack Daniels from the cupboard, he poured himself a drink and tossed it back. He poured another and stood quietly, staring at the wall, then, he turned to face her.

"Jesus, Karen," he groaned. "Why do you want to dredge up all this old stuff again? It's ancient history. She was a friend. That's all. Do you think I had something to do with her death? Is that where this is going?"

"I don't know," she replied. "But there are things you're not telling me and what happened to her is just one of them.

There are events in your background you've been keeping hidden ever since we met. Why didn't you ever mention her before? I think it's time we got this all out in the open. Let in some fresh air so we both can breathe again."

Dex took a sip of his drink, quietly thinking. "You're not making sense. Christ, why would I tell you about Evie? It's not like it's everyday conversation. Did you expect me to look up from the dinner table one day and say, 'oh, by the way, princess, I once knew a girl who was murdered?' And just when was I supposed to drop that bombshell? Before or after we were married?"

"Stop making excuses, Dex. Tell me the truth about her."

Dex took a deep breath. "Okay, I'll say it again, if that's what it will take to get some peace around here. She was a friend and she disappeared one January night and was later found dead in Scarborough Marsh. They said she was pregnant and strangled. I was at a party the night she went missing ... a party here on the island. I have an alibi, if that's what you're getting at."

Karen laughed. "An alibi - right, all your island buddies sticking up for you. I want the truth, Dex. She was more to you than just a friend. I can hear it in your voice every time you say her name. Were you involved, in any way, in her death?"

Dex slammed his fist down on the bar. "Christ, I can't believe you really want to do this. You really want to go there?"

"Yes. Stop lying to me. Just tell me what happened."

He stared down at his drink, then looked up, his face contorted in anger. "ALL RIGHT!" he yelled. "I'll tell you."

He paused, visibly trying to bring himself under control and took a deep breath.

"Okay, you want to know it all - so you can breathe, right? Well, here's your answer - yes, she was more to me than just a friend."

He paused, a look of unbearable sadness coming over his face. "She was ... she was special."

He stared off into space, remembering. It seemed to Karen that he was speaking more to himself than to her.

"I think I actually loved her," he said in a voice barely above a whisper. "But I was too young and stupid to realize it. And, I was there when she died, but you have to believe me, it was an accident."

"An accident?" Karen asked.

Dex slumped down on the couch, his face drained of color. "We started out as friends like I told you, but it changed. We began seeing each other on the sly and, yes, we were intimate. The night she died, I picked her up as usual at the store where she worked. We drove out to the shore and parked in my truck."

He hesitated, taking another drink. "You sure you want to know all this?"

"Yes, go on. Tell me."

He took another deep breath. "She told me that night that she was pregnant. It was a shock. We always used condoms, except for one time. She'd said she wanted to really feel me, you know, inside of her, just once. So, we did it. I tried to pull out, but she didn't let me - she held me to her. It was stupid and careless. And then, a few weeks later, she's telling me she's pregnant and that I have to do the right thing - you know, marry her. We argued."

Karen listened carefully, her heart aching as she realized that Evie, the young girl whom he'd loved, had purposely trapped him.

"Yes, and what happened then?"

Dex looked up at her with eyes pleading for understanding. "I told her we had to get rid of it. That my mother could do it seeing she was a midwife and all. And that it would be safe. But Evie wasn't having any of that. She was real Catholic, you see. Her whole family was. She said she was going to tell her dad and he'd make sure I did the right thing. I tried to reason with her, but she was adamant. I got angry and called her a slut and told her to get out of the truck and that I was through with her. She started crying, but I pushed her away. So, she got out and began climbing the rocks to get back to the road. She screamed at me that I was not going to make her murder her child."

Dex paused, taking a healthy swig of his drink.

"That made me feel ashamed. So, I yelled to her that I didn't mean it. Begged her to come back and talk some more, but she wasn't listening. She just kept climbing on those damned rocks. You gotta understand, it was winter - everything was covered with snow and ice - and she was crying, angry, and not really watching her footing."

Karen frowned, puzzled. "Are you telling me she fell to her death? But she was strangled. At least that's what the police report said. How could a fall do that?"

"Like I said, it was winter. She had a long knit scarf wrapped around her neck. Somehow, when she slipped, the scarf got caught between the boulders and her body's momentum caused it to choke her. When I saw her go down, I got out of the truck and ran to her, but it was too late. She was already dead."

Karen stared at him, knowing how much this confession was costing him.

"Okay, it was an accident. I see that. But how did she get all the way to Scarborough?"

Dex sighed. "My dad. I panicked and called my dad. When he got there, I told him what happened and that she was pregnant. After slapping me around and cursing me for riding the girl bareback, he told me to go home and find some friends to hang out with - anyone who would swear I was with them all night. I assume that after I left, he took her body and dumped it."

"Why did you let that happen? Why didn't you go to the police?"

"Christ, Karen. I was only seventeen! I was going to college - medical school. If I'd told the truth, all of that would have disappeared. So, I did what my dad told me to do. Now are we through here? Are you happy now that you know all this? Does it make things different somehow?"

Karen took a deep breath. She was nowhere near through and knew that going further would put her marriage in even more jeopardy than it already was. But she had to know.

"No, we're not through. Tell me about your mother's friend, the author, Nichols. His bones were found on Puffin. Were you somehow involved in his death, too?"

Dex stared at her, a look of surprise coming over his face. "Howard Nichols? How did you know...?"

Karen closed her eyes. "I didn't really know until right now. But Louise told me he and your mother were close and then that LeVeque woman reported that she had been questioned about his disappearance. I was just putting two and two together."

Dex nodded slowly. "Me and my big mouth. Okay, you want to know it all. I'll tell you. Howard Nichols. You're right, he was a friend of my mom's. They'd known each other since they were kids spending summers on the island. Their families were friends, too. The night he disappeared, I came home from college unexpectedly. You see, my mom and I were close and I knew she missed me. I liked to surprise her; see her face light up when I came in the door."

He took another sip of his drink.

"Go on. Don't stop. Get it out. What happened?"

"Okay, this time when I walked in the door my mom wasn't there. Just Howard Nichols, sitting on the sofa, with a half-full glass of red wine. I wasn't surprised to see him. Like I said, he and Mom were friends. He came over all the time when my dad was fishing or in town. That night, my dad was at a lobstermen's meeting on the mainland. He wasn't expected home until late.

"Well, I said 'hello and how's it hanging' or some other pleasantry and then asked where my mom was. He nodded toward the bedroom. I went inside to see her."

Dex stopped again, his eyes far away, as if reliving what had happened that night. Minutes passed, then he turned his gaze back toward Karen.

"She was packing. Packing her bags. She was going to leave with him. Leave my dad and me. She handed me a letter she said she'd written for me. Said the letter would explain everything. Well, I wasn't having any of that. I got mad and said some awful things to her - accused her of sleeping with Nichols and stuff like that. Then I stormed out of the house. I took my scooter down to the general store and called my dad on the mainland. I told him she was running away with Nichols. He said for me to go back to the house and stall her ... keep her there until he could get home to the island."

Karen looked puzzled. "But aren't there pictures of him in town? And, signed statements that his punt never left the harbor? Are you telling me that's all a lie?"

Dex laughed unpleasantly. "Yeah. It's all a lie. My dad traded shirts and hats with a friend of his who was the same age, build, and coloring. Told that guy to make sure he was 'seen' but not seen too closely. Then he borrowed the same guy's punt. So, yeah, his punt never left the mainland. And pictures were taken that everyone assumed was Pop. But he came home."

Karen leaned forward against the counter. "So, what happened when he arrived?"

"Well, I kept my mom there as he'd instructed. Told her I wanted to hear it from her, not read it in a letter. So, she sat me down and said she just couldn't abide being with him anymore. That he was cruel, had other women, and, most importantly, that he'd done things, bad things, she just couldn't live with. Said there was nothing between Howard and her, that they were just friends and that he was going to take her to her parents' place. She said that once she was safely away, she'd make sure her dad saw to it that I went to medical school - the best in the country. And that I could come live with her and get away from the island for good. I would have done it, too, Karen. My dad was not always a nice man. He had a mean streak in him.

"Anyway, I regretted that I'd called Pop and was about to tell her to leave right away, not bother with clothes and stuff, but it was too late ... the door opened. It was my dad. He took one look at Mom and Howard there in the living room and went berserk. Grabbed Mom by the hair and threw her in the bathroom and locked the door. Then he went after Howard. Beat him to a pulp. I tried to intervene, but he threw me against the wall so hard I saw stars. Then he grabbed the fireplace poker and started hitting Howard with it ... hitting him in the face. Oh, God, there was blood everywhere!"

Tears were running freely down Dex's face as he relived the horror from his youth. Karen wanted to reach for him, take him in her arms, but she knew he had to finish and that when this was done, there was still more they had to get through.

"So, what happened?" she asked softly. "I assume he killed Nichols. What did he do with the body?"

Dex poured himself another drink. "When his rage was over, he unlocked the bathroom and let Mom out. He told her she was to clean up the mess, and, if she didn't and tried to call the police, he would tell the authorities that I helped him kill Nichols. And that I had murdered Evie, too. He said that if she didn't keep quiet, he'd make sure I went to jail and never got out. That was something she couldn't abide, so she did what he said. He took the body - I didn't know for sure what he did with it back then, but there were rumors about Puffin and what went on there. So, you see, I wasn't really very surprised when Susan's little expedition came up with his bones.

"Anyway, like I said, my mom and I did what he told us to do. We cleaned it all up. I told her I would go with her to the police, but she insisted we keep quiet - that it was better that way. She wasn't going to see me sacrificed.

"So, that's what happened. We never talked about it again. Then they were killed in that so-called car accident."

"What do you mean by 'so-called'?"

"Oh, come on, Karen. Isn't it obvious? It was no accident. She committed suicide and took him with her. All to protect me."

He hesitated and, seeing the stunned look on her face, laughed.

"Now, ain't that a bitch? Finally, something you didn't count on. How'd you think I liked living with that all these years? And, I guess that's it, end of story. Are you happy now?"

"No, of course, I'm not happy. It's tragic and keeping all that buried within you for so long ... You should have told someone, me, anyone."

"Yeah, like you should have told me all your secrets. Right, Karen? Now, can I get some peace? I'm tired."

Karen sighed. "There's still more and you know it. We have to talk about Bill."

Dex looked up, startled. "Bill? Why do we have to talk about him? He's off to the nut house where he belongs!"

Karen stared at him icily, all the warmth gone from her eyes. "Yes, we have to talk about him. He would never have done what he did if he hadn't been left to die on Puffin. He had his faults, sure, but he wasn't a murderer. What happened to him at that place ... what he was forced to do to survive, that's what deranged him and I want to know how he got there. And I know you know something you're not telling."

Dex turned from her and walked to the door leading to the deck. He stood quietly looking out at the night sky as Karen waited for him to respond. Finally, he spoke, pleading with her.

"Please, Karen, haven't I gone through enough? Can't we give this a rest, at least for tonight? The man murdered my son."

At the mention of the boy, Karen flinched and tears began to stream down her cheeks. Dex shook his head and walked out onto the deck, leaning heavily against the railing, staring at the rocks below.

For a moment, everything was silent, then he turned again to face her. "At least I think he was my son. Was he, Karen? Was he really my kid? Or was he Bill's?"

Karen's head snapped back as if she had been slapped. "What? Are you accusing me again? I thought we'd settled all this two years ago."

Dex laughed shakily. "It was never settled for me. I had DNA testing done, you know. Had Josh do it when we got here."

"You what? DNA?"

"Yeah. But strange thing, the results were inconclusive. Josh said it was the oddest thing he'd ever seen. Said the sample I brought him must have been corrupted somehow. I was going to get him a new one, but ... but it no longer really matters now, does it?"

"Do you distrust me that much? I'll say it one more time ... I did not sleep with Bill. You are the only man I've been with these past twelve years. What makes you continue to think he wasn't yours?"

Dex hesitated, staring at the wall behind her. "Remember before we were married, before we left for California after Bill disappeared?"

"Yes, but what's that got to do with anything?"

"Didn't you ever wonder why I stayed away for so long after you asked me to leave with you? Why I didn't show up until the very last minute?"

"Yes, I guess. I thought you'd changed your mind about me. I was surprised when you joined us at the airport. Why?"

"After...after Evie, I didn't want to ever have anything like that happen again. You need to understand, I was young and foolish. I convinced myself it was better not to ever have children, and, to make sure, I had a vasectomy. But then when you asked me to come to California with you..."

His voice trailed off.

"Go on."

"Well, the reason I wasn't around after that was I had it reversed. When the doc said I was good to go ... that everything was working again, I joined you. But we tried to make a baby for ten years, Karen, and nothing. I assumed it was my fault. And suddenly, right after Bill..."

"Stop right there. I'm not going to do this, Dex. I've told you the truth. Alex was not Bill's son. Now, I'm sorry about what happened to you, but either you believe me about this or you don't. Right now, I don't really care. And you still haven't answered my question. Were you involved in Bill's disappearance?"

He threw back his head and finished the remains of his drink, then heaved the empty glass off the deck, listening as it shattered on the rocks below.

"All right. You'll get your answer," he replied, his anger returning. "You won't like it, but you'll get it."

Karen stood frozen, waiting.

"Yes, I took him to Puffin. I didn't start it ... I didn't hit him or anything. But, yes, I helped take him there. Does that satisfy you?"

Red blotches of anger stained Karen's cheeks. "But, why? Why would you do something like that?"

Dex walked back into the room and slumped down onto the sofa, his head in his hands.

"It wasn't planned. It just happened. I was with the search party - you know that. We were walking a grid, ten yards or so apart. I went all the way through those damned woods looking for your loser of a husband until I came out on the other side, on the north shore. There's an old abandoned cottage there. Transients sometimes use it in the summer. I looked in the window and saw movement so I went inside. It was Rusty - Maggie's dad. He had a shovel in his hand and Bill was lying on the floor, bleeding from the back of the head. Rusty said Bill came running out of the woods right at him and, well, he just reacted and swung the shovel. He was angry, you see, and the sight of your husband ... He'd only found out his daughter was pregnant that morning. I thought Bill was dead and Rusty was afraid he'd go to jail and, if that happened, who'd take care of Emma, Maggie, and the baby? So, we loaded him onto Rusty's boat and motored him to Puffin. He was dead and it just didn't seem right to hurt any more people by explaining it all. Nothing was going to bring him back."

Karen took a deep breath. "You thought he was dead? You don't expect me to believe that, do you? You, who's always telling me how much he knows about medicine? Give me a break. I want the truth, Dex. Don't keep lying."

He looked up at her. There was no escaping the accusation in her eyes. "Oh, Christ, Karen, do we have to?"

They stared at each other for a moment, neither one willing to give an inch. Then Dex looked away, down at his hands.

"Okay, you win. Yes, I knew he was still alive and that the wound on his head wasn't fatal. But, Karen, I just wanted you so bad. I never wanted any woman the way I wanted you. Not since Evie. I knew if I brought him back, you'd leave Mateguas and stay with him. This was my only chance. He was no good and you know that. He didn't deserve you.

"So, yes, I wanted him to die on Puffin. I knew it was wrong, but I did it anyway. There, that's it. I've said it. You've got your truth. Are you satisfied now? Does knowing this make you feel better? Christ, none of this would have happened if he'd just died."

Karen reached out and gripped the breakfast bar, trying to steady herself. She felt as if all the air had been sucked out of the room and that she was silently suffocating. But in that moment, as she gasped for breath, things began to become clear. She stared at her husband, the man she had loved for twelve years, really seeing him for the first time. He was naked now, like a newborn, having cast aside the facade that he had worn for so many years - the proud islander. And she recognized that everything he had done - Evie, Nichols, and Bill - had been done in an attempt to break away, to be someone else - someone educated, someone respected. And, he had succeeded for a time, using her family and her love.

Steeling herself with this new knowledge, she again confronted him.

"Look at me," she demanded. "Are you listening to yourself? You think Bill's to blame for all that's happened? You're the one who started all this thirty years ago. Now, I'm not going to blame you for what you did with the poor young girl. You were just a kid and the adults around you steered you into making the wrong choices. And with Nichols, too, you really didn't do anything wrong. You were just so young and trying to protect your mother. But Bill? When you made that decision, you were a man, for Christ's sake. No abusive father bullying you then. No, you made a conscious choice. YOU took him to that island. And what had he done to you to deserve that? NOTHING! His only crime was that he was married to me!

"No, none of this would have happened if YOU hadn't intervened. You and Rusty Maguire - just a couple of good old boys, following in your father's footsteps!"

She moved closer to him and put her hands on his shoulders, gripping him forcefully. "I said, look at me, Dex. You say you 'wanted me so bad.' Really? Didn't you realize that once I found out Maggie was pregnant that it would have been over for Bill and me? That you would have had me anyway? I loved you, for God's sake. Didn't you know that? But you couldn't wait. Just like your father, you saw an opportunity and you took it.

"And, now, we've lost our boy, Bill is in an asylum, and you expect me to understand why you did this? God, you disgust me!"

She straightened up, releasing her hold on him, and wiped her hands on her skirt as if trying to remove something unclean. She stared at his bowed head, then opened the hall closet, grabbed a jacket, and walked to the door.

"I'm going out. When, and if, I return, I don't think I want to see you here."

Dex hesitated a moment, then looked up, his eyes following her voice. "Karen, please..."

But she was gone.

KAREN

SHE DROVE AROUND THE island aimlessly, trying to understand and accept the fact that the actions of her husband - the man she loved - had brought all this tragedy down upon them. Despite her suspicions, she had prayed that he would tell her that he wasn't involved or that someone like Rusty Maguire had acted alone. But she had insisted on the truth and, ugly as it was, he gave it to her.

Driving now, with tears in her eyes, she avoided the high-traffic areas near the B&Bs and the wharf, seeking out instead the lonely dead-end roads that usually led to the rows of summer cottages that lined the shore.

She was driving down one such road when she passed a sign, partially obscured by dense foliage. Curious, she hit the brakes and backed up to get a better look. Stepping from the car, she pushed the brush aside. The sign was old and the wood post that held it was rotting away. At one time, she could tell, it had been whitewashed but now most of the paint had flaked off. Taking a handkerchief from her pocket, she wiped away the dirt and debris that concealed the lettering, until, with some difficulty, she could make out the words:

Old Cottage Road
Right of Way to The Shore

How come I never noticed this before, she asked herself, sure that by now she had explored every inch of this island.

Thoughts of Dex and Bill suddenly seemed trivial as she stared down the dark, winding dirt road that lay before her. Something about it seemed familiar, but she couldn't put her finger on it and she felt somehow driven to find what lay at its end.

Without thinking, she reached under her sweater and grasped the tiny carved owl that rested lightly between her breasts. Stroking it gently, she nodded once, then got back in the car, turned on her high beams, and started down Old Cottage Road, heading toward the shore.

It was slow going. Mother Nature's rains had eroded the lane so that now it was deeply rutted. Vegetation on the sides encroached, brushing the windows and hood of the car making it difficult for her to navigate. At one point, she stopped, wondering what force had compelled her to go on this fool's errand. She thought about turning around but knew that would be impossible on this narrow track. And the thought of backing the car out, all the way to the main road, sent shivers down her spine.

Hesitating only for a moment, she forged onward, slowly. A sharp turn loomed ahead. Blindly, she eased the car around it.

As she came out of the curve, she slammed on the brakes.

A giant oak was strangely growing in the middle of the lane and, with no way to avoid it, the car crashed into it. The impact threw her forward, into the steering wheel.

She sat motionless for a moment, catching her breath. Slowly, she leaned back, rubbing her forehead, which had bounced off the wheel when the car hit the tree. She glanced down at her palm, relieved to see there was no blood. Cursing her stupidity for venturing down this road in the first place, she struggled to get out of the car to assess the damage done to the front end.

"Oh, shit! I'll never get this car out of here now," she exclaimed, looking at the crumpled front bumper. "I'll have to call Shawn."

She reached into her pocket for her cell only to remember that in her haste to get away from Dex, she had neglected to take it with her.

"Double fucking damn!" she cried. "I'll have to walk home."

She turned and gazed down the dark road, finally realizing why it had looked so familiar. While it was broader and could accommodate a car, it mimicked that deadly trail behind her old house - the place she had lived with Bill and her daughters so many years before. Fear coursed through her as she thought about the long walk back to the road and what terrors might be lying in wait for her along the way.

She stood frozen in indecision. Should she try to walk home? Or should she try to get the car going and back it out of here?

The soft hoot of an owl disturbed the silence of the woods, startling her.

Again, her hand grasped the little carved totem Harry Three-Feathers had given to her.

He said it wouldn't hurt me, she thought. *That it's my totem and meant to help me on my journey. Should I...*

As if reading her thoughts, the owl hooted again, this time sounding more insistent.

She turned around. It was coming from the woods beyond the oak tree, in the direction of the beach. Listening carefully, she thought she could hear the comforting sound of waves lapping against the rocky shoreline. She sniffed the air and smiled, recognizing at once the tangy, salty smell of the ocean.

If I can make it to the beach, maybe I can find some shelter and wait until daybreak. Then that road won't seem so bad and I can get to Terri and Shawn's place.

She took one last look at the dark, overgrown lane that led back to the road and decided. Returning to the car, she rummaged around in the glove compartment until she found a flashlight. She shook it once, praying that the batteries weren't dead, then turned it on. The light flickered at first, then steadied.

The owl hooted once more as if telling her to hurry and, taking a deep breath, she followed its call into the dense woods.

Gamely, she tried to make her way through the foliage. She was wearing a long peasant skirt, and she swore as it caught on branches and underbrush, tearing the fabric. Stinging nettles attacked her bare ankles and calves and she questioned the wisdom of her decision to follow the owl.

She was about to give up and turn around when her flashlight caught sight of a narrow path directly ahead of her. She hesitated for a moment, shining the light down it. It seemed well-tended and, weighing the alternatives, she decided to take a chance.

Mercifully, the path was short and she was relieved to find it opened out to a small, sandy cove, sheltered on the sides by tall jagged rocks. She gazed around, hoping to see the lights of a cottage or two nestled among the trees behind her, but there were none. The beam of her flashlight only revealed more dense woods and seaweed-covered, black rocks.

Sighing, she sat down in the sand, hugging her knees to her chest.

The moon, in its full phase, shone brightly on the water, creating shimmering patterns in the night sky. On impulse, Karen removed her sandals, stood, and walked to the water's edge. Gingerly, she stepped into the waves, letting them lap at her toes. The water was cold, but somehow it soothed the fever of despair that now came back to her.

She thought about Dex, wishing there was some way she could return to him and take comfort from his warm embrace. But then she remembered Bill and how he had looked at the police station, so lost and alone, and she knew there was no way she could ever let that happen.

She was on her own again and would have to deal with the awful emptiness she now felt clinging to her heart and soul.

Silently, she listened to the soothing sound of the sea. Inhaling its life-giving aroma, she took a step forward, letting the cool water encase her ankles. She looked up and was surprised to see a shadow begin to pass over the brightly shining moon.

An eclipse, she thought, her mind reeling in wonder.

Wordlessly, she continued to walk forward as if summoned, the waves now massaging her calves, her long skirt billowing out around her as it moved gently back and forth with the tide.

The moon was now beginning to glow hotly as the sun passed over it and, acting on instinct, Karen averted her eyes.

Is it safe to watch? I know you can't watch a solar eclipse, but a lunar one? It doesn't seem so bright.

Steeling herself, she looked back up at the sky. The moon had taken on an iridescent reddish color as the sun completed its journey. Now only a familiar sickle shape remained - a shape like the one that was already burned into the palm of her hand and quite possibly deep into her soul.

She stared, mesmerized, at the crescent moon, when suddenly it began to radiate and pulsate with a searing white light. She cried out in agony as the burning light assaulted her eyes and, too late, squeezed them tightly shut.

All movement ceased as the pain abated.

Slowly, she opened her eyes. The world was now dark around her, except for a fiery crescent shape the white light had burned permanently into her retinas.

Staring blindly at the waning crescent moon in her mind, she continued her journey forward into deeper water. It was up to her armpits now, but she didn't seem to notice or care. She stopped for a moment, clutching at the little mother of pearl owl, taking comfort from its warmth.

Then, nodding once, she stepped forward again, turning her sightless eyes to the sky and raising her arms high in acceptance and silent supplication.

The only sound now was that of the sea. When the water reached her chin, she smiled, relishing a sense of sweet surrender as she let the salty waves enfold her in their cold embrace.

And, finally, with her hair floating around her head like a bright, golden mantle, she sank beneath the surface.

As the sea pulled her down, a vision of her daughters flashed before her eyes and she struggled to remember who and what she was.

Oh, my God, she thought, *I don't want to die.*

Consumed by panic and fear, involuntarily she opened her mouth to scream, letting the cold, salt water rush in, filling her lungs, driving her deeper down into the sea.

The little carved owl floating around her neck began to pulsate with light and, as she lost consciousness, she finally knew where she belonged. A feeling of peace settled over her as she gave up the last of her resistance and let the cool waters claim her, knowing she would be reunited with her true husband and blessed son.

And, as the shell of her body finally rested on the ocean floor, the waves that kissed the shores of Mateguas caressed her with reverence, gently lulling her weary soul to a merciful sleep.

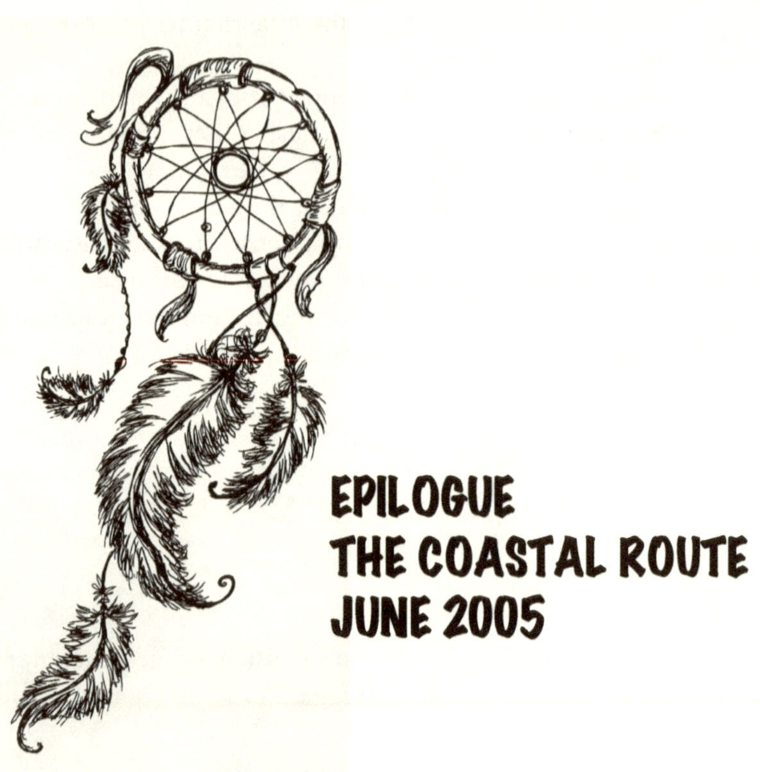

EPILOGUE
THE COASTAL ROUTE
JUNE 2005

"The dead live"
"How do they live?"
"By love."
— John Fowles, *The Magus*

BY THE TIME HE pulled into the parking lot, the fog had lifted. He'd made good time. His appointment was scheduled for eight and he was only fifteen minutes late. He stepped from the car and gazed at the building in front of him. The facade was old, very institutional, dark, and dreary - almost like something out of an old horror movie. But he knew that inside, it was different. The new wing at the rear was spacious and modern with all the conveniences. Large picture windows looked out over the ocean, creating a calm and peaceful environment for the patients.

Again, he relived the phone call.

Urgent - they said it was urgent.

Quickly, he bounded up the steps and into the building. The waiting room was all but deserted at this early hour and he gazed around looking for someone to assist him.

"Mr. Andersen?"

He turned. An attractive redhead dressed in a nurse's uniform was rapidly approaching him from the back of the room.

"I'm sorry there was no one here to greet you," she said. "Our receptionist has been delayed this morning because of that blasted fog. I hope you didn't have any difficulty getting here?

Bill smiled. "No, it was fine. Now, what's so important? The new doctor, I think his name was Todd, left the message that it was urgent. What's happened?"

"I'll have to let the doctor explain. Follow me."

The nurse led Bill through a door and down a corridor lined with offices. The last door on the left held a plaque that read "David Todd, M.D., Ph.D., Chief Medical Officer."

The nurse turned to Bill and smiled. "You go right on in. He's expecting you."

Bill thanked her and opened the door. A distinguished-looking gentleman around fifty years of age, wearing a white coat, got up from behind the desk and came around to greet him.

"Mr. Andersen. So glad you could make it on such short notice. I'm Dr. Todd, the new Chief Medical Officer and lead physician on your wife's case."

Bill shook hands with the doctor. "Your phone call said this was urgent but didn't say why. What's happened? Is my wife all right?"

"Please take a seat, Mr. Andersen. Before we get into the particulars, I'd like to go over with you in some detail your wife's history. I have her files, of course, but I'd like to hear it from you. Can you go through with me the events that brought Mrs. Andersen here?"

Bill sighed, feeling frustrated and a little angry. "Okay, if it's really necessary."

The doctor nodded. "It is."

"It was two years ago. We went to a party my company threw out at the Napa Valley Country Club. Karen didn't want to go because our twin daughters were sick. They were only five years old and Karen didn't want to leave them with a babysitter. But I insisted. You see, it was important to my job that we attend. I was up for a promotion and..." Bill hesitated for a moment.

"But that's not important. Karen had canceled our regular sitter so we had to get a new one. The girl was young, but the neighbors recommended her and she was available. This was a last-minute thing, you see, and we couldn't be choosy.

"So, we went to the party. It was about eight o'clock when the earthquake hit. We couldn't reach the house by phone so we headed home immediately. It took us awhile - all the bridges were closed as a precautionary measure. When we finally got there, it was all over. Apparently, the sitter, who as I said was young, had lit candles all over the girls' room and was reading them some sort of spooky story. The earthquake caused the candles to tumble over and fall. One of them caught the curtains on fire. The sitter panicked and ran from the house, leaving the girls behind."

His voice broke and he again hesitated, staring down at his hands.

"They were gone by the time we got home - smoke inhalation. It was horrible. Karen ... she felt it was all her fault ... that if she'd stayed home, it wouldn't have happened. The guilt ate away at her. Then she found out she was pregnant."

Bill stopped again, closing his eyes.

"Go on, Mr. Andersen. What happened with the pregnancy?"

Bill took a deep breath. "She ended it. Didn't tell me beforehand, but I found out. She said she didn't want to bring another child into the world ... that it would be disrespectful to the twins. I'm afraid I didn't handle it very well. I was upset and we fought."

The doctor nodded, then reached into his desk and removed a stack of notebooks, tied together with a red ribbon.

"Have you read these, Mr. Andersen?" he asked, handing them to Bill.

Bill nodded, setting them on the desk in front of him.

"Yes, she began writing after the fire. It's a novel. There are twins in it ... I guess it was her way of keeping our girls alive. She stopped writing after the abortion. Why? What does this have to do with anything?"

"You don't come off too well in her writings, you know. Is there any truth to what's in there?"

Bill hesitated. "I know. But you have to understand, I was grieving, too. And I felt guilt, maybe even more than she did. After all, it was me who insisted we go to that party. If she'd stayed home..."

He stopped again and gazed down at the notebooks, his hands gripping them tightly.

"Take your time, Mr. Andersen. I know this is hard."

Bill looked back up at the doctor, nodding.

"But I had my work and I threw myself into it. She ... she had nothing. So, she wrote these. The stuff about infidelity - that's not true. Karen was, and is, the only woman I've ever wanted or loved. The inferences to my shallowness, yeah, I'll own up to that. I wasn't there for her and I should have been. But those girls, they were my life, too, and every time I looked at her, I saw them. So, I stayed away - at work - ignoring her pain.

"Then came that day. I went to work as usual but found I couldn't concentrate. I don't know what it was ... something about the way she'd looked at me that morning ... as if with resignation or something. In any case, I couldn't work so I left and came home early. I found her in the bathtub, her wrists slashed. I'd never seen so much blood. I called 911 and they rushed her to the hospital. The doctor said that I got there just in time, that if I'd been five minutes later..."

His voice trailed off as he stared out the window behind the doctor's desk.

"Mr. Andersen?"

Bill shook his head slightly as if trying to wake up from a bad dream. "And that's about it. The doctor at the hospital recommended she be admitted here. Dr. Specks has been taking care of her since. Where is he, by the way? I thought he'd be here, too."

"Thank you, Mr. Andersen," said Dr. Todd, ignoring Bill's last question. "That all tallies with the information in her file."

Neither of them spoke for a moment, then Dr. Todd stood and walked around the desk, taking a seat next to Bill.

"What I have to tell you now is difficult and it has to do with Dr. Specks. You know he's been the lead physician on your wife's case since she was admitted, right?"

"Yeah. I know and he said she was making progress. He was very optimistic last time I spoke to him."

The doctor frowned. "He was wrong to give you that impression. I'm afraid Specks became emotionally involved with your wife; it clouded his judgment."

Bill leaned forward and stared at Dr. Todd. "I hope you're not telling me that he ... he took advantage of her. By God, if he laid on hand on her..."

"No, no, Mr. Andersen. It was nothing like that. Let me put this another way. You know patients often fall in love with their doctors, right?"

"Yeah. I believe it's called 'transference,' isn't it?"

"That's correct. But, in this case, the opposite happened. The doctor fell in love with the patient - counter-transference - and he wanted so badly to believe that she was getting well that it clouded his clinical judgment. Specks truly believed your wife was improving, but that was wishful thinking on his part. Your wife was still clinically depressed. But Specks couldn't see it and, well, he pushed her too hard."

"Pushed her too hard? What do you mean?"

Dr. Todd sighed. "He insisted she talk about that night ... about your daughters and her guilt. He made her relive it. It sent her over the edge."

"What do you mean? Did she try to kill herself again? Is that what you're telling me?"

Dr. Todd shook his head then reached down and picked up the pile of notebooks.

"No, it's nothing like that. But, I'm afraid she has experienced a complete psychotic break. She now believes she's one of the characters in this book and that she's living on an island off the coast of Maine."

Bill stared down at notebooks and opened the top one to its title page: *Mateguas Island, A Novel of Terror and Suspense* by Karen Andersen. He stared at it for a moment, then closed it angrily.

"I want to see her. NOW. I can't believe this has happened. I'll be talking with my lawyers about all this, of that you can be sure."

Dr. Todd eased himself out of the chair, nodding. "I'd be doing the same thing if I were you. Please, believe me, Dr. Specks is being disciplined. He'll most likely lose his medical license over this."

"I want to see her, doctor. Please."

"Okay, I'll take you to her. But don't be surprised if she calls you by another name or doesn't acknowledge you at all. She's deeply immersed in this fantasy and very fragile now. So, please, at this juncture, don't do anything to upset her. Okay?"

Bill nodded. "Take me to her."

The doctor escorted him to the elevator and they ascended to the second floor. It was a locked ward and Dr. Todd used his passkey to gain entry. Karen's room was the third on the right, her windows overlooking the Pacific Ocean. Bill hesitated at the door, not sure what to do.

"Go on in. She'll be most likely sitting by the window. Just don't do or say anything to upset her. I'll be right outside if you need me."

Bill nodded and walked into the room.

Karen was seated by the window just as Dr. Todd said she would be. To Bill, she looked beautiful, calm and serene, with no outward evidence of insanity. Then he noticed her lips were moving as if she were speaking to someone, but there was no one else in the room.

He stood watching her for a moment, then sat down by her side. She turned to look at him and smiled.

Encouraged and hoping that the doctor was wrong about her mental state, he reached out to take her hand, but when their fingers touched, she pulled away. They sat silently, staring at each other and, then, without acknowledging him further, she turned and gazed out at the sea below.

He sat with her for a while, not saying anything. Finally, he reached out again and laid his hand on her arm. He waited, holding his breath, for what seemed a lifetime, trying to will her mind to come back to him. But she remained immobile, gazing out the window, seeing what, he didn't know.

Shoulders slumping, he finally gave up, leaned over and kissed her lightly on the cheek, then walked slowly to the door.

Unbeknownst to him, Karen watched him go. Something deep inside of her urged her to reach out - to stop him - to bring him back. But the call of the waves crashing relentlessly against the rocks was stronger, and, once again, she turned toward the window.

I'll never get tired of this view, she thought as she gazed upon the rocky shoreline of Mateguas Island.

Outside the hospital, Bill walked slowly to his car. The sun was shining brightly on a field of orange poppies planted in front of the building, but their beauty was lost on him.

Sitting in the drivers' seat, he put his key in the ignition. He started the car, listening as the engine roared to life, then reached over toward the gearshift. His hand stopped midair as unbidden tears spilled onto his cheeks. Overcome with despair, he leaned forward and rested his head on the wheel, his body racked by silent sobs.

He remained like that for a while, mourning his lost love, while the car idled. A song came on the radio, filling the air with soft and poignant sadness.

He sat up, recognizing it. It was from a movie he and Karen had seen long ago when they were young and so much in love. He closed his eyes, remembering.

The movie was about a young couple, torn apart by war. They were in love and promised each other that nothing would or could separate them; that no matter what happened, they would wait for each other. Of course, they both broke that promise and the movie ended in tragedy.

He listened to the lyrics, recalling how Karen had sung them on their way home.

The song finally ended and he gazed up at the hospital, knowing she was still there, her mind trapped by grief and guilt. Did he have the courage to wait for her, even if it took forever?

He nodded once, deciding, then backed the car out of the lot and onto the highway.

He would be back next week. And the week after that. No matter how long it took, even a thousand summers, he would wait for her to come back to him. She was his end-all, his be-all, and nothing or no one could replace her, ever.

But as he drove away, somewhere, on a remote island, a young woman walks slowly toward the sea, relishing the sensation of the cool, wet grass beneath her bare feet.

When she reaches her destination, she stops and glances back over her shoulder at the house behind her. On the porch sits a man and two little girls. He's reading them a story and, as he turns a page, one of them says something, causing him to look up from the book.

He gazes at the young woman who is smiling at him, her face suffused with joy.

He returns her smile, his eyes filled with love.

They stare at each other for what seems an eternity, then she turns her head, shifting her gaze to the dark sky above.

The moon, hidden behind a cloud, peeks out as if summoned and shines down, illuminating her. As she looks up at its crescent shape, she rests her hands on her belly, which is now big with child.

Sighing with contentment, she nods once, then raises her arms to the sky and begins to speak,

Oh Mateguas, grand pere de la mort, entend my priere....

THE END

A NOTE FROM THE AUTHOR

I want to thank you, gentle reader, for choosing *GHOSTS OF MATEGUAS* and I hope you enjoyed it. When I began writing this novel, I fully intended that it be the final chapter in the Andersen saga. However, as I progressed, I made the decision to leave some doors ajar, just in case, you wanted more. For example,

Harry calls Terri "The Bringer of Light" - what does this mean?

Dex - will the truth about him ever be revealed?

Terri and Shawn - what path will they choose?

And, Sophie - what's up with her?

So, I'm going to leave it to you, dear reader. Do you want a fourth full-length novel? If so, when you write your review (which I know you all will!), please let me know. Just include, at the end, "yes, I want more" or "no, I'm satisfied."

In the meantime, I will be working on something quite different - a nostalgic romance, set in 1965. The title is *SUMMER GIRL* and it's the story of two teens that meet one summer on (you guessed it!) an island off the coast of Maine. I also have the fleshed out the plot of a gothic mystery, working title either *STORM ISLAND* or *THE CARRIAGE HOUSE*.

Again, thank you for joining me on Karen and Bill's journey. I hope you enjoyed. For me, it's been a blast!

Linda
February 7, 2016

ABOUT THE AUTHOR

Linda Watkins currently resides in Western Michigan and, in another life, was a Senior Clinical Financial Analyst at Stanford University School of Medicine. She was born on the east coast, but grew up in a suburb of Detroit. Upon graduation from college (Carnegie Mellon, '70), she moved to the San Francisco Bay Area where she lived and worked for thirty years. Taking early retirement, she moved briefly to Oregon then to an unconnected island off the coast of Maine (Chebeague Island, ME).

She lived on Chebeague for seven years and it was there that she wrote her award-winning debut novel, *MATEGUAS ISLAND*. The island of Chebeague served as a model for the one depicted in *MATEGUAS* and, in fact, the house the Andersen family inherits was modeled on her 150-year-old home.

She moved back to Michigan in the summer of 2013 and, in 2014, both *MATEGUAS ISLAND* and its sequel *RETURN TO MATEGUAS ISLAND* were published.

Since publication, *MATEGUAS ISLAND* has been the recipient of several major awards:

- 2014 Gold Medal in Supernatural Fiction, *READERS' FAVORITE INTERNATIONAL BOOK AWARD COMPETITION*
- 2014 First Place Award in Contemporary Gothic, *CHANTICLEER BOOK REVIEW, PARANORMAL AWARDS*
- 2015 Outstanding Novel in Horror/Suspense, *IAN BOOK OF THE YEAR AWARDS*

In addition, **RETURN TO MATEGUAS ISLAND** was named 2015 Finalist in Horror by *READERS' FAVORITE INTERNATIONAL BOOK AWARD COMPETITION* and has just been awarded a 1st Place in Contemporary Gothic Fiction by the 2015 *CHANTICLEER BOOK REVIEW'S PARANORMAL AWARDS*.

Today, Linda lives with her three aging rescue dogs (Splatter, Spudley and Jasper) and is a work on her next novel, **SUMMER GIRL**. Serious about dog welfare and rescue, all net proceeds from sales of **THE MATEGUAS ISLAND SERIES** are donated to Linda's charitable trust, the *Raison d'Etre Fund for Dogs, Dedicated to Rescue and Research*.

ACKNOWLEDGEMENTS

I'd like to thank my faithful reader, Marge LeBel, for all her important insights. She is the first person I turn to for advice on my work. Also, I'd like to thank Becky Pellerin for helping me with the sections on meditation and for her knowledge of all things 'baby'! Finally, I'd like to acknowledge all the wonderful friends, fans, and colleagues who have supported and cheered me on my journey. Without you, this would all be meaningless.